Empire of Night

JUSTIN SOMPER

SIMON AND SCHUSTER

First published in Great Britain in 2010 by Simon and Schuster UK Ltd,
A CBS COMPANY

Copyright © 2010 Justin Somper
Chapterhead illustrations copyright © 2007 Blacksheep
Cover illustration copyright © 2010 Kev Walker

www.vampirates.co.uk

Simon & Schuster UK Ltd
1st Floor, 222 Gray's Inn Road, London WC1X 8HB

A CIP catalogue record for this book
is available from the British Library.

ISBN 978-1-41691-652-9

1 3 5 7 9 10 8 6 4 2

Printed and bound in Great Britain.

www.simonandschuster.co.uk

For Sue, Sherri and Scott,
thanks for welcoming me into your crew!

A bay, somewhere off
the west coast of Australia.
The year 2512.

PROLOGUE

The Three Gifts

Connor,
My son, heir to my empire.
Here is the first of three gifts to mark this auspicious first night
of blood-taking. Come to my cabin when the watch shows
midnight and I will present you with your other two gifts.
Your blood father,
Sidorio

Connor stood at the captain's door. Instinctively, his hand dropped to his belt, his fingers seeking out his sword, resting in its scabbard. Connor squeezed the sword hilt, as he often did in times of stress. It reminded him of the moments when he was utterly in control – when his sword was drawn and he was in the midst of battle. If only he could achieve the same simplicity and clarity in the rest of his life as he did when he was engaged in combat.

Adrenaline surged through his body. Adrenaline is a strange thing, he thought. You need it to fuel you in times of pressure. Yet too much of the stuff almost paralyses you. His life had changed and he knew there was no going back. He couldn't even be sure that his sister Grace would still be alive by morning. When he had last seen her, she had observed that they were in control of their own destinies. She could not have been more wrong, Connor thought bitterly now. They were no more than flies, caught in a steel web.

The gold watch that had accompanied Sidorio's note weighed heavily around his wrist. Connor glanced at it now, glimmering under the corridor lights. There were only seconds until midnight. He could delay no longer. He took a breath, lifted his hand and knocked on the metal panel. There was a pause, then the sound of bolts sliding back. The heavy door opened and Connor stepped inside.

"Connor," Sidorio said, pushing the door closed. "Welcome! It's good to see you again. And you found the first of my three gifts. It looks well on you."

"Yes," Connor said. "Thank you, Father."

"Come here," Sidorio said, beckoning Connor deeper into the cabin. "I have the second of your gifts."

Connor walked on. Sidorio was standing in front of a long chest made of blue-lacquered wood with silver characters etched into its surface. "This was the war chest of Kublai Khan," Sidorio said, running his hands along the surface. "It was kept in his battle tent so he could select which weapon he favoured on any given day. This chest was a wedding present from my wife." There was something reverential in the way Sidorio opened the top drawer and pulled it towards them both. Inside was an array of swords such as Connor had never glimpsed before. They surpassed even the captains' swords housed at Pirate Academy and those within Master Yin's workshop.

"These are weapons fit for an emperor," Sidorio said. "And therefore for an emperor's son." He placed his hand on Connor's shoulders. "Choose one for yourself, my boy. This will be the second of my three gifts."

Connor was momentarily dazzled as his eyes travelled across the spikes of polished metal, set amongst a sea of blue silk. Any one of these swords was a rare prize indeed. It scarcely mattered which he chose.

"If none of those take your fancy," Sidorio said, "open the second drawer, or the third. Take your time." He stepped back, allowing Connor full access to the war chest.

Connor did not need to open any other drawers. There, in the corner of the top drawer, was the sword which was calling to him. It was not an obvious choice, being one of the simplest of the weapons, but Connor saw with his experienced eye that this was *the* perfectly designed sword. He knew in his heart it was the one which Master Yin, pirate swordsmith of Lantao Island, would have singled out.

Connor reached into the drawer and lifted his chosen sword. As he clasped the hilt in his hand, he knew he had made the right decision. It felt, like the very best of swords, as if it were an extension of his arm. Should he ever use it in combat, he had no doubt it would prove prosperous for him.

"Is that the one?" Sidorio asked.

Connor nodded. "Thank you, *Father*. It's incredible."

"You've made a good choice," Sidorio said, pushing the drawer closed again. "And now, let's sit."

The words were innocuous enough, but Connor's heart was hammering as he fell into step with Sidorio and walked back to the table. Sidorio nudged Connor gently towards the opposite chair. Connor sat, letting his old sword hang down at his side and laying the newly acquired one at his feet.

On the table was a folded velvet cloth, edged with brocade. Connor's eyes traced the detail in the brocade and then travelled back up to the cloth and what lay upon it. A golden goblet, its handles fashioned to look like two writhing snakes.

Sidorio lifted the goblet in one hand. "This belonged to

Caesar, once." He turned to Connor, his voice proud and strong. "Now Caesar is dust, and the goblet belongs to me."

He placed it back on the table, beside a crystal decanter, which had been filled to the neck with a dark, somewhat opaque, crimson liquid.

Sidorio wasted no more time. Connor watched as his father's hands removed the crystal stopper from the decanter and upended the vessel, pouring a generous amount of liquid into the two-handled goblet. Then he set the decanter back on the table and reinserted the stopper. Sitting down, he lifted the goblet to his thick lips and drained its contents in one. Connor watched. Sidorio swallowed it so easily. It would be his turn next.

Sidorio set the goblet down on the table, then lifted the decanter and refilled it. He held the cup out to Connor.

Connor could see his pale reflection in the ruby-red liquid. He had anticipated that his hand would tremble as he took hold of the goblet, but strangely it did not. He was possessed by a surprising serenity. This was a good sign, he thought; a sign that he was ready. Besides, he figured, it wasn't as if this was actually the first time he had taken blood – he had just never drunk it straight like this before.

"My son," Sidorio said, his lips stained dark by the drink. "Blood of my blood. Heir to my eternal empire. Drink."

Connor lifted the goblet to his lips. He wasn't sure what he had expected but, as he took his first sip, he was surprised at how natural it felt. He took a second sip, aware of Sidorio watching him attentively. The vampirate smiled as Connor finished the contents of the goblet. That wasn't so difficult, thought Connor, pleased with himself. He felt warm, somehow glowing, inside. And he felt strong too, invincible, as if new energy was pumping into him.

"Good?" Sidorio asked.

"Yes." Connor nodded.

"More?" Sidorio's hand was already on the decanter.

"Yes, Father."

"That's my boy!" Sidorio refilled Connor's goblet. "We'll share this one. Half for me, half for you." Smiling, he brought his lips to the cup, then passed it across to Connor.

Connor drank and felt the glow within him expanding and, with it, the energy. He felt very powerful – as if he could fight off a marauding army single-handedly if he had to. If he *chose* to.

"Another?" Sidorio asked.

Connor nodded.

Time blurred, until Connor was suddenly aware of Sidorio tapping the empty decanter. "It appears we've drained this dry. But I can have more sent up, no problem." His expression grew serious. "Next time we feed, my son, we shall dispense with these formalities and hunt for fresh blood together. Side by side."

Connor recoiled at Sidorio's words. Hunting for blood felt like a step too far. But, after everything else that had happened these past six weeks, he couldn't rule it out. As Sidorio had observed – Connor Tempest was long gone. He was Connor Quintus Antonius Sidorio now.

Sidorio had resumed speaking. "Now it is time for your third gift. I think you'll find I've saved the best for last."

"The watch is cool and the sword is awesome, I can't believe it gets much better than this," Connor said, wondering what Sidorio's third gift could possibly be.

Sidorio lifted one of his chains from around his neck. At first Connor was disappointed. After the excitement of the first two rare and luxurious gifts, some second-hand jewellery was a definite anticlimax. Then he noticed that suspended on the chain was a key. And engraved into the metal of the key was a number.

Intrigued, Connor turned the key over in his hand and looked up at Sidorio. "What is this?" he asked.

"The key to cabin number 329," Sidorio said. "Your third gift is waiting for you there. All you have to do is open the door."

"Shall I go now?"

"If you like," Sidorio said. "In fact, I'll come with you."

Connor nodded. "Sure, OK . . . Father."

Once more, his use of the word brought a soft smile to Sidorio's lips. They got up from the table. Connor reached for his new sword. He wasn't about to let it out of his sight. It was way too beautiful.

Sidorio proudly led Connor from the cabin and they made their way out into the corridor. Other crew-members were waiting outside. They made no effort to disguise their interest in Connor. He did not mind or feel at all self-conscious. Who could blame them for being interested in him? He felt as if he was walking in a golden spotlight. In the brief time he had spent in the cabin, his role as their future commander had been sealed. He was the captain's son; heir to the eternal empire of night.

Father and son strode purposefully along the corridor. At the end, they came to another door. Sidorio paused, then pointed. "Cabin 329," he said. "Your gift is waiting inside."

Connor reached forward with the key.

"I should warn you," Sidorio said, leaning closer as Connor positioned the key in the lock. "It isn't *quite* ready for you."

"What do you mean?" Connor asked, turning the key. He felt the bolt turn and the metal door give way. He stepped into the cabin. Sidorio followed.

"There," Sidorio said. "My final gift. Like I say, not *quite* ready for you."

Connor couldn't speak. Looking into the heart of the cabin, every fibre of his being froze. Was this some trick, some hallucination brought on by his first proper taste of blood? No. It was what it was. He could see it and sense it. Sidorio's third gift. This, this *horror*, was truly Sidorio's idea of the best gift of all.

"What have you done?" Connor rasped. "*Why* have you done this?" He shook his head, then opened his mouth once more and let out a deep, keening wail.

Six weeks earlier . . .

CHAPTER ONE

If You Can Keep
Your Head . . .

Sidorio stood on the beach, cradling in his hands the decapitated head of his new bride.

Lola. He opened his mouth to speak her name, but it was too painful to say the word and know that she was gone. To know that she would never again glance up at him, her eyes sparkling with dark purpose. That she would never again smile and take his hand. Never again lift one of her favourite antique glasses, filled with her own special vintage, and sip from it with all the grace of her aristocratic lineage . . .

He gazed down at her in wonder. Even in this state, with her face turning as pale as the reflection of the moon on the becalmed sea, her beauty was peerless. Lady Lola Elizabeth Mercy Lockwood Sidorio. It was not yet an hour since they had been married and already she had been taken from him. Cruelly dispatched at the altar by his own son. A tear welled up in Sidorio's eye. It was not a familiar sensation. The bead of water escaped and fell like a raindrop onto Lola's cheek. Sidorio had a sudden fancy that the water might somehow revive her. That she was not dead but only sleeping. But deep down, in the knot of his stomach, he knew she was gone. He was alone again.

Sidorio lifted his eyes for a moment and saw a small boat skimming away across the water: the pirate squad heading back to its ship, their terrible mission completed. Already, they were too far off for him to distinguish between the silhouettes of the vicious captain Cheng Li and Lola's youthful assassin. But Sidorio held the image of the boy's face clearly in his mind. For it was the face of his own flesh and blood. His son, Connor.

"My boy," he rasped, in agony.

From somewhere came a sound resembling a sigh. Instantly, he glanced down at his wife's head, wondering if there was any conceivable way the sound had emanated from her. But no. It was merely a rogue wave, lapping against the shore. Lola's face was as impassive as ever. Sidorio traced the line of his wife's cheek. Her skin had begun to change now – not only in colour but also in tone – no longer the smooth alabaster he was used to.

Sidorio stared down at the tattoo of a black heart painted around Lola's left eye. That black heart, that closed eyelid, covered the most precious of jewels. Sidorio willed Lola to open her eyes just one more time. If only he could see her beautiful mahogany-coloured eyes for one last, fleeting moment. But no, a single moment with Lola would be too tantalising. He would always want more. Even if he could turn the clock back a mere hour, when all eternity was spread out before them, he would always feel ravenous for more time with Lola. Her skin was growing more wrinkled with every second. Now that the seal of her immortality had been broken, the hungry years were at last racing to catch up with her and consume her. It was a terrible thing to behold.

Sidorio thought back to their first meeting. It had been on

another beach, not dissimilar to this one. She and her crew had been playing games with him, but, as she had confessed that night, it had all been a ploy to catch his attention. How had she put it? She was so dextrous with words. "How else can a minnow signal a whale?" That's right! He could almost hear her voice. He smiled momentarily. How long though, he wondered, before he lost the ability to summon up that distinctive, cut-glass timbre? How long before even this memory was lost?

His thoughts moved on to the time he had trespassed onto her ship, *The Vagabond* – a considerably smaller vessel than his own, the mighty *Blood Captain*. That night, he had interrupted her as she prepared for her nightly blood bath. It was part of her secret beauty regime but she had broken it for him. Instead, they had drunk together from the antique glasses she prized so dearly. She had fed him sweetmeats.

This memory soon spiralled into another – the first time they had gone hunting together. Lola was always clear that she preferred to drink blood from a glass, but still she had hunted with him, telling him she wanted to know his ways – not only to know them but to *experience* them. He had tried to do the same for her, too, though he had never quite understood the appeal of the glass over the human vessel. Those nights they had hunted together, like two rampant wolves, had been nights of the purest joy he could ever remember. To think of them now brought only coldness to his immortal bones and a dull, heavy ache to his head. In his hands, Lola's face grew more wrinkled with every passing minute. Her skin was so dry, it was starting to flake. She was being ravaged before his very eyes. Sidorio began to fear his beautiful wife might simply turn to dust and slip through his fingers into the night air.

He closed his eyes, urging darkness to engulf him. Now, even to think of her was a constant source of pain. But she was within him. Images of her filled his being as completely as blood cells: the time she had helped him pick out new clothes, like the wedding suit he was wearing still, though he would never again have use for such finery; the evening she had placed her tiny hand on his and shown him how to swirl the vintage inside the glass to release its aroma; then that moment – that magical moment – when she had consented to become his wife . . .

She had become his wife but, more than that, she had become his world. Now she was gone.

Sidorio had been lonely before, but never like this. He let out a sorrowful roar.

The wind whispered close in his ear, as if somehow it shared his mourning. The sound came again and Sidorio wondered if it could, after all, be the wind. The beach was calm and the air was still and dry.

There was a third sound, not so much a whisper as a cough. Tempted to believe that some drop of life still remained in Lola, he glanced down, fearful of the bitter disappointment ahead. But, he had no choice. He had to gaze again at her beautiful face. At that perfect tattoo of a black heart.

He contemplated his wife's ruby lips. Was it his imagination or had they parted slightly since he had last looked? And her skin seemed, if not smoother, then at least no more wrinkled and cracked than before. Sidorio shook his head. A man could drive himself mad with such imaginings.

And now perhaps madness *had* taken hold of Sidorio. Because, as he gazed at his wife's face once more, he saw a fragile eyelid flutter. The black heart was broken. And, in its place, he saw the dazzling beauty of Lola's eye.

Sidorio felt himself inextricably sinking into the depths of insanity. "No," he moaned. "Don't play tricks on me! Let me mourn her."

At that Lola's cracked lips shifted into a soft smile. Then he

4

heard her unmistakeable voice. "You're a touch premature in mourning me, my darling husband."

Sidorio froze. "No more tricks!" he cried. "Whoever you are, whoever is doing this, stop! I must let her go!"

Lola's eyes blazed with fire at that. "Darling Sid. I am not going anywhere just yet. Though if you would be a dear and hurry up and reunite me with my body, I'd happily go back to one or other of our ships with you . . ."

This was no dream. No madness. It was a genuine, gold carat miracle!

Sidorio couldn't contain the torrent of joy that swept through him. "You're back!" he cried, tears streaming down his face. "But how? How can it be?"

Lola gazed up at him. Though her face was creased and desiccated, it was still unmistakeably one of rare beauty. "Dear, dear Sid. Did you really think I'd leave you on our wedding night? Not a chance! A man like you is hard to find."

Sidorio shook his head in wonder. Now he knew he wasn't imagining this. Only Lola would say something like that. "You're back," he said. "You're really back!"

"Yes," said Lady Lola Elizabeth Mercy Lockwood Sidorio. "I'm back, husband. So let's not waste another moment. Take me to my body and then I'm going to need something exceedingly strong to drink."

"I know exactly what you mean," he said. As he spoke, Sidorio was already striding across the sand, cradling his precious wife's head in his hands. Joyously, he broke into a run, then propelled himself up into the air. He flew up to the top of the cliff, where Lady Lola's svelte but inert body lay patiently waiting on the cliff-top, ready to be reunited with her wayward head.

Sidorio laid Lola's head down upon the grass, holding it as close as possible to the torn veins and arteries, the broken bone and muscles of her neck. As he did so, Lola closed her eyes once more. She frowned, as if in excruciating pain. Sidorio was struck with fear that this wouldn't work, but soon the fibres of her neck began to knit themselves back together.

Sidorio watched, fascinated, as Lola's bruised and bloodied skin rapidly began to repair itself. The flaking skin fell from her face and the wrinkles ebbed away like the outgoing tide. Her face swiftly regained its customary sheen and suppleness. If anything, she looked younger than before. Throughout this, her eyes remained closed. She looked peaceful now, as if she were taking a restorative nap.

Sidorio laid the palms of his thick hands on either side of his wife's beautiful face, tendrils of her raven-black hair spilling over his grubby fingers. He could scarcely believe she was actually here; that he was not imagining this miraculous reunion. But the mere touch of her flesh felt different now. He could sense a new energy fizzing beneath the surface of her skin. He knew little of vampire biology, but imagined dark cells multiplying, oscillating within her veins.

Lola opened her eyes and an extraordinary light beamed from inside them – a light which seemed to illuminate both the life within her and the journey ahead. Now Lola was back at his side, they could at last embark on their voyage together. Who knew where it would take them?

Sidorio felt himself coming back to life again, along with his wife. Once more, he thought of Connor. If this miraculous reunion with Lola had been possible, why not then a reunion with his son too, however improbable it seemed? And with his daughter, Grace, of course. It was time to unite his whole family.

He became aware of his wife staring up at him, her head pillowed on the soft grass. Sidorio leaned down, carefully stroking a stray wisp of hair away from her eyes, so that her distinctive tattoo was clear to see once more. "What's next for us, I wonder, my black heart?"

Lola's eyelids fluttered as delicately as the velvet wings of a moth. "After a wedding," she said, huskily, "isn't it customary for the groom to take his new bride on a honeymoon?"

"A honeymoon?" Sidorio found himself racing to catch up. "A honeymoon. Yes, of course. Where would you like to go?"

"Somewhere cold," Lola answered. "I'm tired of this incessant heat. Take me somewhere *bitterly* cold."

Sidorio beamed at her, his twin gold incisors glinting in the moonlight. "Whatever your beautiful black heart desires, my love. You know I'd do anything for you."

Lola smiled at that and lifted her hand to Sidorio's. "And I for you," she said. "For all eternity."

CHAPTER TWO

Beach Pirates

Connor Tempest stood poised on the ship's deck, waiting for "Cutlass" Cate Morgan to give the sign. He glanced to his right side, where his friend Bart Pearce gave him a reassuring wink. As usual, he drew strength from his proximity. There was no one you could depend upon more in the chaos of conflict – or, for that matter, outside of it – than Bart.

Turning to his other side, Connor saw Cheng Li up ahead. The Pirate Federation's newest captain had her intense, almond-shaped eyes trained on Cate too. In so many ways, it was just like old times. Cate, Bart and Cheng Li were the first pirates Connor had met and befriended when he had been taken aboard Molucco Wrathe's ship, *The Diablo*.

But Connor was no longer on board *The Diablo*; no longer shackled to Wrathe's erratic command. He and his young comrades had all travelled a long way in a short time; none more so than Connor himself. In many ways, living through these past few months had felt like riding the most extreme rollercoaster ever invented. But Connor didn't want to dwell on the twists and turns of his journey. Now wasn't the time for thought, but for action. His body was poised like a hawk, waiting to pounce on its prey. His mind too was psyched up for the fight. Bring it on! His newer comrades were close by. Connor's eyes skimmed the attractive faces of Jacoby Blunt and Jasmine Peacock. The golden couple. That was how they had seemed when he had first encountered them at Pirate Academy. Jacoby and Jasmine had been two of the most talented and popular students in the graduation class. How carefree they had seemed then. Subsequently, they had served as professional pirates aboard *The Tiger*, commanded by Cheng Li. Their elite training had served them well professionally but, in private, there had been developments none of them had predicted. Yes, Connor thought, as his eyes traced the contours of Jasmine's startlingly beautiful profile, there had indeed been many surprising twists and turns on the journey here.

Cate gave the signal. Without hesitation, Connor ran to the edge of the deck, then propelled himself up into the air, shoulder to shoulder with Bart on one side and Jacoby on the other. Swords in hand, the battle was already underway before they landed on the deck of the adjacent ship.

Steel clashed with steel. There had been times when the noise had made Connor's hackles rise and his head ache. Not today. Today, the merciless noise was welcome, for it instantly shut out the internal din. Here, in the inferno of combat, there was no chance for the icy voices inside his head to be heard. Here, things were simple, achievable. He and his comrades had a job to do – a fight to win. And Connor Tempest was up for the fight.

"Follow me, Tempest!" Jacoby cried.

Connor didn't falter. Jacoby Blunt was deputy captain of *The Tiger*, Cheng Li's second-in-command. Whatever Connor's complicated personal feelings towards Jacoby, in combat there was a simple hierarchy to be adhered to.

The two young pirates raced down from the deck into the

heart of the ship. They were on the tail of their main targets – the ship's captain and his deputy. If – or rather *when* – they surrendered, the battle was over. It was a smaller ship than *The Tiger* or *The Diablo* and Jacoby and Connor had to run in single file, kept at a disadvantage through their lack of knowledge of its particular layout. Their adversaries were young and fast. Cate and Cheng Li had said that this was a straightforward mission. But Connor had already accrued sufficient experience as a pirate to know that no mission is ever entirely straightforward. There is always an opportunity for things to go awry. It had happened when he and the rest of Molucco Wrathe's crew had been surrounded on the deck of *The Albatross*. Connor and Bart's dear friend Jez had lost his life as a result. Blood had flowed again during the pirates' raid on the Sunset Fort, this time through the characteristically selfish actions of Molucco's nephew, Moonshine Wrathe. Connor had had to kill, for the first time, to save Moonshine's life. Afterwards, he had been feted as a hero, but the experience had led him to question his suitability for life as a pirate.

Now Jacoby and Connor came to a stairwell, spiralling down into the bowels of the ship. They could see their targets twisting and turning beneath them. As they shouted abuse up at the pirates, Connor wasn't struck so much by his adversaries' colourful language as by the pitch of their voices. He had known from the outset that their targets were young, but exactly *how* young?

He had to shelve this thought temporarily in view of more pressing concerns. Top of the list was where were the two targets heading – and why? Their actions defied all logic. You never ran down from an open deck to the very bottom of a vessel – it was one of the first aspects of strategy inculcated in pirate apprentices at Pirate Academy. But Connor's opponents had never studied at Pirate Academy. They were "beach pirates" –

opportunistic kids hoping to take the fast track to fame and fortune. A few years back, they just might have succeeded. Might have grown up to receive the adulation afforded to Molucco Wrathe, say. Not now. Things were changing at a lightning pace. The Pirate Federation was coming down hard on non-Federation vessels and their self-appointed captains. With the growing external threat on the oceans, the Federation could no longer turn a blind eye to the rogue elements within the pirate fraternity. Cheng Li and Cate had been crystal clear about the purpose of this mission – to shut down this ship and its young command with immediate effect.

Jacoby threw himself down the stairwell. As ever, Connor was dazzled by his mate's athleticism. Sometimes, Jacoby's lithe and sinewy body seemed to have more in common with a panther than a human. Connor followed, not giving himself credit for the fact he was every bit as athletic as his comrade.

"This way," cried Jacoby, as Connor's feet made contact with the floor of the lower deck. They raced along another corridor, towards the door at the end. Their opponents had to be in the cabin behind it. There was nowhere else for them to go. Connor held Jacoby back for an instant, alert to the fact that they might be racing into a trap. Jacoby got the message without a word being exchanged. It was the Synchronicity of Comrades – Connor remembered Jasmine referring to a lecture at Pirate Academy on that very subject. A lecture given by the academy's recently assassinated headmaster, Commodore John Kuo.

Kuo may have gone, but his teachings lived on. Perhaps that was the best you could hope for by way of a legacy.

Together Jacoby and Connor scanned the terrain, assessing the possibilities. Satisfied that there was only one, Jacoby turned to Connor. Connor nodded in anticipation, and the two of them charged along the corridor and hurled themselves at the cabin door.

Their adversaries had piled up ballast against the other side of the door but it wasn't enough to stop Jacoby and Connor from breaking through. They found themselves crashing into a large, dark cabin. In essence, it was like many other cabins they had seen before. In the centre of the room stood a long, heavy banqueting table, surrounded by tall chairs. But attached to the walls on each side of the cabin were hundreds and hundreds of swords of all shapes and sizes. It looked as if the walls were made of steel. This was a veritable armoury. Their opponents would have no shortage of weaponry with which to threaten them. But where *were* their opponents?

Looking up, just in the nick of time, Connor saw a small but athletic figure curled around the iron chandelier that hung centrally above the table. Catching Connor's gaze, the assailant swung on the chandelier to gain momentum, propelling himself towards him. As he did so, there was a battle cry and the second assailant flew out from under the table with the force of a cannonball, ricocheting into Jacoby.

Without flinching, Connor leaped up onto the table and met his opponent head on. For the first time, he saw his face – the boy could be no more than nine or ten years old. In any other circumstance he'd have applauded the kid's ambition, but now wasn't the time for praise. The beach pirate grinned as he drew his sword. Connor swiftly parried it with his rapier.

He heard Jacoby clash swords with the beach pirate's captain, but couldn't risk glancing away from his own opponent. The young lad was full of raw energy and Connor had no doubt that if he was allowed to gain the upper hand, he would be merciless. Connor wasn't about to let that happen. He drew his adversary in, allowing him to make the moves, confident that sooner or later he would catch the kid out and seize victory.

Connor met every strike of his opponent's sword. The boy

was slight and couldn't rival Connor in force but he utilised his own weightlessness to great acrobatic effect. The lightness and agility of his movements was dazzling. He made Connor, at fourteen, feel old and heavy in contrast.

Connor was impressed both by the boy's nerve and his raw talent as he made a fresh lunge at him. He could imagine the teachers at Pirate Academy piling praise on the lad or Cheng Li taking him under her wing as she had lately with Bo Yin. But, in a flash, the kid's inexperience in combat revealed itself. He had allowed himself to be backed into a corner. The fight was over. The beach pirate had been easily outmanoeuvred by the professional. In the throes of conflict, they had seemed equals, in spite of their difference in age. Now, Connor found himself staring at a terrified kid. Albeit one who spat and hurled a stream of invective at him. Connor decided it was time to teach the kid a lesson.

He extended his blade to touch his opponent's face. Carefully, Connor drew the tip across the boy's cheek, watching as a neat line of blood appeared on his downy skin. He could see the raw terror in the lad's eyes, knew that he had clarified who was now calling the shots. He had the power to choose life or death for his opponent. It was then that Connor realised just how angry he was. Angry that these 'beach pirates' were out at sea, messing with real pirate crews, like his own, who had serious business to accomplish. Angry too, that he had been denied the full, challenging fight that another professional would have given him – a fight he needed; that his body and mind were crying out for. But, mostly, angry at himself. For things utterly beyond his control.

"It's over." He heard Jacoby's voice, addressing the young captain who had been forced equally easily into submission. Now, Jacoby turned to his comrade. "It's over, Connor. Draw down your sword!"

Jacoby's voice was so clear, so confident. It had been an open-and-shut mission for him. That was how Jacoby saw each battle, each mission, each passing day and night. In patterns only of black and white; no grey. Things will never be that simple for me, Connor thought bitterly. For him, there would be no more simple beginnings and endings. Not after what he had learned about himself; about what he was and his inability to do anything to change it. For evermore, for all gnawing eternity, his only truth would be that his name was Connor Tempest and he was the son of a vampire.

CHAPTER THREE
The Honeymooners

The Black Sea, Odessa, Ukraine

"I do so love it here," Lola declared, turning her gaze from Sidorio out to the frozen sea. "I knew you'd choose the perfect spot for our honeymoon." It was so cold that the ocean waves were freezing as they hit the shore. It was a rare and magical sight, made yet more magical by the violet tint of the moonlight and the soft hush of the waves in the distance, sounding their final sighs before they transmuted from liquid into ice.

A fresh drift of snow began to cover the table between them. Lola turned to face her husband, reaching out her hand to him. "How clever you are," she said.

Sidorio smiled. In his achingly long time roaming this world, he could pretty much count on the fingers of one hand the times he had been called clever. He shifted his gaze from his wife's glowing face to the building behind them. A soft light emanated from the windows of the all but deserted hotel. In former times, the rococo building had been a royal palace and it clung on to a certain epic grandeur. The Lockwood Sidorios were the only guests at the hotel and had secured the suite of rooms once used by Peter the Great and his wife, the Empress

15

Catherine. "How fitting," Lola had said as she had snatched the key from the desk clerk, who doubled up as the maître d'.

In the absence of business during the long, harsh winter, the hotel retained only a skeleton staff. This mattered little to the newly-weds. Their needs were quite simple.

Now, the maître d' made his way towards the unconventional but unerringly generous couple, sitting at their table at the edge of the snow-covered beach. Tonight, the woman with the curious heart tattoo was dressed in a full-length sable; the man in a greatcoat, enhancing his somewhat militaristic air.

"Sir." The elderly host cleared his throat, then announced, "The musicians have arrived. Just as you requested." His message delivered, the elderly host began trudging back through the snow.

Lola clapped her hands in delight. Gazing lovingly at her husband, she exclaimed, "Musicians! Bravo!"

"You said you wanted music." Sidorio's eyes bore into hers. "Anything my wife desires, she gets."

Lola smiled. "Anything?"

He winked. "Try me."

"A new ship," she said, not missing a beat. "One like Trofie Wrathe's. *The Typhon*." She paused, then smiled. "No, not *like The Typhon*. I want *The Typhon* itself."

Sidiorio looked amused. "Her golden hand wasn't enough for you?"

Lola pouted momentarily. "Her rancid son stole that back. No matter, it served its purpose." She smiled to remember how she had lately employed Trofie's hand as the centrepiece of her unorthodox wedding bouquet.

"Fine," Sidorio said. "So, I'll get you her ship. What else? Anything I can get for you this very night?"

"Well," said Lola, "I *am* quite thirsty, as it happens. How about you?"

16

Sidorio nodded, smiling. Then, he whistled to the maitre d' who was still forging his way back through the snow to summon the musicians. As Sidorio's whistle whipped through the night air, the old man stopped dead in his tracks, turned and began to plod back, his snowshoes slow and none too steady.

"Bring us a magnum of your finest vintage," Sidorio barked.

The old man raised a wild eyebrow – the wave of white hair encrusted with ice. "Our finest is expensive, sir – in a magnum, especially."

Sidorio shrugged, losing no time in pulling gold from his pockets. "Don't bother me with talk of money. You know perfectly well I have enough gold here to buy this fleapit hotel, if I choose to. Just fetch us the wine." Noticing Lola watching him admiringly, he added, "My wife is a connoisseur. She has a very *sophisticated* palate."

"Very good, sir!" The host gave a nod, then turned to embark on his latest epic journey through the thick falling snow.

Lola slipped off her shoes and let the bare flesh of her soles connect with the icy ground. It felt utterly delicious. Once more, she shivered with pleasure.

The musicians arrived. They were young and clad in coats, hats, scarves and fingerless gloves. They climbed onto the old iron bandstand. With minimal fuss, they took up their instruments and began to play. The music was entrancing, blending the innocent air of an old folk-song with the insistent rhythm of a tango.

Lola stood up, letting her sable coat slide down from her shoulders into the well of her chair. She reached out a hand. "Dance with me, husband!"

Sidorio rose to his feet and enfolded her tiny hand in his powerful grip. They walked across the snow-covered beach, a short distance from the bandstand. The lead singer – a young woman with wild, dark eyes and lashes reminiscent of thick spider's legs – smiled, as the couple began to dance. Their style was unusual but full of flair.

Lola shrieked with delight as Sidorio dipped her low over the ice. She let her head fall backwards, exposing the fresh scars about her neck, while strands of her long, raven hair brushed the snow and her eyes gazed wildly up at the full moon.

After their dance, Sidorio led Lola back to their table. In their absence, the aged host had deposited the magnum of wine and a pair of glasses. Already, the bottle and glasses were dusted with fresh snowflakes.

"I'll pour," Lola said, brushing snow from the wine bottle. Lifting it up to the light, she glanced at the bottle's yellowed label. Then she upended it and poured its dark, glutinous contents out onto the moonlit snow.

Sidorio grinned.

The musicians began a new song – the violin and accordion building the rhythm. The singer slapped her tambourine and stomped her feet with increasing vigour, utterly caught up in the frenzied world of her song.

Lola extended the empty bottle to her husband, swinging it precariously between her elegant fingers. "Lola's thirsty," she declared, mimicking a young girl's voice. Then, reverting to her normal timbre, she smiled prettily and asked, "Won't you fetch me a *proper* drink, dearest?"

Nodding but saying nothing, Sidorio seized the empty bottle and set off through the snow. Lola glimpsed the fire in his eyes; the deep pits of flame which revealed that his own appetite was as strong and deep and demanding as her own.

Inside the warmth of the hotel restaurant, the maitre d' noticed that the music had stopped. He squinted out through the window but a veil of fresh condensation impaired his view. He

18

lifted a feeble hand to the glass, wincing as his old flesh made contact with the freezing pane. Rubbing his fist against it, he cleared a peephole.

Peering out, he saw that the bandstand stood empty. He adjusted his line of vision and corrected himself. The bandstand was not in fact empty but carpeted with bodies. The musicians were slumped on it, lifeless. A river of red, illuminated by the moon, flowed urgently into the virgin snow.

The man – the impossibly tall stranger with the impressively deep pockets – walked back across the snow. Rocking between the thick thumb and forefinger of his left hand was the wine bottle. As he strode on, some of the contents of the magnum spilled over the brim and spattered the ground.

Feeling waves of nausea, the old man frowned. He turned away from the window and sought comfort in the sight of the pile of gold coins. They gleamed in the candlelight, as bright as if they had been minted that very evening. He cupped the coins in his hands and cradled them carefully. This was more money than he had ever seen in his long life; certainly more money than he would ever see again.

Outside, Sidorio offered the bottle to his wife. Lola reached out her glass and Sidorio poured a tasting portion of the liquid inside. She had trained him well. Mouthing her thanks, she swirled the liquid around the glass and lifted it to her nose, the better to savour its distinctive aroma.

Glancing up, she caught her husband eschewing the other glass and, instead, lifting the bottle directly to his thick lips. He drank thirstily. She watched him; half appalled, half entranced.

Sidorio, growing conscious of his wife's glance, drew the bottle away from his mouth and smiled, guilelessly, at her. His lips were smeared with blood. Like a naughty lad caught with a mouthful of chocolate, he extended his tongue to lick up the traces.

19

Lola laughed. "You're such a brute, my darling," she said, her words laced with affection. She reached out her glass once more. "A refill, please, if you've left anything for me! It's a mixed blend, but rather tasty."

"Plenty for us both," he said. "And plenty more where this came from."

Lola sipped her wine, thoughtfully. "You know, Sid, you're the roughest of diamonds, but once I have finished with you, you will shine with all the light of Lucifer."

Sidorio raised his glass. "A toast," he said. "To you and me. Together always. Husband and wife."

Lola raised her own glass. "To us, my brutish darling. Together through eternity." She drank, then gazed at her husband, fresh fire in her eyes. "You asked me before what I wanted. Well, there is one more thing . . ."

Sidorio nodded. "Go on."

"I want to grow an empire with you. Hand in hand."

"I want that too," Sidorio said. He paused. "And I want my children to be part of it."

Lola hesitated. "Grace and Connor?"

Sidorio nodded. "I can't pretend they don't exist. Even if Connor *did* try to destroy you."

Lola considered for a moment. "He did cast a certain pall over our wedding by stabbing and then decapitating me. But," she shrugged, "I'm sure we can forgive such waywardness in the young. Connor and Grace are *your* flesh and blood. And, by marriage, *my* stepchildren. It is only fitting that they should become part of our empire." She smiled at Sidorio. "You should invite them to visit us, when we return. I'd so enjoy getting to know them."

"Would you really?"

As Lola nodded, Sidorio thought his heart might break from happiness. In a short space of time, he had gone from feeling that he had lost everything to the sense now that he was being overloaded with gifts. Fortune's wheel was certainly spinning fast.

"Nothing would make me happier," he said, "than you and I building an empire, with Connor and Grace at our side."

"Let's not waste a moment," Lola said, refilling her glass. "Let's cut short our honeymoon and return to the ships this very night."

Sidorio smiled. "Sometimes it's as if you can read my every thought."

Lola gave a little laugh. "There is no time to be wasted in the quest for world domination . . ." They clinked glasses. "Though there *is* a small supply of vintage still to be drained back at the hotel . . . Perhaps we could finish that first?"

"Indeed," said Sidorio. "We should drink a toast to our family!"

Arms entwined, they turned and headed leisurely back towards the hotel, their footsteps muffled by the snow.

The entrance door closed quietly behind them. And then all that could be heard was the tinkle of gold coins clattering to the floor.

CHAPTER FOUR

Voyagers of the Night

Grace Tempest and her friend, Darcy Flotsam, joined the throng making their way along the corridors of the ship. Dressed in their finery, they were all journeying down to the banqueting hall on the bottom deck, where the weekly Feast would take place.

Scanning the faces of the Vampirates around her, Grace saw clear signs of their hunger – a silvery-grey pallor to the visible flesh and a distant quality to their eyes, as if they were not entirely present in this realm. Such signs were always most pronounced just before the Feast, when the Vampirates were at their lowest physical ebb and in most urgent need of blood. In spite of the Vampirates' evident weakness and pressing hunger, it was a remarkably orderly crowd which made the weekly *passeggiata* through the ship, their footsteps beating time with the percussive music drifting up from below.

Since the Captain's disappearance, Mosh Zu had taken command of *The Nocturne* and it was a credit to the guru's quiet authority that there had been no further rebellions or incidents of random blood-taking on his watch.

Mosh Zu had made it very clear upon his arrival that he

expected members of the crew to exercise self-discipline with regard to their blood-hunger and to confine their blood-taking to the weekly sharing which followed the Feast. He gave them a simple choice: either they respected this *modus vivendi* or they departed the ship and took their chances in the world beyond. A few *had* chosen to leave and seek out Sidorio and his renegade disciples. But that had been during the first nights of Mosh Zu's command. Since then, order had been fully restored.

When the Captain returned, Grace mused, it would be to a ship of Vampirates brought firmly back into line.

Darcy nudged Grace gently. "You look lost in thought," she said. "What's on your mind?"

"I was just thinking about the Captain," Grace said. "I find it impossible not to, on nights like this."

Darcy nodded. "Me too. He's missed so many Feast Nights now." She hesitated before continuing. "I know it's a terrible thing to say, Grace, but I'm starting to doubt he'll ever return."

"Darcy!" Grace exclaimed, in shocked tones, causing some of those walking ahead of her to turn and glance back. Grace lowered her voice before continuing. "He *is* coming back, Darcy. I know it. He wouldn't just go away and leave us. You, of all people, know how weak he was, but Mosh Zu says he is making a steady recovery now. He'll be back soon, I'm sure of it."

"I'd like to believe that," Darcy said. "Truly, I would. It was horrible seeing someone so powerful brought down so low."

Grace nodded. She had experienced the same gut-wrenching emotions, standing over the Captain during Mosh Zu's healing catharsis. But she had to hold on to hope. "He'll be back," she repeated firmly, as much to reassure herself as Darcy.

The two friends had reached the entrance to the banqueting hall. Now, Darcy took Grace's arm and they stepped across the threshold together.

Inside the spacious cabin, the music was louder and there was a hubbub of conversation amongst the well-dressed diners. As usual, a long table stretched down the centre of the room. It was laid with damask tablecloths, fine china, sparkling crystal and shiny silver cutlery. But there were only place-settings on the far side of the table. Standing behind this side of the table, ready to be served a delicious, nutrient-rich dinner, were the donors.

For every Vampirate who travelled aboard *The Nocturne* – with the exception of Mosh Zu – there was a donor. These men and women, of a variety of ages and backgrounds, had each made a pact with the Vampirates to give a weekly portion of their blood in exchange for bed, board and one further gift: immortality, for in return for their blood, the donors remained as ageless as their Vampirate partners.

Looking along the line of faces, Grace remembered attending her first Feast and thinking that she herself was to be a donor. She had even taken her place on the donor side of the table. Initially it had looked as if she was to be Sidorio's donor, or the Captain's. But though it was the Captain who had led her out of the banqueting hall that night, he had had no plans to take her blood. Like Mosh Zu, the Captain was a highly evolved Vampirate – a *pranic* vampire – who had no need to feast on blood. Grace had been let off the hook that night and, though she continued to attend every Feast and to sit on the donor side of the table, ever since it had only been as a guest.

As the Vampirates arrived in the room, each sought out their donor. The pairs bowed before one another, then sat down, ready for the Feast.

"I'll see you later," Darcy said to Grace, gently squeezing her arm. "Enjoy your dinner!"

Grace watched as her friend strode off to meet her donor, James – or "My Jim" as Darcy fondly referred to him. It was easy to misinterpret the relationship between Vampirate and donor as a romantic one but, in the main, this was not the case. The relationships were intimate, certainly, and, for the most part, tender. Every Vampirate, and his or her donor, was aware of the great gift which the Sharing bestowed upon each party. But there was a marked gulf between gratitude and romance. Indeed, thought Grace, the only instances she knew of where the Vampirate/donor relationship had become more complicated had ended in tragedy.

Grace's thoughts turned to Sidorio and his original donor, Sally – Grace's own mother – and then to Stukeley and his donor Shanti. Both Sally and Shanti had passed on now. Sidorio and Stukeley were forging their own, dark, command. And the Captain was missing. So much change but, inside Grace's head, the five of them lingered in the room like ghosts at the feast.

"Grace! About time!" Grace turned her head and saw Oskar, Lorcan's handsome donor, smiling and gesturing towards the seat next to his. Nodding, Grace made her way over to join him.

As Grace slipped into the space beside Oskar, he cast an approving glance over her. "You look *amazing*!" he said. "Great dress! It really brings out the colour of your eyes."

"Thank you," she said, her spirits instantly lifting, as they invariably did in Oskar's sunny company.

Oskar was poised to launch into further conversation but a hush had begun to descend upon the room. Mosh Zu had arrived and was making his way towards the table. At his side was his trusty lieutenant, Lorcan Furey.

Lorcan reached the table first. He bowed to Oskar, then reached out and took Grace's hand, lifting it to his lips and kissing her fingers. His lips were as soft and cool as a mountain stream.

"Hello," she said, suddenly as nervous as if they were meeting for the first time.

"Hello you," he said, in his warm Irish brogue. "I swear, Grace, you look more beautiful every time I see you."

25

Grace beamed up at him. He was dressed in a tuxedo, a crisp white shirt with pearl studs, and, knotted around his neck, a blue silk cravat – an exact match for his twinkling azure eyes. "You look very handsome yourself," she said.

"Blah, blah, blah," Oskar said, with a grin. "*You're so beautiful, Grace! No, you're so handsome, Lorcan!* And what, pray, am I? Chopped liver?!"

Lorcan smiled winningly. "My, my, Oskar. How well you look tonight."

"*Thank you!*" Oskar said, with some emphasis, as if he had waited years for this sole compliment.

Lorcan shook his head from side to side, in mock-dismay, as he sat down. "Of all the donors aboard this ship, how come I ended up with the most high-maintenance one?"

"Just luck, I guess," said Oskar, always intent upon having the last word.

Grace and Lorcan laughed at Oskar's sharp tongue and shameless vanity, then adopted a more serious demeanour as Mosh Zu arrived at the table and stood in the place opposite Grace. Although theirs was not a comparable Vampirate/donor relationship, they still bowed to one another – a mark of respect from both sides. Mosh Zu gestured to Grace that she should sit down. He remained standing.

The doors to the banqueting hall were closed. The musicians in the corner of the room stilled their instruments. The men and women standing along both sides of the table fell silent, their faces bowed over the candles which flickered along its centre. Mosh Zu began to speak. His fellow Vampirates joined in with his stirring words:

> "*I am a proud voyager of the night.*
> *No lesser, nor greater, than a being of the light.*
> *I will not hide in the shadows,*

26

For why should I hide?
Nor shall I stalk the dark places,
With the intention of striking fear into passing strangers.
I will be moderate in my taking of blood,
For blood is a gift above all worldly treasure.
I give thanks for this gift.
I embrace my immortality.
I relish this journey through all eternity.
No lesser, nor greater, than a being of the light.
I am a proud voyager of the night."

As he finished speaking, Mosh Zu paused for a moment, glancing left and right to survey his crew. Then he sat down. The music resumed and the doors to the banqueting hall were thrown open again as the servers brought in vast platters loaded with food.

Feast Night had begun.

"Tut, tut! You haven't touched a thing!" Oskar chided Grace, as the servers began clearing away the main course plates.

Grace glanced down guiltily. Oskar was right. She had cut up her fish and pushed it around her plate but very little had actually reached her mouth. "I'm not very hungry tonight," she said. "And there's such a lot of food!"

"That's why it's called a feast," Oskar said, with feigned patience.

Lorcan and Mosh Zu were deep in conversation. Grace leaned in confidentially towards Oskar. "I think it's because of the changes I'm going through. My hunger is very erratic. Sometimes it's really intense and urgent. Sometimes, like now, I have zero appetite." She paused, locking eyes with Oskar. "But my *other* hunger seems to be rising."

Oskar nodded, unfazed. "Have you thought about getting

your own donor? Or – how about this – why don't you share with me as well?" He smiled at her, invitingly. "I don't know why we didn't think of it before. Of course, you should share me!"

Grace surveyed Oskar's handsome, smiling face but shook her head. "It's very good of you to offer, Oskar, but I'm not ready. Besides, Mosh Zu tells me that I don't need to take blood. As a dhampir, I should be able to master my appetite, just as he and the Captain have done."

Oskar's face was etched with concern. "Are you sure you're not expecting too much of yourself, Grace? Setting yourself the same standards of discipline as the Captain and Mosh Zu?"

Grace shrugged. "I don't know," she answered, honestly. "Sometimes, I don't have a clue who – or what – I am any more."

"Now, now," Oskar said. "No sad face! You look far too beautiful tonight to be sad." He glanced over, as the servers re-entered the room with platters of dessert. "Oh goodie! Chocolate mousse. My favourite!"

The thought of yet more food made Grace feel queasy. "I think I'll go to my cabin for a bit."

As she stood up, Mosh Zu and Lorcan broke off their conversation and turned towards her.

"Are you all right, Grace?" Lorcan asked, looking concerned.

"Yes," she nodded. "Yes, I'm fine. I'm just feeling a bit tired and off-kilter. I think I should go to my cabin and lie down."

Mosh Zu nodded.

Lorcan rose to his feet. "I'll walk you there."

"No." Grace shook her head. "I'll be fine on my own. You stay here. I'll see you later." She turned to Mosh Zu. "I apologise for my bad manners," she said.

Mosh Zu softly shook his head. "Go, Grace. You need your rest."

Grace nodded and pushed her chair back under the table, making her way as discreetly as possible across the floor of the banqueting hall. But there was no escaping the laser-like gaze of Darcy Flotsam, who glanced up at her questioningly from across the table. "I'm fine," Grace mouthed to her, before turning and exiting the room.

Grace felt better as she climbed the steps up to the higher levels of the ship. She considered going out on deck to get some fresh air but decided that she really would be best returning to her cabin. The ship was deserted – everyone was down in the banqueting hall – and she made swift progress along its corridors, gratefully pushing open the door to her room.

The first thing she saw on entering the cabin was the painting which now hung above her bed. The picture had been a gift from Lorcan. It depicted a young man and woman stretched out lazily on a ship's deck. *This* ship's deck. The couple's eyes were fixed on each other, basking in the afternoon sun and the first flush of love. They exuded joy and optimism but Grace knew this was deceptive. The two figures depicted were Grace's mother and the man Grace had thought, until recently, was her father. It captured Sally and Dexter at the zenith of their youth and happiness. Soon afterwards, their lives had veered into dark water.

Grace's eyes locked on the image of Dexter Tempest. He might not be her blood father, but he would *always* be her dad.

She turned away from the painting and approached the dressing table and the mirror which rested upon it. She looked into the glass, scrutinising her reflection. In spite of all the changes she was going through, she didn't look obviously stressed or run-down. On the contrary, she looked rather well tonight. Indeed, as Oskar had noted, the latest dress borrowed from Darcy *had* brought out the subtle colouring of her eyes.

Grace found herself gazing deep into her own reflected eyes, watching the green shift to blue like the ocean waters. Then she felt an increasingly familiar sensation. It began as a certain queasiness but grew into a deep, gnawing hunger. A hunger not for food, but for blood.

As the coil of hunger ricocheted through her body, Grace kept her gaze locked on the mirror, observing herself with horrid fascination, as the familiar emerald green of her irises disappeared and was replaced by dancing orange fire.

CHAPTER FIVE

The Homecoming

"I'm home!" A familiar voice reverberated around the bridge of *The Blood Captain*, as the door was flung open.

Jez Stukeley and Johnny Desperado, Sidorio's two ambitious lieutenants, scrambled to their feet to salute their returning captain as he strode inside to join them. They were somewhat surprised to find Sidorio dressed in a silver fox fur coat and matching hat. Ever since The Big Romance with Lady Lola Lockwood, the captain's dress-sense had taken a turn for the bizarre.

"It's great to be back!" Sidorio declared, dropping two hefty suitcases on the floor and standing, hands on hips, grinning at his two deputies.

"Nice hat, Captain!" Stukeley said. "I take it you didn't honeymoon in the tropics, then?"

"No, the Ukraine," Sidorio said, unbuttoning his coat. "Lola wanted a snow and ice vacation."

"How ... quirky," Stukeley mumbled, whilst nodding agreeably.

Sidorio shrugged off the coat and sent his hat flying through the air. It landed on a protruding part of the ship's steering kit.

31

"How's tricks?" he inquired, rubbing his hands together briskly. "Anything crop up in my absence that I should know about? Anyone misbehaving? Tell me everything!"

Johnny shook his head, exchanging glances with his comrade. "It's all been smooth sailing, hasn't it, Stuke?"

Stukeley nodded, his hand resting possessively on the ship's wheel. "We've kept everything nicely under control, Captain."

"Excellent work, lads," Sidorio said, marching over to the wheel and placing his own hands firmly on its circumference. "I knew I could depend on you both to take care of business for me." He grinned, surveying the vast hulk of the ship beneath him, and the thronging crew below. Then he shifted his bulk, with the result that Stukeley had no choice but to step aside and release his hand from the steering wheel. "I'm home now," Sidorio said, quietly but with unquestionable authority, "and things can get back to normal around here."

Behind Sidorio's back, Stukeley grimaced at Johnny.

Johnny knew how much his friend and comrade had relished taking command of the ship during the captain's absence. Johnny had undeniably got a kick out of it too – and there was no doubt that the crew had been more organised under their command than had previously been the case. The question was: now that Sidorio was back at the helm, would things remain structured or would they slip back into the old chaos? It could go either way. It didn't matter so much to Johnny. He was more than capable of going with the flow. But he had lately detected a new drive and ambition in Stukeley's make-up. He had known there would be tension on the captain's return; he just hadn't expected it to surface quite so soon.

Johnny racked his brains for a way to defuse the air of tension on the bridge. Suddenly he had a brainwave, inquiring of Sidorio, "*Capitan*, where is your lovely wife?"

"Lola's on her ship," Sidorio said. He registered the surprise in his lieutenant's eyes and added, "She has *her* ship and I have *mine*. Just like before we were married."

Now Stukeley's interest was also piqued. "So Lady Lola won't be coming to live with us here on *The Blood Captain*?"

"Not for the time being." Sidorio shook his head, then waved his hand as if swatting away a fly. "Let's not waste time discussing my domestic arrangements. I'm sure there are far more interesting things for us to talk about."

"Sure," agreed Stukeley, exchanging a swift, surreptitious glance with Johnny. "Just so long as Lady Lola is well and quite recovered from the horrendous attack at your wedding." Both lieutenants watched carefully for their boss's reaction. After all, it was Stukeley and Johnny who had instigated the "horrendous attack", though it had been inflicted by the pirates. Did Sidorio know or suspect the truth?

If he did, he wasn't giving anything away – and subtlety had never been his strongest suit. He simply nodded amiably at Stukeley. "Lola's better than ever, thanks for asking. You'll see for yourself soon enough. She's invited you two over to *The Vagabond* tonight for Tiffin."

"*Tiffin?*" Stukeley's face was blank. "What on earth is that?"

Sidorio shrugged. "Search me. I can't be expected to keep track of everything that goes on in that woman's head. All I know is you're due over there . . ." – he glanced at the ship's clock – "oh, about ten minutes ago."

Stukeley made no move to leave. Instead, he inquired casually, "Do you know *why* your wife wishes to see us?"

Sidorio shook his head. "I suppose she wants to get to know you better. After all, you're working for her now, as well as me."

"Working for her?!" This time, Stukeley couldn't keep the irritation out of his voice.

"She's my wife," Sidorio roared, turning to face his deputies.

"Lola and I run this empire together. You report to her now, as well as to me."

Stukeley struggled hard to contain his anger. Both Sidorio and Johnny watched as his face morphed through several contortions.

Sidorio smiled, then broke into a grin and finally a full-bodied laugh. "Had you going, didn't I? Nothing's changed, you *babbo*! I'm still the one in charge of *everything*. But I have a wife now and I have to make her *think* things are different. It's the secret to a successful marriage."

The relief was immediately evident on Stukeley's face.

Sidorio shook his head and lifted his huge left arm, drawing his deputy into a hug. "Did you really think I was demoting you, *compadre*? After everything we've been through together? You were my very first sire, remember? You'll always have a place right at the heart of my empire."

He held Stukeley in something approximating a headlock, then hoisted his other arm and grabbed Johnny simultaneously. "You too, Stetson. You came to us later but I knew you had leadership potential from the very first – like it was branded on your forehead." He chuckled. "No, nothing changes. You two are my *compadri* as well as my lieutenants and that's exactly how it's going to stay. Don't you worry! Even after my son and daughter come to join us, there'll always be a place here for you both."

Stukeley's face froze once more. "*Your son and daughter?*" he rasped.

Johnny looked equally dumbstruck.

Sidorio released the two lads from his clutches and sent them both flying forwards. They spun around to face the captain as he continued.

"My son, Connor, and my daughter, Grace, will be joining us here soon. Well, actually Connor will bunk here with us and

34

Grace will stay with Lola on board *The Vagabond*. We think it'll work best that way . . ."

"Sorry," interrupted Stukeley, frowning as if in acute pain. "You're saying Connor is your *son*?"

Johnny faced Sidorio, his head tilting to one side. "Grace is your *daughter*?"

Stukeley raved on. "Connor Tempest? My old mate, Connor Tempest?"

"Yes," Sidorio boomed. "Though, strictly speaking, his name is Connor Sidorio."

"And Grace too?" Johnny said, as Sidorio nodded again. "But how?"

"It's a long story," Sidorio said, closing his dark eyes momentarily, then opening them once more. "The twins' mother was a donor on board *The Nocturne. My* donor."

"You've never mentioned this," Stukeley said, his mind whirring away furiously. "And you and Connor have had run-ins before. *More* than run-ins. He tried to kill you! And me too, come to think of it!"

Sidorio nodded. "You speak the truth."

"And Grace . . ." Johnny added, "she's not exactly your number one fan. She and I got pretty close during her stay at Sanctuary and she confided in me a lot."

Surprisingly, in the face of this volley of objections, Sidorio remained perfectly calm and spoke with equanimity. "No one's denying that we've had our differences in the past. That was before we all knew where we stood. What we are to one another."

"Connor tried to set fire to us both!" Stukeley protested. "He succeeded in destroying three of our comrades. And *he* was the one who stabbed Lola . . . *twice* at the wedding. Captain, he sliced off your wife's head."

Johnny couldn't look at Stukeley, but he marvelled at his gall.

Yes, it was true Connor had stabbed Lola, but he'd been doing *their* bidding. They had made a pact with Connor's commander, Captain Cheng Li – the spunky young pirate who led the dedicated Vampirate assassination squad.

Sidorio simply shrugged. "Every family goes through rough patches. Connor didn't know who or what he was then. Now he does – he is my son and heir. Grace is my daughter and my other heir, equally important. That's why we're inviting them to come and stay, so we can all get to know each other better. It was Lola's idea."

"I'll bet," Stukeley muttered, under his breath.

"A family reunion," Johnny said, smiling guilelessly. A fresh thought occurred to him. "So, if Grace and Connor are your children, are they like us? Are they vampires?"

"No." It was Stukeley who answered the question. He was already ahead of his comrade. "They aren't vampires, they're *dhampirs* – half-mortal, half-vampire. Incredibly powerful beings."

"What else would you expect?" Sidorio declared, proudly. "Connor and Grace are *my* children – blood of my blood. You couldn't ask for more powerful genetics. And Lola will be their stepmother." His face lit up. "You know, I expect *that's* what she wants to talk to you about. Making the twins welcome, that kind of thing."

"It will be good to see Grace again," Johnny said, with a grin. "I always felt I had unfinished business with her."

"Careful, Stetson," Sidorio said, giving him a swift clip around the ear. "That's my daughter you're talking about."

"We'd better go," Stukeley said, ushering Johnny towards the door. "We shouldn't keep Lady Lola waiting any longer."

Sidorio nodded. "Quite right," he said. "Enjoy your Tiffin, boys!"

As his lieutenants departed, Sidorio turned and glanced back down at his ship, his nascent empire. He felt a rare excitement running through his veins. Times were changing. He had Lola at his side now, as well as his trusted lieutenants. Soon, Connor and Grace would be here too. And wait until he shared more of his and Lola's Grand Plan with Stukeley and Johnny. It would send their heads spinning.

CHAPTER SIX

Tiffin

Sidorio's two lieutenants were met on the deck of *The Vagabond* by one of Lady Lola's officers. Zofia was an attractive, young-looking woman whom Stukeley remembered seeing, but not talking to, at Sidorio and Lola's wedding. Now, he took the opportunity to strike up friendly conversation, but she resisted his advances. Perhaps she was shy. She led the two lieutenants down the ship's main corridor, walking ahead of them until she came to a standstill in front of a cabin door. "The captain is waiting for you in here," she announced, knocking twice on the door.

After a brief pause, the door opened and Lady Lola herself appeared on the threshold. Her face was bright. "Stukeley! Johnny! How lovely to see you both." She kissed the air on either side of their cheeks, then ushered them inside.

"Will that be all, Captain?" Lola's underling inquired.

"Yes, thank you, Zofia. I'll be taking Tiffin with the boys now. I don't wish to be disturbed. You know how I hate Tiffin to be interrupted!"

"Very good, Captain," answered Zofia, nodding and turning away.

A fresh thought occurred to Lady Lockwood. "Zofia, dear, would you ask Mimma to come and see me later, before she goes off duty?"

"Aye, aye, Captain." Zofia saluted Lady Lockwood, then exited the cabin, closing the door behind her.

"Well, don't stand on ceremony, boys," Lady Lola said, beaming at Stukeley and Johnny. "Take a seat. Make yourselves comfortable. I've prepared some Tiffin for us."

"What exactly *is* Tiffin?" Johnny asked, sitting on an antique love-seat upholstered in silver velvet.

"Tiffin is a term for a light meal or snack," Lola explained. "It originated at the time of the British rule in India." She held out a small silver platter. "Blood jelly, Johnny? I think you'll find them absolutely delicious. It's my own recipe."

Intrigued, Johnny lifted a jelly from the plate and slipped it into his mouth.

Lola watched as his face registered delight at the new and exquisite taste. "Good, aren't they? Stukeley, would you care to try one?"

"No thanks," Stukeley said, wrinkling his nose.

Unfazed, Lola set the platter down in front of Johnny. "Help yourself," she said. "They're there to be eaten."

Now Lola herself sat down on an elegant chaise and continued her companionable chatter as she inspected the decanter and glasses that had been set out on the low central table before her. "I gather that originally there was a slang term – *Tiffing* – which meant to take a little drink or sip." She smiled, extracting the stopper from the cut-glass decanter and pouring the dark liquid inside carefully into three glasses. "I'm sure you'd agree," she continued, "that we all enjoy a little drink, don't we?"

She passed a glass to Johnny and another to Stukeley. After a moment's hesitation, he accepted.

Lola wrapped her long fingers around the third glass. "Anyway, one of the traditions I uphold on board *The Vagabond* is the nightly taking of Tiffin with various members of my crew. It's a chance for us all to get to know one another better." She raised her glass, poised, it seemed, to make a toast.

"We're not your crew," Stukeley said, bluntly.

Johnny flashed a look at his comrade, then glanced apologetically at Lola, before smiling amiably and taking another blood jelly from the platter.

Lola sipped her drink calmly, seeming only amused. "You may not like it, Jez—"

"Please don't call me that," he interrupted her. "That's my old, mortal name. I'm called Stukeley now."

"My sincere apologies," Lola said. "As I was saying, *Stukeley*, you may not like it, but the fact is, now that Sidorio and I are married, we are all part of the same crew."

"Perhaps." Stukeley shrugged. "But from what he tells us, you'll continue to be based here and he'll remain on *The Blood Captain*."

"For the time being, yes," Lola said, calmly. "We'll continue to run our parallel operations until we have expanded the fleet and fully integrated our command structures. But don't be under any illusions, Je— I'm sorry, *Stukeley*. I must get that right! Don't be under any illusions, my dear – the day that my husband and I integrate our commands is not so far away."

"We'll see," Stukeley said, swigging defiantly from his glass.

"I'm not sure I care for your tone," said Lola, returning her own glass to the table with some force.

Johnny glanced anxiously from Lola to Stukeley. In his view, this confrontation could only end badly.

"Come on, mate." Stukeley addressed him directly. "I knew this Tiffin thing was overrated. Let's get back to our own ship. We have decisions to make." He stood up and was halfway to the door when Lola spoke.

"Not so fast," she said. Something in the tone of her voice succeeded in rooting him to the spot, just as deftly as if she had lassoed him. "The three of us have unfinished business."

"The three of us?" Johnny echoed, his anxiety increasing.

"Yes," Lola nodded. "Like I said before, Tiffin is a chance to get to know each other better. To share some secrets. And we three have one very big secret between us, don't we? A veritable elephant in the room, you might say."

"What secret?" Stukeley asked, regaining some of his former bluster, though he stood rooted to the spot.

"Think," Lola said, standing and striding towards him, her long tulle skirt swishing against the polished floorboards. She came to a standstill beside Stukeley, extended her forefinger and tapped his skull. "Think *hard*, Jez!"

"Ouch!" Stukeley said, raising his hand to push her away.

Lola laughed. "*Ouch*, he says. Ouch! *This* from the man who plotted for me to be destroyed on my own wedding day."

Johnny gasped.

Stukeley's mouth hung open.

"Well," Lola said. "At least neither of you insult my intelligence by trying to deny it." Seeming suddenly calmer, she returned to the centre of the room and lifted her drink. "Why don't we all sit down again?"

Stukeley followed and sat, carefully, opposite her – as if fearful that the antique chair he perched on might be embedded with a land-mine. "You said before that this was a secret we three shared." He paused. "Does that mean that you haven't revealed your suspicions to your husband?"

Lola smiled, her dark eyes scrutinising first Stukeley, then Johnny. "My husband does not know of your dastardly plot. And I have no intention of telling him – why, the last thing I want to do is upset him." She sipped her drink. "I'm sure that's the very last thing any of us would want."

41

"There's a price to this," Stukeley said, "isn't there? A price to your silence."

Lola laughed, but it was a hollow laugh – devoid of warmth, somewhat mocking. "Yes, Stukeley. There is a price. There's always a price to pay for your actions. Especially when your actions include attempted murder."

"Let's not beat around the bush," Stukeley said. "What *is* your price?"

Lola refilled her glass, drawing out the moment. "It's very simple," she said at last. "Like I say, my husband doesn't know what you arranged for me and I have no intention of telling him. Just as long as you do exactly what I say."

Johnny finally mustered the courage to speak. "Exactly as you say?"

"Yes, Johnny, dear," Lola said. "Oh, don't look so worried! I'm not going to command you to set fire to yourself or anything extreme like that." She shook her head. "I just have a few bits and pieces – a few matters of ship's business – with which I could use a helping hand from two talented young Vampirates such as your good selves."

"You have plenty of crew, already," Stukeley said. "Why do you need us? Ask whatshername . . . Zofia."

"I need you two boys for a special mission," Lola said. Safe in the knowledge that she had their full attention, she rose and walked across the room to a small bureau. On it was a silver salver and on this were two envelopes. She picked up the envelopes and passed the first to Johnny and the second to Stukeley.

The lieutenants glanced down at Sidorio's distinctive handwriting.

"Grace," Johnny read.

"Connor," read Stukeley.

"Invitations," Lola said. "Your first job will be to deliver them by hand." She sipped her drink. "Your second job is to ensure that both invitations are accepted."

"We can't force them to come with us," Johnny said.

"Now, Johnny," said Lola, smiling broadly. "I've heard you can be very persuasive. You too, Stukeley."

"So we go to their ships, give them their invitations and bring them back with us?" Stukeley said.

"Quick on the draw as ever," said Lola, miming releasing the trigger of a gun with her fingers.

"I don't know about this," Johnny said.

"Don't you see, Johnny," Stukeley answered, turning the envelope over in his hands, "we don't have a choice. She's outplayed us."

Lola reached out her hand and laid it on Stukeley's shoulder. "Now, now," she said. "There's always a choice. Just like there's always a price. You just have to weigh up your odds."

"You mean if Sidorio finds out we tried to kill you."

"If Sidorio finds out you plotted to spoil the happiest night of his life and take away from him the very thing he holds most dear." Her eyes sparkled. "Me!" Laughing, she snatched up their glasses. "I think that's enough Tiffin for one night, boys." She set the glasses on the tray and began propelling them towards the door. "What's that old saying? Fish and visitors stink after three days. In your case, I'm afraid the stink has come a little sooner. Goodnight!" With that, she pushed them out into the corridor and closed the door firmly behind her.

Hearing their receding footsteps, she returned to the centre of the room, lifted the decanter and refilled her glass. She had earned another drink and there was nothing better to soothe her frazzled nerves than a nice glass of Commodore Kuo. What a shame this was the last bottle of that rare and pungent vintage.

It was high time she restocked the cellars.

CHAPTER SEVEN
Worse Than Dead

"We are gathered here tonight to bid farewell to two members of our crew." Cheng Li's eyes sparkled in the candlelight as she gazed across the dim tavern at the subjects of her speech. They stood arm in arm beside the bar, surrounded by crewmates who had swiftly become good friends. "Cate, Bart, we are all exceedingly grateful for your crucial input into Operation Black Heart. It was a complete success and our work has been recognised by the Pirate Federation as one of the single most important missions in Federation history."

At her words, there was an enthusiastic burst of applause from the room full of pirates.

Cheng Li nodded, waiting for the noise to subside before continuing. "Speaking personally, it has been wonderful to have you both as colleagues once again. I only wish your stay aboard *The Tiger* could have been longer." A wry smile played on her lips. "I don't suppose if I stand another round of drinks, you might reconsider?"

Over the ripple of laughter, Cate called back. "As good as the ale is here, if you want to extend our contract, you'll have to speak to Molucco!"

Cheng Li's nose wrinkled, as if assaulted by a particularly noxious smell, at the mention of her fellow captain's name. "Yes, well," she pushed on, somewhat flustered, "that's all I had to say . . . Except to wish you both well. Oh yes! And also . . ." She paused, gaining her composure once more. "To raise a toast to the rest of you." She lifted her tankard. "To the crew of *The Tiger* – the most kick-ass bunch of pirates on the ocean!"

As the crew roared its approval with shouts, whoops, stomps and fresh applause, Bart leaned closer to Cate. "Did she *actually* say kick-ass?"

Cate nodded, smiling. "I fear Jacoby's *patois* is rubbing off on her."

Cheng Li waved at the pair and began moving briskly through the crowd.

"Thank you both for everything," she said, arriving at their side. "I truly wish I could persuade you to stay on a more permanent basis. We may have successfully eliminated Lady Lockwood but our larger mission regarding the Vampirates is only just beginning."

Bart nodded. "I think I speak for us both when I say that we've enjoyed working with you again. You were born to be a captain, Cheng Li. But like Cate said before, the terms of our loan were for a specific mission – Operation Black Heart. If you want to discuss extending our contract, you'll have to go back to . . ."

"Molucco!" Cheng Li said sharply, as if keen to get the name out of the way as quickly as possible. "Yes, well, perhaps I shall."

Cate reached out her hand to Cheng Li's shoulder. She smiled softly at the Federation's youngest and most ambitious captain. "Thanks for bringing us in on this mission, Cheng Li. I must say, I found the challenge of developing combat techniques against a new kind of adversary quite intriguing." Cate's eyes twinkled. "I'd certainly be open to taking that a stage further, if something could be worked out."

Cheng Li nodded. "I'm delighted to hear that." Her eyes darted across the tavern. "Look, there's Jasmine and Bo Yin, wanting to talk to you. Let's go over, if you can bear to leave your *boyfriend* for five minutes."

Cate and Bart exchanged a glance. He released her from his embrace.

Cheng Li looped her own arm through Cate's. "You're such an important role model to the next generation of young women pirates, you know. Well, I suppose we both are!"

Before Cheng Li and Cate could move, Jacoby and Connor appeared, their arms laden with foaming tankards. Distributing fresh drinks amongst the group, Jacoby turned to Cheng Li. "Hot diggity, Captain, what *is* this place? The Full Moon Saloon! Deeply ironic, given the paucity of lighting in here. When you said you were taking us out to celebrate, I felt sure we'd be heading back to Ma Kettle's Tavern."

Cheng Li raised her eyes exasperatedly. "Why does everyone act like Ma Kettle's is the *only* tavern around? Can't we broaden our horizons and try somewhere different for a change?"

Jacoby was unconvinced. "But Captain, Ma Kettle's has such a rich piratical history!"

"*Precisely!*" Cheng Li said. "It's more like a museum than an inn these days. It's where the old fossils go. It's impossible to have a conversation there without turning around and finding one Wrathe brother or another sticking his beak into your business." She turned to Cate. "No offence."

"None taken," said Cate, stifling a laugh.

Cheng Li had one further pearl of wisdom for her deputy. "We're the new wave of pirates, Jacoby. We don't follow tradition. We make our own way!"

With that, she propelled Cate forward towards Jasmine and Bo Yin.

Once the women were out of earshot, Bart grinned at

Jacoby. "Face it, buddy, the only reason you're angling for Ma's is because you're hoping for a sight of the delicious Sugar Pie."

Connor grinned at the mention of Ma Kettle's trusted second-in-command. Sugar Pie made pirates from all around go weak at the knees but, that aside, she had become a good friend and trusted confidante of Connor's.

Jacoby shook his head emphatically at Bart's accusation. "That is *so* unfounded. I only have eyes for Jasmine."

Connor listened to this exchange warily. Jacoby was still blissfully ignorant of his own fast-developing relationship with Jasmine. They had kissed. Twice. And it had changed everything. He knew it and Jasmine knew it. But, for now, Jacoby was still in the dark.

Bart grinned at Jacoby. "Jasmine's a wonderful young woman, no question, but few pirate lads have been able to resist the charms of Sugar Pie." He tapped his own chest. "I know whereof I speak." He shook his head and glanced fondly towards Cate. "Of course, that was in my younger and wilder days, when I was footloose and fancy-free. That's all behind me now."

"Yeah right," Connor interjected. "You're the grand old age of *twenty-three* now!"

"Exactly!" Bart said, taking a draught of beer before continuing. "Tempest, cast your mind back to the very first night we met. Remember what I told you then?"

Connor knew exactly what his mate was alluding to. "A pirate's life is a short but merry one."

Bart nodded, wiping the beer-foam moustache from above his lips. "Spot on, mate! I've been luckier than most in avoiding the enemy cutlass all these years I've roamed the oceans. But who knows how much longer my luck will hold?" His expression became more sombre. "After all, think of Jez."

"Who's Jez?" asked Jacoby, unaware what a loaded question this was.

Connor and Bart exchanged a glance, both waiting for the other to take the lead. After an awkward silence, Connor spoke. "Jez Stukeley was a good friend of ours, aboard *The Diablo*. He was the most talented fighter on the crew. He got killed in a duel on board *The Albatross*, the ship captained by Narcisos Drakoulis."

Jacoby was confused. "If Jez was such a great fighter, how come he lost the duel?"

"You should have seen the guy he was up against!" Bart said, "Drakoulis's prize-fighter, Gidaki Sarakakino. He was like a gladiator – twice the size of *me*, if you please, but incredibly agile with it."

Connor picked up the story, his expression dark. "We should never have been on that ship anyhow. It was a trick – an act of revenge against Molucco Wrathe. Jez died because of Molucco's shortcomings, not his own." Frowning, he took a deep draught from his tankard.

"Jez sounds like a great guy," Jacoby said. "I can tell how much you both miss him."

Bart's eyes suddenly brightened. "They had a nickname for us. *The Three Buccaneers*. Catie came up with it."

"The Three Buccaneers," Jacoby repeated, nodding. "I like that." He raised his tankard. "A toast, my friends! To Jez and the Three Buccaneers!"

Without hesitation, Connor and Bart lifted their tankards and slammed them against Jacoby's. "The Three Buccaneers!" they bellowed as ale slopped over the floor, then slipped down their throats.

"I haven't heard *that* expression in a while," Cheng Li said as she, Cate, Jasmine and Bo Yin returned to join the lads.

"The boys were just telling me about Jez," Jacoby informed the newcomers.

"Poor guy!" said Jasmine.

Cate laid her hand on Bart's arm. "Did you see him at the wedding?"

Bart nodded, glumly.

"I don't understand," said Jacoby. "How *could* you have seen him at a wedding, or anywhere else for that matter, if he's *dead*?"

"Think!" Cheng Li said. "Which wedding did we all recently attend together?"

Jacoby racked his brain for a moment. "Sidorio and Lady Lola's?"

Cheng Li nodded.

"I still don't understand," Jacoby said. "If Jez is dead, how could he be at a wedding . . . Oh! Oh, I think I get it." He trembled as he spoke.

"He was killed," Bart confirmed. "We buried him at sea. But Sidorio found his corpse and sired him to be his lieutenant. He's known as Stukeley now and he's Sidorio's joint deputy."

Every time Sidorio's name came up, Connor felt as though he was being stabbed in the heart. Did the others have any sense of his discomfort? It seemed not.

Bart's eyes were sad and empty, whilst Jacoby's were as wide as portholes as he questioned Bart further. "Your old mate Jez is working for Sidorio, King of the Vampirates?!"

Once more, Connor felt a stab in the heart. Yes, he thought. King of the Vampirates and, by the way, my father.

"Well," Jacoby breezed on. "Look on the bright side . . . at least he's not dead . . . only resting." His attempt at levity was lost on the others.

Bart shook his head. "There's no bright side, mate. Jez is worse than dead."

Connor turned to Bart, his heart racing. Before he knew it, he had opened his mouth and was asking Bart a question — a question he felt compelled to ask even though he was far

49

from sure he was ready to hear the answer. "Do you really think that? That it's worse to be a vampire than to be dead?"

"You saw what he was like, Connor, when he came to us and asked for our help. He was in torment. Every day, every night of his *life* – for want of a better term – is torture, now. If he was dead, he'd be at peace. He was a good and honourable man. He deserved the right true end to a noble life. That . . . *monster*, Sidorio, denied him that."

Connor shivered at the word "monster", for if it applied to Sidorio, then it certainly applied to Connor himself. Bart didn't yet know that Sidorio was Connor's true father. Nor did he know that Connor was a dhampir and therefore half-vampire. But Bart's impassioned words left Connor in no doubt. If he had known, he'd have turned those same heartbroken eyes on Connor and pitied him for a fate worse than death. Connor felt queasy at the thought, and queasier still at the fact he was keeping such a big a secret from so close a friend.

Jacoby pressed on, oblivious to Connor's meltdown. "Suppose it had been you, Bart? You, instead of Jez, killed in that duel. Would you really prefer to be dead and buried than brought back from the brink – to walk and talk and sail the oceans again?"

"Absolutely!" Bart said, smashing his fist down into the palm of his other hand. "I told you before. *A short life but a merry one.* That's what I signed up to." His eyes blazed with fire as he gazed at his comrades. "When I die, bury me deep as hell where no vampire can dig me up and have me join his crew. Deal?"

No one answered.

Bart's eyes roved across the group. "I asked you all a question. Do we have a deal?"

"Yes," Connor said, his voice overlapping with those of his comrades. He felt really sick now, and intensely claustrophobic. He had to get out of the tavern, away from this conversation. He couldn't take it a moment longer.

As Cate reached out a soothing hand to Bart, Connor was quick to seize his opportunity. "I'm not feeling so good," he mumbled to Bo Yin. "I need some air."

"I'll come with you, Connor Tempest," Bo Yin said, her face etched with concern. But Connor shook his head and held up a hand to deter her.

He strode away from the group and made his way towards the back of the saloon. The back door was ajar and Connor slipped outside.

He found himself on a small beach, strewn with litter from the tavern. Waves lapped, like whispers, against the sand.

Connor breathed in the night air. He kicked off his shoes and socks and rolled up the bottom of his trousers. Weaving his way through the debris, he walked out into the water. The first caress of the cool liquid around his ankles was instantly soothing. He closed his eyes and willed the toxic thoughts raging in his brain to drain out into the waves and be carried away on the tide.

When he opened his eyes again, he felt momentarily dizzy. The sea below and the stars above seemed to be sliding towards each other. He had lost his footing and prepared himself for an imminent dunk in the cold, oily water. But somehow he remained upright, suspended in mid-air. It took him a moment or two to come to his senses. Glancing down, he saw that a pair of pale hands had reached out to steady him.

"All right now?" asked a familiar voice, presumably belonging to the slowly retracting hands.

Connor nodded. "Yes," he said. "Yes, thank you." He twisted around to face his rescuer.

51

As he did so, his heart missed a beat and he felt dizzy again. Even though he had suspected it, the reality was nevertheless a body-shock.

There, standing beside him in the ocean, was his old friend and former comrade, Jez Stukeley.

CHAPTER EIGHT

The Sharing

Grace waited for a bowl of cherry pie to be cleared from her place. She had barely touched her food at tonight's Feast. It had looked and smelled as delicious as usual but she had taken only a mouthful or two of first the scallops, then the lamb, and perhaps half a spoonful of dessert. The rest of the food had ended up being pushed around her plate or lingering uneaten in the bowl, under her cutlery. None of this escaped eagle-eyed Oskar's notice.

"Still not hungry, I see," he said, a dark eyebrow raised interrogatively.

Grace shook her head. "Not for food, anyhow."

Oskar looked her directly in the eye and nodded, slowly, thoughtfully. He understood. Leaning closer, he spoke in confidential tones. "Remember what we talked about before? You should join us – Lorcan and me – tonight. I have more than enough blood for both of you." His brown-black eyes seared into Grace's. "Share me."

Since he had first made this proposition at the previous week's Feast, Grace had turned the idea over constantly in her head. It was unthinkable, wasn't it, to take blood? If she did,

53

there would no turning back. She would be accepting that she was a dhampir – half-vampire, half-mortal – and that this was the way she lived now.

On many levels, she *did* accept it. What was the point in even trying to deny it? She was not, as she had thought for the first fourteen years of her life, the daughter of a lighthouse keeper from a dead-end coastal town. No, she was the daughter of a Vampirate, Sidorio – the result, like her brother, of a spell cast by Sidorio on their poor mother, Sally.

Grace looked down to find that the long banqueting table had been cleared. The servers had disappeared back to the kitchens. She had been so lost in her own thoughts, she hadn't noticed any of this. Now, the musicians took up their instruments again, playing more and more loudly. Glancing along the table at the faces reflected in the warm glow of the candlelight, she saw that the men and women on both sides of the table were waiting silently. The Feast – at least this phase of the Feast – was over.

At the far end of the table, nearest to the door, Darcy and her donor, James, rose together from their seats and began walking away from the table, their footsteps beating time with the percussive music. Their neighbours followed, moving in unison. The exodus continued like a wave as each vampire and their donor left the banqueting hall – no one hurrying, no one missing a beat. Though Grace had seen it many times before, it still fascinated her – now perhaps more than ever.

The wave reached them and now it was Lorcan and Oskar who rose and each began walking along their side of the table towards the exit. Then, Mosh Zu and Grace stood. Though they were not vampire and donor, they would exit the cabin together, so as not to break the symmetry.

As Grace followed in Oskar's path alongside the table, she couldn't help but smile at the irony that she still sat on the donor side of the table. She didn't even register leaving the banqueting hall, so deep was she in her own thoughts, so she was surprised to find herself out in the corridor. Was this what it was like for the Vampirates? She had seen the distant, empty look in Lorcan's eyes when his hunger was most urgent. Like now.

Glancing over at him, Grace saw that his usually blue eyes had changed. They now looked like deep pits of fire. It didn't scare her or freak her out. She had seen him in this condition before. All he needed was the gift of Oskar's blood to sate his hunger. Grace found her gaze turning to the tanned skin on Oskar's neck. Suddenly, it was as if his skin was transparent and she could see the blood flowing within the veins beneath it. She could see it. Smell it. Taste it . . .

They climbed the stairs to the next deck – the donors' deck. Along the corridor, doors opened and quickly closed, like the beating wings of moths, as the vampires and donors disappeared inside. Grace felt her heart racing. Her head was pounding with the strange, driving music of the Feast, now intercut with Oskar's words. *You should join us . . . share me. Share me. Share me. Share me.*

Oskar reached for the door. He opened it, and Lorcan walked purposefully inside. Oskar followed. The door began to close.

Grace faltered. *Share me*, he had said. What was she supposed to do? She should talk to Mosh Zu about this but, as she turned, she saw that he had continued on along the corridor. Now she was separated from him by other vampire and donor pairs making their way to their cabins.

Oskar's door was still ajar. Grace felt a powerful heat coursing through her, followed by as sudden and penetrating a chill right along her spine.

Share me. Inside her skull, Oskar's voice grew stronger. Her head would surely explode if the music didn't end; if this feeling didn't subside. This feeling which she now understood to be her hunger. There was only one way for such a hunger to be quelled, wasn't there? Grace saw the sliver of candlelight spilling out into the corridor. She stretched out her hand and pushed the door. Taking a deep breath, she entered the room.

The cabin was suffused with a red glow. Grace couldn't be sure if this was the lighting within or if it was a further effect of her hunger. Each of her senses seemed heightened. Time seemed to lurch from running at increased speed to suddenly spooling very slowly, like an out-of-control film. Through all of this, she felt the alternating heat and chill, and the relentless throbbing in her head. *Share me.*

It took all Grace's strength to gather her focus. At last she began to make sense of what was happening around her. There was Oskar, leaning against the wall, Lorcan to his side. So this was how it happened. This was how they shared. Grace had glimpsed Lorcan sharing with Shanti from outside in the corridor once before, but then she had been quick to turn away. Now, she opened her hungry eyes to the scene before her, fascinated to see how it worked. Once again, it seemed to her that Oskar's skin had become completely translucent and she could see the blood coursing from his heart and through his veins towards the punctured skin of his thorax. Looking up, she was surprised to find him smiling at her and beckoning her closer.

"Come," he was saying. "Share me."

Grace stepped closer. She moved forward until she was standing only a breath away from Oskar. He smiled at her again as she looked into his eyes. There was fire there, as in Lorcan's eyes, but more distant somehow. It confused her, distracting her from her hunger for a moment. She stared deeper into the black slicks of Oskar's pupils, seeking out the fire. Then she recoiled, understanding. There was no fire in Oskar's eyes; they were simply a mirror, reflecting back to her her own deep hunger.

The realisation made her gasp and step backwards, stumbling towards the door. The room suddenly felt utterly airless. She needed to escape. "I'm sorry," she said, unsure whether there was any volume to her words. Oskar was turning towards Lorcan now, as the Vampirate prepared to take his blood.

She had to get out. Now. She wasn't ready for this. Yet.

Grace wasn't sure of the sequence of events which followed. Somehow, she managed to locate the doorknob and twist it open. Somehow, she made it into the corridor and found herself pushing open another door – though she had no recollection of having climbed up any flights of stairs – onto the main deck. It was only as she stepped out into the air that she began to breathe with any semblance of normality and to start to pull together her thoughts into some kind of shape.

She knew she had done the right thing, removing herself from Oskar's cabin. She was not yet ready for this. Her hunger had fallen away as steeply as her appetite at dinner. Now, as she reached out to the deck-rail, the thought of what she had been on the verge of doing shocked her to her very core. She took in a deep lungful of air, then exhaled just as slowly. The vicissitude of heat and cold had receded. Her body felt released from the thrall of her hunger. She felt normal again, though this seemed a relative state and quite possibly a transient one. She stood at the guard-rail, the breeze caressing her hair and skin, growing calmer with each passing moment.

She wasn't sure how long she stood there before she heard footsteps and became aware of someone joining her at the guard-rail. She smiled, preparing herself for the sight of Lorcan. He must have broken off the sharing to come after her. How typically selfless of him, even in the moment of his most urgent hunger, to come and check on her. Truly, he was the perfect gentleman.

But when she turned, it wasn't Lorcan's face she found gazing back at her, though it was still familiar, still handsome. Instead it was a face she hadn't expected to see again – or not for a good while, at least, and not here, of all places.

Johnny tipped his hat and grinned at Grace appreciatively. "Well, look at you, little lady! Heaven must be missing an angel tonight!"

CHAPTER NINE

The Invitation

Connor stood in the icy water, outside the Full Moon Saloon, staring at Jez – or rather, he corrected himself, at Stukeley. His former comrade was wearing a red shirt, sleeves rolled up to the elbows, and beaten-up black leather breeches. Since the last time Connor had seen him, at Sidorio's wedding, Stukeley's hair had been closely shaved. From his left ear dangled a tiny skull. On the back of his neck was a fresh tattoo – of a wave, in the style of a Japanese woodcut. Lower down, on the inside of his forearm was the tattoo of three cutlasses which identically matched the tattoo on Connor's own arm. Connor, Bart and Jez had each woken up to find them there after their "lost weekend" in *Calle del Marinero*. It remained a complete mystery to them as to how the tattoos had gotten there.

"How do," said Stukeley, with a nod.

"We were just talking about you," said Connor.

"Well, you know what they say," Stukeley grinned. "Speak of the devil and the devil appears."

Connor shook his head. "You're not the devil. You've got some wacky new habits and strange new people to hang around with but you're not the devil."

Stukeley shrugged. "Thanks . . . I think." He smiled. "Shall we go ashore?" He put his arm on Connor's shoulder and led him out of the cold water onto the sand.

Amongst the rubbish on the beach were a couple of rusting oil drums. Stukeley leaned back against one and Connor sat down on the other. "What are you doing here?" he asked.

"I came to find you," Stukeley said. "To give you this." He reached inside his shirt pocket and produced an envelope. In the starlight, the vellum shone like a sliver of white gold.

Connor took the envelope and saw his own name written on it in ink, in wild, curling letters. He had a deep sense of foreboding about what lay inside. He let it rest in his hands for a time.

"Open it," Stukeley said.

His heart beginning to race, Connor tore open the envelope and pulled out the folded parchment. He unfolded it and scanned the brief letter . . .

Dear Connor,
I hope this finds you well. My son, you have been much in
my thoughts of late. Our reunion was interrupted. We should
get to know each other. My wife and I would very much like
you to come and stay with us aboard our ships. Come as
soon as you can and stay as long as you wish.
Your blood father,
Sidorio

Having read it, Connor instantly folded up the letter and reinserted it into the envelope. He set it down on the rusting oil drum and began walking away.

"You can't ignore this," Stukeley said, coming to walk alongside him.

"I can try." Connor's eyes were fixed ahead.

"It won't change anything," Stukeley said. "Sidorio *is* your blood father. You're one of us now."

Connor said nothing, just kept walking. He was in imminent danger of running out of beach.

"Wait!" Stukeley said, jumping in front of him. "Look at me, Connor!"

Reluctantly, Connor lifted his eyes to face Stukeley once more.

"We were friends once," Stukeley said. "We said that our friendship transcended life and death, remember? When I came back to find you, you helped me. You took me to the Blood Tavern and then to *The Nocturne*, so I could get help from the Captain."

Connor nodded. "I remember." He shivered at the thought of the Blood Tavern.

"You helped me," Stukeley repeated. "Now it's my turn to help you." He reached out his hand to Connor's shoulder. "I know you must be reeling from all this – discovering that Sidorio is your father, that you are a dhampir. It changes everything."

"Only if I let it," Connor said, defiantly.

Stukeley shook his head. "No, Connor. You're not in control of this. It's bigger than you. Trust me, I know what I'm talking about."

Connor thought about Stukeley's words. He thought of how he had watched Jez die and of the lavish funeral they had staged for him on the deck of *The Diablo*. He thought of how Jez's journey had ended there, but Stukeley's had just begun as they had tossed his coffin into the ocean and unwittingly sent it travelling on the tide into the grateful arms of Sidorio.

"I didn't ask to be on this side of the fence either," Stukeley said, as if reading his thoughts. "But Connor, I've learned that the only way through this is to accept what you are."

Connor hung his head, letting his eyes close. A fresh thought occurred to him. He opened his eyes again, frowning.

"What's the matter?" Stukeley inquired.

"I don't understand," Connor said. "I thought I destroyed Lola Lockwood at the wedding. But, in the letter, Sidorio says, 'my wife and I', as if she's still around."

Stukeley's nod confirmed it. "Lady Lola is very much still around," he said. "In spite of your best efforts to the contrary."

Connor shook his head in disbelief.

Stukeley leaned in closer. "You saw how she managed to recover from your first attack, didn't you? You stabbed her but she removed the sword from her own chest."

"Yes," Connor thought back to the events of that night, "but then I decapitated her and we separated her head from her body. That should have proved fatal."

Stukeley shrugged. There was a look in his eyes Connor couldn't decipher. "You'd certainly have thought it was enough but Sidorio brought Lola's head and body back together and before you could say, 'Mazel Tov', they were bound for their happy honeymoon."

"That flies in the face of all our research," Connor said, shaking his head again.

"You can't trust what you read," Stukeley said. "Sidorio and Lola break all the rules. The closer they come to destruction, the more powerful they seem to emerge."

This struck a chord with Connor. He thought of how the captain of *The Nocturne* had once counselled Connor to attack the renegade Vampirates with fire. The Captain had said that fire would be fatal to Sidorio but, though it had destroyed some of his fledgling crew, it had left Sidorio – and indeed Stukeley – somehow stronger. Like metal, forged in the flames. Connor could see the hungry fire in front of his eyes now, and in it the faces of Sidorio and Stukeley and Lola.

"I can't come with you," Connor said.

"No such word as can't!" Stukeley grinned.

"Think about it," Connor said. "I'm the one who attacked Lola. I tried to destroy her. She can't possibly want to see me." He had a fresh thought. "Unless she wants to take revenge."

Stukeley shook his head. "She wouldn't dream of taking revenge on you. You're much too important to Sidorio. And, before you go there, I can assure you that revenge is the furthest thing from *his* mind. He genuinely wants to get to know you, father to son."

Far-fetched as they sounded, Stukeley's words rang true. Connor remembered the last time he and Sidorio had faced one another, on that other beach, after the pirates' disruption of the Vampirate wedding. Sidorio had drawn Connor towards him, his twin incisors bearing down towards Connor's thorax, poised to kill. Then Cheng Li had spoken and everything had changed. Not just for Connor, but for Sidorio too. He remembered the look in Sidorio's eyes as he had stared at Connor and declared, "He's my son."

"Trust me," Stukeley said now, "Sidorio only wants the best for you, and for Grace too. He talks about you both as heirs to his empire."

"Grace?" Connor said, feeling a flash of fear for his sister. "Are you going to invite her too?"

"Already on it," said Stukeley, with a wink. "Same invite, different postman."

Connor scolded himself for his knee-jerk reaction of fear for Grace. When it came to the Vampirates, she was far more comfortable in their company than he was. Then another thought occurred to him. "Grace doesn't know," he said. "She doesn't know that Sidorio is her father. I have to tell her. *I* have to be the one . . ."

Stukeley shook his head. "Grace knows," he said. "She found out *before* you did." His eyes met Connor's. "That shouldn't surprise you. Grace was always a step or two ahead of you with the Vampirates."

Stukeley turned away. He crouched down and reached for a pebble, then took a swing and sent it skimming across the water. Connor smiled. This was something he'd watched Jez do many times before.

As Stukeley turned to reach for another stone, he caught Connor watching him. "What?" he asked, one eyebrow raised inquiringly.

"Nothing," Connor said.

Stukeley clasped the stone but instead of skimming it, he crouched down in front of Connor. "Talk to me, old buddy. Tell me how you feel about all this."

"I feel numb," Connor said, though as he started talking, he already felt some sense of relief. "I don't know who I am any more. There was a kid called Connor Tempest but I feel like he's still in the lighthouse in Crescent Moon Bay. I left him behind when Grace and I headed out to sea and got caught in the storm." He sighed. "Ever since I landed up on *The Diablo*, I feel like I've been growing up at an accelerated rate. That was fine. At last, I began to see who I really was – who I might be. Connor Tempest – the pirate." He was aware that Stukeley was watching him carefully. "There were some jolts along the way, like when I killed for the first time." Stukeley's gaze remained steady, even with this fresh information. "But I guess I just had to wake up to what being a pirate meant. And to make sure I was signed up to the right captain." He stopped speaking, turning from Stukeley and looking out at the dark, lapping water.

"And now?" said Stukeley.

"Now I'm back to square one," Connor said. "Turns out that I'm not Connor Tempest, pirate, but Connor Tempest, Vampirate. Everything is turned upside down. My true father is a Vampirate who I tried to kill at least once before. And the only time I met my stepmother, I stabbed her and sliced her head off." He gazed back at the saloon door. "The people who

I thought were my friends are back inside this tavern, but they don't know who or what I really am." This, he realised, wasn't quite true. But he saw no need to share with Stukeley that Cheng Li, alone of the pirates, was in on his dark secret.

"Connor," Stukeley said, softly, "I know exactly what you're going through, mate. I've been on this exact same voyage myself. You have to let me help you." He brought his arm around Connor's shoulder once more. "We'll get you through this, old buddy. You see if we don't."

Connor wasn't sure how long they'd been standing there, when he heard the door squeak open behind them. As he turned, Stukeley disappeared into the shadows. He hid behind the door as two figures stepped onto the beach: Jasmine Peacock and Bo Yin.

"Here he is!" Bo Yin declared.

"Yes," Jasmine said. "Go back inside and tell the others we'll be along in a minute."

Bo Yin nodded. With obvious reluctance, she ducked back inside again as Jasmine strode across the beach to join Connor.

"Hey, stranger," said Jasmine. "We wondered where you'd got to."

Connor turned, his heart racing. "I just needed some air and some time to myself. It's kind of claustrophobic in there."

Jasmine smiled. "Whatever Captain Li says, it's no Ma Kettle's!"

Connor returned her smile.

"There you go," Jasmine said, reaching her arms around him. "I knew there was a smile buried somewhere deep inside."

Connor noticed Stukeley watching from the shadows. His smile faded. "We should get going."

"Are you OK, Connor?" Jasmine asked. "You look really tired."

Connor smiled weakly. "I am really tired, actually."

Jasmine looked into his eyes searchingly. "You seem kind of wired at the moment," she said. "You were like a coiled spring during that attack the other day. Tonight, it's like all your energy has left you, but you don't seem relaxed at all. Just flat."

Connor nodded. "That's about right," he said.

Jasmine's voice was uncharacteristically small as she continued. "Are we OK, Connor?"

"Sure," he said, robotically, his hands resting on her shoulders. "We're fine. We're good."

She looked unconvinced. "I'm not going to push you," she said. "I know you have a lot going on right now. And I'm patient enough to know it's worth waiting for you to work through whatever it is." She sighed. "But Connor, please remember that I'm here for you. We all are. You have to learn to lean on your friends when you need to."

He nodded and drew her into a hug. But as she burrowed into his chest, his eyes were met once more by Stukeley's. His old comrade began walking towards him. The alarm must have been evident in Connor's eyes, for Stukeley smiled and shook his head, walking past Connor and Jasmine and soundlessly blending back into the night.

CHAPTER TEN

Persuasion

"Johnny, what are you doing here?" Grace asked. "No, before we get to that, *how* did you get here?"

Johnny smiled at Grace but did not answer either of her questions. Instead, he reached into the back pocket of his jeans. "Got a little something for you," he said, lifting out an envelope and handing it over to her.

"What's this?" Grace asked, taking the envelope. She saw her name, written in ink on the front, but she did not recognise the handwriting.

"An invitation," Johnny said. "Why don't you open it up and read it?"

Shrugging, Grace turned the envelope over. It had been sealed with wax, into which had been pressed some kind of crest, with writing – in Latin, at a guess – which she did not understand. She peeled away the wax and lifted the flap, then took out the letter and unfolded it. As she began to read, Johnny wandered over to stand beside her, leaning against the deck-rail and lighting a cigarillo.

When Grace turned to him, he was concentrating hard on

blowing a perfect smoke-ring over the guard-rail. He glanced over at her, raising an eyebrow.

"Sidorio," she said, almost lost for words. "Sidorio wants me to go and stay with him. To get to know him better."

Johnny nodded. "He is your father, Grace."

"In name only," Grace said, crossly, thinking of Dexter Tempest, her true dad.

"Like it or not," Johnny said, "Sidorio is your blood kin. You always knew there was something different, special, about you. We all did. We just didn't realise quite *how* special."

Grace frowned, glancing down at the letter once more. "Sidorio has a wife now? He got married?"

Johnny nodded once more, taking another pull on the cigarillo and then breathing out the smoke into the night air. "Lady Lola Lockwood. Quite a lady! The invitation is from both of them." He grinned. "If this was a fairy tale, I reckon Lola would be your wicked stepmother."

"This isn't a fairy tale," said Grace. "This is my life."

"Exactly," said Johnny. "Which is why you owe it to yourself to get to know Sidorio. He's really quite something when you get close to him."

"I've been close to him," Grace said, with a shudder. "When I first arrived on *The Nocturne*, he got it into his head that I was going to be his donor." She paused, then added bitterly. "Just like my mother before me."

"Just like Sally," said Johnny, with a nod.

Grace leaned closer to him. "You know about my mother?"

"Sure, I know some stuff. The captain told me and Stuke – Stukeley, that is, we're joint deputies to Sidorio. He told us both about your mother. How much he loved her. How she was taken away from him, and you and Connor too."

Grace was dumbstruck. "*Sidorio* told you about us? He told you he was in love?"

68

Johnny smiled. "I know you, Grace. I know your head is just spinning with questions. Questions about Sidorio and Sally; about yourself and Connor too. Don't you owe it to yourself to accept the captain's invitation to come and spend some time with us?" He smiled. "And, might I add, I'd certainly enjoy the opportunity to renew the pleasure of your acquaintance."

Grace stared back down at the letter. Johnny knew her well. Her head was so full of thoughts that she could no longer focus on the words Sidorio had written on the page. Part of her was tempted by the invitation. Johnny was right. Sidorio *was* an undeniable part of her history, a vitally important piece, and she owed it to herself to get some answers from him. Maybe it would help her to understand herself better. But the thought of journeying right into the heart of the renegade empire was crazy, wasn't it? She'd be throwing herself into the path of danger. Even if she *was* reckless enough to do so, there was no way that Mosh Zu or Lorcan would agree to let her go.

She shook her head. "Tell Sidorio, thanks for the invitation, but no thanks."

"Grace," Johnny said, shaking his head. "Please don't do this to me. If I go back without you, he's going to be really mad at me."

"Sorry, Johnny, but that's not my problem." Grace folded the letter and slipped it back into the envelope. She pressed the wax down again over the join. It looked as if it had never been opened. Grace held the envelope out to Johnny. "It was good to see you again, but I don't want to detain you here unnecessarily."

"It's OK, I'm not in any kind of hurry." Johnny didn't take the envelope. He didn't even reach out his hand. Instead, he took another pull on his cigarillo.

His butter-wouldn't-melt demeanour was starting to enrage

Grace. "I need to go back inside," she said. "My *boyfriend* is waiting for me." She waited, hoping that her dart had hit home.

Infuriatingly, Johnny remained as cool as a watermelon. "Boyfriend, eh? I guess you're talking about good ol' Lorcan. Well, I'm happy for you, Grace. I know you always had strong feelings for him. After all, it's why nothing ever transpired between us."

Grace couldn't believe his arrogance. "Johnny, nothing could have ever happened between us. Lorcan has no bearing on that!"

Johnny shrugged. "Suit yourself. But I know *I* enjoyed all our late-night chats and, without wanting to parade this ol' heart of mine on my sleeve, I've missed you." His eyes bore into hers. "Besides, from what I can see, you've done quite a bit of growing up, since last we met."

Grace couldn't help but smile at his bravado. He didn't give up without a fight. "Johnny, it's always fun seeing you, but I really do have to go. We're not part of the same world now. You made your choice the night you hitched your star to Sidorio's. There's no place for you here on *The Nocturne*."

Johnny had come to the end of his cigarillo. He dropped the stub to the deck and ground it into the deckboards with the toe of his boot. "I never was a man to outstay my welcome. I'll get going and go break the unhappy news to Sidorio." He hung his head, lifting his Stetson. But before he slipped it onto his head, a fresh thought occurred to him. His words were mumbled but Grace caught each and every one. "I'll be sure to send Connor your regards."

"When will *you* be seeing Connor?" she asked, suddenly on red alert.

"Later tonight, maybe," said Johnny, with a grin. "I got the job of delivering the invitation to you. And Connor's old mate Stukeley went to hand over his invite. Only, unlike you, Connor is bound to say *yes*."

"You really think Connor would accept Sidorio's invitation to come and stay on his ship?" Grace shook her head. "There's no way Connor would do that. He can't stand the company of any Vampirate, let alone Sidorio . . ."

"That was before," Johnny said. "All bets are off now Connor's found out he's one of the team." He glanced at his watch. "Which should be happening around about now. I'm sure Connor and Stukeley – who you might remember as Jez – are having quite a heartfelt reunion. And seeing as Stukeley has recently been on the journey from mortality into the after-death himself, I'm sure you'd agree that he's the ideal person to act as Connor's guide to *Vampireville*." Johnny grinned once more. "You know what I think? I don't think you realised that Connor even knew he was a dhampir. But you see, Sidorio and Connor had another run-in – at Sidorio and Lady Lola's wedding, as it goes. And that's when it came out that Connor was Sidorio's son . . . and heir to his building empire. At least, that's how the Captain's been talking it up."

"Sidorio thinks of Connor as his heir?" Grace was incredulous.

"*One* of his heirs," said Johnny. "Though I guess if you aren't interested in getting to know him, he'll just have to make do with the one blood heir."

"I'm *not* interested in getting to know Sidorio," Grace said, vehemently. "And I certainly don't want a part of whatever empire he's building. Besides, do the maths, Johnny. As Sidorio and Lady Lola are immortal, they're never going to die, so there's no logic in talking about heirs, is there?"

"Grace, you're very new to this world. It's true that vampires don't exactly die but they *can* be destroyed. Why, poor Lola almost perished on her wedding day. Imagine that! Besides, maybe Sid and Lola will want to retire someday. Find a place in the moon and kick back for a few centuries. Then you and

71

Connor – and me and Stuke – could have our run of things. I reckon we could have some fun with that, don't you?"

"No!" Grace said. "How many times do I have to tell you: Sidorio is nothing to me. Less than nothing." She exhaled deeply. "I have *nothing* against Vampirates and I'm *proud* to be a dhampir. It's all very new but I'll adapt, I always have before. But the one thing I can tell you with complete and utter clarity is that I abhor everything Sidorio stands for and I don't want any part of his empire now . . . or ever."

"Bravo!" said Johnny, bringing his hands together, clapping and whooping as if he was at a rodeo. "All right, Grace, I get the message. Guess I'll be on my way." He set his Stetson back on the crown of his head and climbed up onto the guard-rail, standing there proudly as if he was lord of all the oceans. Clearly spending so much time with Sidorio was rubbing off on him. He nodded at Grace before executing a double back-flip over the side of the ship.

"Wait!" she cried. "You forgot something." She waved the envelope containing the invitation from Sidorio and Lola. Grace tore the envelope in two and tossed it over the side in Johnny's wake.

"Grace!" Turning, she saw Lorcan striding across the deck towards her. Her heart was racing from her encounter with Johnny and all that he had told her.

Lorcan came to a standstill before her. His cravat was unfastened but, other than that, he looked as pristine as when he had arrived at the Feast earlier that evening. He was always meticulous about removing every last trace of blood post-sharing, although this time Grace noticed a dot of red on his dress shirt. The spot of blood took her back to the image now imprinted in her brain of the dark, claustrophobic cabin below. Now, Lorcan reached out his hand to her. "Grace, what is it? Are you OK?"

72

"I'm a little shaken up," she said. It was nothing less than the truth.

"By what you saw earlier?" he said. "I knew it was too soon. Oskar was trying to be helpful, but he lets his wild ideas run away with him." Lorcan opened his arms and drew Grace into them, enfolding her. He kissed her on the head. "Everything's changed so fast for you. For me, too. It's going to take us some time to make sense of this."

Grace nodded.

"But we will adjust," he said, with conviction. "And remember, however strange things seem to you now – however scary, however impossible – I'm here for you. I'll be with you every step of the journey."

Again, she nodded. She felt safe now, protected. She looked up into Lorcan's eyes. All traces of his rampaging hunger were gone now. His eyes were as blue and infinite as the oceans. Just like the first time she'd seen him. Just like the first night he'd kissed her.

"Come on," he said, reaching out his hand. "Let's get you back inside. It's a little unchivalrous of me to say so, but you do look about ready to drop."

Lorcan took Grace back to her cabin and they talked for a while. Then, she had to confess that she really *was* very tired and, with daylight on its way, she was more than ready for a good, long sleep. Lorcan kissed her good-day and left to make his own way back to his cabin.

After he'd gone, Grace didn't even bother undressing. She just drew the covers up over herself and snuggled down into the comfortable bed, closing her eyes tightly shut. Almost immediately, she fell into a dream. But it was not a restful dream. It was feverish, seen through a haze of black and red. There was Oskar, standing in his cabin, his shirt flapping as he lifted his arm. On his tanned forearm were two words, written in blood. *SHARE ME!*

She glanced at Lorcan, who was wiping traces of blood from his lips. "Grace!" he said, tossing his cravat over his shoulder and walking towards her. "Grace, I'm here for you."

He reached out his arms and she ran into them, desperately needing his protective hug. He kissed her head.

She looked up at him, yearning to see his cool blue eyes. But as she glanced up, it wasn't his face that she was looking into, but Sidorio's. He hugged her tighter and tighter, suffocatingly so, and smiled down at her. "I'm here for you," he said. "Every step of the journey."

Grace woke from the dream, drenched in perspiration. It took her a while to steady her breathing. It was only a nightmare. What else could she expect, after everything she had been through? She got her breath back. Only a nightmare. There was a glass of water at the side of her bed. She reached towards it, desperate for a draught of the cool liquid. But as she made contact with the glass, she froze. There, on her bedside table, was the invitation. The one she had torn in two and thrown after Johnny into the sea. Grace frowned, her hand reaching out for the envelope. It was in one pristine piece and it was bone-dry. Was this some kind of magic?

As Grace leaned forward, she realised she wasn't alone in the cabin. Someone was sitting in the chair at the foot of her bed. Unnerved, Grace reached for a match and lit the oil-lamp at her side. As she did so, the room was illuminated with a soft glow. It was faint but quite sufficient to reveal the striking features of the person sitting, arms folded, staring right at her. Now, the woman leaned forward and addressed her directly.

"Grace, what is all this nonsense about you declining our

invitation? I can't condone this kind of behaviour. You're my stepdaughter. Don't we deserve the chance to get to know one another?"

"Lady Lola?" Grace rasped.

Lola smiled and unfolded her arms. "I was hoping you might call me Mummy."

CHAPTER ELEVEN

The Wicked Stepmother

Lola shook her head. "I don't know why I said that. About you calling me 'Mummy', I mean. Of course, that's not at all what I expect, or what I want."

"What *do* you want?" Grace asked, sitting up in bed and feeling at a distinct disadvantage, given that Lady Lola had quite literally caught her napping. "What are you doing here?"

Lola smiled. "I shouldn't have entrusted the cowboy with such an important task. Oh, I know he's pretty and perfectly charming and I'm aware that you and he have a certain history, but, as I have learned to my cost – and perhaps you are already on the way to learning, my dear – if you want a job done, it's generally best to do it yourself."

Grace stared at Lady Lola, her "wicked stepmother". Lola was stunningly beautiful. When she had crossed from mortal life into the Vampirate realm, she must have been in her late thirties or perhaps very early forties. Her skin was as white as alabaster, her hair raven-black and her eyes a deep, velvet brown. She had the kind of otherworldly beauty reserved for movie stars or fairy-tale queens and princesses. Every detail was flawless – from her full lips to the beauty spot which punctuated her creamy cheek.

The only thing which jarred was the tattoo of the black heart around Lola's left eye. True, the heart was perfectly drawn and the effect striking. But there was something about it which set Grace's nerves on edge. She couldn't help but gaze at the tattoo. As she did so, the heart shape began to melt away and Grace found herself staring at a much less appealing mark. The slightly blurry crescent shape was black in the centre but bled to neon green and purple around the edges. Grace realised she was looking at a nasty bruise.

"Don't you know it's rude to stare?" Lola's cut-glass voice pulled Grace back into the moment. Lola began walking towards her and Grace was suddenly aware of the heady, almost hypnotic, scent of roses.

Lola had moved closer and was now standing directly above her. She placed a hand on Grace's shoulder. "You have a certain wild look in your eyes, Grace. Perhaps you should take another sip of water?"

Grace glanced away momentarily but did not reach for the glass.

"What is it?" Lola inquired, sitting on the bed and smoothing down her full skirt. "What's stirred you so?"

Grace hesitated, weighing up just how much she was willing to share. She decided to take a gamble. "I see things," she said. "I have a gift."

Lola nodded. "I hear that you have many gifts, my dear. Your father speaks most highly of you."

Grace found the word "father" unsettling. "You mean Sidorio?"

Lola nodded once more. "That's right. Sidorio. My husband, your father. We'll come to him in a moment. First, tell me what you saw before."

Again Grace hesitated, then decided to risk it. "I see

beneath the surface of things," she said. "I saw beneath your tattoo." Lady Lola's face froze as Grace continued. "I saw your injury."

"Fascinating," Lola said, somewhat defensively. "What exactly did you see?"

"Just the bruise," Grace said. "It was crescent-shaped." She leaned forward. "I wonder . . . is it connected to your death and how you crossed?"

Lola folded her arms across her chest. "I remember now, Sid told me that you were fascinated by crossing stories. Aren't you compiling a book of them, or some such?"

Grace was surprised, and strangely flattered, that Lola knew this. She nodded. "I like to talk to all the Vampirates I meet and find out how they crossed. Sidorio was one of the first to talk to me, about how he was killed by Julius Caesar." As she spoke, she reached over and opened her bedside drawer. Reaching inside, she grabbed her latest notebook and held it out to Lola.

Lola opened the volume and scanned the pages with interest. As she did so, Grace again marvelled at her stepmother's beauty. In the light of the oil-lamp, Lola's long lashes were elongated by shadows, extending across her angular cheekbones. Grace's eyes travelled once more to the black heart tattoo. As if reflexively, Lady Lola glanced up at her.

"You have very neat handwriting," Lola said, smiling prettily as she closed the notebook and set it down on the bedspread.

To her surprise, Grace felt crushed. She had hoped for a fuller response. She was proud of the work she'd amassed to date on the Vampirates' crossing stories. And, more than that, for reasons she couldn't fathom, she wanted to impress Lady Lola. She found herself gazing at the heart-shaped tattoo once more.

"What are you doing?" Grace heard Lola's voice but it was muffled now, as if far in the distance. As the voice decreased in volume, another noise grew in intensity inside her head. It was the sound of horses' hooves. Drumming on earth. There was another sound too – smaller, softer. Rain. A mizzly country rain. Interspersed with the occasional cry. A bird call, perhaps? Intrigued, Grace tuned in her senses more deeply. As she did so, she realised it wasn't a cry, at least not an animal cry, but rather a mechanical squeak.

"Stop it! Whatever you're doing, stop it!" The voice was no more than a whisper now and Grace had no intention of stopping. Her vision was becoming more and more complete. Now, she could see horses' hooves thundering over uneven ground and rain collecting in swollen puddles on a country track. The squeak she had heard, she realised, belonged to the wheels of a carriage being pulled by the horses. The carriage wheels were rusty and needed oiling.

Suddenly, Grace felt a searing pain and the vision was instantly lost. Opening her eyes, she found Lady Lola standing over her, her palm stretched out close to Grace's stinging cheek.

Grace stared up in disbelief. "Did you just *slap* me?"

Lola made no attempt to deny it. "You left me no choice. You were being very discourteous. I'm an absolute stickler for good manners."

"Good manners!" Grace stared up at Lola, her cheek still smarting from the slap. "I don't see how you can lecture me on *any* kind of manners!"

Lola sat down again. "Get over it, Grace. I did what I had to do. We don't have much time. I need you to stop drifting off and focus on what I have to tell you."

Grace folded her arms defiantly. "Give me one good reason why I should give you five seconds of my time."

"Oh, Grace," said Lola. "You know as well as I do that you're in a bind and I'm the only one to help you out of it."

Grace shook her head. "I don't know anything of the sort."

"You're a *dhampir*, Grace. Half-mortal, half-vampire. *I* know that and *you* know that. The only problem is, you really don't understand very much about what that means. You need help to discover your true being, to come to maturity as an immortal."

"And you're offering that help?"

"You could do a whole lot worse," said Lola.

Grace rolled her eyes, but Lola proceeded, unperturbed. "You've spent most of your life living a lie. You thought Dexter Tempest was your father. Not so. Whilst he was a nice albeit unambitious man, who loved your mother and raised you and your brother as best he could, there was no authentic blood connection."

"Dexter was my dad," Grace said. "Whatever Sidorio is doesn't change that."

Lola shook her head. "Your relationship with Sidorio changes everything. Sidorio is your blood father. And Sidorio is a very powerful being. He is High King of all the Vampirates."

Grace snorted with derision, then froze, fearing another slap from Lola's vicious hand. But this time Lola only looked at her questioningly. Grace felt suddenly emboldened. "Sidorio is captain of a ragtag army of renegades," she said. "The ones who couldn't deal with the discipline of this ship or Sanctuary. He certainly *isn't* the King of the Vampirates. *This* is the one, true Vampirate ship – not yours, not *The Blood Captain*. This ship – *The Nocturne!*"

Lola shook her head. "Once, perhaps, that was true. But this ship no longer even has a captain." She smiled, mirthlessly. "I see you don't even try to deny that."

"The Captain is . . . away," Grace said. "But he'll be back soon. And, in the meantime—"

"Stop!" Lola raised her palm. "Before you waste precious breath telling me how Mosh Zu is keeping the Captain's throne warm. You've fallen into the same trap again, Grace. You're living another lie. Oh, I know that you feel loyal to the poor Captain and others aboard this ship. But *The Nocturne* is dying, Grace. Half the crew have deserted it to join Sidorio. Not because they are lacking in discipline but because they have finally woken up to what they are and accepted the nature of their true being. It was no longer appropriate for them to report to a captain who hid for all those years behind a mask, even before he completely disappeared from view. His time is over."

Grace felt a visceral reaction to Lola's brutal words. "Mosh Zu . . ." she began, but faltered.

Lola didn't miss a beat. "Mosh Zu is here, yes. And he has many gifts, Grace. But he is no leader. Remember, Grace. What did Mosh Zu do when Sidorio stormed Sanctuary? He just let more Vampirates flee. The world of the Vampirates is changing, Grace, and *you* have to make a decision. Are you going to fade into obscurity here, out of some misguided sense of loyalty, or are you going to take your rightful place at your father and brother's side, at the heart of a new empire? The empire Sidorio and I are building together. For you and for Connor. For all of us." Lola's eyes blazed with ambition. "Our empire of night."

Grace lowered her eyes. "Please leave," she said softly, but with utter conviction.

"I'll go in a moment," Lola said. "It's time I returned to *The Vagabond* in any case. There's just one more thing I want to say to you before I go."

Grace waited as she felt Lola's piercing gaze on her once more. "Face up to who you are, Grace," Lola said. "*What* you are." She reached out to the bedside table and lifted the

81

envelope that still rested there. "Don't be so quick to dismiss an invitation which others would kill for." She held the invitation out to Grace but Grace made no move to accept it.

Grace found she was trembling, but whether from fear or anger, or a combination of the two, she was unsure. "I didn't ask for this," she said, her voice tight. "I didn't *ask* to be different. I was happy before. Just being ordinary. Back with Dad and Connor in the lighthouse. Home in Crescent Moon Bay."

Lola snorted. "You don't believe that any more than I do. You may not have asked for this but you're fascinated by the world you've discovered and which you now find yourself a part of. You've been showered with the rarest of gifts, Grace. But this bounty doesn't come without a price. You have an obligation — to yourself and to your father."

"Sidorio?" exclaimed Grace. "I owe him nothing!"

Lola's eyes were on fire as she stared once more at Grace. "On the contrary, my dear, you owe him *everything*. You owe him life. You owe him your immortality. Don't be under any illusions, Grace, darling. If you had been a regular mortal you wouldn't have lasted a single night on this ship before someone had drained your blood. They all knew you were different, special, from the very start. It was only you who was voyaging alone in the dark." Lola strode forward and reached for Grace's notebook. Grace watched with alarm as Lola opened the book and began riffling through the thin pages. Grace had poured a lot of time and energy into the book of crossing stories and she couldn't bear for Lola to tear it, just to make her point.

"It's all right,' Lola said, closing the book between her palms. "I'm not going to harm your precious opus. But, don't you see, Grace? You're so fascinated by everyone else's story that you've missed the point. Yours is the best crossing story of all."

Lola dropped Grace's notebook down onto the bedclothes once more. "I've said all I came here to say. When you're ready to stop scribbling your jottings and start living your life – your *true* life – we'll look forward to welcoming you, your father and I."

Lady Lola Lockwood Sidorio, Grace's wicked stepmother, opened the cabin door and made her exit. As the door swung to behind her, Grace stood reeling in the centre of the cabin. She had the sense of being caught amid omnivorous, circling currents, preparing to tear her apart.

CHAPTER TWELVE

Divided Loyalties

"You're lucky to catch me," said Cheng Li as Connor stepped into the captain's cabin. "I'm about to jump on a taxi-boat." She glanced at the clock above her desk. "Which is already three minutes late! This isn't the first time this has happened. One more strike and I'm changing ferry companies."

Connor was dismayed. He had been psyching himself up for this meeting for the past twenty-four hours and had hoped that by rising so early, when the ship was mostly silent, he'd have managed to secure some private time with Cheng Li.

"Where are you going?" he asked.

Cheng Li smiled. "I have a meeting with our old friend, Commodore Black. After our successful execution of Operation Black Heart, it's time to plan our next move against the Vampirates."

Connor's heart lurched to his stomach like an out-of-control elevator.

"You know," Cheng Li said, "you look a little peaky. Are you sickening for something? I hope you haven't caught that nasty Crustacean Flu that is doing the rounds. Perhaps you had better sit down." She pointed to the chair on the other side of her desk.

Connor hesitated, leaning against the chair. "We *really* need to talk," he said.

Cheng Li smiled. "You know I always enjoy our chats," she said. "But I'm afraid this is just really bad timing. We can schedule a meeting this evening if you like, when I get back from the academy."

Connor shook his head. "Actually, we need to talk *before* you meet with the Federation."

Cheng Li arched an eyebrow inquiringly. They had worked alongside each other long enough to read one another's body language. He knew that he now had her full attention. But he was going to have to talk fast.

"Lola Lockwood isn't dead."

Cheng Li's face froze.

There was a knock at the door, then it pushed open and Bo Yin poked her smiling head around. "Captain, just to let you know that your taxi has arrived."

"Thank you, Bo Yin," Cheng Li said, her voice surprisingly calm and normal. "Will you tell him that he's already five minutes late and he now needs to give me five minutes more, which I have no intention of paying for."

"Yes, Captain! No problem!" Bo Yin gave a salute, then grinned at Connor and hurried off merrily to execute Cheng Li's command. There was no doubting how much Bo Yin was enjoying every aspect of belonging to the crew.

Cheng Li sat down behind her desk. "OK," she said to Connor. "We have five precious minutes. Clearly, you have important information for me. Spill."

"Lola Lockwood wasn't destroyed the night of the wedding," Connor said, feeling the adrenaline coursing through him. "Operation Black Heart failed. Sidorio reunited Lola's head with her body and revived her. She's alive and well and, evidently, just back from a most enjoyable honeymoon."

Cheng Li frowned. "And you know this how?"

There was no time to waste. Connor reached out his hand and dropped the envelope on Cheng Li's desk. "Stukeley came to see me," he said. "He brought me this invitation."

Cheng Li unfolded the letter and slipped on her reading glasses. Her brow furrowed as she read Sidorio's words. Then she set the letter down, locked her hands together and rested her chin on them. "It appears we have a situation," she said.

Connor nodded. "I'm sorry. I should have told you sooner."

"When did Stukeley deliver this?"

"The night before last. At Bart and Cate's send-off at the Full Moon Saloon. I went out the back to get some air and he was waiting for me there on that scuzzy beach."

Cheng Li frowned.

"I know I should have told you straight away," Connor said. "I'm really sorry."

Cheng Li gazed at him. "You're right, Connor. You should have. But doubtless you had good reason not to. I'm just grateful that I found out before I stood up in front of that stuffed shirt, Ahab Black."

Connor was amazed how well she was taking the news. Their mission, which had been so meticulously planned, and for which praise had been heaped so lavishly upon both Cheng Li and her crew, was now revealed to be a failure. Connor frowned. His own actions had deprived Cheng Li of twenty-four hours of valuable thinking time.

Suddenly, she stood up and reached for her satchel. Was that it? Was she leaving already?

"I'm really sorry," he repeated.

"Do stop apologising," Cheng Li said, lifting her satchel over her shoulder. "And wipe that sad-sack look off your face. The nature of this mission is constant flux, Connor. This was inevitable. We are not dealing with any regular enemy."

Connor was flummoxed by her balanced reaction. "What will you tell them?" he asked.

"I don't know," Cheng Li said, pushing open the cabin door. "You can help me work that out on the way."

Suddenly, the penny dropped. "You want me to come with you to your meeting?"

"Try eating fish for breakfast, Connor," said Cheng Li. "It should make you sharper in the mornings. Come on, we're now officially ten minutes late. This taxi sailor had better be on top of his navigation."

As the taxi-boat skimmed the ocean, Connor found himself calmed by the small craft's smooth and rapid motion and its proximity to the water. It was a warm morning and the ocean spray was refreshing on his face and arms. He and Cheng Li were sitting at the opposite end of the vessel to the driver, where they could talk further without being overheard. Nevertheless, for the first part of the journey, both passengers were silent, as if they had all the time in the world simply to enjoy the scenery and mull over their private thoughts.

"So," Cheng Li broke the silence, "this invitation from Sidorio and Lady Lola. Are you thinking of accepting it? Is that why you kept it to yourself?"

Connor shook his head. "No," he said, honestly. "No, it's the last place I want to go and they're the very last people I want to spend time with."

Cheng Li lifted her sunglasses for a moment. "Don't be too hasty, Connor. There are no rights or wrongs here. After what we discovered about your parentage, I'd say that both of us, but you especially, are sailing in uncharted waters."

Connor frowned. She could have picked another time to be so uncharacteristically understanding. What he needed from her now was the typical Cheng Li response, full of certainties – do

87

this, don't do this – not this new, hippy-dippy *laissez-faire* attitude. If anything made him feel he was in uncharted waters, it was this.

"I know Sidorio is my blood father," Connor said. "And I know that that makes me different. I'm not happy about it – far from it – but I'll work through it. Whatever – and however long – it takes. I'm so grateful for your support. I don't want to enter into their world. I want to be here. Surrounded by my friends and comrades, in the world I know."

"Hmm." Cheng Li slipped down her shades and considered his words. "The thing is, Connor, you really are between Scylla and Charybdis. I hear what you are saying about your friends and comrades but the fact is *we* are on a mission to destroy the Vampirates – at least the renegade Vampirates, including Sidorio, Lola and Stukeley. You have to think through whether you can still be part of that mission, when your loyalties may be divided and your effectiveness compromised."

Connor felt his blood rise. "My loyalties aren't divided," he said angrily. "Not one bit. They mean nothing to me. Less than nothing. I want them destroyed every bit as much as you do. Probably more." He stared Cheng Li directly in the eyes. "I'm ready to see the destruction of every last Vampirate and to play my part in it. You have to believe me."

"I do believe you," Cheng Li said, reaching out her hand to his shoulder, and lowering her voice. "But you need to be clear about this. Even if our mission is successful and we take out every last one of them, that won't change your genetic make-up, Connor. You will still be a dhampir – as will Grace – and Sidorio will still be your father." Her tone was soft, sympathetic even, but her words stabbed at him like a freshly-sharpened épée.

"I'll deal with that," he said. "First, let's destroy them. Then I'll have all the time in the world to work through my identity crisis."

88

"All right," Cheng Li said. "If you're sure. But be in no doubt, if you're on my side in this mission, then I expect you to do everything I ask of you. I can't make any exceptions for you on account of our secret."

"I don't want any special treatment," Connor said. "I'm one hundred per cent committed to the mission. All I'm asking is that you keep my secret from the others. Until I'm ready to tell them." He dropped his head. "If that day ever comes."

Cheng Li extended her hand. "You have a deal," she said.

Connor took her hand and shook it. He was trembling with emotion but he felt her firm hand enclose his and squeeze it tightly. It steadied him and he felt his heart-rate beginning to slow down at last.

A shout came from the other end of the boat. "Look, boss! There's the Pirate Academy arch. I got you here with a good twenty minutes to spare." The sailor opened his mouth and grinned a toothless grin. "I hope you're a generous tipper, Captain Li."

As Cheng Li and Connor stepped out onto the familiar landing-stage at Pirate Academy, Connor sighed deeply, letting go of some of the stress he'd been carrying since Stukeley's visit. He felt better for his talk with Cheng Li. She was there for him, just as she had always been since the night she had rescued him from the raging ocean.

"Come on," she said, striding ahead up the hill. "Let's not keep Black waiting." She waved to the diminutive figure of Lisbeth Quivers, who was standing on the terrace at the top of the hill. Quivers was one of the former pirate captains who now played a key role both within the academy faculty and in the Pirate Federation. Connor had little love for the majority of the teachers here but he felt a certain warmth towards Quivers, who seemed to have a more fully-developed human side than her colleagues.

Connor increased his pace to catch up with Cheng Li. "Have you worked out what you're going to tell Commodore Black and the Federation?" he asked.

"Just about," she said, with a nod. "I'm sure the rest will come to me once we're in the room. Just remember what you agreed to before, Connor. To do everything I ask of you."

Connor nodded soberly. "I remember, Captain. I won't let you down."

CHAPTER THIRTEEN

An Audience with the Federation

Cheng Li knocked briskly on the panelled door of the headmaster's study.

"*Entrez!*" called a familiar voice. The door opened and Captain Rene Grammont ushered them inside.

"Cheng Li and Mister Tempest. *Bienvenue!* Welcome back to your old stomping ground." Captain Grammont kissed Cheng Li on each cheek. "And one more for luck, *n'est-ce-pas?*"

Then he extended his hand and gave Connor an eye-wateringly firm handshake. There was something reassuringly old-school about Rene Grammont, from his ruddy, immaculately-shaven cheeks to the soft smell of pipe-tobacco which mingled with his lime cologne.

"Congratulations on succeeding John as headmaster," Cheng Li said, stepping deeper into the study. "I know it's what he would have wanted."

"*Merci*," Captain Grammont said, smiling with pride. "It is a great honour for me to build on all the *incroyable* work John put in here."

"You were with him every step of the way," Cheng Li said. "I'm sure it will be the most seamless of transitions."

"You're too kind!" Rene Grammont's blue eyes twinkled. "How well you look. And of course, you are doing such great things with your young crew. Everyone at the academy, and in the Federation too, is very much in awe of your recent exploits."

Cheng Li bowed her head, modestly. Connor couldn't help but wonder if the powers-that-be would be quite so awed when Cheng Li revealed that Operation Black Heart had not, after all, been one of the most successful campaigns in Federation history. Hopefully, they would take the news in their stride, as Cheng Li had done. But whilst Rene Grammont might well be sympathetic and supportive, it was anyone's guess how the enigmatic Commodore Ahab Black, his senior officer in the Pirate Federation, would react.

Captain Grammont glanced at his highly-polished fob watch. "*Alors*, much as I'd like to sit and have a chinwag with you both, I suppose we really should get a move on."

"Indeed," Cheng Li said. "Where are we meeting Commodore Black?"

Grammont raised an eyebrow. "In the vaults," he said.

"The vaults?" Cheng Li didn't mask her surprise.

"He's stepped up security to level six," Captain Grammont explained. "Come on, I'll lead the way."

Connor and Cheng Li had previously accessed the academy vaults through a secret door in the floor of the Rotunda. They had made the journey down there to visit the Federation's secret cache filled with research materials and artefacts relating to the Vampirates. Now, a more direct route was revealed as Captain Grammont leaned forward to a silver globe and spun it three times upon its axis. As he did so, behind the globe, one of the leather wall-panels swung open, revealing a dimly-lit spiral staircase.

Captain Grammont held open the wall-panel, allowing the others to enter first. "I do hope neither of you has dust allergies," he said, brushing a cobweb out of his perfectly groomed hair.

The spiral staircase led down to a familiar subterranean corridor with a number of identical doors on either side. Connor glanced at the door numbered 8. Behind it lay the cache where they had slaved long and hard in their mission to research the Vampirates' vulnerabilities. They had emerged with what they had hoped was a foolproof plan. Events had unfortunately proved otherwise.

Now, though, Captain Grammont led them past this door and on to Room 13. He knocked to signal their presence, waited a moment, then pushed open the door. He crossed the threshold first, signalling Cheng Li and Connor to follow. As they entered the dark room, Captain Grammont formally announced them: "Captain Li and Mister Tempest of *The Tiger*." The door swung closed behind them, with a snap.

Room 13 was, like the other rooms in the vaults, poorly lit. The air felt thicker down here, colder too, as if you were underwater. Dust-mites floated in front of Connor's eyes. He looked beyond them to the long table which extended along the length of the room. It was covered with papers, as well as carafes of water and bowls of fruit. Commodore Black was at the far end. He stood up to welcome the new arrivals – the most minimal of smiles forming under his trim moustache. Connor gazed at Black's one visible eye, which shone more violet than ever in the gloom. His other eye was, as usual, shielded by a patch.

Connor had been under the impression that Cheng Li was expecting a one-on-one meeting with Commodore Black. Evidently, this was not the case. Ranged along both sides of the table were all the other members of staff at Pirate Academy, each serving a dual role as high-ranking officers within the Federation. Connor followed Cheng Li towards the table, casting his eyes over the familiar faces. On the left side of the table sat Pavel Platonov, Shivaji Singh, Francisco Moscardo and Apostolos Solomos. On the opposite side sat Floris van Amstel, Kirsten Larsen, Wilfred Avery and Lisabeth Quivers, who had evidently made a swift descent from the academy terrace. The captains all greeted Cheng Li and Connor. Clearly, Connor's presence at the meeting had not been expected but no one seemed perturbed that he was there. Indeed, Captain Platonov himself sprung to his feet and drew forward an extra chair. Thinking back to his first encounter with arch-disciplinarian Captain Platonov, Connor realised just how far his stock within the Federation, and the pirate world as a whole, had risen.

Connor sat down next to Cheng Li at the near end of the long table. Captain Grammont went to join Commodore Black at the other end. As Grammont moved, Connor noticed four more high-ranking pirates sitting close to Ahab Black. He could tell from Cheng Li's sudden change of posture that she too had clocked the additional personnel. Before they could comment, Ahab Black called the meeting to order.

"Welcome, Captain Li and Mister Tempest. As you can see, we are quorate today with the full staff of Pirate Academy. We are also joined by four celebrated pirates who will be well known to you – Barbarro Wrathe and his wife Trofie, captain and deputy of *The Typhon*. And Molucco Wrathe and Cate Morgan, captain and deputy of *The Diablo*."

At his words, Cate smiled and raised her hand at her former comrades. The three Wrathes also turned towards Cheng Li and Connor. Surprisingly, they too were smiling.

"Perhaps I should explain," Commodore Black said.

"That would be useful," Cheng Li said, her voice measured.

Black went on. "I need hardly tell you that the world of piracy is changing fast, Captain Li. As such, we need to strengthen the alliances within the Federation. That means reaching out to talented pirates who have, for one reason or another, parted company with us in recent years." Black glanced at Molucco. "Earlier today, we concluded a deal welcoming Molucco Wrathe back into the fold." Molucco nodded and grinned, running his fingers through his rainbow-coloured dreadlocks. As he did so, Scrimshaw, the captain's pet snake, emerged and coiled himself about the captain's arm. Across the table, there was a corresponding ripple in Barbarro Wrathe's dark locks and his own pet snake, Scrimshaw's brother, Skirmish, emerged, slinking down the captain's velvet sleeve.

Ahab Black paused only momentarily at the distraction. "The loss of our colleague John Kuo left a significant gap in the hierarchy of the Federation – a gap which I feel cannot be filled by one person alone. That is why I am delighted to tell you that, as of today, Commodore Barbarro Wrathe and Commodore Molucco Wrathe will be jointly sharing John's former Federation duties. Meet your new commanders, Captain Li."

Cheng Li was speechless. She couldn't seem to take her eyes off Molucco. He was stroking Scrimshaw contemplatively but now looked up and smiled at her. "Good to have you working for me, again, Cheng Li."

The still, stale room was filled with an uneasy silence. Finally, Cate spoke. "I think you mean that it's great to have Captain Li working *with* you again," she said.

"Do I?" responded Molucco, a mischievous glint in his eye.

Barbarro Wrathe took up the baton. "Captain Li, I know my brother and I have had our differences with you in the past. But we're ready to bury the hatchet and come together for the common good. You impressed us all enormously with your work on Operation Black Heart. Not that it was anything less than we expected of you." He shuddered, and placed his hand on Trofie's shoulder. "My wife and I had a particularly nasty encounter with that Vampirate monster, Lola Lockwood."

Trofie Wrathe brought her golden hand up to her cheek, the ruby fingernails glinting.

"Your encounter was not quite so nasty as John Kuo's," observed Cheng Li.

"Granted," acknowledged Barbarro. "We were lucky to escape with our lives, but we are deeply appreciative of your work," his eyes turned to Connor, "and that of your crew, in ridding our oceans of this vile scourge. Now the mission continues. As you know, Molucco and I had a brother, Porfirio. Our dear baby brother. A pirate captain with the brightest, most glorious of futures ahead of him. Porfirio was slaughtered by the Vampirates, by this Sidorio, with whom you have previously tangled. Now that you have dispatched the she-devil, we must turn our attention to Sidorio himself. This will be your next mission."

Connor was struck dumb. Things were moving so fast. He thought of his conversation with Cheng Li on the voyage that morning. She had seemed bullish, then. Now, he wondered how on earth she was going to respond.

All eyes were on Cheng Li as she began speaking. "I had anticipated that today's meeting would be a private audience with you, Commodore Black," she said, "but it is always good to see my old teachers, comrades and friends. Indeed, it is opportune to have you all here today as I have important news, both bad and good, to bring you up to speed on."

Cheng Li's confident tone had captured everyone's attention. Not least of all Connor's. He was still unsure how she was going to play the difficult hand she had been dealt.

"I shall begin with news which I know will be a bitter blow

to you all," Cheng Li said. "Lola Lockwood has not been eliminated." There was an immediate chorus of gasps from around the table.

Cheng Li nodded. "I'm afraid it's true. Operation Black Heart was not, as we initially thought, one hundred per cent successful."

Molucco didn't miss a beat. "If Black Heart herself has not been eliminated then, *de facto*, Operation Black Heart was zero per cent successful."

He smirked at Cheng Li's obvious discomfort, but suddenly an unlikely voice came to Cheng Li's rescue. Barbarro Wrathe boomed from across the table. "Let Captain Li have her say, brother!"

Cheng Li nodded towards Barbarro. "The fact is, that the Vampirates have certain capabilities which we are only just beginning to understand. I might add that in the past weeks and months, my crew and I have got further than any Federation enquiry has previously managed. Our knowledge and experience now outstrips the secret cache in Room 8, compiled by countless Federation officers over many years. And I should like to acknowledge here Cate Morgan, who was nothing less than brilliant in devising a revolutionary attack strategy with which to fight this new enemy."

"Hear, hear!" came the voices of several of the captains.

Cheng Li paused before continuing, her eyes taking in all of her comrades. "We have to face facts. The Vampirates are no regular adversary. It was complacent of us to think we could simply swing in and defeat them in one fell swoop. In short, we need to stop thinking about one decisive battle and prepare instead for a period of more prolonged war."

"I don't like the sound of that," said Wilfred Avery.

"Nor I," said Shivaji Singh. "Wars are expensive."

"Hear, hear!" added Floris van Amstel.

"None of us likes this," piped up Captain Larsen. "But we turned a blind eye to the threat from the Vampirates over a number of years, which led to this state of affairs."

"That's not *quite* right," interceded Lisabeth Quivers. "The Vampirates posed no obvious threat until recently."

"Yes," agreed Francisco Moscardo. "Unless you are suggesting we eliminated the threat before it happened, I don't see what we were supposed to have done."

"That doesn't make sense!" objected Apostolos Solomos.

"My point precisely!" rejoined Moscardo.

"Cheng Li is right," said Pavel Platonov. "We need to step up to the new order of things."

"Agreed." Ahab Black spoke with calm authority, drawing the captains back to order. "Captain Li, you spoke before of bad news and good. Presumably, your revelation that Lockwood is alive is the bad news?"

Cheng Li nodded.

"That being the case, shall we move on to the good?"

Connor watched Cheng Li take centre-stage once more. "I said before that the Vampirates are a different kind of enemy. They have certain capabilities which we have underestimated. For instance, in Lockwood's case, her ability to repair herself after decapitation. *However*, we also know now that this enemy exhibits key weaknesses. Chief amongst them being, if I may be so blunt, stupidity."

There was a hubbub amongst the captains at this. Black raised his palm to silence them once more. "Stupidity?" he said. "Please explain."

"The Vampirates are quite gullible," Cheng Li said. "Susceptible to stories which a mortal enemy would see through in an instant. For instance, you mentioned Sidorio before, self-styled King of the renegade Vampirates. Well, we have managed to convince him that Connor is his son."

Connor was shocked to his core. *She couldn't be saying this.* He must have dozed off and was dreaming.

"I'm not joking," Cheng Li continued. "We have convinced Sidorio that he has two children – Connor and his sister Grace. I can fill you in further on the details later." Her eyes swept across the captains' faces. "We'll also need to discuss some key staffing issues. For instance, I'm going to need Cate Morgan and Bart Pearce back on my crew on a more permanent basis." As Molucco opened his mouth to object, Cheng Li powered on. "The important thing for you all to take on board is that Sidorio completely believes our cover-story and has invited Connor and Grace to stay with him and Lola Lockwood. This, I'm sure you'll agree, gives us an incredible opportunity to send a spy into the very heart of the enemy camp."

"Wouldn't that be sending Connor into terrible danger?" asked Lisabeth Quivers.

"Connor has proved his mettle on more than one occasion," Cheng Li ploughed on. "And as long as Sidorio is convinced that Connor is indeed his son, he will be in no danger at all." She reached into her satchel and withdrew an envelope.

Connor couldn't believe it. He didn't remember giving the invitation to her, though it was possible. His mind and emotions had been all over the place earlier in the day.

"Exhibit A," announced Cheng Li, opening the letter and tossing it triumphantly on the table. "Read it. I think you'll agree it changes everything."

Molucco shook his head. "It doesn't change the fact that Operation Black Heart failed. You're not having Cate and Bart back again. They belong to me."

"Oh, stop being so cheap!" Trofie snapped at her brother-in-law, darting out her golden hand and snatching up Sidorio's letter. "This is indeed a remarkable opportunity to spy on the Vampirates and gather more intelligence from which to plan their final destruction." She turned to Cheng Li. "This is yet more excellent, innovative work, Captain Li."

"I agree," Black said. "You have snatched a greater victory from the jaws of an understandable defeat. The Federation will give you the team you request and whatever else you need to proceed. The way forward is clear. Connor accepts Sidorio's invitation and finds out every last thing he can about how their operation works."

Connor could feel the eyes of the captains upon him. He couldn't believe the position Cheng Li had placed him in. He was eager to see how she justified this move. But, as he turned to her questioningly, he heard her earlier words once more.

"Be in no doubt, if you are on my side in this mission, then I expect you to do everything I ask of you."

He shook his head. He really should have seen this one coming.

CHAPTER FOURTEEN

News of the Captain

Grace lay on her bed, turning the envelope containing Sidorio and Lola's invitation over and over in her hands. Her head was a jumble of thoughts and feelings in reaction to the invitation and all it represented, which, combined with the surprise visits from Johnny and Lola Lockwood, had meant a sleepless night and day. As if she didn't already have enough on her mind, after what had happened on the night of the Feast!

Grace still hadn't had the chance to talk properly to Lorcan about her spontaneous decision to join him in Oskar's cabin, nor her equally precipitous exit. She realised that she also needed to talk to Mosh Zu about her growing hunger. So much had happened in such a short space of time, it was hard to know where to start.

There was a knock on the door. "Come in!" Grace cried, slipping the envelope between the pages of her notebook and reaching for a pen, as Darcy pushed open the door and stepped inside.

"Hello, Grace," Darcy said, buzzing with nervous energy. "Oh, I'm sorry! I hope I'm not interrupting your writing."

Grace shook her head, feeling a little guilty at her charade.

She closed the notebook and placed it and the pen back on her nightstand.

Darcy closed the door behind her and swept into the room with characteristic drama. "I've been sorting through some of my old jewellery boxes – you know what a magpie I am – and I found these." She extended her right arm towards Grace's face, her hand clenched in an upturned fist. As she opened her fingers, Grace gasped. Lying there in Darcy's doll-like palm was the most stunning pair of aquamarine drop earrings. They seemed to contain an infinite depth and variety of blues and greens, as if they had been distilled from the ocean waters themselves.

"They're a little too classic for me," Darcy said. "But the minute I saw them, Grace, I thought of you. Now, lift up your hair and let's see how they look!"

"They're beautiful!" Grace exclaimed, obediently lifting her hair. She realised she had let it grow quite long of late. Darcy fastened the earrings for her and Grace let her hair fall down again behind her ears.

"Perfection!" proclaimed Darcy with a smile. "Stand up and have a look in the mirror!"

Grace approached the mirror. She felt a momentary jolt. It was as if her mother was looking back at her. She had never looked so grown-up before. Behind her, Darcy smiled and lifted a hand to Grace's shoulder. "The earrings are pretty, Grace, but *you* are beautiful," she said. "No wonder Lorcan has fallen so hard for you."

Grace couldn't hold back the solitary tear which slid across her cheek.

"Now, Grace, why are you crying?" Darcy asked, busily searching for a handkerchief.

"I'm sorry," Grace said, as fresh tears coursed down her cheeks. "I'm trying really hard not to get emotional but there's an awful lot going on at the moment."

"There, there!" Darcy dabbed away the remnants of Grace's tears. "Why don't you sit down and tell Auntie Darcy all about it?"

"Auntie?" Grace said, laughing through her tears and lying back down on the bed. "You're a bit young to be my auntie! I mean you *look* too young. Oh, you know what I mean . . ."

"I'm laying it on a bit thick, aren't I?" Darcy said, lying down beside Grace. "I'll level with you, pal. I know something's going on with you. The earrings were . . ."

"A pretext?" Grace asked, amused.

"A Trojan horse, if you like," Darcy said. "I just wanted to check you were OK and jewellery seemed a good way in."

"Oh Darcy," Grace said. "You didn't need jewellery, though I do love the earrings so don't even think about taking them back! But you're my friend. In fact, you're really like the sister I never had."

"Oh Grace!" Darcy said, raising the hankie to her own eyes. "That's the nicest thing . . . just the nicest thing."

Grace smiled. Darcy's arrival was a blessing. She could talk things through with her and get a better idea of how to approach both Lorcan and Mosh Zu. Darcy had proved an excellent sounding board in the past.

"Well?" Darcy said, her chocolate-brown eyes wide open and her bow-shaped mouth pursed. "I think it's about time I heard what's on your mind, don't you?"

Grace opened her mouth to speak, but she was silenced by another knock on the door. Before she could say anything further, Lorcan strode into the cabin.

"Aha!" he said, with a smile. "Two for the price of one!"

"Lorcan," Grace said. "Come on in. Darcy and I were just having a chat."

"That's right," Darcy mumbled, sitting up straight and unruffling her hair. "Just a little chat. Nothing important.

Nothing which can't wait until later." She began tapping her fingers on the counterpane, in a display of feigned, or indeed strained, patience.

"I'm sorry to interrupt you, ladies," Lorcan said. "But I need you both to come with me. Mosh Zu wishes to see all three of us at once."

"What for?" Grace asked, sliding off the bed.

Lorcan looked them both in the eye and spoke in measured tones. "I don't know any details except that it concerns the Captain."

"The Captain!" Grace's heart missed a beat. Her first thought at hearing his name was excitement but then she felt a flash of fear. It had been some time since Mosh Zu had shared any news about the Captain. Her mind was racing now and she saw that Darcy was trembling. Grace reached out her hand once more to her friend.

"Now, Darcy, don't look so worried," Lorcan said. "You too, Grace. It could very well be good news."

Darcy's voice was strained. "Mosh Zu wants to see the three of us – the last three people who saw the Captain at Sanctuary." She shook her head. "Oh, don't you see? It can't be good news. It just can't . . ."

"Darcy!" Grace pressed her friend's hand tightly. "Keep calm. Please. Mosh Zu needs us to be strong. The Captain does too." She drew Darcy into a hug, wrapping her arms around her. "Oh, Darcy, I know how much the Captain means to you. He means so much to us all. But we have to go on together – whatever Mosh Zu has to tell us."

Lorcan nodded. "She's right, Darcy. We're in this together and we'll get through it together." He turned to Grace. "I think we should go now, don't you? We'll only fill our heads with needless fears if we drag our heels here."

Grace nodded. In spite of the brave face she was showing to

the others, cold shivers ran up and down her spine. She was unable to tell whether it was this new worry about the Captain or a fresh manifestation of the state of flux within her. As she followed the others out of the room, she glanced over her shoulder at the painting of her parents. As she did so, she heard her dad's voice. "Trust the tide!"

She nodded, feeling a current of calm cut through her rising panic. Turning, she followed the others out into the corridor.

Hand in hand, the three of them approached Mosh Zu's cabin – the suite of interlocking rooms which had formerly been inhabited by the nameless captain of *The Nocturne*. Grace thought back to the first time she had come to this door and sought out the Captain, determined to find out just how much danger she was in aboard the ship. It seemed so long ago now; a world away. She had been surprisingly brave then, under the circumstances. If only she felt half as brave now, coming as she was to learn the Captain's fate. It would be such a terrible blow to lose him, she reflected. To lose him and never to have even known his name. With these thoughts rushing around her head, Grace wasn't even conscious of Lorcan knocking on the door or Mosh Zu calling for them to enter. Before she knew it, she was inside the cabin, still holding tightly on to the hands of her friends. Mosh Zu stood up to greet his guests.

"It's good to see you all," he said. His expression was, as usual, impossible to read. "Perhaps you'd like to sit down?"

"Well, now we know!" Darcy cried. "It can't be good news. That's what people always say when they have something bad to tell you. Sit down. Have a cup of sweet tea! As if it will somehow cushion the blow!"

Grace saw her own fear reflected back through Darcy. Turning to Mosh Zu, she saw him smile softly and shake his head. "I just thought you'd like to be comfortable," he said. "We have much to discuss."

CHAPTER FIFTEEN

A Council of War

"Thank you for coming so swiftly," Mosh Zu said. He remained standing as Grace and Darcy sat down, side by side, on a long couch. Lorcan settled himself in the adjacent chair as Mosh Zu continued. "I can see in your faces how concerned you are for our dear friend, the Captain. I know how much he means to you all. So I am very happy to bring you news of him."

With these words, Grace's fears subsided. Lorcan was glowing with relief. Grace glanced at Darcy, seeing that she too was alert and poised for Mosh Zu to continue.

"The Captain is in the final stages of his recovery," Mosh Zu said. "Very soon, he will begin his journey back to us."

"Where is he now?" Grace asked, but Mosh Zu raised the palm of his hand to still this and further questions. "The Captain and I have been in regular communication these past few nights and we are agreed that things are coming to a severe pass. We need to take decisive action and that's why I have gathered the three of you here tonight, our most loyal and trusted crew-members."

Grace felt a deep sense of pride at his words. Tears pricked her eyes once more, this time from relief, but she fought them back and steadied herself. She needed to focus. Clearly, Mosh Zu had important information to share.

"The world of the Vampirates is changing," Mosh Zu said. "In former times, we kept ourselves to ourselves and our presence went generally unnoticed by the mortal world. We created a sea-shanty to strike fear into the hearts of mortals and persuade them to keep their distance. But, at the same time, we never sought to harm them."

Grace thought of the shanty her dad had sung to her and Connor throughout their childhood.

You'd better be good, child,
Good as gold,
As good as good can be.
Else I'll turn you in to the Vampirates
And wave you out to sea!
Yes, you'd better be good, child,
Good as gold,
Because – look, can you see?
There's a dark ship in the harbour tonight
And there's room in the hold for thee.
Plenty of room for thee!

So the familiar shanty had been penned by the Vampirates themselves! Grace's head was filled with the comical image of Mosh Zu at the piano, working away at the tune while the Captain scribbled down lyrics. She smiled to think of it, then dismissed this highly inappropriate thought as Mosh Zu resumed speaking.

"*The Nocturne* provided a refuge for vampire outsiders – those who did not fit in with conventional vampire society, based as it is on a mania for blood. In the beginning, there were other ships besides *The Nocturne*. This is a subject for another time. For now, my point is this. These ships sailed through eternity, providing safe harbour at last to those vampires oppressed, persecuted and experiencing the very worst of times since crossing over from mortality into the vampire realm."

Lorcan nodded in recognition at this.

"The same was true at Sanctuary, where I have worked for many centuries now, helping vampires to understand their appetites and, if not control them, then at least break through the feeling that they are being controlled *by* them. I have prepared crew-members there, both Vampirates and donors, prior to them joining these ships." Mosh Zu's eyes ranged across the three members of his audience. "But now things are changing – and fast."

"Sidorio," Grace said. "And his new empire. The empire of night."

Lorcan glanced curiously at her. She wasn't ready to meet his eyes and turned back to Mosh Zu, who nodded. "It all began to change when Sidorio rebelled against the Captain and went into exile. We hoped that would be the end of him, but it wasn't. We underestimated him. In his time of exile, he has only grown stronger."

Mosh Zu shook his head, sadly. "Sidorio's rebellion has provided a magnet for other Vampirates who cannot make peace with what they are, who see their condition as licence to behave like demons. They live up to the horror story we spun through the shanty. Their way is not our way, but we cannot expect mortal eyes to draw a distinction."

Mosh Zu had come to stand in front of the hearth. The fire in the grate was unlit but there was hot anger in his eyes as he continued. "A time of war is coming, my friends. We did not invite this war. Nor do we welcome it. But, make no mistake, we will fight it. And we will win it. This message comes to you from me and from your Captain. It is the reason why he had to go away. Before, he was too weak to fight the growing forces of darkness. When he returns, things will be very different."

"This war," said Lorcan. "So it's between us and Sidorio's forces? Between us and this empire of night?"

"In part," said Mosh Zu. "But Sidorio's actions have opened up a further rift between us and the mortal pirate world, which even now is preparing to attack us."

Grace thought of Connor and shook her head. "The pirates won't attack us," she said. "It's Sidorio they have in their sights. *They* must be able to draw the distinction, surely?"

"This is how wars begin," Mosh Zu said, "but not how they end. We will do what we can to avoid war with the pirates but, at the same time, we must make ready for it."

"How?" Lorcan asked.

"Each of you will play a key role," Mosh Zu said. "That is why I summoned you here tonight."

"Us?" Darcy said. "What can *we* do?" She glanced at her friends. "I'm not putting you two down but given the general doomsday scenario, what hope do we have?"

"Plenty," Mosh Zu said, breaking into a smile. "The immortal future begins with the three of you. Your Captain and I have complete faith in you."

He turned towards Lorcan. "Lorcan, your mission relates to combat. *The Nocturne* has always been a ship of pacifists. Because we have steered clear of trouble and kept ourselves to ourselves, we have not had to fight before. Now, we find ourselves in a position where we must defend ourselves. You will develop combat techniques and train the crew to fight, both against Sidorio's forces and, if required, against the pirates."

"That's quite a job!" Lorcan exclaimed.

"Which is why we need someone of your talent and character in charge," said Mosh Zu. "I will work with you, of course, and the Captain too, once he returns."

Lorcan nodded. "I shall do what I can," he said, "and gladly."

"Very good." Now Mosh Zu turned to Darcy. She crossed and uncrossed her legs nervously, then began twisting a strand of her hair.

"Darcy, you are much stronger than you think. Why, you saved the Captain's life when he was at his weakest. You must have greater belief in yourself." He smiled. "Now, no one could disagree that you are a great communicator, Miss Flotsam. You like to talk, am I right? To gossip and chat with all and sundry on the crew?"

"Well, yes," Darcy said, flushing with embarrassment. "I like to be *au courant* with my fellow travellers. Guilty as charged."

"Which is what makes you perfect for your mission," Mosh Zu said. "There are two parts to your task. Firstly, you will be my eyes and ears throughout the ship. You will talk to each and every member of our crew. You will listen to them and watch them and, if you have the merest suspicion of a new rebellion, you will tell me. We cannot afford another insurrection at this point."

Darcy nodded. "I understand," she said.

"There is another facet to your role," Mosh Zu said. "The Captain and I have taken an important decision. It fills us with a certain sadness and it is not one we have taken lightly."

Grace, Darcy and Lorcan exchanged a glance, wondering what he was going to say.

"Sidorio has laid claim to the name 'Vampirates'. He has sullied it beyond repair," he said. "Henceforth, we will make a distinction between his forces and our own. From now on we will call ourselves the Nocturnals, after our ship *The Nocturne*."

"The Nocturnals?" Darcy repeated.

Mosh Zu nodded. "The second part of your mission is to instil this word among the crew. Help them to embrace this new identity. Can you do that?"

"I shall do my best," Darcy said, with some zeal.

"Now you, Grace," Mosh Zu said, turning to face her. "In many ways, your mission is the hardest."

She shivered at his words. What did he and the Captain intend for her?

"You will accept Sidorio's invitation," Mosh Zu said. Grace was struck dumb. How did he know?

Mosh Zu smiled, but when he spoke his voice was icy and humourless. "Does Sidorio think he can send his lieutenant and his wife to prowl about my ship and consort with my crew and I will not know about it?"

Grace could feel the gaze of the others burning into her.

"Johnny came to see me," she explained. "And then Sidorio's wife, Lola Lockwood. They've invited me to join them on their ships." She turned to Lorcan. "I was going to talk to you about it, but it only happened a couple of nights back, on Feast Night, and I had a lot of thinking to do."

"A lot of thinking!" Lorcan exclaimed. "What thinking did you have to do? Of course you cannot accept the invitation!"

Grace felt herself flush but Mosh Zu answered for her. "On the contrary, Grace *must* accept their invitation."

"No!" Darcy exclaimed.

"For what good reason?" inquired Lorcan.

"For *two* very good reasons," Mosh Zu said. "Firstly, it will give us an unparalleled opportunity to spy on Sidorio and his misbegotten crew. Secondly, it will give us the chance to destroy the empire of night from within."

Lorcan was aghast. "It's not fair to ask Grace to do all that. It's too big a task. And it's dangerous. Let me go instead."

Mosh Zu shook his head. Lorcan's face was like thunder. Darcy was in tears.

Grace felt suddenly calm and stoic. "Don't you see?" she said, addressing her two friends. "I must go. I'm the only one of us who can do this. It's my responsibility. I'm Sidorio's daughter."

CHAPTER SIXTEEN

Secret Agents

"I hate to leave you here, all on your own," said Lorcan.

Grace glanced along the desolate beach, shivering in the night breeze. "I'll be all right," she said, glancing at her watch. "Besides, I won't be alone for long. The ship should arrive soon enough to pick me up."

Lorcan frowned. "In fact, I really hate you having to do this at all."

Grace dropped her suitcase down onto the sand and reached out her arms, resting her hands around Lorcan's slender neck. "I have to," she said. "I'm . . ."

"I know," he said, frowning again. "You don't have to say it again. You're Sidorio's daughter."

Grace shook her head. "I was going to say that I'm ready to do whatever it takes to secure the future of the Vamp—" She broke off, then corrected herself. "To secure the future of the *Nocturnals.*" It was still a mental adjustment using the new term, though she completely understood Mosh Zu's reasons for the change. Grace looked up into Lorcan's achingly handsome face. Concern was etched into every pore. "Please try not to worry," she said. "I can take care of myself, you know."

He nodded. "I know that. Truth is, I've grown rather fond of taking care of you." His blue eyes glowed with intensity as he leaned forward to kiss her.

"It's only for a while," she said, as his lips lifted from hers. "I have to do my duty just as you're doing yours. Besides, you'll be so busy training up the Nocturnals in combat, you won't have time to notice I'm not around."

Lorcan drew her close again. "I shall notice," he said. "I shall notice your absence as if a star is missing from the sky. But I shall know that my star is coming home soon and I will be strong for her."

Grace smiled and snuggled against the familiar harbour of his muscled chest. If only they didn't have to part. If only things hadn't reached this impossible pass. But there was no future in "if only". They had to go forward, do their duty and carve out a new future. It was the only way. Reluctantly, she broke free of Lorcan's hold. "You had better go," she said. "They won't come to get me if they see *The Nocturne* lurking in the shallows."

"You're right," Lorcan said. He drew her close once more and kissed her again. Then he gently released her, smiled and turned away. She couldn't be sure but, as he turned to head off across the beach, she thought there was a trace of water in his eyes. As he made his way across the sand, his old military greatcoat flapping in the breeze, she realised how deep her connection with Lorcan had become. They were inextricably bound together and, in spite of her brave words, it was going to be very hard being apart.

Grace stood watching *The Nocturne* slip away into the night. She felt a shiver run down her spine and was unsure whether it was the breeze cutting across the exposed stretch of beach or the sudden realisation that she was now alone. She drew her own coat closer around her. As she adjusted her scarf, she felt a hand on her shoulder.

113

"Grace." The voice, as well as the unexpected touch, made her jump.

She turned to find her brother standing at her side.

"Connor!" she exclaimed, suddenly filled with joy. She opened her arms and they hugged. "It's so good to see you again!"

"You too!" He nodded vigorously, beaming. He was dressed warmly in a parka, his kitbag strung over his shoulder. The kitbag reminded her of their last goodbye, at the gates of Sanctuary. She had been angry with him then, but there was no residue of that anger now. Now she no longer felt alone. There was so much to share with him, not least the change of name from Vampirates to Nocturnals. And she wanted to know how he was dealing with the news that he was Sidorio's son, and a dhampir. Was he experiencing the same blood hunger she was? If so, how was he dealing with it?

"I knew that they'd invited you too," she began, "and they told me you were coming, but I wasn't sure. I mean, I know how you feel about the Vampirates!"

Connor's face was serious. "My feelings about the Vampirates haven't changed," he said.

"Even though . . ." Grace began.

"Even if I *am* a dhampir," he acknowledged. "Grace, I know what we both are. I know that Sidorio is our blood father."

"I think it's important to remind ourselves," she said, "that though we have a blood connection to Sidorio, Dexter Tempest was – and always will be – our dad."

Connor smiled. "Yes," he said. "Yes, you're absolutely right." His expression grew serious again. "Grace, I'm not sure how much time we have before they come to get us, and there's a lot to fill you in on."

She nodded. "I have loads to tell you too," she said. "But there'll be plenty of time, once we're on the ship together."

114

Connor shrugged. "Perhaps, but we'll have to be careful," he said.

"What do you mean?" Grace asked.

"You need to know something," he said. "I haven't accepted this invitation because I want to get to know Sidorio, his wife or his crew. I'm not here to come to terms with my new identity, either. I'm here as a spy. I'm on a mission for the Pirate Federation." He paused and took a breath. "I've told you before that the Federation is changing its stance on the Vampirates. I've warned you. I know that you feel a strong attachment to Lorcan, Darcy, Mosh Zu and the Captain, but war is coming, Grace. Everything is changing. You have to prepare yourself and be ready to make some tough decisions." There was a pleading in his eyes.

Grace nodded. "I *am* prepared," she said. "And just so we're clear, I'm not here to get to know Sidorio or Lola Lockwood *either*. As for coming to terms with my new identity, I'll do that with my friends who I can trust." She gazed deep into Connor's eyes. "I'm here on a spying mission too. The Vampirates know about the war." She saw Connor's eyes widen. "The Captain and Mosh Zu are implementing far-reaching changes. It's vital to them that the pirates do not regard all Vampirates as the same. That's why their crew, *my* crew, will now be known as the Nocturnals. We need the pirates to understand that there's a difference between us and Sidorio's mob."

"Well!" Connor said, letting out a breath. "That's quite some news."

Grace nodded, pleased with herself. "When you next pass information back to the Pirate Federation, you must make that clear. The sooner they recognise the distinction between the Vampirates and the Nocturnals, the better."

Connor nodded, but frowned. "Grace, I will tell them. But I've tried to make them aware of the different factions before."

"You have?"

He nodded. "I had to protect you and do everything in my power to stop you coming to harm through any pirate offensive. Besides, I know that Lorcan and the others have been good to you and I'm grateful to them."

Grace smiled. "Actually, there's something else I need to tell you—"

Connor raised his hand. "Please, Grace. We don't know how much time we have left before the Vampirates arrive. And we don't know how safe it will be to talk once we're on board. This could be our last opportunity to exchange meaningful information."

Grace was irritated that, as usual, Connor was trying to take the upper hand. How did he know whether what she was going to tell him did or did not qualify as meaningful information? In her view, news of her relationship with Lorcan was very meaningful.

"Like I say," Connor continued, "I've tried hard to make the pirates distinguish between the two factions. I'll carry on emphasising that but, if it comes to a full-blown conflict, those lines of distinction will inevitably become blurred."

Grace shrugged. "Then it will be up to us to unblur them," she said. She had the sudden realisation that she and Connor were not on the same side. She felt foolish for not having absorbed that before. Now, it was all too clear. Whilst he was genuinely doing his best to look after her, when war did eventually come, he would be on the side of the pirates and she would be on the side of the Nocturnals. If he was right, and the pirates failed to distinguish between the Nocturnals and the Vampirates, then she and Connor would be in opposite armies. The thought filled her with a deep sadness.

"Hey," Connor said. "What's wrong? You don't look so pleased to see me any more."

Grace shook her head. "I'm always pleased to see you. I was just thinking that we're on opposite sides now."

"You're right," Connor said. "And that's driven me mad in the past. That's why I've tried so hard, and often ineptly, to tear you away from the Vamp— from the Nocturnals. But I know now that I can't. And I don't expect you to leave them either."

Grace was surprised by his honest assessment of the situation, but it didn't offer any easy solution. "So, what *do* we do?" she asked.

"We may not be on the same side in this conflict," Connor said. "But we're both here to spy on Sidorio and his operation. To work out how best to take him down." He reached out his hand and took hers, giving it a squeeze. "When you think of it like that, we're here to do exactly the same thing, aren't we?"

He smiled at her. Grace smiled back, thinking how much more grown-up her twin brother looked since she had last seen him. He was changing, just like her. The thought reminded her that they hadn't yet spoken about being dhampirs. But he was right. Time was short and this was a big subject to start exploring in the fleeting moments which remained. She squeezed his hand and grinned. "Who ever would have thought it?" she said. "The two outsiders from Crescent Moon Bay now heading into a war zone as secret agents!"

Connor turned his whole body to face her. "Grace," he said. "We must do everything we can to prevent it from coming to that." He sighed. "I may as well tell you this: the pirates are training up to fight the Vampirates. I led the first assault on Sidorio's wedding. It wasn't a complete success – we failed to eliminate Lola Lockwood – but our intelligence and attack strategies are getting more sophisticated all the time. Going forward, no Vampirate, no Nocturnal, will be safe."

Grace received this body blow with a nod. She wondered if

she should return the favour and inform him that the Nocturnals were also accelerating their combat training. Part of her wanted to deliver a reciprocal punch to his gut. But a calmer voice within her head cautioned her to keep quiet for now. Turning her eyes away from him, she saw that they were now indeed running out of time. Two ships, side by side, were making their way into shore.

The ship on the left-hand side was ugly, brutish and significantly larger than its companion. The smaller vessel, a traditional galleon, was far more appealing to Grace's eyes.

Connor turned to Grace. "The bigger ship is *The Blood Captain*," he said. "It was a prison hulk but Sidorio and his crew took it over. It's his base of operations now. The other ship, *The Vagabond*, belongs to Lady Lola Lockwood. I thought maybe she'd have let it go now they are married."

"Evidently not," said Grace, her eyes fixed on the elegant *Vagabond* as it dropped anchor. There were figures on the deck, outlined in the moonlight. They were dressed similarly but still she thought she could discern the imposing figure of Lady Lola amongst them. After all the grand talk of war and secret missions, suddenly this was starting to feel very real. Grace thought of her first run-in with Sidorio – the time he had held her captive in her cabin aboard *The Nocturne*. Then her thoughts turned to Lola and her own visit to Grace's cabin. Grace could still feel the sting of Lola's palm across her cheek. She flushed cold. She had been so gung-ho about this mission, but was she really up to it and all it entailed?

Grace was distracted by the sight of two small launches, separating from the larger ships and making their way rapidly towards the beach. Each was occupied by just one person. As they came nearer, Grace recognised both faces. In spite of herself, she found herself raising a hand in welcome.

"Well," she said to Connor. "I guess this is it."

He nodded. "Let's make Dad proud of us," he said. "And I don't mean Sidorio."

"Yes!" she smiled, grateful for the thought.

The figures in the boats were beckoning to them. Grace turned to Connor and nodded, then they ran across the sand. They came to a standstill in front of the pair of boats.

"Grace!" called out Johnny, with a smile. "Jump aboard. You're coming with me to *The Vagabond*."

"Connor!" cried Stukeley. "Over here, mate! We're heading out to *The Blood Captain*."

The twins turned towards each other. They had only just been reunited and now they were heading off again in separate directions. It was ever thus. Connor looked towards Grace, his expression pained.

"No need for the big farewell scene," Stukeley said. "You'll be seeing each other again in a couple of hours max."

"That's right," Johnny said. "We'll just get you settled in your quarters then we'll all get together on *The Vagabond* for Tiffin."

"Tiffin?" Grace and Connor asked, simultaneously.

"All will be explained!" cried Stukeley, beckoning to Connor. "Come on, mate, don't dawdle."

Johnny reached out his arm to Grace. "Jump in, angel," he said. "Lady Lola hates to be kept waiting."

CHAPTER SEVENTEEN

The Perfect Hostess

Darling Grace,
Welcome, welcome welcome! I wish you a blissfully happy
stay on my little ship. The entire crew is at your service so if
you need <u>anything</u> just ring the bell! We are having an
informal gathering tonight to celebrate your and Connor's
arrival. Once you have unpacked and had a chance to
freshen up, slip on something fabulous (I've taken the liberty
of putting a few clothes and accessories in your wardrobe)
and join us in my cabin. It's the one at the end of the main
corridor – with the gold doors.
Yours in eager anticipation,
Your "wicked stepmother"
Lady Lola Lockwood Sidorio xxx

Grace had found the handwritten note propped against a glass
bowl of glossy red apples on the dresser in her new cabin. It had
reassured her – to a degree – that she was welcome aboard *The
Vagabond* and that Lola's intentions were good. The red apples

and Lola's reference to the "wicked stepmother" seemed a good omen too. At least she had a sense of humour about the situation.

Nevertheless, a half-hour or so later, as Grace knocked on the gilded doors of the captain's cabin, she couldn't help but think of her one previous encounter with Lady Lola Lockwood. Hearing the murmur of voices and the click of footsteps from within, she recalled the raw viciousness of Lola's slap. An instant chill sprouted in Grace's cheek, as if she had been struck anew. This dart of ice travelled down her neck and along her spine. Grace smoothed down the floral tea-dress she had chosen from Lola's generous selection, trying to steady her nerves and encourage the shivers to exit her body.

As the door opened, she found a very different Lady Lola waiting to meet her. When they had last met, Lola's hair had been pinned up in a chignon, adding to the impression of severity. Now, soft raven locks tumbled down either side of her razor-sharp cheekbones, making her seem both younger and warmer. This impression was heightened by the flowing red dress Lola wore, accessorised by bright red stilettos and an elaborate necklace resembling a spider's web of rubies. Smiling at Grace, her hands outstretched, Lola strode forward to kiss her. "Grace! Welcome aboard!"

As Lola released Grace from her perfumed embrace, she stepped back to study her. "Don't you look just darling in that dress! I knew it would look well on you."

Lola took Grace's arm and drew her into the cabin. Behind her, the gilded doors were closed once more. Grace's eyes ranged around the captain's cabin. It was the first time she had seen a female captain's quarters and they were absolutely stunning – opulent but at the same time refined. The elegant room, furnished in beautiful antiques, was lit by hundreds of candles. They gave off the softest of light and the heady scent of an abundant flower garden at night.

"I hope your cabin is to your liking," Lola said.

"Oh yes," Grace said. "Yes, it's lovely. And thank you so much for letting me borrow some of your clothes."

Lola laughed. "No, dear, those aren't *my* clothes. I had them made for you."

Grace was bowled over by her stepmother's surprising generosity. "I don't know what to say."

Lola shook her head. "Enjoy them," she said. "We had fun picking them out for you, didn't we, ladies?"

As Lola spoke, Grace suddenly became aware of three members of Lola's crew. They had been lingering in the shadows around the edges of the room but now, at Lola's words, they stepped out into the warm pool of candlelight. Lola glowed. "Jacqueline, Nathalie, Mimma, come and meet our special guest – my beautiful stepdaughter, the very aptly named Grace."

As the three women stepped closer, Grace noticed that each of them sported the same heart-shaped tattoo as their captain – but while Lola's was around her left eye, the others wore theirs on the right. Presumably, this was a reflection of rank.

As each of the women came to say hello to Grace, she was wowed by their beauty. Jacqueline's hair was the colour of ripe plums, swept up from her aristocratic face in a series of intricate plaits. Nathalie had bitter-chocolate curls, which tumbled down to her shoulders. Mimma's tousled locks rested on her shoulders, her blue eyes sparkling like sapphires. All three of them wore exquisite dresses, shoes and jewellery. As Grace greeted each in turn, she reflected that even Darcy, with her seemingly infinite wardrobe, would be given a run for her money in the fashion stakes aboard *The Vagabond*.

"What's with all this grub, Captain?" Mimma inquired, stepping away from the group.

Grace saw that behind the girls was a table positively

groaning with plates of food. In the centre of the table was an abundant bowl of roses – ranging from the palest pink to the deepest crimson.

Lola gestured to the table. "Doesn't it look delicious? I've engaged a chef for the duration of your stay – a very famous chef during his mortal days – and in honour of your arrival, he has recreated one of his most celebrated feasts." As Lola pointed to the dishes, Grace noticed that each dish was, like the flowers, coloured a varying shade of pink. "To start, a bowl of Borscht, followed by chicken à la paprika, and then spring lamb in milk. And later, two of Chef Escoffier's signature desserts – peach melba and strawberries with pineapple and sorbet."

"Wow!" exclaimed Grace. "You must be expecting a lot of guests."

"A few, my dear." Lola looked momentarily confused. "But this food is only for you and Connor. I'm sure you must both be famished after your journeys."

Grace stared at the massive spread. "All *this* is for the two of us?"

Lola nodded. "I do hope it's to your taste. It's such a long time since I ate food. You must tell me all your likes and dislikes and I'll be sure to pass them on to Chef Escoffier. I do so want you to feel perfectly at home here."

Grace nodded. She had the sense that Lola was doing everything she could to be hospitable. Her eyes swept across the table. "It all looks delicious. I think it will be enough to keep Connor and me going for a week or two!"

Lola laughed lightly. "If what I've heard about the appetite of teenage boys is true, I'm sure Connor will have no trouble cutting a swathe through this."

Just then, there came a swell of noise from the other side of the gilded doors.

"Well, speak of the devil!" Lola smiled. "That must be the

boys now. Jacqueline, Nathalie, would you do the honours?" The two women moved swiftly into position, drawing back the gilded doors just in time as Sidorio and his crew swept into the room. Grace turned to face the new arrivals, a shiver of fear darting down her spine once more.

Sidorio was flanked on one side by Stukeley and Connor. On his other side was Johnny – who doffed his Stetson and grinned at Grace – and an older-looking man with dark, shoulder-length hair and piercing almost black eyes. Grace found herself transfixed by the newcomer, though he seemed to look straight through her. Who was he?

Johnny and Stukeley sauntered past Grace to greet Mimma, Jacqueline and Nathalie. Feeling a flicker of envy as Johnny kissed Nathalie hello, Grace turned back just in time to see Sidorio put his hand on Connor's shoulder and present him to his wife.

"My darling, I'd like you to meet Connor," he said, his voice raw with emotion. "My son."

Connor looked sheepish. He well remembered the last time he'd seen her – when he'd separated her head from her body with his sword. "Umm, we've met before," he said.

Lola shook her head. "No," she said, her hand lingering for a moment on her ruby necklace, a necklace that concealed the livid scars that Connor himself had put there. "We've never met properly. All past transgressions are forgotten now. Our relationship begins anew tonight. You are my husband's son, my stepson. And you are very welcome aboard *The Vagabond.*" To Connor's surprise, she reached out her hand to him. Grace watched as he shook it.

Sidorio smiled. Then, spying Grace, he crossed the room.

"Grace," he said. "I'm so pleased to see you again. Thank you for coming." He opened his arms and she realised he wanted to embrace her. It would be churlish to resist.

As Sidorio released her and stepped backwards, his eyes lingered on her face. Though they had met before, it was as if he was seeing her for the first time. "You look so beautiful," he said, tears in his eyes. "So like your mother."

Grace felt a lump in her throat at his words and their obvious sincerity. This demonstration of real emotion was the very last thing she had expected from Sidorio. She realised she was going to have to put aside everything she thought she knew about him and start from the beginning again. Nevertheless, she reminded herself, she must tread carefully.

Lady Lola walked over to join them, putting a hand on Sidorio's shoulder. "Husband," she said. "You didn't tell me you were bringing a guest tonight."

"A guest?" Sidorio's gaze remained upon Grace for a moment. Then he turned back to his wife.

Lola nodded towards the stranger, who remained in the shadows at the far end of the room. Grace too studied him. He was rather like a statue, she thought. She wasn't sure he had moved at all since arriving at the soirée.

Now, Sidorio called out to him. "Obsidian. Come forward! Meet my wife and family."

The man hesitated. Then, his expression unchanging, he strode formally across the room to join the two captains.

Sidorio addressed his wife. "This is Obsidian Darke, a lieutenant on my crew. He's a fairly new recruit but he's already marked himself out as a future star. Commands great respect in the ranks."

Darke's thin lips smiled at this. When he spoke, his voice was gruff. "Lady Lockwood, it's a pleasure to meet you." He bowed stiffly before her, as she reached out her hand. He was wearing gloves but had the presence of mind to remove them before taking her hand.

Grace observed Lola's reactions to the newcomer. The gracious hostess was on her mettle now. Grace couldn't blame her. The stranger had gatecrashed the family reunion Lola had planned with obvious care. More than that, there was something about Darke which immediately raised Grace's hackles – perhaps Lola sensed it too. He had an air of cold menace about him. His eyes were as dark as his name suggested and yet Grace felt they were merely a hint of the violent tides within him.

"Lieutenant Darke," Lady Lola said. "If my husband rates you so highly, then I am assured of your rare capabilities." She scrutinised his face a moment longer. "You are welcome to take Tiffin with us, sir, and to join our special celebrations tonight."

During this exchange, Connor had come around to Grace's side. "You certainly got the better end of this deal," he whispered. "Your ship is way plusher than mine. *My* cabin is a glorified prison cell."

Grace smiled, turning to her brother. "Bad luck," she said. "I'll certainly think of you when I slip into my Egyptian cotton sheets."

She glanced up to find Sidorio and Lola's eyes trained on her and Connor. Unnerved, Grace found herself blustering, "Connor, look at all the food Lady Lockwood's chef has prepared for us!"

"Wicked!" Connor stepped towards the table. "I'm starving."

Lola winked knowingly at Grace. "Don't stand on ceremony. Take a seat, dear. You too, Connor." She pointed to where two place settings had been laid. As Grace and Connor went to sit down, Lola addressed the others. "Well, now, as the twins tuck into their vittles, why don't we all have a drink, eh?" Her dark eyes connected with her comrades, old and new.

Sidorio slapped Obsidian Darke on the back. "My wife has a winery," he said.

"So I've heard," said Darke. He shook his head. "I don't drink."

Sidorio chuckled. "It's not a regular kind of winery, you clot! Someone fetch him a glass."

"Allow me," Lola said, stepping forward with the decanter and one of her favoured antique glasses.

"Really," Obsidian Darke said, with no apology. "I'm a man of simple needs."

"That's evident," Lola said, "but you're part of our crew now. And a guest on my ship on a night of rare celebration." She extended the glass. "It would be rude, sir, not to drink – if not out of need or desire, then out of fellowship."

Darke's expression was unchanged. He studied the glass in Lola's hand. Finally, he reached out. "You're right, Captain," he said. "I am your humble guest, and I thank you sincerely for your hospitality." He lifted the glass to his thin lips and downed the drink in one.

Lola smiled and joined her crew-members. "Did you see that, ladies? They're all the same, these men! They say they don't drink and then they drain the glass as if it's the last drop of water in a desert." Though her words were harsh, her tone was light, as she turned. "Not Johnny, though. Johnny's a little more refined, I'm pleased to say. He knows what it is to circulate in mixed company. Don't you?"

Johnny bowed, smiling at Lola and her crew.

Watching this exchange, Grace couldn't help but smile.

Lola addressed her crew. "Help me out, ladies." At her word, Mimma, Jacqueline and Nathalie began circulating with silver trays, each bearing a decanter and glasses.

Grace watched the Vampirates around her taking their glasses of blood. It was easy to imagine it was something else – fine wine or vintage port – but she was under no illusions. It might come in a decanter and be served in the most exquisite glasses but it was still blood, which had until recently flowed through someone's body. Where had it come from, she wondered. *Who* had it come from?

Connor seemed oblivious to what was going on around

them. He had piled his plate high with all manner of delicacies and was making short work of it. It was as if he hadn't eaten in a month. "What?" he asked, noticing her staring at him, as a prawn dangled from his lips.

"You're certainly hungry tonight," Grace said.

Connor swallowed the prawn and reached for a lobster claw. "Are you kidding? This food is amazing! Cheng Li has us on a macrobiotic diet right now. I can't tell you what a relief it is to see real food again."

Grace smiled at him. So much had changed – both around them and within – but at moments like this he was the same brother he had always been, clearing his plate in a jiffy and then swiping food from hers. He was right, though. This food *was* delicious. Grace was relieved that she was hungry tonight. Her appetite had been so up and down recently and it would have been as discourteous as Obsidian Darke rejecting Lola's drink, for her not to have done justice to the feast Lola had laid on in their honour.

"Well," Lola said, stifling a yawn. "I don't know about the rest of you but I'm about ready for a siesta."

Sidorio laughed. "The night is but young, my dear."

Lola shook her head and swiped his glass. "Time to drink up, everyone." She turned to the twins. "I'm sure you two are more than ready for a rest."

Grace nodded. Connor took a last mouthful of dessert, then glanced up. "I *could* do with a bit of shut-eye," he said. "That was the best meal I've had since . . . well, since for ever!"

Lola laughed and clapped her hands with delight. "I'm so pleased," she said. "I'll be sure to pass on the compliment to Chef Escoffier." She turned. "Mimma, would you escort Grace back to her cabin? And Stukeley, perhaps you'd help Connor find his way back?"

"It's all right," Connor said. "I'm sure I can—"

"I'm sure you can too," Lola said. "But you are our guests and we have certain ways of doing things aboard both *The Vagabond* and *The Blood Captain*, don't we, my darling?" Lola turned to her husband, her eyes sparkling. Sidorio nodded obligingly.

Connor voiced no further protest. "Thanks for the excellent dinner," he said, as Stukeley held open the door. "Goodnight, everyone!"

Mimma took Grace's arm and propelled her towards the golden doors, which Jacqueline and Nathalie held open. As she reached the threshold, Grace glanced back at Lola. "Thank you again," she said. "For everything."

"You are more than welcome," Lola said. "It's simply wonderful to have you with us. Rest up, my dear. We're going to keep you busy with all kinds of fun."

Then the four young people headed out into the corridor and the gilded doors closed behind them.

Sidorio turned to face his wife. "You're not *really* tired, are you?"

Lola shook her head. "Of course not," she said. "I just thought we should send the twins to bed so we could get down to discussing strategy."

"Ah," Sidorio said. "I see."

Lola leaned close to Sidorio and whispered in his ear. "Perhaps you'd like to send Lieutenant Darke on his way?" The two captains looked deep into each other's eyes for a moment, then Sidorio stepped aside and went over to talk to Obsidian.

Lola watched for a moment as her husband addressed his lieutenant. Then, satisfied that her will had been done, she turned and saw that Johnny, Nathalie and Jacqueline were chatting animatedly at the side of the table. She strode over to join them.

"Well," she said. "I think we gave Grace and Connor a good welcome, don't you?"

"Yes," Jacqueline and Nathalie nodded.

"You certainly fed them well," Johnny added, with a grin.

Lola smiled to herself, then to the others. "They don't call me the perfect hostess for nothing. I wonder . . ." She was interrupted by the satisfying sound of Obsidian Darke making a discreet exit, then Sidorio coming to join her. She felt her husband's hands encircling her waist and smiled.

"You were about to say something, Captain," Jacqueline said. "Before Captain Sidorio joined us. What was it?"

Lola shrugged, her eyes ranging across the array of empty plates. "Oh, only that I wonder how Grace and Connor enjoyed their first taste of blood."

CHAPTER EIGHTEEN
Business of the Night

Stukeley jumped back onto the deck of *The Vagabond* to find Mimma waiting for him. She was standing against the deck-rail, her tousled hair and the soft material of her dress shifting in the ocean breeze. Hearing him, she slowly turned and smiled.

"All done with your babysitting duties?"

Stukeley nodded. "And you?"

Mimma smiled. "For now."

"Well, then," Stukeley said, holding out his arm to her. "As tempting as it is to linger here and count the stars with you, we have a meeting to get to, don't we?"

Mimma locked eyes with Stukeley. "You're a charming man," she said. "But you're right, of course. No rest for the wicked!" Looping her arm through his, she led him across the deck and down to the captain's cabin.

"Now that we're all here, we shall begin," Lola said, addressing the key personnel of *The Blood Captain* and *The Vagabond*. "There is much to discuss." She turned to Sidorio, who was sitting beside her at the head of a long, highly-polished wooden table.

Sidorio rose to his feet and cleared his throat. "When we returned from our honeymoon, my wife and I told you of our plans to expand and fortify our empire. We charged each of you with a key part of the jigsaw."

Now Sidorio nodded to his wife. Lola rose from her seat and walked a few paces across to an easel draped in black cloth. Lola removed the cloth and picked up what looked like a riding crop. She pointed at the distinctive red lettering on the board.

"In a nutshell," Sidorio continued, "we want . . . more ships . . ."

There was a thwack as Lola struck the board to emphasise his words.

". . . more blood . . ."

Thwack.

". . . faster recruitment . . ."

Thwack.

". . . and more leaders."

Thwack.

"Thank you," Sidorio said, winking at his wife. Smiling, she set down the crop and returned to her seat. Sidorio's eyes sought out Stukeley, who was sitting beside Mimma at the other end of the table, a sheaf of papers spread out in front of him. "Stukeley, you were charged with the task of expanding our fleet."

Stukeley nodded sharply, as all eyes turned to him. "Yes, Captain. And, since we last met, I've been looking into commissioning a fleet of ships to be built for us."

"Progress?" Sidorio barked.

"Costly," Stukeley said, "but, more importantly, too time-consuming." He lifted a handful of papers. "I got quotes from three shipyards but we're talking months before they can get the first ship ocean-worthy. Part of the problem is that the pirates are also commissioning more ships."

Sidorio was unimpressed. "You got *three* quotes? You offered *money*? What were you thinking? We're Vampirates! We don't buy – we take!"

There was a ripple of laughter around the table, just enough to acknowledge the captain's joke without seriously undermining Stukeley's authority.

Stukeley took it in good humour, quietly shuffling his papers. "As it happens, Captains, I've come up with a new plan, which I believe will achieve our goal of a rapidly expanded fleet with the minimum of time and expense."

Lola raised an eyebrow. "This sounds interesting. Tell us more."

"We steal the ships," Stukeley said, "from the pirates. We kill two birds with one stone and we diminish the Federation fleets and gain access to a portfolio of the most top-of-the-range vessels on the oceans."

"I like it," Lola said, clenching her fist.

Sidorio grinned. "Good work, Stukeley."

Stukeley passed a piece of paper along the table to the captains. "I have a working knowledge of the Federation's fleets. I've drawn up a list of some initial targets."

Sidorio snatched the paper and glanced at the list of ship names on it. But Stukeley hadn't finished. "There's another aspect to this situation, for which I would now like to pass you over to my colleague, Mr Desperado."

Johnny grinned and stood up, as was his wont at meetings. "As you all know, I head up the Inhuman Resources department on our ships." There were smiles around the table – Johnny's contributions were always laced with humour. "In other words, I'm in charge of recruitment. There are two recruitment streams in the Vampirate empire. Firstly, your landlubber vampires. I've recently conducted meetings with several key leaders of vampire cells along the coast. They know darn well that the real power is on the ocean these days and they are about ready to join up."

"Really?" Lola asked. "Just like that? We've had problems before with all their terms and conditions."

Johnny nodded. "Quite so, Captain. Quite so. And you're right, we're still in the middle of negotiations but I've left them in no doubt as to how big we're getting . . . and how much bigger we're gonna get. I'm confident that I'll be bringing you confirmation of one very major acquisition deal real soon."

Lola scribbled a note on her pad.

"Of course," Johnny continued, "When we recruit vampires with no previous marine experience, there's a steep learning curve for them, which brings me to our second recruitment stream. In many ways, it works better for us to take pirates, who are familiar with the ways of the sea, and sire them. It's an adjustment for them in other ways but at least they know how to sail." He grinned. "Here's where Stuke's ideas and mine dovetail. As we acquire each pirate ship in turn, the crews will be given a very simple choice . . . join us or die." On that note, Johnny sat down again.

Sidorio clapped his hands. "Excellent work, as usual, Stetson." He turned to Lola. "Don't you think so, my dear?"

Lola nodded. "Very impressive, Johnny."

"Now then," Sidorio said, glancing at the easel. "What's next? Ah . . . more blood. Over to you, my love."

"Thank you," Lola said. "Obviously, blood acquisition and storage is under the control of the Black Heart winery team." She gestured to the five young women who sat beside her. "Jessamy, you have the latest blood yields, I believe."

Jessamy stood and went over to the easel. Removing the list of key objectives and setting it to one side, she revealed a graph. Lola passed her the riding crop so she could explain the coloured markings. "The blue line marks our current stock levels. As you can see, these are good but, since we merged command of the two ships, we've been getting through stocks at an accelerated rate." She glanced at Sidorio with a smile. "You, sir, have some thirsty crew-members!"

Sidorio shrugged. Jessamy waited for the ripple of laughter to subside before continuing. "Look at the red line! This is our projected increase in production over the next six months. I'm sure you'll agree it's impressive."

"It certainly is," Sidorio said. "But is it viable?"

"Oh yes," Jessamy said. "We've been developing some new toolkits, which will be supplied to all crew-members involved in blood harvesting Camille?"

Now Camille pushed back her chair and reached behind her. Standing up, she put what looked like a chunky briefcase on the table. All eyes zeroed in on it, as Camille slipped the catch and revealed its contents. "As you can see, this lightweight, durable case holds six standard bottles – which as you know is our typical yield per capita."

Lola raised her hand to speak. "This state-of-the-art portable unit will revolutionise our harvesting. We no longer need to harvest solely on *The Vagabond*, which was previously the case. We've tried portable kits before but there's always been too much wastage in transit. Not any more! Outstanding work, ladies."

Camille smiled and lifted the bottom of her shirt. "The rest of the harvesting equipment will be carried in these new tool-belts we've been developing simultaneously. Again, each of the hunting team will be equipped with one."

"Bravo!" Lola beamed and led a round of applause.

"This is all going swimmingly," Sidorio said. "Now we charged you *all* with identifying potential new leaders. As the Vampirate fleet expands, we need the right men and women in

135

charge of the ships." His eyes ranged along the length of the table. "Thank you for all your input."

Sidorio turned to his wife. "Tell me, my dear. What did you think of Obsidian Darke?"

Lola raised her eyes and chose her words carefully. "Cold. Lacking in manners or any residual human warmth. Charmless. Somehow disconnected. Potentially brutal." She smiled sweetly. "I think he's exactly the kind of leader we're looking for."

"I agree," Sidorio said. "And now I've heard Stukeley's idea of acquiring ships from the pirates, I've come up with a gem of an idea myself. We'll put a different Vampirate in charge of each attack mission. That way, we'll not only make swift progress at acquiring the ships; we'll also see who's got the *cojones* to take a senior position in our organisation."

Lola coughed. "Darling, since when have *cojones* been a key requirement for running this organisation?"

"Just a pattern of speech, dearest," Sidorio said. "Obsidian Darke can lead the first attack. That'll show us what he's made of."

Lola shook her head. "No," she said. "*You* must lead the first attack. And then Stukeley and Johnny. It's vital that the rank-and-file Vampirates see the existing team demonstrating authority at this point. By all means, you can *then* get Obsidian Darke to step up to the plate."

"I think you're right, Captain Lockwood," Stukeley said. "If we develop the fleet as swiftly as is our intent, we risk confusing the crew. It's a good idea to reinforce the command structure before we do so."

"That's settled then," Sidorio said. "I'll lead the first attack, then Stukeley, then Johnny. And then Darke! Is someone taking minutes?"

"Yes!" Nathalie cried from the other end of the table, her pen flying across the yellow legal pad in front of her, as it had been since the meeting began.

"Well, then," Sidorio said. "That's about it, I think. Unless anyone has any other brainwaves?"

"Captains!" Jacqueline's arm shot up. "I want to ask about our plans to contain the pirate threat. It seems like they are getting smarter and more ambitious in their attacks on us. Look at what happened at your wedding."

Lola nodded, exchanging a quick knowing glance with Stukeley and Johnny, unseen by the others. "You're right to ask the question, Jacqui. Of course, we should be on our mettle but I tend to think that the incident at my wedding was a one-off." Once more, she glanced along the length of the polished table. "With Stukeley's plan to decimate the pirate fleets and build our own, the pirates should have plenty on their minds besides attacking us."

Now Nathalie spoke. "But Captain, isn't Connor himself part of a Vampirate assassination squad? That's the rumour going around. Should we be at all concerned for our safety?"

Lola shook her head. "These are valid concerns, but you needn't worry about either Connor or Grace for now."

"It's just that we know they're dhampirs," Nathalie persisted. "And dhampirs have special powers to destroy vampires."

"Only if they choose to," Lola said, exchanging a glance with Sidorio. "We weren't going to get into this tonight, but since you've brought it up and I can see some of you are concerned . . ."

Sidorio took over. "A dhampir, being half-mortal and half-vampire, has a choice when he or she reaches adult maturity – the point at which Connor and Grace are arriving now. They can either be a very powerful advocate for the Vampirate cause or, as you say, they could turn against us."

There were some anxious faces around the table. Lola smiled at them, reassuringly. "Don't look so glum, everyone. We've thought this through and we're on the case. Tonight, we began surreptitiously feeding the twins blood. This will continue, without them noticing, for several nights to come. The blood will stoke their appetite for more and this hunger will bring them very firmly over to our side once and for all."

"What are Connor and Grace doing here?" Mimma asked. "I mean, they're surely not just here because they're curious about their parenthood?"

"I honestly think that's part of it," Lola said. "But you're right, Mim, to suspect there are other factors at play. Connor *is* currently attached to a boat of would-be assassins. Is he spying on us? More than likely. Does it matter? Not a jot. He's going to have a whole lot more on his mind by the time we've finished with him."

"And Grace?" Johnny asked.

Lola was visibly amused. "I rather thought *you* were the expert on Grace. Why do *you* think she's here?"

Johnny shrugged. "She's incredibly open-minded. I think she might well be here to get to know you both better." He paused. "But it is also true that she has strong attachments to members of the crew of *The Nocturne*. Lorcan Furey, for instance."

Once more Lola smiled. "It's your job, darling, to break those attachments. Just as it is Stukeley's to work on Connor." Lola made sure she had everyone's attention before continuing. "Connor and Grace have the power to destroy us all. We need to eliminate that threat before it arises by convincing them that they belong here with us." She raised her head, imperiously. "Does everyone understand?"

"Yes, Captain," came the answer from all around the table.

"This meeting is over," Lola said. "Good work, everybody. Now back to business! Seize the night!"

It took a matter of moments for the deputies to clear up their various papers, charts and samples and exit the cabin.

When they had gone, Lola poured two fresh glasses of blood, extending one to Sidorio and taking the other in her own hand.

"That went well," Sidorio said, sipping from his glass. "We have an unbeatable team."

Lola swallowed a mouthful of liquid. "In the main," she agreed. "But, darling, you must keep an eye on those two deputies of yours."

Sidorio frowned. "You've never liked my boys, Lollipop, have you?"

Lola shuddered. "Don't *ever* call me that," she said. "And it's not a question of like. I simply don't trust them. I'm not asking you to choose between them and me . . ."

"I'd choose you," Sidorio said. "Always you. Over anyone. Even my son and daughter." His voice was raw. She had no doubt that he was speaking the truth.

"No one is asking you to choose," she said in soothing tones. Then her voice grew sharper. "Just keep them busy."

CHAPTER NINETEEN

Contact

Connor broke into a jog around the edge of the deck, finding an easy rhythm. His body had been crying out for exercise and the afternoon sun was pleasingly strong on the back of his neck. Though his footsteps were light, still they echoed on the metal floor. He thought of the Vampirates sleeping down below and hoped the sound wouldn't wake them.

He was surprised that he felt *so* awake. By the end of a day's labours aboard *The Tiger*, he was normally so in need of rest that he was capable of lying down and sleeping on bare deckboards if necessary. Yet here, on this ship, he didn't seem at all tired. Quite the reverse. Right now, he could feel his body pulsing with energy. He realised that he might also be having trouble adjusting his rhythms of waking and sleep. He wondered if Grace was experiencing similar issues aboard *The Vagabond*. But then, he reflected, she had travelled on a Vampirate ship for so long that he imagined the exchange of day for night – and night for day – must come easily to her now.

As he ran around the perimeter of the deck, Connor's eyes took in the expanse of the ship and the emptiness around him.

Its size seemed the perfect symbol of his mission. He felt dwarfed by it. How on earth could he, working solo, hope to effect change here? The key thing was to keep Sidorio, Stukeley and the others firmly on side and build their trust.

That part of his mission seemed to be going well so far – but it occurred to Connor that the Vampirates might also be working hard to build *his* trust. He knew there was a good chance that *they* might be spying on *him*. So be it. Uppermost in his mind was the fact that he still had no idea how he was supposed to keep Cheng Li informed of his progress. She had promised him a contact but left him in the dark regarding who it might be and when he or she might arrive.

After three circuits of the deck, Connor paused to catch his breath and wipe away the beads of perspiration on his forehead. The sun had already dropped close to the horizon behind him, causing the ship's shadow to stretch across the surface of the ocean. He had hoped the run might tire his restless body but, if anything, he now felt even more energised. Perhaps it was the adrenaline, induced by the importance of his mission and the need to be on his mettle 24/7. He turned and glanced over the edge of the ship. It was like looking down a sheer black cliff. It surprised him that he didn't feel any sense of vertigo. If anything, the sparkling turquoise water seemed to beckon to him. A cooling dip would be a great way to burn off his excess energy.

He untied his shoelaces and peeled away his sweat-soaked tank-top, leaving it beside the plimsolls at the deck-rail. Then he climbed over the side of the ship, his feet reaching for the metal ladder which led down to the ocean. It was a long way down but, where once he might have hesitated, Connor felt his body moving down the rungs with calm and confidence.

By the time he'd got halfway down, he couldn't resist another glance at the cool, glittering waters below. Once more, he anticipated a wave of vertigo but, again, there was none. Instead, as he glimpsed the waters below, he felt only adrenaline. I really am changing, he thought, as he released himself from the ladder and pin-dropped down into the chill water, feeling the thrill of exhilaration.

He entered the water cleanly and, as his body ceased its motion, he realised he had gone quite deep. It was so quiet and peaceful here, another world entirely from that above the surface. For a moment, he felt sheltered from all his worries. He lingered for a time, his lungs feeling full and strong. Then he began a calm, slow ascent.

Breaking through the surface, back into the air, he found himself in the shadow of the vast ship – but the shadow was already less defined as the day's light began to fade. He began swimming along the edge of the creaking hull. As he swam, he had the sensation of something slipping past him in the water. He hesitated, treading water for a minute or two, searching for signs of a fin. There was none. Connor realised he was getting too close to the barnacle-encrusted metal and kicked out, intent on putting some distance between himself and the ship.

He turned back to face *The Blood Captain*, treading water once more. The ship looked even more gargantuan from this perspective, dominating his view like a killer whale. His thoughts returned to his mission. Was he really up to this?

Suddenly, his gnawing anxiety was banished by a more pressing concern. Something – or someone – had grabbed onto his ankles and was dragging him underwater. He only had time to mumble, "What the—" before his head was pulled beneath the surface.

Connor instinctively kicked out with his legs, trying to throw off whatever it was that had latched onto him. The grip around his ankles felt human and, if this was the case, then a kick seemed as good a defence as any.

His vision underwater was limited. As he was dragged further down, his movements and those of his assailant created a screen of air bubbles. Through them, he could just about make out a tail-fin. It didn't make sense to him. He knew that the hands which had moved from his ankles to his waist were human. Confused, he managed to wrench himself free from their vice-like grip. He didn't wait to get another look at the fin. He swam hard back up to the surface. His instinct was to gasp for air – but, strangely, he didn't seem to be out of breath. Whoever or whatever had attacked him couldn't be far away. He'd have to swim fast to avoid a second attack. He began a powerful freestyle towards the ship and safety.

Something swam past him again. Then a shimmering tail arced through the water's surface, and disappeared again below. Just ahead of him, a head pushed up through the surface into the air. Connor froze. It was a girl's face. He was immediately struck by her elfin beauty. She had intense eyes, which seemed to shimmer all the colours of the rainbow, and close-cropped, bright-blue hair.

The girl smiled warmly at him. "Connor!" she exclaimed. "Long time no see."

"Who are you?" Connor asked, wincing as a draught of salt water sank down his throat.

She laughed. "I was just having fun before, trying to get your attention."

Connor pushed the hair back out of his eyes and took a good look at the strange girl. "I asked you a question," he said, on his guard. "Who are you?"

They stared at each curiously for a time, until the girl broke the awkward silence.

"You really *don't* remember me," she said, "do you?"

He shook his head.

"Hmm," she said, somewhat deflated. "Then I'm going to have a fair bit of explaining to do." As she spoke, a shimmering tail rose from the water.

Connor realised with a jolt that it belonged to the girl. He gazed at her in wonder. "Are you . . . some kind of mermaid?" he asked.

"I'm a fishtail," she said. "My name's Kally. I won't pretend I'm not disappointed that you don't remember me." She shook the water from her spiky hair. "But first things first! Captain Li sent me. I'm a fellow agent of the Pirate Federation and I'm going to be working with you on this mission, carrying messages between the two of you." Kally winked at him. "Guaranteed same day delivery."

Connor studied Kally in wonder. Cheng Li had promised him she'd find a safe way of keeping the lines of communication open between them. Even in his wildest dreams, it hadn't occurred to him that it would be via a mermaid – he corrected himself – via a *fishtail*.

He noticed that what was left of the day's light was almost gone. "We don't have much time," he said.

As Connor climbed up the ladder leading back to the deck of *The Blood Captain*, his head was spinning with everything Kally had told him. They hadn't had much time and he suspected that the fishtail had taken advantage of that to draw him away from certain lines of enquiry. Never mind, there would be other meetings. Indeed, Kally explained that she was charged with checking in with Connor on a daily basis. And, for now, she had left him with plenty of information to ponder.

According to Kally, she had met him, Bart and Jez (for that's what he'd been called then) in a dingy bar, when they were on weekend shore leave from *The Diablo*. Kally maintained she had taken on each of the Three Buccaneeers in an arm-wrestling contest. Afterwards, there had been "some kind of aggro with a greasy punk by the name of Moonshine". Connor's ears pricked up at this. Whilst he might not remember the details, it wasn't a stretch to conjure up aggro with Moonshine Wrathe, Barbarro and Trofie's teenage son. Suddenly, the animosity that Moonshine had shown towards him when they first met aboard *The Typhon* made sense – if it *hadn't* in fact been the *first* time they'd met.

The way Kally told it, Connor, Bart and Jez had ended up spending the weekend on *The Lorelei*, the ship belonging to Kally and her dad, Flynn, and crewed by fishtails. Then, she went quiet and said there had been a misunderstanding. It was as if the light had gone out from behind her unusual eyes. She didn't want to talk about it. The boys and the fishtails had evidently parted company not on the best of terms. Soon afterwards, Sidorio himself had attacked and taken over *The Lorelei*.

Climbing higher, Connor could see the lights coming on around the vast deck above. He was returning in the nick of time. Kally's tale was too much to take in. Did Bart or Stukeley, he wondered, remember anything of *Calle del Marinero* and the fishtails? He had no doubt that Kally's hatred for Sidorio was genuine. She had fought back tears as she recalled how the Vampirate had brutally killed her father. Connor shook his head. There seemed to be no end to the trail of destruction and sorrow that Sidorio had wreaked across the land and oceans. But, thanks to the Pirate Federation, that era was coming to an end – at last the net was about to close on the self-proclaimed King of the Vampirates. Connor no longer felt so isolated. His meeting with Kally had renewed his determination to complete his mission.

He leaped over the ship's railings onto the deck, filled with exhilaration. As his feet touched the ground, the tip of a sword pressed into his bare chest. And at the other end of the sword was Sidorio.

CHAPTER TWENTY

Duel

Connor looked down the length of Sidorio's sword. There was something familiar about it but he couldn't allow himself to be distracted. He remembered his earliest weapon training by Bart and Cate. *Always look at your opponent's face – not the tip of their weapon.* However tempting it might be to focus on the blade, you had to keep yourself fixed on your opponent's eyes – the window to their dark intent. Determinedly, Connor locked eyes with Sidorio.

The first thing he needed to assess was how much danger he was in. Had Sidorio witnessed his meeting with Kally? It had been conducted in the light, albeit the dying light, so surely he couldn't have?

"Are we going to fight?" Connor asked, his tone a mix of innocence and cheekiness. It seemed to hit the right note, for now Sidorio grinned.

"Quick on the uptake, aren't you? Yes, my son, we're going to fight. I'm keen to see if you live up to all the hype. It's you versus me. *Mano-a-mano.*"

Connor's face remained a mask but inside he felt relief. This was a test. Not a punishment; not a death-threat. Connor

147

Tempest had been put to the test before and never yet found wanting.

"Could I have a sword?" he asked.

Sidorio smiled, then nodded. Drawing down his own weapon, he turned and called out. "Stetson, bring my boy his sword."

Now Connor allowed himself to glance at Sidorio's sword. In a flash, he was able to identify it. It was the Toledo Blade – the iconic weapon wielded by the late Commodore Kuo. Connor recognised the distinctive stingray-skin bindings glittering beneath Sidorio's thick fingers. No doubt Lola had seized the sword after slaughtering Kuo. This rapid succession of thoughts flared like fireworks in Connor's head but he remained detached. His feelings about Kuo or, for that matter, Lola, were of no consequence. Right now, all he needed to know was that Sidorio was using the Toledo Blade. It was a sword Connor knew about; one he had himself used in a duel. He knew its strengths and its weaknesses. This gave him his first advantage.

Now, Johnny was at their side and extended Connor's own sword to him. As Connor accepted the sword from Johnny, he saw that the deck was suddenly crowded with the Vampirate crew, swarming around them in a hungry circle. All their eyes seemed to be trained on him. This must qualify as the most dangerous sitiuation he had ever found himself in. Yet, for some reason, he did not feel fear; only adrenaline.

"First to draw blood wins round one!" Johnny declared.

"Ah, here she is!" announced Lola, rising from her seat, side-saddle on the cannon, as Mimma led Grace out onto the deck of *The Vagabond*.

The centre of the deck was lit by pretty fairy lights. A large chequered picnic blanket had been laid out, with heaps of silk cushions around it, many of them occupied by members of Lola's crew. They turned and looked at Grace, then waved politely, as graceful as a pack of swans. Grace smiled and waved back.

In the centre of the rug were a number of china and silver pots and an elegant five-tiered cake stand, covered in bite-sized cupcakes with pink icing.

"We're having a little tea party," Lola said, beckoning Grace into the circle. "In your honour."

"Thank you," Grace said, sitting down on a cushion between Nathalie and Jacqueline.

"Would you like some tea?" Jacqueline asked, lifting a clean cup and saucer and reaching for one of the pots.

Seeing Grace hesitate, Jacqueline smiled prettily. "We made up some Lady Grey just for you," she said.

Grace smiled with relief. "In that case, yes please."

Jacqueline filled Grace's cup, then inquired, "Milk or lemon?"

"Neither," said Grace. "I prefer to savour the taste without."

"You see," Lady Lola said, sitting back down amongst the group. "Grace shows every indication of becoming a connoisseur, just like her old stepmum."

As Grace took the cup, a wave of laughter passed amongst the others. They were a curious lot, she thought, taking the opportunity to scan their faces. As her eyes came to rest on the two young women she had yet to meet, their right eyes similarly enclosed by a black heart tattoo, she heard a gasp from Lola.

"Oh dear! How unforgivably rude of me. Grace, I forgot to introduce you to Leonie and Holly."

The two young women smiled and nodded politely at Grace.

"Would you like a fairy cake?" Holly asked her, passing a fluted plate to Grace.

"I'm really not very . . ."

149

"They're quite delicious," Leonie said. "Trust me, dear, you won't have tasted anything better."

"We made them specially," Holly added. "We do so want you to feel welcome here."

Grace looked at the tower of fairy cakes. They did look quite enticing. Almost unconsciously her hand reached out for one and set it on her plate.

There was a hush of expectation and Grace realised the others were waiting for her to bite into the cake. She took the tiny cake in one hand and peeled away the paper cover. Then she popped it into her mouth and felt the most exquisite flavours explode against her tongue.

"Good, aren't they?" Leonie said, nodding and smiling.

Grace nodded her agreement. She noticed that Lola was now standing, a pair of field-glasses trained to her face. She was gazing across to the deck of *The Blood Captain.* Grace got up to join her.

"What are you looking at?" she asked.

Lola lowered her field-glasses and passed them to Grace. "Take a look," she said. "It would seem that the boys are having a little sport tonight."

Grace stared through the glasses at the brightly-lit deck of the prison hulk. It was crowded with crew-members but the glasses were strong and Grace could make out two swords clashing through a gap in the crowd. She saw Sidorio swing his sword at his opponent. Connor. Grace let out a gasp, but then she heard her brother's voice clear as a bell in her head.

"*Don't worry, Gracie. I know what I'm doing.*" He sounded so calm and assured.

As his voice faded, Grace watched Connor swing his sword at Sidorio and land a clean strike on the Vampirate's bicep. A slash of red appeared on Sidorio's glistening flesh. Grace was stunned. *What had happened to bring them to blows so soon?*

*

150

"First blood to Connor!" Johnny called.

A wall of noise erupted from the Vampirate crowd. Initially, Connor had assumed that they'd all be supporting the captain but now he realised that this wasn't the case. From their cheers and colourful chants, it was clear that they relished a good fight. Connor felt like he and Sidorio were locked in a gladiatorial duel. He'd have been glad of some armour, he thought, suddenly conscious of his bare chest, limbs and feet, which contrasted with Sidorio's leather and chain-mail. Again, Connor banished the negative thought. He hadn't needed armour to win round one. He was lighter than Sidorio to begin with and, without heavy clothing or boots to slow him down, he gained his second advantage.

"Change of weapon!" Johnny cried, striding back across the deck bearing a metal box. He approached Connor first and offered the open box to him.

Looking down at its contents, Connor grimaced. "What *is* this?" he asked, lifting out a weapon composed of a wooden haft, attached to a metal chain with a spiked iron ball at its end.

It was Sidorio who answered the question, as he reached into the box and took hold of a matching weapon. "The flail," he announced. "Sometimes referred to as the chain-morning-star. A personal favourite of mine."

The Vampirate crowd were stomping their feet and chanting louder, eager for the second stage of the duel to commence.

"They don't get out much," Johnny said, with a wink.

Connor weighed the vicious-looking flail in his hand. "I've never seen one of these before, let alone used one." He instantly regretted the words.

Sidorio was grinning. "This should be interesting, then," he said.

"May I have my glasses back?" Lola asked Grace.

Grace was still mesmerised by the activity on the deck of *The*

151

Blood Captain. What on earth were the weapons which Connor and Sidorio were now brandishing at one another?

Suddenly, Grace felt the glasses being wrenched from between her fingers and the vision was lost. "Manners, Grace!" Lola said in hushed but severe tones. "The girls have gone to a lot of trouble to host this party for you. Don't you think you should repay them by giving them your undivided attention?"

"My brother seems to be fighting some kind of duel with Sidorio," Grace said, breathlessly. "It looks dangerous."

Lola rolled her eyes. "Just boys being boys," she said, spinning Grace around and directing her back to the picnic blanket, then pushing her firmly down onto her cushion. "Pass Grace another cake, if you'd be so kind, Holly."

Obediently, Holly lifted the tiered cake stand.

Grace took another cake and stared sullenly at Lola as she bit into it. If anything, each cake seemed more delicious than the one before. They were utterly addictive. As she marvelled at the complex flavour, her thoughts of what was happening on board *The Blood Captain* receded. Instead, she found herself staring at Lola's face and, in particular, at the black heart tattoo. Now, the tattoo began to fade and, once more, Grace saw the bruise underneath, just as she had the first time they met. Now, as then, the crescent-shaped bruise served as the gateway into a deeper vision. Grace heard horses' hooves drumming on the earth and the squeak of carriage wheels.

Lola was frowning at her. Grace remembered how angry the Vampirate had been when Grace had read her before. She had a sense memory of Lola's vicious slap, but she didn't care. The vision was strong and she was going in deeper this time. Now, her eyes traced up from the wheels to the doors of a carriage. There was a window and a pale, frightened face pressed to the glass.

Grace heard a familiar voice. "Halt! Halt, I say! Your money or your life!"

Then the same voice – Lola's, unquestionably – shrieked loudly inside her head. "No!"

Snapping out of the vision, Grace looked up to find Lola smiling serenely at her. Now, Lola clapped her hands. "Everyone! Grace has the most marvellous party piece, don't you, my dear?"

"I do?" Grace said, reaching nonchalantly for another fairy cake.

"You know you do," Lola said playfully. "Now, we need a volunteer. Hands up, ladies." Her eyes ranged around the party. "Ah yes, Mimma. Perfect!" Lola put her hands on her hips. "Go on, then, Grace. Get to work!"

Connor had encountered few more forbidding sights than Sidorio brandishing the terrifying-looking flail. The Vampirate was spinning the wooden haft faster and faster, sending the spiked ball into a deadly orbit. Once more, Connor made himself focus on Sidorio's eyes, as hard as it was to remove his own from the spiked missile that was spinning ever nearer to his head. Once more, he was aware of his lack of armour.

Dismissing this thought, he spun his own flail. As vicious as the weapon looked – as vicious as it *was* – the technique of agitating it was simple enough to master. Now, it came down to which combatant was cleverest at invading his opponent's space and who was more fleet of foot in evading his enemy's strike.

A game of cat and mouse developed in the centre of the deck. The crowd obligingly edged backwards to give the two combatants more room – and to evade the path of the deadly flails. Connor found himself circling Sidorio, each man keeping the flail agitated at such speed that the spikes seemed invisible. Feeling emboldened, Connor let out a roar and made the first move – directing the flail at Sidorio's shoulder. But something had gone wrong. Where was the ball? It had caught. Connor had been watching Sidorio so closely, that he hadn't noticed how he'd been led astray, right into the rigging – where the fighting end of his flail was now trapped, in a tangle of rope.

Sidorio did not waste his advantage. As Connor helplessly tried to extract his flail, the ball attached to Sidorio's weapon came spinning through the air and grazed the outside of Connor's thigh. He felt a flash of pain and looked down to find a river of blood coursing down his leg and over his bare feet.

Behind him, some of the Vampirates edged forward. He could see the telltale signs of hunger in their eyes as they stared at the pool of crimson collecting on the deck.

"Second blood to Sidorio!" Johnny announced to the frenzied crowd.

Connor was surprised at how quickly the pain subsided. His wound was soon staunched too – with a cloth helpfully provided by Johnny. Within moments, the remaining blood began to dry and his leg looked as if it had been savaged by a tiger's claw. But it was only a shallow wound. Under the circumstances, Sidorio had been kind to him.

Johnny returned with the metal box. Gratefully, Connor dropped his flail inside it and watched as Sidorio did the same. Surely this had to mark the end of the battle?

"Change of weapon for round three!" Johnny announced, setting down the first box and lifting up another, smaller, one.

Connor shook his head. What was next? Johnny extended the metal box. As Connor glanced down, he felt a cold dread descend through his insides and settle in his gut.

The *yawara*. They looked innocent enough – like two small wooden dumb-bells. Utilised in various Japanese martial arts, in pairs, to initiate throws, bone breaks and pressure points, amongst other delights. As Connor took the pair into his hands, he grimaced. The *yawara* looked far less vicious than the flail, but they signalled that round three would be fought hand-to-hand. Glancing, in spite of his better instincts, at Sidorio's towering body, Connor realised that he had no chance of victory in this round.

Grace studied Mimma's face. It took her a moment to tune in her focus, then she felt a familiar calm sweeping over her.

"You're dressed in black lace," she said. "It's a baking hot day but you're dressed in an elaborate outfit with a veil covering your face."

Mimma leaned forward, excitedly. "Yes, yes," she urged, "go on!" Grace was aware that every one of Lola's crew, the captain included, hung upon her every word. She couldn't deny that she enjoyed their attention and the feeling of power it gave her.

"In your hands is a posy of flowers. Like a wedding bouquet. But there's something else there too." She paused, allowing the vision to sharpen. She was aware of all eyes watching her in wonder, none brighter or more engaged than Mimma's.

"Yes," Grace continued. "Underneath the flowers, you're holding a gun."

"That's amazing!" Mimma cried. "Did you tell her, Captain?"

Lola shook her head and raised her palms. "Not a word," she said. "It's Grace's gift. Isn't she a wonder?" She brought her hands together to clap and the others joined her in polite but enthusiastic applause.

As the applause died down, Jacqueline raised her hand. "Now me!" she said. "Read me next!"

"Just one more cake," Grace said, reaching out to help herself. She tried to savour this one a little longer but it slipped down all too quickly. It was as if they were truly made of fairy-dust.

Grace turned and focused on Jacqueline's eyes. After a moment, she nodded and smiled.

"I know this city," she said. "It's Paris. You're dressed in rags and your feet are bare. You're very hungry. And angry, so angry . . ."

"Go on!" Jacqueline said, her eyes wide as saucers. "Go on!"

The third round of the duel had already lasted twice as long as the two previous rounds. Initially, Connor had been nervous and tired, conscious of the wound on his thigh and of the odds stacked against him as he squared up to Sidorio. But from somewhere deep within had come fresh reserves of calm, energy and strength. Connor was on fire. He knew that he was using his dexterity to maximum advantage. His opponent had struck out several times with his fists clenched around the punishing *yawara*, only to find that Connor had slipped out of his clutches. Connor could see the frustration on Sidorio's face. He knew that, after his triumph in the second round, the Vampirate was now keen to lock down his victory.

Connor's only previous knowledge of the *yawara* was by reputation and he had some basic knowledge of anatomy through his combat training. But now, as he approached Sidorio, he felt an inner voice guiding him towards pressure points he had never been aware of before. The doubts he'd been harbouring about his ability to fight Sidorio melted away. He stopped seeing his opponent as a vast hulk, as strong as the ship he ruled over. Instead, he now saw a mass of potential targets and prepared to land the victory blow. It happened almost in slow motion. He reached out and landed two precise punches, his fists wrapped tightly around the yawara. The next thing he knew, Sidorio's eyes rolled and he crashed down onto the deck.

The crowd gasped as Connor stood over the fallen Vampirate captain. Then there was applause and cheers. Johnny stood over Sidorio, counting out loud. Then he reached out his hand for Connor's and lifted it, crying out, "The victor!"

As a wall of noise erupted around him, Connor glanced down at Sidorio. The Vampirate's eyes flickered open once more. He was staring at Connor. Connor could feel the intensity of his gaze but found it difficult to read his expression. Then Sidorio's lips curved into a soft smile.

"I'm so proud of you, my son," he said.

Lola entered Sidorio's cabin and strode over to his bedside. He was lying down, his head propped up on vast gold pillows, but his eyes were open and bright.

"I gather you've been through the wars, dearest," Lola said, brushing her cool hand over his temple.

Sidorio twisted his head so that his eyes met hers. "Connor was magnificent," he rasped. "As exceptional as we predicted. No, scratch that. More so! In all these years, I've never seen anything like it."

"That's nice," Lola said, kicking off her heels and lying down beside him.

"Nice?" Sidorio sat up. "It's a bit better than *nice*, my dear. Do you know what it feels like to be reunited with my only son? To find out he's as gifted as I am? Possibly more so."

Lola nodded. "I understand," she said. "But don't forget, Sid, you have *two* children. And Grace is every bit as extraordinary as her brother."

Sidorio smiled. "Connor's so strong. Like a fighting machine . . ."

"Yes, yes," Lola said. "But physical strength is a lot like physical beauty. It easily impresses but it's on the surface. Grace's talents lie a little deeper but, I suspect, given time, we'll see that she has even more to contribute."

Sidorio shrugged. "Well, as you say, they're both my kids. It's a win-win situation."

Lola laughed. "Yes, my dear, it's a happy time for the

Lockwood Sidorios." She laced her fingers through his. "Our little empire is coming together quite nicely, don't you think?"

"Oh yes," Sidorio said, grinning, bringing her hand to his lips and kissing it.

"And don't forget," Lola added. "They're my children too. Not by birth, perhaps, but nurture can be just as important as nature. And I think I have a vital role to play in grooming the twins for their future."

"Of course," Sidorio said. "Of course you do."

CHAPTER TWENTY-ONE

Daybreak Rendezvous

"You're sure this is the place?" Jacoby asked, striding along the deserted pier.

"Of course I'm sure," Jasmine said, tapping her map. "Are you forgetting who thrashed you in navigation seven years running?"

"OK, only asking!" Jacoby said, raising his palms in defence and walking out to the end of the pier.

Jasmine strode after him, checking her watch. "We're a little early is all."

Jacoby looked out across the still water, which reflected the purple cliffs and the pink-tinged light of the breaking dawn. He turned his face back to Jasmine, smiling. "It's rather a romantic spot, don't you think? Exactly how early are we . . .?" He reached out his arm to Jasmine but she gently brushed it away.

"Not now," she said. "What has Captain Li told you about Kally?"

Jacoby shrugged. "She's a fishtail – in essence, a kind of mermaid. She was part of a pack, or shoal – or whatever the collective term for fishtail is! But their boat was taken over by Sidorio and he killed several of the crew, including her father."

Jasmine shuddered. "How awful."

"The father, FYI, wasn't a fishtail," Jacoby continued. "Just a regular guy who fell in love with a merm— erm, a fishtail. Anyhow, Sidorio took over their boat – *The Lorelei* – and it was, *unsurprisingly*, a grim experience for Kally. She and her comrades staged an escape. She managed to get away but the others were not so lucky. To the best of her knowledge, she's the very last of the fishtails."

Jasmine nodded. "So she offered herself up to the Pirate Federation as a unique asset in the fight against the Vampirates."

"Pre-cisely," Jacoby said. "And Cheng Li thought she'd be the ideal conduit of communication between Connor, whilst he's stuck out at Vampirates Central, and us."

Jasmine frowned but she was no longer thinking of Kally's history. "Jacoby," she asked, "do you buy Captain Li's story about Connor?"

Jacoby raised an eyebrow. "You mean about the two of them convincing Sidorio that Connor is his son and heir?"

She nodded. "Exactly!"

"It sounds far-fetched," Jacoby agreed. "At least until you stop and reflect that we're waiting to rendezvous with a mermaid."

"A *fishtail*," Jasmine corrected him. "It *is* far-fetched," she persisted. "In so many ways. For one thing, when did they have the opportunity to present this whole crazy story to Sidorio?"

"That's the easy part of the puzzle," Jacoby said, his eyes bright. "You remember after our attack at Sidorio and Lola's wedding that Cheng Li and Connor were left behind with Vicious Sid? He was cradling his wife's severed head – one for the wedding album, that. We had made our escape with the rest of Team Tiger and were waiting for Connor and the captain in the launch. We saw Sid attack Connor but somehow he and Cheng Li repelled him and made their escape. The captain didn't go into detail but evidently that's when she told

Sid that Connor was his son. Apparently, she thought it up on the spot. You've got to hand it to her. Genius piece of improvisation!"

Jasmine decided to reserve her judgement for the time being. There were many unanswered questions. "How could Sidorio be so gullible?"

"Two possibilities," Jacoby said. "First, Vampirates are just plain dumb. That's Captain Li's theory and, I have to say, I'm inclined to agree with her. Remember when we had those three Vamps trapped in cages on board *The Tiger*? They weren't exactly brimming over with the smarts, were they?"

Jasmine cast her mind back. "To be fair, one of them did escape."

Jacoby was unfazed. "Yes, but that was a basic error on *our* part. I'm with Cheng Li on this – the Vampirates may look like adult men and women and they may be physically strong but they have a reduced mental and emotional capacity."

Jasmine considered his words. They were silent for a moment, both looking out at the water, watching for signs of any ripples that might signal Kally's arrival.

Jasmine put her hand on Jacoby's shoulder. "You said that there were *two* possible reasons why Sidorio believed the story that Connor is his son. The first reason was that he's plain stupid. What's the second?"

Jacoby raised his eyes. "Isn't it obvious, Min? That Cheng Li was telling Sidorio the *truth*. Connor's not the son of a lighthouse keeper. He's son and heir to the evil Vampirate dynasty. Grace too, of course. We shouldn't forget her in all this."

"You really think that Connor and Grace could be Sidorio's children?" Jasmine frowned. It couldn't be true. "If, and it's a big *if*, it were true, what would that make Connor and Grace? Are you suggesting that they're vampires too?"

Jacoby shook his head. "Think back, Min. You remember when Captain Li set us those research projects? And I came up with a list of the big three ways to destroy a Vampirate . . ."

Jasmine nodded, a little impatiently. "Burning, sunlight, stake through the heart."

Jacoby grinned. "It's kind of sexy to know you still hang on my every word, Min. Well, there was a fourth way which I didn't bother including." Jasmine's eyes were fixed on him as he explained. 'The fourth way to destroy a Vampirate would be by employing a dhampir."

"A what?"

"A *dhampir*," Jacoby repeated. "The child of a mortal mother and a vampire father. According to my research, dhampirs have exceptional powers."

Jasmine's eyes were wide. "If you knew this all the time, why on oceans didn't you share it with the rest of us?

Jacoby looked flushed for a moment. He reached out his hand to Jasmine but she clenched her fist as he continued speaking. "I figured that it didn't matter. We were hardly going to run into a dhampir, were we? Little did I realise there might already be one on the crew!"

Jasmine turned away and laughed. "You really think Connor could be the son of a vampire – Sidorio's son? For real?"

When she turned back, she found Jacoby shaking his head. "No way," he said. "Connor's just a regular guy like me and Bart. I've spent enough time around him to see that. Otherwise, I'd have picked up signs. We all would. You know: snacking on blood; keeping out of the light – that kind of thing would give him away."

"Exactly!" Jasmine was reassured to hear it. But her feeling of relief soon dissipated. She suddenly thought how glum Connor had been in the aftermath of his encounter with Sidorio. She remembered how disconnected he had seemed, sitting on the hillside, looking down at the academy harbour. There was no question that he had had a lot on his mind. She remembered the shock of him crying and her efforts to soothe him. Was it possible that there was a genuine connection between Connor and Sidorio? And where did that leave Connor now? How much danger was he in? She couldn't believe she was even entertaining such crazy thoughts.

"They didn't teach us about Vampirates and fishtails at Pirate Academy," Jasmine said. "Perhaps they should have done."

"They did teach us to deal with ever-changing threats," Jacoby said. "Maybe they thought that would cover it."

"I don't know," Jasmine said, shaking her head. "Do you ever feel that our world is changing a bit too fast?"

Jacoby reached out his hand to Jasmine again. This time, she took it and squeezed it, just for a moment.

"Look!" Jacoby said, pointing as the water in front of them became rippled. "Something's coming."

A second later, a girl's head popped up from beneath the surface.

"Kally, I presume?" Jacoby said.

She nodded, shaking the water from her spiky blue hair. "You're Jacoby and this must be Jasmine."

"That's right," Jasmine said, her thoughts still far away, with Connor. "It's nice to meet you," she mumbled, still on auto-pilot.

"You too," Kally said. "Guess we'll be seeing quite a bit of each other as this mission progresses. Well, I don't have much to report on this occasion. Just to confirm that I've made contact with Connor. Our communications set-up is in place."

"Good work!" Jacoby said. "Captain Li will be delighted to hear it."

"How is he doing?" Jasmine asked.

"He's good," Kally said. "Given the decidedly weird circumstances. A bit surprised to see me, I think. But we're cool." Her bright eyes shimmered in the daylight. "Well, I guess that's us done and dusted for today. Same time, same place tomorrow?"

"How are you able to navigate so precisely?" Jacoby inquired.

Kally winked. "My sonar is off the charts, dude."

Jacoby grinned. "Your tail's very colourful too," he said.

"If you gave me a pearl for every time I've heard that!" Kally said, with a laugh.

Jasmine watched the exchange, wishing she could somehow find a way to get some time alone with Kally. The fishtail gave them both a thumbs up, then turned to duck her head back under the water.

"Wait!" Jasmine called out to her, unable to help herself.

Kally turned, surprised. "Was there something else?"

Jasmine nodded, crouching down and speaking low in the hope that Jacoby wouldn't hear her. "I have a private message for Connor."

"Sure," Kally said. "Shoot!"

"Would you tell him that what I said to him at Pirate Academy, well, it's still true." She blushed as she finished speaking, but Kally nodded matter-of-factly. "Got it, dude!"

Then the fishtail turned, ducked her petite blue head under the water and disappeared once more. Jasmine watched the trail of ripples on the surface, then calm was restored.

Jacoby stepped closer to Jasmine. "I guess we're done here. Let's go and report back to the captain. Unless there's time for breakfast first? I'm positively ravenous, though strangely not in the mood for kippers."

Jasmine nodded. Her thoughts were still with Connor. When Jacoby had first used the word dhampir it had seemed too ridiculous. But the more she thought about it, the more it started to make a crazy kind of sense. She realised that it was time to accept two truths. One, Connor Tempest and his sister might actually be dhampirs. Two, whatever Connor might or might not be, she was falling in love with him.

CHAPTER TWENTY-TWO

Changes

As Lorcan stepped into the Captain's cabin (he couldn't help but think of it this way, even though it had been occupied by Mosh Zu for a good while now), he found Mosh Zu and Darcy waiting for him, sitting in chairs by the hearth. Darcy glanced up, with evident relief. Though she smiled, it was all too easy to detect the stresses and strains beneath the surface. Mosh Zu's smooth features were harder to read. He nodded to Lorcan and raised his hand in welcome.

"I'm sorry I'm late," Lorcan said. "And for the state I'm in." He looked dishevelled, his hair plastered to his forehead and his clothes damp from the rain, which had begun falling heavily out on deck. "I intended to clean up after combat training but time ran away with me."

Mosh Zu shook his head. "No problem. You made it ahead of Grace's expected arrival. How did the latest training session go?"

Lorcan sighed as he sat down on the sofa, his wet boots resting on the rug. "The usual mixed bag," he said, stretching one arm along the sofa's edge. "Some of the crew are really throwing themselves into it. They understand how important it is and how much things are changing in our realm."

166

"What about the others?" Darcy inquired.

Lorcan shook his head. "They don't get it at all. Their heads are buried in the sand. They want, and expect, things to be just as they always were."

Darcy frowned and shook her head. "Don't they remember what it was like when Sidorio and the others rebelled?" Her face grew yet more troubled. "And when he came back and Jez . . . I mean Stukeley . . . when Stukeley led the revolt against the Captain himself? It was on a Feast Night. They were all there. How could they not remember?" Darcy was looking at Mosh Zu as she finished speaking, but it was Lorcan who answered her question.

"They choose not to remember. They shut it out. Pretend that everything is just as it always was. When I tell them that the Captain has sent word that we must prepare ourselves for a new era, they just look vacant. It's as if some of them have already forgotten him."

"No!" Darcy gasped.

"And others just assume that when he does return, the old routines will continue. They can't accept that things will never be the same for us." Lorcan looked up guiltily into Mosh Zu's almond eyes. "I'm sorry to complain," he said. "I am doing my best, but this isn't an easy mission."

Darcy shook her head. "It's *my* fault. I was charged with persuading the crew that times are changing and that they need to change with them. I thought I was making inroads but I see now that most of them have just been turning a blind eye."

Mosh Zu rose to his feet, smiling beatifically. "Please, both of you, don't be so hard on yourselves. This was never going to be a swift process and from my observations you are both doing a far better job than you give yourselves credit for." He stood by the mantel, looking warmly at them both. "I never expected this to be easy, my friends, but I do believe that you will succeed. If

167

I have any advice for you both, it is to focus first on those who *do* understand the situation. Get them ready and then let them spread the knowledge to the others, like ripples in a pool."

Lorcan nodded. He noticed Darcy looking strangely at him for a moment, but as he met her glance, she pulled away and addressed Mosh Zu.

"Do you have any more news of our Captain? Of when he's coming back? I'm sure Grace will ask us when she arrives."

"Yes," Mosh Zu said. "I expect she will."

Just then, he looked to the door. "Come in!" he said.

The door did not open but, suddenly, Grace was inside the cabin, standing before them. She was smiling broadly. "I made it!" she said. "I wasn't sure if I could do it but I can see the three of you and the cabin."

"And we can see you," Mosh Zu said. "Welcome, Grace. You look well." Smiling at her, he sat down again and beckoned to her to come closer.

Grace walked towards the others, though in reality she was still in her cabin aboard *The Vagabond* and this was only an astral projection of herself. She was dressed in a long white toga, embroidered in gold and silver thread. Her hair had been teased into elaborate ringlets and plaits. Gold earrings dangled from her ears.

Darcy clapped her hands. "That's quite an outfit you have on, Grace. And your hair!"

Grace lifted her hand to her head, smiling. "Do you like it?" she asked. As Darcy nodded, she continued. "It took absolutely ages to do. Nathalie and Jacqui did it for me, while I did readings of them and some of the other girls to pass the time. Oh, and the toga was made for me by Lola's favourite designer. We're having a portrait painted later – me and Connor, Sidorio and Lola. Lola thought it would be fun if we dressed up in Roman outfits. The stitching is *real* gold."

Darcy reached out her hand, frustrated that she couldn't actually touch the fabric. "It looks amazing," she said. "I can tell how fine it is just by looking at it."

Lorcan stared at Grace, wondering what had happened to the feisty companion he'd left on the beach only a few days previously. He saw Mosh Zu observing her shrewdly too. At last, she paused to notice Lorcan. She turned and looked directly at him. Though it was what he'd been waiting for, the strength of her gaze unsettled him. He felt deeply self-conscious. "I look rough," he said, apologetically. "I just came from training."

"You look good," she said, her eyes seeming to trace every line of his body. There was a new look in her eyes that could only be described as hungry. She smiled and sat down in the seat beside him. "All that training is doing wonders for your physique."

Lorcan flushed, anxious to change the subject. "So you're having a portrait painted with the others?"

"Yes," Grace said. "A family portrait. Lola's idea *of course* – she's into that kind of thing. I'm sure Connor's dreading the thought of sitting still for hours on end, but apparently Lola's got some legendary artist to do it. Caravaggio, I think he's called."

Her words rushed out at breakneck speed and Lorcan struggled to keep up, let alone stem the flow. At last, she drew breath, allowing him to speak. "It sounds like you've settled in well," he said. Looking at Mosh Zu, he added. "A bit too well, perhaps?"

Mosh Zu smiled and shook his head. "We wanted Grace to infiltrate the renegade empire and it sounds as if she is doing that very successfully."

Lorcan noticed Darcy giving him a knowing look once more as Mosh Zu turned to Grace. "How are *you* finding the experience so far?"

Grace smiled brightly at Mosh Zu. "It's fine," she said. "To be honest, it's much less scary than I expected. In their own way, Sidorio and Lola are doing everything possible to make me feel welcome. And the girls – Mimma, Nat and Jacqui – well, they're really friendly to me." Seeing Darcy's eyes drop, she added, "They'll never be as good friends as *you*, though." Darcy smiled fleetingly, then shot Lorcan another glance.

"How's Connor faring?" inquired Mosh Zu.

"He's good, too. Though, to be honest with you, I haven't seen that much of him. He's been kept busy on *The Blood Captain* and I'm mostly on *The Vagabond*. We see each other at Tiffin – this nightly get-together for key personnel of both ships – but that's about it." She raced to get the words out.

She had, thought Lorcan, a new energy to her; a somewhat nervous energy. Maybe it was the stress of being somewhere new and bearing the burden of such an important mission. He fervently hoped so.

"Have you seen much of Johnny?" he asked her.

Grace reached out her hand and, though she couldn't touch him, laid hers on top of his. "Not so much," she said. "Except to say hello to." Lorcan bit his lip. Noticing this, Grace added, "Trust me, you have nothing to worry about."

"I do trust you," Lorcan said. "Of course I do." He frowned. "It's Johnny I don't trust."

"Tell me what's going on with all of you," Grace said, brightly. "How's your combat training going, Lorcan? And Darcy, what about your mission? Oh, and tell me, Mosh Zu, has the Captain returned yet?"

Her words were spilling out faster and faster now. Lorcan and Darcy looked at Mosh Zu with dismay.

Mosh Zu replied to Grace, seemingly unconcerned by the change in her demeanour. "The Captain has not yet returned," he said. "But he will, very soon. He is getting stronger night by night. He is looking forward to being amongst us all again."

"That's good," Grace said. "Please, when you next see him or talk to him, send him my—" She broke off, distracted. "Did you hear that? Someone's at my door."

Mosh Zu nodded. "You had better go," he said.

"Grace!" It was Mimma's voice. "They're all waiting for you in the Captain's Cabin. Signor Caravaggio is setting up his paints and Lola says to get a move on."

Grace looked apologetically at her comrades. "I'm sorry. I had better go. I wish . . ."

"It's OK," Mosh Zu said.

"We'll see you tomorrow night," Darcy said, firmly. "Same time."

"Yes," Grace said, a touch absent-mindedly. Then she called out to Mimma, "I'm coming, hon!"

Frustrated, and overflowing with emotion, Lorcan reached out to Grace. "Be careful, Grace! Please, be careful!" But his hand fell straight through her image and, before he had even finished speaking, she had completely faded from view.

Lorcan stood up and smashed his fist angrily against the arm of the sofa. He let out a strangulated sigh, then turned to face the others. "I'm sorry," he said, "but I'm really worried about her. They're getting to her. She looks different. She sounds different. She has this weird new energy. I knew it was a mistake sending her in."

"You underestimate her," Mosh Zu said, rising to his feet once more. "She's the only one of us who could have undertaken this mission. And, don't you see, she only seems different because she is adapting to her surroundings, like a chameleon? She's doing just what she needs to in order to win their trust."

"How can you be sure that's all it is?" Lorcan asked.

"We'll keep a close eye on her," Mosh Zu said. He crossed the room to stand beside Lorcan. "You're tired," he said. "No wonder. We're only halfway through the night and look what you've already achieved. Go and get some rest. Your worries will weigh on you less." He rested his arm lightly on Lorcan's shoulder.

"All right," Lorcan said. "But if we think Grace is getting out of her depth, you must let me go and fetch her back. Will you promise me that?"

Mosh Zu seemed to weigh up his words. "I don't believe it will come to that," he said. "But, be assured, my friend, that I would never place Grace in a position I did not think she could handle."

"Come on," Darcy said, taking Lorcan's arm. "Mosh Zu's right, you need your rest. I'll walk you to your cabin." She nodded formally at Mosh Zu as she propelled Lorcan towards the cabin door.

"Good work, my friends!" Mosh Zu called after them.

Once they were a safe distance away from the Captain's cabin, Lorcan turned to Darcy. "I'm worried about Grace," he said. "You and Mosh Zu might not be, but I know her better . . ."

"Excuse me!" Darcy exclaimed, huffily. "You might be Grace's boyfriend but I'm her best friend so I think I know her *just* as well as you, maybe better. And I'm every bit as worried about her as you are. Something was up with her tonight. I can't put my finger on it exactly but something wasn't right."

Lorcan was relieved someone else shared his concern. "How come you and I saw it but Mosh Zu didn't?"

Darcy leaned against the corridor wall. "I know that Mosh Zu is incredibly wise and has many powers, and I'm going to sound really disloyal with what I'm about to say . . ." She hesitated.

"Go on," Lorcan urged her.

"I think that Mosh Zu has been so far removed from real life, up high in the clouds at Sanctuary, that he's finding standing in for the Captain a huge stretch. I think he's struggling. He's a healer, not a leader. He doesn't understand the complexities of running a ship and I actually don't think he relates to people that well on a night-to-night basis. If I hear him tell me to watch the ripples spreading in a pool again, or any more of that stuff, I think I may scream." She drew to an abrupt halt. "Oh dear, you're thinking dippy Darcy's really lost the plot this time, aren't you?"

Lorcan shook his head. "On the contrary," he said, his voice firm but soft. "You've articulated it better than I ever could have. I feel just the same. I have the utmost respect for Mosh Zu but he isn't the Captain, *our* Captain." He frowned. "We've been given this impossible task. For as long as *The Nocturne* has sailed, the crew has been conditioned to abandon violence and conflict and embrace ways of peace. Now, all of a sudden, we have to turn pacifists into a fighting force to rival not only Sidorio and his henchmen but the pirates too. We're doomed to failure."

"No," Darcy said. "Mosh Zu was right about one thing. The task might seem daunting but we *are* starting to make progress. We must carry on our work, making things right for the Captain's return."

"Yes," Lorcan said, Darcy's belief reigniting the fire inside his own soul.

"Mosh Zu wasn't the right choice to deputise for the Captain in his absence," Darcy said. "It should have been someone who knows this crew, and the ways of this ship."

"What are you saying?" Lorcan asked.

"I think you know what I'm saying." She spoke softly and slowly, her wide eyes boring into his.

Lorcan frowned, dropping his voice to a whisper. "You're surely not suggesting that *we* rebel against Mosh Zu?"

173

"No!" Darcy shook her head vigorously, her sleek bobbed hair swinging around her face. "Of course not! We have to sit tight for now. Keep a close eye on Grace – a *very* close eye – and patiently await the Captain's return. In the interim, we must do Mosh Zu's bidding but that needn't stop us thinking our own thoughts, or talking to one another like this, need it?"

"No, Darcy," Lorcan said. "No, indeed not." He looked at her and shook his head. "You've changed," he said. "You're changing."

She nodded. "It's true. And I'm not the only one, Mister Muscles." She reached out and lightly prodded his bicep. Then her tone grew more serious. "Oh, Lorcan," she said. "Don't you see? We have to change. All of us. And fast. Otherwise, there is no future for this ship, or for any of us. Everything that the Captain worked so hard to build, for so long, will all just fall away. We can't let that happen."

Lorcan nodded, drawing her towards him. "You're right," he said. "We can't. And we won't."

CHAPTER TWENTY-THREE

First Blood

"Nice outfit!"

Connor cringed as he heard Stukeley's voice behind him in the corridor. He turned and found Stukeley and Johnny striding towards him.

"It really shows off Connor's legs, don't you think, Johnny?"

"Oh yes!" Johnny said. The two Vampirates cracked up laughing.

Connor stood there, nodding and waiting for their laughter to subside. They weren't telling him anything he didn't already know. He did look like a prize plonker in the toga Lola had insisted he wear for the family portrait. It was bad enough he'd had to sit in it for the better part of two hours. He couldn't wait to change out of it.

"You know the best bit—" Stukeley began.

"Well, obviously, it's the gold laurel wreath!" Johnny exclaimed.

Connor flushed. Was he still wearing that? He reached up and grabbed it.

"No, mate," continued Stukeley. "No, the best bit is that when the portrait is finished, we'll be able to look at Connor dressed in all his finery every single night!"

Connor groaned. He hadn't thought of that before. Worse and worse. "Thanks, lads," he said. "You've really made me feel better. Nice work!"

"We're only teasing!" Stukeley said, nudging Johnny. "Except the part about your legs!"

"OK," Connor said. "That's enough! I'm going to my cabin to get changed into something normal and then we can continue this conversation."

Connor couldn't get the toga and assorted Roman accessories off quickly enough. He was tempted to throw the hellish outfit away but suspected that Lola had paid a tidy sum for it so, instead, he slung it to the very back of his closet. Then he took out a selection of his regular clothes and carried them over to the bed. As he did so, he caught sight of his reflection in the mirror. He noticed that the outside of his thigh, where Sidorio had wounded him with the flail a few nights before, no longer showed any trace of the wound. He ran his fingers over his skin. There was a slight scar where the flesh had knitted itself back together but it was amazing how quickly and cleanly the deep wound had healed.

As he stepped into a fresh pair of trousers, he felt the ship lurch into motion and had to steady himself to remain balanced. It wasn't unusual for the ship to move off during the night, though he hadn't expected them to ship anchor so soon. He buttoned up his trousers and reached for his shirt.

There was a knock on the cabin door.

"Give me a minute!" Connor called. "I'm still getting changed out of my fancy dress!"

No doubt it was Stukeley and Johnny back for a few more easy laughs. Well, at least he wouldn't be fuelling their fire any more by wearing a gold-embroidered dress. In truth, he didn't mind the lads' jokes. Stukeley was an old friend and Johnny already felt like one. It made Connor think back to the days of the Three Buccaneers. He missed Bart, but maybe it was time for a new configuration of the trio. After all, Bart was mortal. These days, Connor had rather more in common with Stukeley and Johnny.

Another knock at the door.

"All right!" Connor yelled. "Keep your hair on!"

His boots still unlaced, he strode over to the door and opened it. But it wasn't Stukeley and Johnny. It was Sidorio who stood leaning against the door jamb, arms folded. He grinned at Connor.

"I see you've changed out of your toga," he said.

Connor nodded. "You too." Sidorio was back in his trademark metal-and-leather armour.

"I never liked wearing a skirt, even when it was considered socially acceptable," Sidorio said. "I'm sorry, son, I could see you enjoyed that portrait sitting about as much as I did. But sometimes I have to do things to keep the wife happy!"

Connor nodded, feeling a surprising sense of fellowship with Sidorio. Although, now he thought about it, Sidorio had been on good form throughout the portrait sitting, alleviating the serious mood and terminal boredom by cracking jokes. At one point, he had made Signor Caravaggio drop his palette, he was laughing so much. Lola had had to instruct them all to take the sitting more seriously or it would never be finished. It was at that point that Sidorio had asked his wife, "Couldn't you have found us a Vampirate *photographer*?" Lola had just scowled at him, so he had apologised and promised to behave himself.

"Anyhow," Sidorio said now. "I don't know about you, but after standing still for two hours I'm more than ready for some physical exercise."

Connor laughed and finished lacing his boots. "You're not suggesting another duel, are you? I've only just recovered from the last one."

177

Sidorio grinned, his now-familiar gold incisors gleaming in the light of the corridor. "No, son, not a duel. Something rather more exciting than that. Come with me." He had a sudden thought. "Oh, and bring your sword."

Intrigued, Connor grabbed his sword and joined Sidorio out in the corridor. The interior of *The Blood Captain* was empty. Walking shoulder to shoulder with Sidorio across the high metal grid, Connor felt no vertigo. On the contrary, it was as if they were walking on air through the deserted ship. He could tell from the way they were going, that they would end up out on deck.

As they walked along, they chatted away. Part of Connor observed the conversation at a distance and wondered how he could have fallen into such an easy camaraderie with the most vicious of Vampirates. One element of it was simple necessity – to do a good job for Cheng Li and the Federation he had to bond as convincingly as possible with Sidorio, Stukeley, Johnny and the rest of the crew. And yet, Connor realised, as Sidorio cracked another joke, he was actually enjoying the captain's company. It was hard to square this Sidorio with the monster he'd once attempted to destroy. Of course, he wasn't blind to the violence and mayhem of which Sidorio was capable, but now he saw another side to him. He knew that Stukeley and Johnny felt the same way. Sidorio was, strange though it was to admit, an easy kind of father figure. Then it struck Connor, like a star shooting across the night sky. He *is* my father. Before, the thought had filled him with horror and disgust. Now, he felt a real connection.

As they stepped out on deck, the mystery of where the crew had disappeared to was immediately solved. The upper deck was thronging with a capacity crowd. The Vampirates were swift to register the captain's presence and a pathway opened up through them, like a red carpet unrolling. Connor couldn't help but feel a sense of pride. He knew that he was being accorded the same respect as Sidorio, on account of being his son. It reminded him of the first time he had passed beyond the velvet rope at Ma Kettle's Tavern. He felt in a position of rare privilege; he was a pirate VIP and now, by some strange symbiosis of birth and destiny, a Vampirate VIP too.

Sidorio marched through the crowd with easy authority. It was as if he'd been born to reign. At last, he came to the bow of the ship, where Stukeley and Johnny were waiting. They raised their hands in salute and it seemed that this mark of respect was not only for Sidorio but for Connor too. He smiled to himself. No more taking the mick about what I'm wearing now, he thought.

"Is everything ready?" Sidorio inquired of his lieutenants.

"Yes, Captain," Johnny said. "Look, there's the ship. It won't be long now."

Sidorio stepped forward and Connor followed in his wake. Johnny had pointed in a north-north-easterly direction, where a sizeable galleon was cresting the night waves. The galleon was flying the familiar skull and crossbones insignia. A pirate ship. Connor felt an immediate wave of alarm.

"How long until we're adjacent?" Sidorio asked Stukeley.

"Less than ten," Stukeley answered. "We're closing in."

"What is that ship?" Connor asked, as salt spray came up and splashed his face.

"It's called *The Redeemer*," Stukeley said.

"It's a Federation ship, isn't it?" Connor's voice was hoarse. He could taste salt water at the pit of his throat. He could barely get the words out.

Stukeley nodded.

Sidorio put his hand on Connor's shoulder. "It's so good to have you here with me. This will be the first of many battles we fight side by side. Forget the portrait. *This* is where our legend begins." Sidorio continued as his eyes met Connor's. "It is time that you had a name befitting your status and destiny. Connor Tempest is no more. From now on, my son, you will be known as Connor Quintus Antonius Sidorio."

Connor registered the words numbly. Was it true? Was Connor Tempest really gone? And, if so, who – or what – had taken his place?

Connor didn't take part in the attack, despite Sidorio's promise that they would fight alongside one another. He didn't need to. Within moments of the Vampirates' descent onto *The Redeemer*, the nameless captain and his crew were overpowered. At first, Connor felt utter revulsion, as the crew of *The Blood Captain* cut a swathe through the subjugated vessel. But, as bodies crashed onto the deck and blood began to spill, he felt himself suspending judgement. Was this so very different from any other attack he had witnessed, or been part of? Attacks were always brutal, whether your weapon was a sword slashing a man's chest or a pair of sharp incisors bearing down on his thorax. He couldn't understand how he could be so resigned to it. Around him, bodies seemed to fall in slow motion, spurting blood. He stood there, frozen to the spot, feeling a strange sense of dislocation. He was both there but utterly absent. It was a strange privilege to be at the heart of a battle yet not even have to lift a sword.

In his head, he heard Cheng Li's voice admonishing him. Why hadn't he acted to prevent this attack? But what could he have done? The first he had heard of it was less than an hour ago, when Sidorio had rapped on his door. Even if, by some miracle, he had gotten word to Kally, the fishtail couldn't have swum to *The Tiger* in time to alert them. Nor could the Federation have got word to *The Redeemer* or sent in reinforcements. Connor knew that Cheng Li and the

Federation would be fuming but there was nothing he could have done.

He felt a strange sense of calm, which he struggled to understand. It was a numbness which held him there at the centre of the deck – a passive witness to the bloodshed around him. But then, he felt a new sensation. It had something in common with a rise in adrenaline, but it wasn't exactly the same. His senses were on full alert: sight, sound, smell, taste, touch. Each of them were reaching out for one thing and one thing only. Blood.

Now, as he glanced about the deck, he no longer saw the fallen bodies, or the impotent swords. All he saw were the splashes of red – small spatters on white linen shirts; larger pools spreading across the deck-boards. Rivers of blood flowing together into an ocean of red.

Seeing this, smelling this, feeling each of his senses open up to it, Connor felt only one thing, resonating through him in a way that nothing had before.

Hunger.

Cheng Li strode along the main deck of *The Tiger*.

"Jacoby! Where's Jacoby?"

"Don't know, Captain," Bart called, as he polished a cannon.

"Haven't seen him, Captain Li," cried Bo Yin, high up in the rigging, where she was making repairs.

"Somebody find him!" Cheng Li bellowed. "Now!"

Her cry seemed to echo not only around the ship but across the vast ocean that surrounded them.

Jacoby flung open the door leading out onto the deck and ran towards her. Jasmine followed after him, a few steps ahead of Cate.

"Captain!" Jacoby called.

"How could this happen?" Cheng Li barked, as they met each other at *The Tiger*'s main mast.

181

"It took Connor completely by surprise," Jacoby said. "He didn't have time to find Kally until afterwards. He promises he'll do better next time."

"*Next time?*" Cheng Li screamed. "Next time?! How many more ships does the Federation have to lose before you, Connor and that fishtail start to raise your game?"

Jacoby had never seen the captain quite so angry. She marched past him back inside the ship.

Jasmine came over to Jacoby and hugged him. They were joined by Cate and Bart and then by Bo Yin, who had deftly swung down the rigging.

"You did your best," Jasmine said. "That was all you could do."

"She's right, buddy," Bart said. "You have nothing to beat yourself up about."

Cate nodded. Bo Yin shook her head sadly.

There were tears in Jacoby's eyes and he was shaking. "One ship lost and a hundred crew missing, presumed dead or, worse, *undead*. And it's my fault." Breaking free of Jasmine's arms, he ran inside to find Cheng Li and determine their next move.

CHAPTER TWENTY-FOUR

Manoeuvres

Connor had been nervously anticipating Tiffin. It was his best – often his *only* – chance to talk to Grace during his day, or rather night. In between, he was kept busy on *The Blood Captain* just as she was on *The Vagabond*. For the past forty-eight hours, since the attack on *The Redeemer*, Connor had been building up the nerve to talk to his sister about his new hunger for blood. The strength of the hunger had overwhelmed and unsettled him. It hadn't happened again since but somehow he was certain that it would return; that it hadn't disappeared but rather lay dormant. He wondered if the sight of blood was needed to stoke the hunger or if it would simply come of its own bidding.

Had Grace experienced the same hunger? It seemed likely. She was a dhampir too. They were the exact same age and, if anything, weren't girls supposed to mature physically a little sooner than boys? The best way to find out was to talk to her. Connor knew that. But he was scared, somehow. He had the sense that once he talked to her – or indeed anyone else – about his hunger, that his words would make it real. For now, he could kid himself that he wasn't really a dhampir, that Sidorio wasn't his biological father – that it *was* merely a ruse conjured up by Cheng Li to help them infiltrate the rebel Vampirate empire. But, deep down, he knew there was no running away from it. The blood hunger had been powerful enough to convince him of the fact. He was changing; becoming a dhampir. There was no denying it.

As soon as he arrived at Tiffin, Connor broke off from the other members of his party and went to find Grace. She was, as he expected, seated at the dining table. They remained the only two who ate at these gatherings and Chef Escoffier's generosity and inventiveness showed no signs of waning. If anything, his offerings seemed to grow more lavish each night. As Grace glanced in his direction, Connor smiled weakly and, taking a deep breath, walked over to join her. As he stepped closer to the table, he realised that she was not alone. Her new friends from *The Vagabond* were sitting around her and it was very clear that they had settled down for a good gossip. There was not going to be an easy way to get her alone.

Feeling a mixture of disappointment and relief, Connor sat down to eat. Initially, the girls acknowledged him but it soon became clear that they had many hot topics to discuss that did not involve him. He tucked into his food with relish, aware that his appetite for regular food seemed to be growing apace.

As Connor watched Grace chatting with the girls, he realised how much she too was changing. It was only a short time since they had arrived on the vampirate ships, but already she was looking and acting differently. Today, she had barely acknowledged him. He knew that she had her own mission to infiltrate the Vampirate ranks and report back to her comrades on *The Nocturne*. But either she was way off track with that or she was far better at acting than he'd given her credit for.

On balance, he thought, it was probably a good thing that

he hadn't blurted out his concerns about his blood hunger to her. The days of sharing everything with his twin sister were over. He'd been slow to recognise this but it was the truth. She had other confidantes now. And so, come to that, did he. He looked up and saw Stukeley and Johnny joking away over on the other side of the room. Stukeley had been on a similar trajectory to Connor – from mortal life to vampirism. He would know what it was like to experience the physical changes involved in the metamorphosis. He was the one Connor should talk to about his hunger. Not here, not now, but soon.

Grace was in fits of laughter, prompted by one of Nathalie's hilarious stories, when she felt a hand on her shoulder. Turning, she found Sidorio standing over her.

"I wonder if I might have a moment alone with you?" he said.

Grace was taken aback but nodded. "Yes, yes of course," she said, allowing him to pull back her chair. The girls were silent for a moment as Sidorio led her away, then they bowed their heads and she could hear their familiar laughter continuing. Their company was addictive. Already, she missed them.

"Let's go up on deck," Sidorio said, opening the doors of Lola's cabin.

"How are you liking life on board *The Vagabond*?" he asked her as they made their way along the corridor.

"Very much," Grace said, pleased that she could add with genuine feeling, "I've made some good friends here."

Sidorio nodded. "I see that. And I hope that you are enjoying getting to know your stepmother, too."

Grace nodded, deciding not to elaborate on this. Her jury was still out on Lola.

"I'm sorry that you and I have not had more time together since your arrival," Sidorio said.

Grace shook her head. "It's really not a problem."

185

"I don't want you to think that I have chosen Connor over you. You are equally important to me, Grace. We just thought that you would be more comfortable here with Lola, and it made sense for Connor to be with me on *The Blood Captain*."

Grace nodded. "I understand," she said.

Sidorio pushed open the door out onto the deck. Grace noticed that several of Lola's crew were patrolling outside. She exchanged a smile with first Holly, then Leonie. Silently, Sidorio placed a hand on her shoulder and led her gently over to the prow of the ship. Then he withdrew his hand and reached into his pocket.

"There's something I want you to have," he said. He opened his fist to reveal a small brooch. "It belonged to my mother . . . your grandmother." Compared to the lavish jewellery worn by Lola and her comrades, the brooch was very simple and *naïf,* but there was something about it that Grace found instantly appealing.

Sidorio placed it into her hand. "It was the only piece of jewellery my mother had. My father – your grandfather – gave it to her on their wedding day. He made it himself. She always treasured it."

Grace looked at the small brooch, then up at Sidorio. Suddenly, a heritage that she had never known before fell into place. She was looking at the face of her father but in her head was a link to her grandparents and the lives they had lived *centuries* ago.

"I let my parents down," Sidorio said. "I went away to make something of myself. I became a pirate. But by the time I'd made a pot of gold and gone back for them, they were already at death's door. My gold was no good to them. It was too late. When they needed me, I was out robbing ships. I let them down and they were the only family I had . . . until now."

Grace lifted up the brooch. "Would you pin it on my dress?" she asked.

He nodded. The pin was tiny and Sidorio's thick fingers fumbled with it for a moment. Grace waited patiently as he finally fastened it to her dress.

"Thank you," she said. "I shall treasure it."

For a moment, they stood side by side, in silence. Then Sidorio turned to Grace once more. "I know that this isn't the life you would have chosen for yourself. Or Connor for himself. But I want you to both know that I will do everything in my power to make you happy here."

He reached out his hand to Grace. To her amazement, she snaked her fingers through his. It felt like the most natural thing in the world.

Connor was talking to Stukeley and Johnny when Mimma came over to them.

"All right, lads? More vino?"

"Sure," Stukeley said, reaching out his glass as Mimma lifted the decanter, with a wink.

"Rude not to," Johnny said, extending his own glass.

"How about you, Connor?" Mimma asked. "Where's your goblet?"

"Not for me, thanks," he said.

Mimma arched an eyebrow defiantly.

Connor shook his head. "Not tonight," he said.

"Please yourself!" Mimma proceeded on her way. Then, she turned and retraced her steps. "Hey, Stukeley, I hear that you're to lead the next attack. Can I come with? There's nothing I like better than a bit of bloodshed before bed."

Stukeley grinned. "I'd be pleased to have you at my side, Mim," he said.

"Now, now, sailor, don't get carried away. I said I'd like to join you in the fight. Not walk down the aisle with you. Not yet, anyhow." Winking, Mimma turned and strode off again.

Connor turned to Stukeley, his heart racing. "There's going to be another attack? And you're in charge?"

Stukeley nodded. "Oh yes, my friend. Tomorrow night. And you'll never guess who the target is." He pulled Connor towards him and whispered in his ear.

"There you both are!" Lola said, as Sidorio and Grace arrived back in the captain's cabin. "I was about to send out scouts to find you!" She smiled, then her eyes narrowed as they locked onto Grace's brooch. "Ah, Sid, you gave her your mother's pin."

Sidorio nodded.

"I think it's beautiful," Grace said. "Both the pin and the story behind it."

"It looks well on you, my dear," Lola said. As she spoke, her eyes were already circling the room and she reached out her hand and waylaid Obsidian Darke, who was heading for the cabin door. "Where do you think you're going, Lieutenant Darke? The night is but young."

Grace watched as Obsidian Darke stared distantly at Lola. "I have business to attend to back on *The Blood Captain*," he said.

"Plenty of time for that," Lola declared, beckoning Mimma over. "Stay a while. Have another drink." By the time she had finished speaking, Darke's glass had been refilled. He did not seem at all pleased by the fact.

"Lieutenant Darke, I'm not sure that you've been properly introduced to my charming and talented stepdaughter, Grace." Lola ran a maternal finger through Grace's hair.

Running his cold eyes over Grace, Obsidian Darke turned back to Lola. "We've met," he said.

"Well, you may have said 'hello', 'how do', that sort of

thing," Lola said, "but you've never *truly* met Grace until you've let her do a reading of you. It's rather remarkable. She's done it for me and all of my ladies, haven't you, dear?"

Grace shrugged. She was growing a little resentful of Lola having her perform at the click of her fingers, like some kind of carnival act. But her feelings softened as she noticed Sidorio looking at her with undisguised paternal pride.

"Go on, Grace," Lola said. "Tune into Lieutenant Darke's dim and distant past and see if he's as mysterious and forbidding as he'd have us all believe."

Grace addressed Darke directly. "Would you mind?" she asked.

Lola laughed. "I don't remember you asking *me* that before you poked around inside my head!"

Darke gazed coldly at Grace.

"All right then," Grace said, irritated but feeling that she had no choice but to proceed. She focused on Darke's eyes. They were usually the best way in. But as she stared into them, she found that they were like mirrors reflecting her own image back at her. He was putting up some kind of block. How was he able to do that? Lola may not have welcomed Grace's reading, but she had been powerless to prevent it.

Grace made a second attempt to get through Darke's defences. But, this time, she recoiled at the force of the barrier he had somehow brought up.

"It's no good," she said. "I'm not getting anything."

"How disappointing," Lola said, draining the remains of her glass.

"On the contrary." Obsidian Darke extended his own untouched glass of blood to Lola. "I must go now." He turned and saluted Sidorio. "Captain!"

Sidorio nodded as Lieutenant Darke made his exit.

Lola exchanged a glance with Sidorio. "He's beginning to

grate on me," she said. "Must we put up with him any longer? At least Johnny and Stukeley are pretty."

"He's a good pirate," Sidorio said, smiling at his wife. "One of the best we have. What he lacks in small talk, he will make up for in battle."

"We'll see," Lola said, dropping her eyes to Grace once more. "Well, missy, it seems your talent isn't quite as boundless as we previously thought." Her tone was jokey but Lola had hit a nerve. Grace had never been blocked like that before. She didn't like it. Not one bit.

"Maybe it's time to find yourself a new performing monkey," Grace snapped, turning away and heading out of the cabin in Lieutenant Darke's slipstream.

Lola grinned at Sidorio. "*Someone's* a little highly strung tonight. And after you gave her such a pretty trinket." Lola leaned closer to Sidorio's ear. "Did she really believe it was your poor dear mum's only jewel?"

Sidorio nodded. "As a matter of fact, yes."

Lola laughed throatily. "How marvellous! Zofia will be so thrilled. She knocked it up in half an hour last night. I knew it would be the perfect catalyst to bring the two of you together."

Sidorio frowned. "I shouldn't have listened to you, Lola. Grace is my daughter. I'm not comfortable playing these games with her."

So saying, he too walked away, leaving Lola on her own.

Frowning, Lola lifted the glass abandoned by Darke and drained it in one. The taste of the blood, warmed perfectly to room temperature, calmed her frazzled nerves. She smiled as Johnny came by, and reached out her arm. "Wait up, cowboy!" she called.

Johnny grinned haphazardly. "What can I do for you, Captain Lockwood?"

Lola smirked at him. "Ask not what you can do for the

190

captain, dear Johnny, but what you can do for the captain's stepdaughter."

"Grace?" Johnny said.

Lola nodded. "She's in a bit of a mood, Johnny. She needs a little fun. F-U-N. That's your department, remember?"

"You bet your—"

"Quite so!" Lola cut him off. "Well, off you go then. Don't let the grass grow under your spurs – or whatever it is you cowpokes say. Go and plan something fun for Grace – something to put a smile back on that pretty face of hers. I want her fully occupied. Things are about to step up a gear here and I can't have a loose cannon in our midst."

CHAPTER TWENTY-FIVE

Johnny's Surprise

"You can open your eyes, now," Johnny whispered in Grace's ear.

As Grace did so, her eyelashes brushed against Johnny's hands, which remained gently pressed against her face. All she could see were slivers of starlight flickering through the slim gaps between his fingers.

"Not fair!" she said. "Let me see!"

Johnny laughed. "All right!" he said. "You've been very patient, Grace. I'll take away my hands on the count of three. One . . . two . . ."

He kept his hands in place for one more tantalising moment. "Three!"

At last, he drew his fingers away from Grace's eyes and rested them on her shoulders.

"Oh, Johnny!" Grace exclaimed. There, standing on the sand, by the water's edge, was a horse. Its body looked bright gold in the moonlight, all except for its mane and tail, which were both pure white.

"Is *that* my surprise?" Grace asked. "It's so beautiful. Its body looks like gold."

"She's not an 'it'," Johnny laughed. "Her name's Nieve. And her body *is* gold; she's a palomino."

"Nieve," said Grace. "That's an Irish name, isn't it?" Instinctively, she thought of Lorcan.

Johnny shook his head. "I named her Nieve. It's the Spanish word for snow."

"Oh, I see! Because her mane and tail are as pure white as new-fallen snow." Grace turned to Johnny.

He looked distant for a moment. "Well, yes, that's part of it."

Then Grace remembered her vision of Johnny, riding through the snow. His story had begun and ended in the snow. She remembered the terrible ending – him hanging by his neck from a tree as the snow fell all around him. She felt terrible for having missed the connection at first but, as she looked up at him, she found he was smiling and his eyes were bright once more.

"Now, either we can stand here and admire Nieve's beauty from afar or we can go and take her for a ride across the beach. What do you reckon?"

Grace felt her heart began to race. "I've never ridden a horse before." The thought of doing so made her nervous, but exhilarated too.

"Piece of cake," Johnny said, reaching out for her hand. "I'll do all the work. Besides, Nieve won't give us any trouble. She loves a midnight run. Come and meet her."

Johnny led Grace across the sand. When they were a few paces away from Nieve, he began talking to the horse. Immediately, Nieve responded. Grace could see the strength of the bond between the horse and the one-time *vacquero*.

"Now, Nieve," Johnny said, his voice low and soft. "I know how you like to go galloping across the sand and to dip your feet into the cool ocean waters. And I know how you usually like it be just the two of us, Nieve and Johnny. But tonight, see, I've brought a very special friend of mine to come along with us."

Hearing Johnny talk to Nieve took Grace back once more to the time at Sanctuary when she had read the ribbon containing Johnny's memories. Then, she had not only seen him on horseback but also ridden for a time in his shoes. She knew that his bond with horses was a deep one.

All the time he was talking to Nieve, Johnny was stroking the palomino's face and rubbing her nose. Now, he reached into his pocket and produced a sugar cube. He laid it out on his palm and Nieve gently licked it up.

"Now you," Johnny said, glancing over to Grace. "Reach out your hand."

A little apprehensively, Grace stretched out her palm. Johnny dropped a second cube of sugar into it. "Introduce yourself to Nieve," he whispered in Grace's ear.

Grace looked into Nieve's soft brown eyes. "Hello," she said, stretching out her hand. "My name is Grace and I'm kind of nervous because I've never been riding before."

Nieve nonchalantly bowed her head and eagerly took the second sugar cube from Grace's palm.

"Well," Johnny said, "I think we're about ready, don't you, girls? Grace, I'll help you up first."

Grace turned to him, confused. "There's no saddle."

Johnny nodded. "Safer that way. If you fall, you'll fall clear. The stirrups won't drag you along. All you'll hurt is your butt and your pride." Seeing her tense expression, he added, "Don't worry, Grace. You're *not* going to fall."

Still Grace hesitated. Before she could voice any further protest, Johnny hoisted her up so she was sitting astride Nieve.

"There you go," he said. "Sit centrally, with your elbows in.

Excellent. Make sure you're gripping Nieve with your legs, it will help your balance."

Grace squeezed her legs together. As she did so, she felt Nieve move forward. She felt a wave of panic, but immediately Johnny was there, telling Nieve not to even think of going anywhere without him. The horse seemed to understand fully. Now Johnny turned to Grace. "Mixed signals," he said. "You squeezed your legs against her a little too tight and that's the signal to go."

"Oh," Grace said, "I'm sorry."

Johnny grinned. "*No problema!* Take a grip of her mane, Grace. That's it, nice and tight – she won't mind."

Grace felt surprisingly anxious and far out of her comfort zone. In spite of Johnny's calm instructions, she could sense that Nieve was desperate to break into a run across the sand. She dug her fingers more deeply into Nieve's mane, intent on making herself as secure as possible. "Come on up!" she urged Johnny.

"No place I'd rather be," he said with a wink, using a nearby rock to propel himself up behind her. "That's a good girl, Nieve," he said. As he spoke to the horse, his breath was warm against Grace's ear. She hadn't realised how close they would be once he joined her. Now, they were drawn closer still as Johnny reached his arms around Grace's waist and took up the reins.

"Lean back against me, Sugar, so you're nice and stable," Johnny told Grace.

She did as instructed, feeling a spark of electricity as her back made contact with Johnny's chest. Thinking suddenly of Lorcan, she momentarily recoiled.

"What's wrong?" Johnny asked.

"Nothing," Grace said, deciding she was being silly. Everything he was telling her to do was for her own comfort and safety. She was only going for a horse-ride with a good friend of hers. She had nothing to feel guilty about. When she next spoke to Lorcan, she'd tell him all about this. There would be no secrets between them.

Grace leaned back further so that she was completely enclosed by Johnny's chest at the back and his arms on either side. Glancing down, she could see the muscles in his forearms as he took up the slack in the reins.

Already, Nieve was beginning to walk forward across the sand. Grace laughed with pleasure and surprise. "This is easier than I thought it would be!"

"Nothing to it!" Johnny said. Though her face was turned away from him, Grace knew he was smiling.

She felt herself relax and leaned further back into Johnny's chest. Even as Nieve began to move a little faster, Grace felt perfectly comfortable. Her initial nerves had swiftly dissipated, and were replaced by a sense of exhilaration and anticipation.

"This is a trot," Johnny told Grace. "It's about the same speed as a healthy human can run. About thirteen kilometres an hour. If you listen, you can hear Nieve's hooves marking out two beats on the sand. You hear that?"

"Yes," she cried. "I can hear it . . . and I can feel it too." And, though she didn't say so, it felt pretty uncomfortable. At this rate, she wasn't sure how long she would last up here on Nieve's back without the comfort of a saddle.

Johnny was unaware of her discomfort. "Now, we're going up to what we call a collected canter. That means that Nieve is still under our control. Now you're going to hear three beats instead of two."

Grace felt their pace increase with great smoothness and, sure enough, she could hear the three beats of Nieve's gait. She glanced to her side at the waters of the bay shimmering in the starlight. It was wonderful to see it from this completely new perspective. She could see the silhouette of *The Vagabond* and the vast hulk of *The Blood Captain*, moored side by side.

Already, they had travelled some distance away from the ships. The ocean was deserted here. It was a tranquil sight, a mirror reflecting the star-filled sky above. Once more, she felt their speed increase. This time, she welcomed it.

"And now, we're in a full canter," Johnny confirmed. "This is what Nieve was wishing for, isn't it, girl?"

Now they were travelling faster, Grace was surprised to find that she felt more, rather than less, comfortable. Pressed back tight against Johnny, she felt as secure as if she was sitting in an armchair.

Grace gave herself over to the smooth, hypnotic rhythm of the ride. She felt her cares melt away. For a spell, neither she, nor Johnny, spoke. The drumming of Nieve's hooves upon the sand blended with the rush of the night air and the crashing of the ocean. It was a symphony of music guaranteed to thrill and soothe her senses.

Grace turned her face to let the ocean breeze cool her. As she did so, her cheek brushed against Johnny's. She was surprised how comfortable she felt being so close to him. Once more, she thought of Lorcan and felt a flash of guilt. She reminded herself she was doing nothing wrong. And she was having more fun than she could remember. She had been through such dark times of late. She had forgotten how it felt to be carefree. What a precious gift Johnny had bestowed on her. Why spoil it?

Nieve's long strides powered Grace and Johnny across the sand, towards the edge of the ocean. As the palomino's hooves pounded through the shallows, she sent salt water flying up into the air. Grace could taste the ocean on her lips. Her own heart was racing now, beating out the exact same rhythm as Nieve's movements.

Nieve sent a fresh spray of water over Grace and Johnny's faces. The cold shower made Grace laugh with surprise and pleasure. She turned and saw that Johnny was laughing too. His

197

face was slick with salt water. Suddenly, she felt an overwhelming desire to kiss him. They were so physically close, all she had to do was lean back a touch and . . . Johnny smiled at her, his eyes dancing with light, his lips looking more inviting than ever. Grace forced herself to turn away again, feeling flushed. She wanted to kiss him but she mustn't. It was a step too far. They rode on in silence.

After a short while, Johnny encouraged Nieve to slow down. The rhythmic pounding of the hooves turned into a regular four beats as they slowed down to a gentle walk.

"Good girl," Johnny said, softly rubbing Nieve's flank. "Time for you to rest up a while."

They came to a standstill and Johnny jumped down, then held out his arms to help Grace dismount.

Grace took a moment to adjust to standing on solid ground again. Johnny reached an arm around her shoulder. "You're trembling," he said.

"Am I?" She was – and his touch was doing nothing to calm her, quite the reverse. "I guess I'm still full of adrenaline from the ride."

Johnny laughed happily. "I knew you'd be into this," he said. "Ever since we met, I've been wanting to take you out riding. You can't really get to know me until you've been riding with me. It's who I am." He looked suddenly bashful and continued speaking, perhaps in an effort to cover his emotions. "Once we've given Nieve a little rest, we'll climb on again and ride back along the beach."

Grace smiled at the prospect.

"So," Johnny said. "Was this a good surprise?"

"Yes." She looked into his eyes. "Yes, Johnny, this was a lovely surprise. Thank you!" Feeling a surge of emotion she could no longer fight, she leaned towards him and planted a soft kiss on his salt-slicked cheek.

He grinned. "Well," he said, bringing his hand to his cheek. "That was a nice surprise too. A mighty nice surprise."

He looked more handsome than ever before. Maybe it was the moonlight. Maybe it was getting away from the ships and from the others. Maybe it was seeing him at his most natural – the way he was supposed to be. She felt as if he was lassoing her in towards him, drawing her closer and closer with every hungry second, but in truth all he was doing was smiling.

Fighting temptation like this was far from easy. Grace pulled back.

"What's wrong?" Johnny asked, his gaze steady but penetrating.

"I got carried away," she said sheepishly. "I'm having such a great time that I forgot myself."

"You're *allowed* to have a good time," Johnny said.

"Yes," Grace answered, carefully. "But I have to be fair to you . . ."

Johnny smiled. "Do you hear me complaining any?"

"*And* to Lorcan," Grace said. When Johnny didn't react, she added, softly. "My boyfriend."

Now Johnny nodded. "I understand," he said. "But Lorcan's a long way away and he wouldn't begrudge you a little harmless fun, now would he?"

Grace looked deep into Johnny's eyes and shook her head. He wasn't going to make this easy for her.

"Shouldn't we be getting back to the ships?" she said.

Johnny gazed at her. For a moment, he said nothing. Then he nodded. "All right," he said. "If you're ready. I think we've given Nieve a good enough rest, don't you?"

He went over and drew Nieve gently away from the edge of the water. "I know you're thirsty but don't even think about drinking that," she heard him say. "Salt water would play havoc with your insides."

Watching his tender approach to Nieve, Grace felt awkward.

She had kissed Johnny. Not the other way around. If anyone had taken advantage, it was *her* not him. Johnny had offered her this amazing treat and she had repaid him with churlishness. That hadn't been her intention. She decided to clear the air before the ride home.

"Johnny," she called, walking over to him. "You know that I like you, don't you?"

He smiled up at her. "I'm happy to hear that, Grace. I thought maybe you'd made your mind up about me and it was a closed book."

She nodded. "I had made up my mind, after you left Sanctuary like that. But since we've met up again, I've realised I was too quick to judge. There are lots of different sides to you."

"Well, thank you," he said. "For taking the trouble to look again." He held out his hand towards her.

She hesitated. Once more, she had the sensation of the lasso tightening.

He smiled. "I'm just helping you up onto Nieve's back, Sugar," he said.

Of course he was. She was mortally embarrassed. Bowing her head, she stepped forward and allowed him to help her up into the saddle once more.

This time, sitting up there, astride Nieve's golden back, Grace felt perfectly at home. In a trice, Johnny was up behind her, once more circling his arms around her and reaching for the reins. Grace leaned back against him, like he had told her to do before.

As Nieve began to walk back across the sand, Grace closed her eyes, savouring the moment. Things were getting complicated. She knew it. But she hadn't felt this good in a long time and she wanted to enjoy every last second of their journey home.

CHAPTER TWENTY-SIX

No Way Out

"How did Grace seem to you tonight?" Lorcan asked Darcy, as they walked away from the Captain's cabin.

"Better," Darcy said. "Back to her old self, I'd say. Calmer. Much calmer." Catching Lorcan's expression, she added, "You don't agree with me, do you?"

He shrugged and shook his head. "Maybe I'm imagining things," he said. "I just feel there's this distance growing between the two of us. I wish she would visit me on my own sometime."

"I'm sure she'd like that too," Darcy said. "But remember these astral visits are very draining for her. Maybe she hasn't built up enough reserves of energy yet."

Lorcan nodded. "Perhaps *I* should visit *her*, then?"

Darcy shrugged. "My gut tells me that you're better off letting Grace take the lead here. She's in a very dangerous position on board that ship. If you suddenly arrived at the wrong moment, though of course she'd be delighted to see you, it could throw her off track and set her back in her mission."

"You're right," Lorcan said. "I wish you weren't, but I know you are." They had already reached Lorcan's cabin. He held open the door. "Would you come inside, just for a minute? I could use the company."

Darcy nodded and stepped across the threshold.

"Apologies in advance for the mess," he said, as he shut the door behind them. His hand swept around the room, which was filled with weaponry, boots and other combat gear, piles of books and pages and pages of jottings in Lorcan's distinctive spidery writing.

Darcy's wide eyes took it all in. "Looks like your cabin's become the ship's armoury," she said.

Lorcan moved quickly around the room, doing his best to organise things into piles so that he could clear a space for Darcy to sit down. He indicated the now empty chair. As she sat, Darcy smiled warmly at her friend. "You know, it's pretty amazing how you've taken up the call to arms. I'm exceedingly proud of you."

"Thanks, Darcy," Lorcan said, smiling back at her. "You're a pal."

"It sounded from what you told Mosh Zu that your combat training is going better," Darcy said. "Is that the whole truth or were you humouring him a little?"

Lorcan sat down on the edge of the bed, stretching out his legs. "No, things are going a bit better. Thanks to you as much as anyone. Our last chat was like an injection of steel into me. I threw myself back into the job with renewed vigour."

Darcy smiled. "Glad to be of assistance!" She leaned forward, her face resting in her hands. "I'm always here for you, Lorcan. You know that, don't you?"

He nodded. "And I for you. It cuts both ways." He looked up into her eyes. "Truth is, it's going a *bit* better, but I'm a long way off transforming this ragbag crew into a viable fighting force." He paused. "I feel like I've hit a wall." Now he rose to his feet and grabbed one of the swords from the floor. He removed the sheath and executed a few moves before Darcy's eyes.

"Very impressive!" she said, clapping her hands enthusiastically.

Lorcan sat down again, the sword resting in his hands. "You're kind, Darcy, but the truth is simple. Sure, I know how to use a sword to defend myself or even initiate a one-on-one attack. But I haven't got anything like the repertoire of fighting skills or know-how required to lead a full crew into battle."

Darcy lifted a book from the pile at her feet. "*The Science of War*," she read, flipping through some dense pages and noting Lorcan's many inked annotations. "Well, no one could accuse you of not doing your homework."

"I'm doing my best," Lorcan said. His eyes, she noticed, were tired, doubtless from long reading marathons as well as combat sessions.

"That's all anyone can ask of you," said Darcy.

Lorcan shook his head. "You're wrong there, Darcy. The Captain sent word that when he returns he wants the crew of *The Nocturne* to be a viable fighting force. Ready to defend itself against attack from pirates, Vampirates, whoever. I'm charged with making that happen. It's *not* good enough merely to do my best. I've got to find some way to make a real breakthrough." He shook his head. "Reading these books is all well and good, but nothing short of a miracle is going to turn this situation around."

Darcy considered his words. Then she shut the heavy pages of *The Science of War* with a loud snap. "I've got it!" she said. "You don't need any more books. You need to draft in some genuine, first-hand military expertise."

"Darcy!" Lorcan exclaimed, "I swear, you're a genius!" He hung his head. "But how exactly do I go about finding some?"

"Good point," Darcy said, a little deflated. She drummed her fingers on the heavy tome and began racking her brains. Suddenly, her fingers became still again. "Maybe we're tackling this problem from the wrong direction," she said.

Lorcan looked at her curiously. "What do you mean?" he asked.

Darcy leaned forward, her eyes wide and bright. "Maybe we should ask ourselves . . . in this kind of situation, what would Sidorio do?"

"Hmm." Lorcan considered her words. "What *would* Sidorio do, indeed?" He nodded, mulling this over for a minute or two. Then he raised the sword once more. "I've got it!" he said.

"What?" Darcy inquired, excitedly.

"He'd kidnap a pirate captain," Lorcan exclaimed.

"Oh," Darcy said, trying to sound supportive. "So is that what you'd like to do?"

Lorcan shook his head, despondently. "Kidnap isn't really my style."

Darcy nodded, opening up *The Science of War* once more. "Back to the drawing board, then, I guess."

"The next attack is scheduled for tonight," Connor told Kally as they sat on a rocky beach, a safe distance away from *The Blood Captain* and *The Vagabond*. "The target is *The Albatross*."

Kally nodded. "*The Albatross*. Got it."

Connor ran a hand through his hair. Despite the swim, it was already almost dry from the heat of the morning sun. "Stukeley's going to lead the attack. He has a particular grudge against the ship's captain, Narcisos Drakoulis – a nasty piece of work." His hand gripped a rock at his side. Now he grabbed it and hurled it into the ocean.

Patience was not Kally's strong suit. "Spill, Connor! What went down between this Drakoulis and Stukeley?"

"It's really very simple," Connor said. "*The Albatross* is the ship Jez Stukeley died on."

Kally let out a whistle and shook her head. "This is one messed-up set of circumstances, dude."

Connor nodded, a grim smile playing on his lips. "You're right about that. And there's no easy way out of it." He looked despondently across the water to where the two Vampirate ships sat, dormant during the hours of light.

Kally nudged her friend. "Don't look so glum, Tempest. Even if the attack *is* set for tonight, we've got time. I'll set off now to rendezvous with Jacoby and Jasmine. They'll relay the intel to Cheng Li and she can get word direct to *The Albatross*. Why, I can take it to Drakoulis myself if need be." She smiled. "There's no speedier, more reliable means of communication than sea-mail!"

Connor ignored her joke. He shook his head.

Now Kally frowned. "You said before that this Captain Drakoulis was a nasty piece of work. Are you saying that you actually *want* this attack to go ahead?"

Connor conjured up a vision of Drakoulis, bragging to Molucco Wrathe as Jez Stukeley lay bleeding to death. There would be worse things than knowing that Drakoulis had gone to meet his maker. But that wasn't what was on his mind.

"It's not a question of what *I* want, Kal. If Cheng Li tips off Drakoulis and he's prepared for the attack, then Stukeley and Sidorio will know that someone close to home broke ranks. It won't take them more than five seconds to work out the most likely candidate."

Now Kally understood. "You!" she said.

Connor nodded. "Either we let this attack go ahead and do nothing to prevent it and the whole crew will be killed or converted to Vampirates . . ." He paused. "Or we tip off Drakoulis and my cover is blown."

"Let me get this straight," Cheng Li said, frowning at Jacoby and Jasmine from the other side of her desk. "The Vampirates' next attack will happen tonight. The target is *The Albatross*. And

Connor is desperate – your word – for us to turn a blind eye and just let it go ahead?"

Jasmine nodded. "That's about the sum of it, Captain."

"Connor makes a good point," Jacoby added. "If we act to prevent this attack, his cover is immediately blown. We'd have to be ready to pull him out from behind enemy lines PDQ."

"Of course, we could do that," Cheng Li said. "If we chose to."

Jasmine was disconcerted by the captain's words. Why wouldn't they choose to?

Cheng Li made a steeple of her hands and rested her chin on them, as she often did when she was sifting through complex problems. "In the scenario you present, not only would we have to rescue Connor but any inroads that he has made within the rebel camp would be instantly and irretrievably lost." Cheng Li sat silently for a moment, then pushed back her chair and rose to her feet. "From Kally's reports, it would seem that Connor has now established himself strongly with Sidorio and key Vampirate personnel on both *The Blood Captain* and *The Vagabond*." Now Cheng Li turned to Jacoby, her almond eyes boring into his. "Wouldn't you agree?"

Jacoby nodded. "Yes, Captain. It's my impression that he has successfully convinced the crews of both ships that he is Sidorio's son and is fully a part of the family."

Jasmine wondered how hard a job that had been. She pushed the thought away, determined not to reveal her suspicions to her colleagues.

"Having played the Vampirates for the fools they are," Jacoby continued breezily, "Connor is now privy to information at the very highest level."

Jasmine nodded. "As our early warning regarding this attack demonstrates."

Cheng Li's eyes were bright. "In other words," she said, "we have succeeded in our mission of placing a Federation operative right at the very heart of the Vampirate command. From hereon in, they can't make one move without us knowing about it." She snapped her fingers with satisfaction.

Jasmine's eyes remained fixed on the captain. Cheng Li returned to her desk. For a moment, she stood in front of her father's portrait and Jasmine could see the identical look of strong-jawed determination in father and daughter. Then Cheng Li sat down behind her desk once more.

"I've made my decision," she said. "Listen carefully. Here's what we're going to do."

CHAPTER TWENTY-SEVEN

Blood Brothers

"Connor, open up! Hey, Connor, let me in!"

Connor opened his eyes, wincing at the sound of a fist hammering on the metallic cell door.

"Open up!"

Recognising that the voice belonged to Stukeley, Connor rolled off his bunk and staggered, bleary-eyed, to his cabin door. The hammering continued, unrelenting.

"OK," he cried. "Wait up, I'm coming." He opened the door and his friend charged into the cell, a ball of energy and excitement, his eyes bright.

"I'm back!" Stukeley declared.

Connor nodded. "So I see. But from where?"

"*The Albatross!*" exclaimed Stukeley.

The words cut through Connor's confusion. Immediately, he understood. Stukeley had returned from his takeover mission. The Vampirates had successfully claimed their second pirate vessel.

"You should have seen him!" Stukeley said. "*Narcisos Drakoulis.*" He spat out the captain's name with obvious disgust. "Cowering at my feet – begging for mercy." There was a grim

208

smile on Stukeley's face as he continued. "I never begged *him* for mercy, did I, Connor? You remember that day."

Connor nodded, frowning. Of course he remembered that day. Jez Stukeley had fought and lost a duel with Drakoulis's prize-fighter and bled to death on the deck of *The Albatross*. That had been one of Connor's darkest days; a day that had woken him up to the brutality of his new profession. The match between Jez and Drakoulis's champion, Gidaki Sarakakino, had been unevenly matched. Jez had never stood a chance. But now the tables had been turned.

"Did you kill Sarakakino too?" Connor asked.

Stukeley met his stare. "Actually, no. I let him go." Connor was surprised. "You know why? Because he was only doing his job. Doing his captain's bidding, just as I was acting out of duty to Captain Wrathe."

Connor nodded. "You won't know this," he said, "but after you died, straight afterwards, Sarakakino came over to us. He said that you fought well, that you carried no shame."

Stukeley nodded, smiling. "I'm glad I spared him. And *only* him." There was a distant look in his eye, then it passed and he shook his head. "But look, I'm in the mood to celebrate and who better to party with than my old mucker, Mister Connor Tempest?"

Connor was unsure. "What exactly did you have in mind?"

"You and me are going to the Blood Tavern. The one at Limbo Creek. You remember the place?"

How could he ever forget? "I'm happy for your victory," Connor said, aware that he sounded far from joyous, "but I'm not really comfortable in that place."

Stukeley's face fell.

"Couldn't Johnny go with you?" Connor suggested. "Or Sidorio?"

Stukeley shook his head. "Johnny's off gallivanting with your sister. And Sidorio, well, I'll give you three guesses as to whose company *he's* keeping."

"Lady Lola's," Connor said.

"Bingo!" Stukeley mimed the release of a gun. "Anyhow, it's you I want to celebrate with, Connor. You're my mate." He stepped forward and enveloped Connor in a bear-hug, whispering in his ear, "We're blood brothers, you and me."

Connor felt his insides run cold at the words. But, like it or not, there was a certain unshakeable truth to them. Once, they had been as close as brothers; now perhaps they would be once more. And what, if not blood, united them?

As Stukeley released him from his clutches, he stared into Connor's eyes. "What's up, mate?" he inquired.

Connor weighed up his options. He needed to talk to someone and there was no better confidant than Stukeley on this particular subject.

"My hunger for blood has risen."

Stukeley nodded, waiting for his friend to elaborate.

Connor felt some of his burden lift as he continued. "It happened when Sidorio took me along on the first attack. It was one of the reasons I was so freaked out. Not just by the bloodshed around me but the fact that I . . ." He faltered. "That I could feel my own hunger for it." He dropped his eyes.

"Connor." Stukeley's voice was softer now. "This isn't something to feel bad about. It's a cause for celebration."

"Is it?"

"This, my friend, is a red-letter day." Stukeley looped his arm around Connor's shoulder. "Come on! Your old pal Stuke is going to take you out to the tavern and treat you to your first pint of blood."

Connor shook his head. "No," he said. "I'm not ready. Not yet."

"We'll see," Stukeley said. "But either way, you're coming

with me. I'm not taking no for an answer. I told you before, there's no one better than me to guide you through these changes. Talking of which, mate, would you *please* change your shirt? That one stinks worse than mine and you haven't even come from a battle!"

The Blood Tavern had seemed an alien environment to Connor the first time he had escorted Stukeley there, and it was still a forbidding place. The same milky eyes greeted them through a gap in the door on their arrival. And, as they stepped into the vestibule – resembling an old, neglected cinema – Connor recognised the strange and unique figure of Lilith, the woman who ruled the tavern from her glass pod in the centre of the foyer. Since their last visit, she had dyed her hair red, but still wore it in a distinctive beehive. Her eyelids were caked in turquoise glitter.

The last time he had come here, he and Lilith had had quite a heart-to-heart. But if she remembered him, she showed no signs of recognition. Instead, she seemed preoccupied with counting Stukeley's money.

"You're sure you don't want a go?" Stukeley asked. "There's plenty of gold in my pockets. Drakoulis was uncharacteristically generous in death."

Connor shook his head. "It's OK," he said. "I'll just wait for you to . . . finish."

Stukeley examined his friend's face, perhaps poised to try one last attempt at persuasion.

"Room Seven!" Lilith announced, inclining her head towards the velvet curtain. "Get a move on, luvvie. There are others waiting their turn."

Stukeley sauntered over to the curtain, turning to salute Connor before he disappeared into the gloom beyond. Connor retreated to the worn velvet sofas in the anteroom and watched the parade of Vampirates making their way beyond the red-velvet doorway.

"Next!" Lilith screeched from inside her gilded cage.

Connor couldn't pull his eyes from the red-velvet door. He realised that a seismic shift had occurred since his last visit to the Blood Tavern. Then, he had felt the division between himself and Lilith's clientele. The door had served as the divider. On this side, normality, mortality: on the other, a world beyond his imaginings, chaos. Now he might be sitting in the very same seat as before, but it was clear he belonged on the other side of the door. He might have eschewed Stukeley's offers of blood tonight but Connor felt in his heavy heart that it was only a matter of time before he caved in.

"You still don't feel like you belong, eh?" Stukeley asked, finding Connor waiting for him back at the boat.

Connor shook his head. "The opposite," he said. "I feel like I *do* belong. And it freaks me out."

Stukeley nodded, manoeuvring the boat away from the rock. He seemed more robust, more like he had been in mortal life. It gave Connor pause for thought. Maybe he should just give in to his hunger. But, as he thought of this, a face appeared to him in the darkness. Jasmine. He could see her as clearly as if she was standing there, watching him from the rock. Her dark, intelligent eyes were trained on him, wide with concern.

He considered their relationship. Surely it was doomed now. She had once told him that he could tell her anything and that he was not alone. Although he knew Jasmine's words were genuine, he was just as certain that her feelings would change if she ever found out the truth about him.

"Hey," Stukeley said, placing his hand on Connor's shoulder. "What's up?"

Connor sighed. "There's this girl," he began.

Stukeley smiled and rolled his eyes. "There's always a girl."

"Things are complicated, but we have this special connection," Connor said. "At least, I thought we did, but she doesn't know the truth about me and, if she did, I know that would be the end of it."

"No." Stukeley shook his head. "You don't know that at all, Connor. You're just tormenting yourself. You have a lot on your plate right now. You're only beginning to come to terms with your real identity. Getting to know your biological father and your stepmother. You're just taking your first steps through this new world. Give yourself time. And don't try to second-guess this girl . . . what's her name, by the way?"

Connor hesitated, but as he spoke her name, he couldn't help but smile. "Jasmine," he said. "Jasmine Peacock. She's really something . . ." He frowned again. "But I know her, Stuke. I know her and how she feels about Vampirates . . ."

"You're not exactly a Vampirate, are you, mate?"

Connor shrugged. "Vampirate. Dhampir. What's the difference?"

"I know you don't believe me," Stukeley said, "but I can assure you that being a Vampirate hasn't hurt my success with women any. Quite the opposite, my friend. Fighting them off, I am." He sent a couple of punches into the air. And then lost his balance. For a moment, it looked like he was going overboard. Connor laughed.

"That's better. Good to see a smile on that ugly mug of yours, young Tempest."

"You're a Vampirate," Connor said. "And the girls you like are Vampirates too. So of course there wouldn't be any issues between you. It isn't the same with Jasmine and me. We belong to different worlds."

"Oh, I see," Stukeley said. "Well, to be frank with you, even between us Vampirates the path of true love doesn't always run too smoothly."

Connor grinned. "Sounds like *you* have a story to tell! How about some details? I told you all about me and Jas."

Stukeley shrugged. "Not much to tell. Except her name is Darcy Flotsam and she's the figurehead on *The Nocturne*."

"Darcy!" Connor said. "I know her!"

"You do?" Stukeley's eyes lit up momentarily. "Well, you probably also know that I let her down. Big time. But I hope one day to convince her how crazy I am about her." Stukeley smiled at Connor. "I reckon this Jasmine must be a pretty amazing girl if she's having this effect on you. Have faith that you'll be able to make it work, mate, just like I do with Darcy. You can't keep a good buccaneer down!"

Connor felt his spirits lift. Maybe Stukeley was right. Even if there was only the merest glimmer of a chance, it was enough for him to seize onto.

Connor and Stukeley were met on the deck of *The Blood Captain* by Johnny. He waved to them and ran over.

"Stukeley, *mi amigo*, I hear congratulations are in order!" He smiled and shook his head. "You took *The Albatross* and all its crew. The captain is pleased as punch."

"Is he?" Stukeley couldn't keep the pleasure out of his voice.

"Oh yes," Johnny said. "Yes, you've certainly set a benchmark for the rest of us. I can't wait for my turn!"

"Your turn?" Connor said. All his feverish thoughts of the night were displaced by this new seed of information. Clearly the next attack was already being planned.

Johnny nodded. "Yes sirree, I'm going to be in command of the next takeover mission and I do not intend to disappoint."

"Any idea which ship you're going after, mate?" Stukeley asked.

Johnny's eyes shone in the moonlight. "The captain and Lady Lola are still making their final decision, but they've narrowed it down to two." Connor felt tense beyond measure as he waited for Johnny to continue. "Either *The Typhon* or *The Diablo*."

"*The Diablo*?" Connor and Stukeley exclaimed in unison.

"You know it?"

"Erm, yes," Stukeley said. "That was our ship. Back when we were pirates."

"Your ship?" Johnny let out a whistle. "So if I get it, should I be merciful to the captain?"

"Molucco Wrathe?" Stukeley said, turning to Connor. "Show mercy to Molucco Wrathe? The man who was responsible for getting me killed? What do you reckon, Connor? What would *you* do if you were taking a walk in Johnny's shoes?"

Connor thought of Molucco. The man whom he'd first viewed as a loveable rogue, then as a substitute father. Increasingly, however, he had come to view Molucco as something else. Someone more dangerous and irresponsible. It was true that if anyone was responsible for Jez's death, it was Molucco. Even so, the thought of him being slaughtered by Johnny and the Vampirate crew made Connor feel sick.

"Go on, Connor," Johnny said. "Tell me what you think."

Connor pointed up above his head. "I think we should get back down below deck. The sky is beginning to lighten. Night is fading."

"As ever, young Tempest makes a good point," Stukeley said. "Come on, my two blood brothers." He stretched out his arms and propelled his comrades towards the door leading down and away from the danger of the fast-gathering light.

CHAPTER TWENTY-EIGHT

Code Silver

Cheng Li pushed open the doors to her cabin. Cate followed her inside and closed the double-doors carefully behind her.

"Have a seat," Cheng Li said, gesturing to the round table she often used, in preference to her desk, for strategy discussions.

Cate sat down.

"Water?" Cheng Li lifted a carafe. "Or I could offer you something stronger from my private bar?"

Cate shook her head. "Not for me, Captain," she said. "Water is just fine."

"You're probably right," Cheng Li said, pouring herself a glass. "Well, then, you were going to debrief me on the latest developments in combat training. What's the story?"

Cate nodded. "It's going well. Should the need arise to defend ourselves against Vampirate attack, I think we could fight a good fight . . ."

"It's not a question of *if*, Cate, but when. And to *think* we can fight isn't good enough. I need to be *certain*, which means *you* need to be certain."

Cate nodded. "I completely understand your position, Captain

Li," she said. "My problem is that we haven't yet tested my training against any Vampirates. Until we do, I have no absolute way of knowing whether we're on the right track or not."

Cheng Li took a sip of water and lifted her pen to scribble a note on her pad.

Cate tried to read the writing upside down but was interrupted by a sudden hammering at the cabin doors.

Cheng Li frowned. "I specifically asked *not* to be interrupted," she said, rising to her feet. "Who is it?" she called.

In answer, the doors opened and Jasmine and Jacoby strode in.

"We're sorry to interrupt your meeting," Jacoby said.

Now Jasmine spoke. "We have a Code Silver situation."

Cheng Li nodded. "Cate, we'll have to resume later. Jacoby, Jasmine, what's going on?"

Cheng Li strode along the grand hall of the Pirate Academy, flanked on either side by Jasmine and Jacoby.

"Captain," Jasmine said. "Before we go in, could I have a moment alone with you?"

"No," barked Cheng Li. "In a Code Silver scenario, every second counts. If you wanted to raise something with me, you should have done so on the journey here."

Jasmine flushed. "I was hoping to be able to talk to you *alone*, Captain," she said. "It's about Connor."

"Why would you want to talk to Captain Li without me?" Jacoby asked.

"It doesn't matter now," Jasmine said.

"No," agreed Cheng Li. "It doesn't. Whatever this is about, it will have to keep."

Jasmine and Jacoby exchanged strained glances as Miss Martingale sped towards them, her heels clicking on the black-and-white chequered marble tiles.

"Captain Li," Miss Martingale said. "Captain Grammont, Commodore Black and the others are waiting for you in the vaults," she said. "I'll take you down." She pushed open the door to the headmaster's study, which was currently deserted. Marching briskly to the headmaster's antique writing desk, she reached out for the hole-puncher and depressed it five times. As she did so, one of the leather wall-panels obligingly swung open.

"Follow me!" chirruped Miss Martingale, twisting her brooch until it illuminated. She led the way down the spiral staircase into the vaults below.

"They're in Room 9 today," Miss Martingale said.

"Thank you," said Cheng Li. "We'll take it from here, Frances."

Miss Martingale stood still and gave Captain Li the Federation salute. "Always a pleasure to see you, ma'am," she said. "Whatever the circumstances."

"Likewise," said Cheng Li, returning the salute and knocking on the door to Room 9.

"*Entrez!*" called Rene Grammont.

Cheng Li led Jacoby and Jasmine into the room, which – like many of its neighbours – housed a long meeting table, composed from the timber of former pirate vessels. Stretched along the table were the great and the good of Pirate Academy and the Pirate Federation.

"*Bienvenue!* Welcome!" exclaimed Captain Grammont. "Under the circumstances, we'll keep introductions brief."

"Understood," Cheng Li said. "I believe you all know my deputy captain, Jacoby Blunt, and I'm sure Lieutenant Jasmine Peacock is no stranger to you either."

"Indeed not," said Lisabeth Quivers. "We never forget our straight-A students! Of which we now have three in the room."

There were nods and murmurs all around the table. "Please,"

Captain Grammont said. "Take a seat and bring us up to date on the latest developments."

Cheng Li and her comrades sat down. "As I indicated in my message, we have a Code Silver scenario. I could have sent word via Kally—"

"She's the undercover fishtail you've been using, *oui?*" Grammont said.

"Quite so," Cheng Li said with a nod. "And I could have sent her with a full message but I thought it best to talk to you in person."

"We're all ears," said Commodore Black, blunt as ever.

"This situation concerns the whole Pirate Federation," Cheng Li said. "But three of us in particular." She glanced to the far end of the table, speaking the names as she met the faces. "Trofie Wrathe, Barbarro Wrathe and Molucco Wrathe." She paused. "Our intelligence reports that tomorrow night one, possibly both, of your ships will be attacked by the Vampirates."

There was a sharp intake of breath around the room.

"You'll be aware," Cheng Li said, "that two Federation vessels have already been attacked and commandeered by Vampirate forces – *The Redeemer* and, latterly, *The Albatross.* To the best of our knowledge, the captains and crews of both these ships have been killed, though our intel suggests that efforts are underway to revive certain pirates in an effort to recruit them to the Vampirate ranks."

"By intel," Barbarro Wrathe spoke now, "I assume you are referring to your undercover operative, Connor Tempest?"

Cheng Li nodded. "As you know, we have persuaded Sidorio – self-styled King of the Vampirates – that Connor is his son. Connor's mission is proceeding extremely well and the intelligence he is sending back via Kally is of a higher and higher calibre."

Molucco Wrathe gave a hollow laugh.

Cheng Li's eyes flashed lightning at him. "Do you have something to contribute, Captain Wrathe?"

"Why yes, Captain Li." Molucco's eyes sought out his old sparring partner. "If Mister Tempest's intelligence is so very good, how do you explain the fact that he did not relay information ahead of the attacks on the other two Federation vessels?"

Cheng Li did not miss a beat. "I'd like you all to imagine the perilous position in which Connor is working. Never, in the history of the Federation, have we had a spy in the enemy camp before. Connor is risking life, limb and blood vessels for the Federation – for each and every one of you."

"We do understand that," Lisabeth Quivers said, her voice – as usual – pouring balm on troubled waters. "And we greatly appreciate both Connor's bravery and your *coup-de-grace* at finding a way in for him."

Jasmine frowned. Cheng Li hadn't found a way into Sidorio's lair. The door had already been open. She was sure of it. And Captain Li had sent Connor into the inferno without a thought for his safety. She would have this out with her – as soon as the opportunity presented itself.

"Captain Quivers speaks on behalf of us all," said Captain Grammont. "We salute you, Captain Li, and your young and superlatively talented crew." He smiled inclusively at Jasmine and Jacoby.

"Thank you," said Cheng Li. "The fact is that Connor had no prior warning of the first attack on *The Redeemer*." She hesitated. "As for the second . . . on *The Albatross*. Well, as a matter of fact, we did have prior warning of this . . ."

Jacoby turned to Cheng Li, open-mouthed. He couldn't believe she was going to surrender this information so willingly. To say that she had a captive audience was an understatement.

"Yes," continued Cheng Li, "we *were* warned about the attack

220

on *The Albatross* but I myself took the decision to withhold the information."

There were gasps around the table.

"You sent Captain Drakoulis to his death!" exclaimed Apolostolos Solomos.

But support came from a surprising quarter as Commodore Black piped up. "Don't you get it? Captain Li was caught between a rock and a hard place. If she tipped off Drakoulis, then she might have saved his ship but she'd have blown Tempest's cover. His mission – which, as Captain Li says, is unprecedented in Federation history – would have ended before it began."

"All the same—" protested Francisco Moscardo.

He too found himself cut off by Commodore Black's reedy voice. "Captain Li took a decision that every military commander, myself included, has to take at some point in their career. She elected to lose a battle to win the war."

Cheng Li found herself in the unfamiliar waters of feeling grateful and well-disposed to Commodore Black. "Exactly so," she said.

"And yet," Captain Kirsten Larsen said, entering the fray, "you took the decision to alert us today to the fact that either *The Diablo* or *The Typhon* is next on the Vampirates' list?"

"Would you rather she had kept silent and allowed us to die?" snapped Trofie Wrathe.

"Of course not," Captain Larsen continued calmly. "I'm just trying to understand Captain Li's rationale. What makes you and your ship different to Captain Drakoulis and *The Albatross*?"

"It's a fair question," Cheng Li said, glancing from Trofie to Barbarro to Molucco. "And I confess I was torn. By preparing you, I am still risking Connor's personal safety – which, of course, I take very seriously – and, more fundamentally, the ongoing success of his historic mission." She sighed. "However, when Jasmine and Jacoby brought me news of the attack plans, it seemed to me that I had to share the information with you. Either of your ships – possibly both – will be targeted tomorrow night. The situation with the Vampirates is escalating."

Commodore Black nodded. "You made the correct call," he said. Then he addressed the group as a whole. "We'll supply both crews with the Vampirate defence kits created by Captain Li and her team."

"I'm happy to stay on and talk you through the new weaponry we have created and our defence procedures," Cheng Li said. "It won't take long and it would be preferable to reading it from a manual."

"Thank you." Barbarro and Trofie Wrathe spoke in unison. All eyes turned to Molucco.

"Erm, thanks but no thanks," he said. "I have some pressing business of my own to attend to."

Barbarro turned to his brother. "What on oceans could be more urgent than preparing your ship and crew for imminent attack by these demons?"

Molucco was already standing. Now he placed a hand on his younger brother's shoulder. "What is *always* the most urgent thing on a pirate captain's mind? Treasure! My new acting deputy has identified a very promising lead, which I intend to follow up on, swiftly."

"Please reconsider," Cheng Li said. "This will only take a few minutes of your day. And the work we have done could save your life and those of your crew – my former comrades."

Molucco gazed at Cheng Li and shook his head. "I've given you more minutes out of my days than I can bear to contemplate," he said. Turning to the others, he waved his arms in the air. "Haven't you all forgotten something? A pirate's life was ever a short but merry one. We've faced dangers before and lived to raise the sail again."

"Brother!" Barbarro exclaimed, rising to his feet. "This is a new kind of danger altogether. Have you forgotten Porfirio? *You* may be ready to lose another brother but I certainly am not. Reconsider. At least take the defence kit with you."

"All right," Molucco said, impatiently. "I'll take the kit if it makes you all feel better and, later on, *after* my business is concluded, I promise to read Mistress – I'm sorry, *Captain* – Li's latest manual from cover to cover."

With that, he swaggered towards the door. As Molucco passed Cheng Li, Scrimshaw leaned out from amongst Molucco's dreadlocks for a moment. Jasmine thought there was a pleading look in the snake's eye. She shook her head – she was letting her imagination get the better of her now.

After Molucco departed, Captain Grammont spoke. "Might I suggest that we all stay for Captain Li's briefing. It's clear to me that the stakes have indeed risen and we should all be as familiar with the new weaponry and procedures as possible."

There was a rousing chorus of "hear, hear" along the table.

"Twenty-minute break," Commodore Black announced. "Then we all reconvene."

Jasmine finally got a chance to talk to Cheng Li alone on the academy terrace during the break.

"I'm sorry about earlier," Jasmine said. "I was worried about Connor, but now I know that we're pulling him out, everything's fine."

Cheng Li looked at Jasmine curiously, sipping a refreshing bowl of sea-urchin tea.

"We *are* pulling him out," Jasmine said, "aren't we?"

Cheng Li shook her head. "The intel he's delivering is too valuable to us to abort his mission at this point."

223

A searing pain shot through Jasmine's head. She couldn't believe what she was hearing. "But what you said in there – about how seriously you take Connor's safety . . ."

Cheng Li nodded. "I'm one hundred per cent committed to each and every member of my crew."

"Then you *have* to pull him out," Jasmine said. "Today!"

"No," Cheng Li said.

Jasmine's face was steely. "I'll break rank and brief Kally myself if I have to," she said.

Cheng Li smiled softly and took another sip of tea. "Jacoby's already on his way to brief Kally," she said. "I've removed you from that duty. From now on, Jacoby will liaise with Kally solo."

Jasmine's eyes frantically scoured the terrace for a glimpse of Jacoby. He was nowhere to be seen. It must be true, then. He was already on his way to meet Kally.

Jasmine shook her head. "You knew," she said. "Somehow you knew that I'd worked this out. That you didn't come up with this brilliant ruse that Connor is Sidorio's son. He really *is* a dhampir. You've just played the situation for all its worth."

Cheng Li smiled at Jasmine. "If anyone was going to work it out, it was you. I know how close you've grown to Connor, even if Jacoby is blind to this development. You're the sharpest mind on my crew. That's why I need you close. Like now. You're going to come back inside and join me in briefing the captains on all our thorough research."

Jasmine bit her lip. "Give me one good reason why I shouldn't leave you here and go after Jacoby. Or, better yet, go after Connor myself."

Cheng Li set down her tea-bowl. "Lieutenant Peacock, the depth of your loyalty is one of your most impressive traits," she said. "But, number one, you signed up to the articles of *my* command and, number two, you have spent your entire life

224

training to play a vital role in pirate history. Since you were a child of seven and first sailed through the academy arch, you have been waiting for your moment. That moment is now. There are bigger issues at stake here than one young pirate or, indeed, young dhampir."

Jasmine shook her head and a single tear rolled down her cheek. Cheng Li knew that her words had hit home. When push came to shove, Jasmine Peacock was made of the exact same material as herself. Her every bone, and her every impulse, was committed to the cause.

"No doubt you're feeling a mixed bunch of emotions towards me at this precise moment," Cheng Li said. "Trust me, this will soon settle. And please be assured that I have no intention of losing Connor at this point. If you want to play a role in keeping him safe, stay close to me and do as I say."

"Do I have a choice?" Jasmine asked, lifting her thumb to wipe away the tear.

"Do any of us?" asked Cheng Li, turning and leading the way back inside.

"Well, Cate," Cheng Li said, hours later, as she pushed open the doors to her cabin. "Ready for that drink now?"

Cate shook her head. "Water's still good for me. After your meeting with the Feds, I'm sure to be working late tonight. I intend to keep a clear head." She sat back down at Cheng Li's conference table and found herself looking at the captain's notepad and the brief scribble made during their earlier meeting.

As Cheng Li sat down opposite her, Cate laughed. "Did you actually write: *action, CL – kidnap Vampirates for CM?*"

Cheng Li looked across at Cate, puzzled. "Yes," she said. "Do you have a problem with that?"

The two women locked eyes. Cate shook her head. Every

time she thought she had the measure of the captain, something happened to force her to reassess.

"*She* may not have a problem with it, but I surely do."

The voice came from the other end of the cabin. Both Cheng Li and Cate were immediately on guard, their eyes sweeping the room, swords at the ready. It was then that they noticed that the chair behind Cheng Li's desk was out of its usual position. It slowly spun around towards them.

"You!" exclaimed Cheng Li. A smile broke across her face. "Well, if I can forgive *anyone* for trespassing into my cabin, it's you." She locked eyes with the interloper. "Though, really, we have to stop meeting like this!"

He nodded, stood up from the chair and made his way over to join the women.

"Cate Morgan," Cheng Li said, with an air of formality, "I'd like you to meet Lorcan Furey. Lieutenant Furey, this is my combat consultant, Cate."

Lorcan reached out his hand and gripped Cate's. "Ms Morgan, your reputation precedes you," he said. "In fact, you're the reason I'm here. I need your help."

Cate looked as if her eyes would pop out of her head. "*You're* the Vampirate Lorcan Furey?" she stammered. "And you came to see *me*?"

He nodded, fixing her with his piercing sky-blue eyes. "One and the same," he said. "Though to bring you up to speed, we are now calling ourselves the Nocturnals, so as to distance ourselves from Sidorio and his kin."

Cheng Li nodded, approvingly. Just like the last time they met, she found it impossible to take her eyes off the young Vampirate. If anything, he seemed to have grown *more* captivating since that visit. It was an effort to compose herself but somehow she managed. "Take a seat, Lieutenant Furey. What did you mean before, when you said you needed our help?"

"It would perhaps be more accurate to say that I've come, on behalf of the Nocturnals – the benign Vampirates, if you will – to propose an alliance."

"An alliance?" Cheng Li considered the delicious possibility of an alliance with Lorcan Furey.

"Let me guess," Cate said. "You want to kick Sidorio's sorry butt out of the oceans but you can't do it alone."

"Bingo," said Lorcan, smiling and nodding at Cate. "I rather thought you might be feeling the exact same way."

CHAPTER TWENTY-NINE

Slumber Party

Once more, Grace was out riding on the beach through the darkest hours of the night. With every night, she was becoming a more assured horsewoman. Tonight, at last, Johnny allowed Nieve to increase her pace from a canter to a gallop. Grace flushed with pride and excitement; she knew that it was a mark of his confidence in her. It felt second nature to her now to entwine her fingers through the soft strands of Nieve's snowy-white mane and lean back into Johnny's chest. As Nieve thundered across the border of land and water, Grace tightened her hold but felt a deep thrill pulse through her. Salt spray splashed up onto her face. She turned to Johnny and saw that he was drenched too. He was laughing, his mouth open to reveal teeth as smooth and white as Nieve's mane. These midnight rides had become so special to the two of them. It was a secret they shared; a deep and powerful secret. As Nieve increased her pace once more, Grace was thrown back into Johnny's arms. He caught her and steadied her. Then he leaned forward and kissed her hungrily on the mouth. She did nothing to resist . . .

Grace awoke with a start, her heart still hammering as if she truly had just been out riding. It was a shock to find herself alone and still within the confines of her cabin aboard *The Vagabond*. She had grown accustomed to taking a siesta after Tiffin, finding that a little nap left her feeling refreshed and full of energy for the rest of the night. But tonight, she felt far from refreshed. Her dream had seemed very real. She could smell the sea air and taste the salt on Johnny's lips. Lips that she ought not to have been kissing, even in a dream.

She took some calming breaths and came to a decision. She had to talk to Lorcan. She couldn't remember the last time they had talked properly – not since she had arrived on *The Vagabond*. She had allowed herself to get distracted – initially by Lola and latterly by Johnny. She realised that, with everything going on here, she had convinced herself that checking in with Lorcan wasn't important. She felt guilty admitting this even to herself. Right now, there was nothing she wanted more than to hear Lorcan's voice, see his face, feel his arms encircle her.

She closed her eyes and spoke his name. Wherever he was, he would hear her calling to him. As she had been trained, she visualised his cabin door before her. With every second, she made it more and more concrete in her head. Once more she spoke his name. Still, there was no response. She tried a third time. Silence. She drew her focus even more deeply into the vision until she could see her own hand on the door, twisting the handle and pushing it open.

"Grace!"

It wasn't Lorcan's voice but that of a young woman. Grace frowned.

"Grace! Wakey, wakey!"

She realised that the voice was coming not from within her vision but from outside her cabin. Frowning, she opened her eyes and looked over to the doorway. It was ajar and

Mimma's head was poking around, an amused smile playing on her lips. "Sorry, hon, I didn't mean to interrupt your slumber . . ."

"It's OK," Grace said. "Actually, I wasn't sleeping."

"No?" Mimma said, breezing into the room as if she owned it. "What exactly *were* you doing then, sitting there with your eyes tight shut? Meditating?"

Though she had grown to like her and, to some degree, to trust her, Grace was reluctant to tell Mimma the truth. Instead, she raised her palms. "It's a fair cop," she said. "I *was* sleeping."

Mimma laughed. "I knew it!" she said. "You can't pull the wool over old Mim's eyes." She plonked herself daintily down on the bed and unzipped her bag, busily removing handfuls of items and laying them out on the bed.

Grace watched her with curiosity. As she did so, the door opened again and Jacqui and Nathalie swept into the room. Both were carrying bags – Jacqui's was like a small briefcase; Nathalie's was broader and made of wicker.

"Hi, Grace!" trilled the new arrivals in unison as the cabin door swung shut behind them.

"Hello," said Grace, adding, rather unnecessarily, "do come in!"

Jacqui and Nathalie came to stand on either side of Mimma, nodding approvingly at the array of make-up she had lined up on the eiderdown. Then they set their own bags down on the bed. Jacqueline snapped open her briefcase. Inside its dark interior, various strips of sharp, shiny metal flashed. Grace leaned forward to get a better look but before she could do so, Jacqueline stepped in front of her. What was going on? Grace was a little unnerved as Jacqueline began running her fingers through Grace's hair. "Like this," she heard Jacqueline say, "or like that?"

"Like that!" Nathalie said.

"Definitely," agreed Mimma.

Now Grace saw Nathalie lift a box out of her own bag, followed by a glass cake stand. Winking at Grace, Nathalie set the cake stand on the low table by Grace's chair. "I just love a slumber party, don't you?" she said, arranging tiny pink macaroons on the cake stand.

"Slumber party?" Grace said. "I don't think I've ever been to one before."

"You're joking?" Jacqueline said, turning towards her. It was then that Grace noticed the rather large pair of razor-sharp scissors Jacqueline was brandishing in her hand.

"What are those for?" Grace asked, somewhat nervously.

"Why, to cut your hair, of course," Jacqueline said, brandishing them as if they were a lethal weapon. "We thought it was time to sharpen up your look."

Mimma nodded. "You're quite a natural beauty, Gracie, but even natural beauty needs a little work to bring it out."

Nathalie smiled and held out a tea plate and napkin to Grace. "Have a macaroon. They're to die for and – you know what they say – pink calories don't count!" Grace found herself reaching out to the stand and taking a macaroon from it. She didn't even bother setting it on the plate, instead dropping it straight into her mouth. It was absolutely delicious, as light as air.

"Another?" Nathalie grinned, pushing the cake stand in Grace's direction.

As Grace nibbled more politely on the second cake, she found that Jacqueline had already draped a towel around her shoulders and spritzed her hair with water. Now, she was combing it out busily.

"Now then," Mimma addressed her, kneeling at her feet. "Time for an important decision!" She held up two small glass bottles of nail polish. "Which do *you* prefer?" Grace was surprised that her own preference was being sought. She pointed to the vial in Mimma's left hand. "That one, I think. The darker one."

"Good choice," said Mimma, throwing the other bottle over her head.

Grace reached out and helped herself to another macaroon. "Would anyone else like one?" she asked, realising that she had consumed almost half of them single-handedly.

Seeing her expression, Nathalie smiled. "Don't worry, Grace. There's plenty more where those came from. Enjoy! This is a night of treats for you!"

"It certainly is," said Mimma, holding Grace's big toe steady as she applied the first drop of paint. "Now, tell us about you and Johnny!" she said, with a wink.

Grace felt suddenly hot. Her head raced with images of herself and Johnny on horseback. The dream she had not long woken from.

"You're blushing!" Nathalie said, in her sing-song voice.

"Of course she's blushing," Jacqueline said, from above Grace's head. "She likes him. And who can blame her? Johnny's hot!"

"We're just friends," Grace protested.

Mimma said nothing but her raised eyebrow spoke volumes.

"He certainly seems to enjoy taking you out riding," said Jacqueline.

"You know about that?" Grace said, deflated. "That was supposed to be our secret."

"Now don't look so dejected," Mimma said, the red of Grace's toenails reflected in her eyes. "*He* didn't say anything."

"We saw you," Nathalie explained. "You looked like you were having heaps of fun. And, from what I could see, you're quite an accomplished horsewoman."

Grace blushed, partly from the memory and partly from the compliment. "I really shouldn't be talking about Johnny," she said. "And I shouldn't have gone riding with him. I already have a boyfriend. His name is—"

"Now, Grace, we're all friends here." Mimma's voice drowned hers out. "So no one's going to judge you. That's right, girls, isn't it?"

Nathalie and Jacqueline murmured their assent.

"Johnny is quite a catch, I reckon," said Mimma. "We've all been batting our lashes at him since we made his acquaintance but it seems he only has eyes for you!"

"You know he used to ride rodeo?" Jacqueline said. "He's as wild as a stallion, Grace, but maybe you can tame him."

"He's the most dreamy-looking of Sidorio's crew," added Nathalie. "There's no question about that. His skin is like caramel – and those eyes!"

Nathalie passed Grace another cake. "So?" she said.

As Grace lifted it to her lips, she found that all the frantic activity around her had suddenly stopped. Mimma had frozen, brush in hand. Nathalie was dead still, her hand on the cake stand. Even Jacqueline had put down her scissors and gone to join the others. Now, all three girls gazed at Grace expectantly, their eyes bright and hungry for answers.

Grace looked from one black heart to another. "I'd be lying if I said I wasn't interested in him," she found herself confess.

"One final touch," said Mimma, nodding happily, then reached inside her bag. "Perfume!"

She dabbed the glass stopper behind Grace's ear lobes and on her wrists. "Isn't it delicious? I reckon it smells like a summer's afternoon – not that I've seen one of those in a long time!"

The perfume did indeed smell delicious – a fragrant blend of nectarines and honey. Mimma reinserted the stopper in the bottle and stepped back to survey her work. "Pretty as a picture," she declared, holding out a hand to Grace. "Come and take a look at yourself in the mirror, missy."

Grace had been sitting for such a long time that she felt rather giddy as she crossed the room to the dressing-table mirror.

At first her appearance was a shock, but then Grace smiled. The girls had done a wonderful job. Jacqueline had left most of the length of her hair but had cut into it and given it a much sleeker and more sophisticated shape. It made her look like a young woman – like the other three, in fact. She brushed her hand through it, noticing with pleasure her painted fingernails. Then she looked straight forward to appraise her face: her eyes looked bigger, her lips a little fuller, her cheekbones sharper.

"Thank you," she said, overcome with emotion. "Thank you all. I feel wonderful."

"Wait 'til Johnny cops sight of you," said Jacqueline.

"He'll swoon," agreed Nathalie.

Grace blushed, but found herself laughing with the rest of them. "Actually, I have an idea." She leaned forward to whisper in Mimma's ear.

"Not fair!" said Jacqueline. "No secrets!"

Mimma laughed. "Be quiet, you! Grace, that's a wonderful idea. Of course, I can do that." She reached for her brushes and set to work.

"What did she ask for?" Jacqueline persisted.

It didn't take Mimma long to complete the job. "Perfect!" she proclaimed.

The other girls turned at her words and gasped.

"What is it?" Grace asked.

"You're . . . you're one of us now!" Jacqueline stammered.

"Let me see!" Grace said, excitedly.

Just as she had requested, there, around her right eye, was the black heart tattoo. Not a real tattoo, of course. Not yet. But it looked just the same. There was no doubt it suited her. It made her eye look even more like a glittering emerald.

Grace sighed, turning from the mirror to her friends. "Thank you all so much. What shall we do next? Are there any more of those delicious macaroons?"

"Actually, honey, we've got to run," Mimma said, dropping the last of her supplies into her bag and zipping it shut.

"Look at the time!" Jacqueline said, grabbing her own case. "Lola will be waiting for us."

"She certainly will," said Nathalie, slipping the empty cake stand back into her bag, leaving one solitary macaroon on the coffee table.

"I'll come with you," Grace said.

"Oh no," Mimma said. "No, sweetie, you may have a black heart but I don't think you're ready for where we're going." Kissing the air on either side of Grace's cheeks, she slipped out through the door as swiftly as she had arrived.

Jacqueline kissed Grace in a similar fashion, then followed in Mimma's wake.

Grace reached out a hand to Nathalie's wrist. "Tell me," she said, "where are you going?"

Nathalie considered the question for a moment. "On a kind of hunt," she said, smiling softly. Then she too kissed Grace goodbye and departed, closing the door tight shut behind her.

Grace felt the emptiness and silence of the cabin which, only seconds before, had been filled with the girls' voices and laughter. She crossed the room to look at her reflection once more. She found herself pouting into the mirror. Why had they left her like this? She had the black heart now. She was ready to go hunting with them, whatever that entailed.

She folded her arms crossly and turned away from the mirror, taking stock. Seeing her robe sprawled across the chair, she remembered that she'd been trying to reach Lorcan when the girls had surprised her with their impromptu slumber party. She could try him again now, she thought. But, as she settled back down into her chair, she realised that it was no longer Lorcan she wanted to talk to. There was only one Vampirate on her mind. She smiled. Johnny.

Lola laughed with delight as Mimma updated her on the slumber party. "This is proving easier than I thought," she said. "Don't you see, my dear? Grace longs to be one of us. She aches for it."

Mimma shrugged, gratefully accepting the glass of vintage blood which the captain now held out to her. "That's not the only thing Grace longs for. A certain former rodeo star has got your stepdaughter a little hot in the saddle."

Lola beamed with pleasure. "Is that so? Well, it seems as if the cowboy is holding up his end of the bargain." She sipped her own drink. "Tell me, how did Nathalie's special patisserie go down?"

Mimma smiled. "Grace couldn't get enough of them. She has an appetite, that one."

"Yes." Lola nodded, decisively. "I believe we have Grace exactly where we want her," she said. "No more blood for the next few nights. Do you understand?"

Mimma nodded. "Yes, Captain."

"No more blood," Lola repeated, smiling. "That should send little Grace's burgeoning appetite through the roof!"

CHAPTER THIRTY

Under Attack

"I don't like this," said Trofie Wrathe, pacing up and down the captain's cabin in what appeared to be a silver catsuit but was, in reality, her new made-to-measure lightweight battle armour.

"I know, my dear," answered Barbarro. "But we have clear instructions. We have to operate on a constant state of red alert. We're in direct danger. Either our ship or my brother's is the Vampirates' next target. We won't know which until it happens."

Trofie sighed. "We've faced off that ghastly Lady Lockwood before. Why must we hide down here? If she or her consorts dare to board *The Typhon* again, I want to be the one to throw the first weapon." As she spoke, she ran the fingers of her golden hand over her new silver sword, with which the Federation had lately equipped her.

"Captain Li is the leading authority on all matters Vampiratical," Barbarro reminded his wife. "She and her team have devised the template for fighting these creatures. What Li and her crew don't know about Vampirates isn't worth knowing." He shook his head. "Frankly, my dear, I'm as uneasy as you about all this. It's not in my nature to hide away below decks and wait to be attacked. But we are dealing with a new kind of enemy and I'm ready to listen to those who have more experience of them than us."

Trofie stretched out her golden hand, its ruby fingernails shimmering in the candlelight. "Need I remind you, husband, that I myself have direct and personal experience of those vile creatures."

Barbarro shook his head, soberly. "No, *min elskling*, you do not need to remind me. It cuts to the very core when I think what that harpy did to you." He drew his wife to his broad chest, wrapped his arms around her and kissed her porcelain-smooth forehead.

Trofie's frown became a smile. "You *never* call me *min elskling*," she said. "I like it."

Just then, there was an almighty thud on the ceiling above them. The captain and his deputy froze. A cacophony of shouts, several crashes and cannon-fire followed.

Trofie leaped out of her husband's embrace and reached once more for her new silver sword, drawing it from its sheath. "So," she said. "It appears that the Vampirates have made their choice."

"Yes," said Barbarro, his voice strong as steel. "And now we act to defend not only our ship but our entire way of life. And to avenge my brother's death."

"Yes," agreed Trofie. "Let's destroy Porfirio's murderers and waste no time about it!"

Hand in hand, they pushed open the cabin door and, with a speed belying their years, raced to join the fight.

The Friday night crowd thronged into Ma Kettle's Tavern, having been frisked by the tough but exceedingly charming Pieces 08. "Enjoy your night!" he called after the latest arrivals, tossing their confiscated swords into a numbered chest for safe keeping.

238

Ma Kettle herself stood stock-still in the centre of the main bar-room, surveying the scene around her. She felt as if she was the fixed point at the centre of a carousel. Around her, everything was moving, loud and blazing with colours. Ma's team of serving girls and boys were athletic, almost balletic, in their movements as they ferried drinks to the insatiably thirsty customers and collected up the empties. Ma watched it all as she had done night after night, year in, year out for as long as she could remember. They said that times were changing in the pirate world but Ma knew one thing for certain: whatever new dangers there might be, pirates would always have need and want of a tavern like this where they were assured of a warm welcome and a well-priced drink.

Ma's reverie was broken by the arrival at her side of her trusty second-in-command, Sugar Pie, who held an improbable amount of empty glasses in her fingers.

"A busy old night, tonight!" Ma declared. "How's my crew bearing up?"

"We're fine," said Sugar Pie who, like Ma, had the capacity to remain calm and collected whatever mayhem was going on around her. "After all the dark murmurings of late, I think everyone's pleased as punch to see so many punters in."

Ma Kettle nodded. "Just like old times," she said, a flicker of sadness in her eyes.

Sugar Pie caught the change in her boss's expression. "Are you all right, Ma?" she inquired.

"Oh yes!" Matilda Kettle said, coming back strongly, as was her wont. "Yes, my dear, I'm fine. Just can't help getting a little nostalgic on nights like this. You wait until you get to my age . . ."

"You're *not* old, Ma!" insisted Sugar Pie.

Ma gave a shrill laugh. "If I'm not old, I must be dead because I've been hanging around this blessed bar-room for the best part of a century!" She smiled tenderly at Sugar Pie. "You're young, dear. We look at life from different ends of the spectrum. You see what's up ahead; the future is exciting to you. But I can't help but look backwards." She paused, looking out once more at the giddy carousel of the tavern. "Sometimes, on nights like this, I look around and everyone seems so young. Everyone but me. Maybe I'm getting too old for this game. Maybe it's time to cash in my chips and buy a little place in the sun."

Sugar Pie shook her head and, setting her empty glasses onto the bar, drew Ma into her arms. "Maybe you just need a night off. Can you remember the last time you put your feet up? No, I didn't think so."

"I'll be all right," Ma said. "Look, isn't that the crew of *The Diablo* coming in now?" She raised a smile. "Lucky will be here soon. He'll cheer me up."

"Yes!" Sugar Pie said. "Molucco always cheers you up. I've an idea. You go and freshen up your make-up. And I'll pop a bottle of his favourite oyster champagne on ice in his VIP booth. What do you say?"

"All right,' Ma said, her eyes brightening. Sugar Pie watched as she hurried away to make herself look nice for Molucco. Ma had told no lie – she was no spring chicken. Yet, beneath the lines and the layers of make-up, her face still lit up like a young girl's when she talked of Molucco. It was, Sugar Pie reflected, a shame that the pirate captain had never made an honest woman of the tavern owner. She smiled. Maybe there was still time.

"Moonshine!" exclaimed Barbarro and Trofie in unison.

They had reached the upper deck on *The Typhon*, expecting to encounter the first vanguard of Vampirates making their attack. Instead, they found members of their own guard surrounding their teenage son, who looked decidedly peeved about it.

"What's going on?" Barbarro demanded of his son. "Where have you been? You were supposed to stay in your cabin tonight. Do you have *any* concept of the danger we're all facing?"

Moonshine ran a hand nonchalantly through his hair. It didn't get very far – his hair was thick with grooming product. "Not that it's really any of your business, Pops, but I was out on a date."

"A *date*!" Barbarro was incredulous, his face the colour of overripe plums. "We're in danger of attack from the Vampirates and you slip out on a date?!"

Trofie couldn't help but smile. "Who's the lucky girl? Anyone we know?"

"Classified information, I'm afraid, Ma." Moonshine folded his arms across his chest. "And just because we may – or may not – get attacked by demon goths, is that any good reason for me not to pursue a healthy and active social life?" He glared at his father. "Pops, do you think you could order these goons off me?"

"Erm, yes," Barbarro said gruffly. "Stand down, crew!"

"I'm sorry, Captain." The leader of the brigade turned and strode over. "But we were under strict instructions to fire the cannon and initiate the defence strategy the moment we were boarded." He shook his head. "Please believe me, Captain, we had no idea that it was Master Moonshine."

Barbarro nodded and squeezed his lieutenant's shoulder. "I do believe you. You have nothing to reprimand yourself for, Lieutenant. You acted exactly as instructed. It seems that, *once again*, it is *I* who must apologise for my son's incomprehensible behaviour." He gazed with fury at Moonshine. "Rest assured, he will be *severely* punished for this."

"Oh Daddy, please don't take the t-bird away!" Moonshine rolled his eyes. "Like my life could *get* any worse!"

"Go to your cabin!" bellowed Barbarro with such force that, for once, his son made no protest but simply slunk away across the deck. His mother turned and watched him go, her mind running through an inventory of talented young daughters of pirates who would make a suitable match for her son and heir.

Barbarro stepped forward, clapping his hands and calling the crew to attention. "Good work!" he cried. "Let's treat this unfortunate incident as a successful rehearsal. You did exactly as instructed in an attack scenario. We're not out of danger yet so reload the cannon and resume your positions. The night is still young."

The united cry of "Aye, Captain" was thunderous. The pirates of *The Typhon* moved swiftly to fulfil their captain's command and resume their positions.

"Come, Trofie," said Barbarro. "We must return below."

"Yes," said Trofie, marching briskly along at his side. For a moment she was distracted, thinking about the dress she would commission to wear to Moonshine's pirate wedding. Time for some silkworms to get to work. Then she brought herself back to the matter in hand. As ever, Trofie Wrathe possessed a keen sense of priorities. First slay every last bloated bloodsucker. *Then* put in a call to her personal stylist.

Sugar Pie noticed that Molucco's VIP booth was still empty. She decided to refresh the ice in his champagne bucket – when he arrived, late and thirsty, he would not take kindly to drinking lukewarm champagne. As she slipped under the velvet rope to retrieve the ice-bucket, she heard a voice behind her.

"Has he *still* not arrived?"

Sugar Pie turned to see Ma Kettle. Anxiety was etched across her painted features.

"He'll be here soon," Sugar Pie said, slipping back from under the velvet rope. "I'm sure of it. I was just going to fetch some fresh ice."

In spite of Sugar Pie's light tone, Ma's expression remained grave. "You'll think I'm a foolish old woman," she said, "but I have a feeling things aren't right with him. That he needs me."

"Molucco?" Sugar Pie said. "Why would you say that?"

Ma shrugged. "He's always been a wild one, my dear. That's one of the things I love about him. But wild ones like Lucky need steady people around to fence them in and protect them from their wilder instincts. He *had* good people – Cate Morgan, Bartholomew Pearce, Jez Stukeley – God rest his soul – and young Connor Tempest. Why, even Cheng Li was a good influence, though Lucky wouldn't thank me for saying so. But, one way or another, they've all gone now and I'm worried that Molucco's lost the vital balance he needs."

As she said the name, a young pirate came over to join them. "I couldn't help overhearing," he said. "Are you talking about Captain Wrathe?"

"It was a private conversation," Ma snapped at the newcomer. Seeing first his youthfulness and then the deep red of his blush, she softened. "Yes, as it happens, we were talking about Molucco. What's it to you?"

"I'm on Molucco's crew," the young man said, bowing before her. "Kane Eden Charles . . . the Third."

Ma shook her head. "I thought you looked familiar. I remember your father and grandfather." She was lost in thought for a moment.

Sugar Pie took the opportunity to address the young pirate. "We were just wondering whether Captain Wrathe might be coming in tonight?"

Kane Eden Charles the Third nodded and smiled. "I'm sure

he will, but I surmise it will be a while longer. We had a very successful raid today and the captain is in his cabin, counting his booty."

"There you go!" Sugar Pie punched the air with relief. "Do you hear that, Ma? The pirate king is in his counting house, counting out his filthy lucre!"

Kane Eden Charles the Third suddenly smacked his hand to his forehead. "You're Ma Kettle . . . I mean *the* Ma Kettle! I've heard so much about you, from my pa and grandpa, and others besides. You're a pirate legend!"

"Thank you, dear," said Ma. "I was feeling old before you arrived. Now, I feel positively mummified."

"No offence intended!" said Kane Eden Charles, blushing furiously once more.

"None taken," said Sugar Pie, smiling softly and drawing Ma away. "Look, if Molucco's going to be a while in his cabin, why don't you take a bottle of fizz over and keep him company?"

Ma considered the proposition, then shook her head. "No," she said. "He won't want interrupting. I know him. I know him better than anyone. I shall wait for him here."

Sugar Pie gazed at Ma. "In that case, I think you should go and have a rest. I can manage things out here quite well. The minute he arrives I'll come and find you."

Ma seemed about to protest but instead nodded gratefully at Sugar Pie. "You're a good girl," she said, lifting a strand of Sugar Pie's silky blonde hair and brushing it tenderly behind her ear. "The daughter I never had but always dreamed of." Her eyes budded with tears. "Oh dear, waterworks! What on earth's gotten into me tonight?"

"You're just tired and emotional," said Sugar Pie. "Go and put your feet up in your cabin. Even if it's just for twenty minutes, you'll feel restored. I'll brew up some reviving sea-urchin tea and bring it in."

Ma smiled. "A little disco nap. That's what we used to call it. Maybe that's all I need." She turned and looked imploringly at Sugar Pie. "You'll come and find me the minute Lucky arrives?"

"The very second he walks in," Sugar Pie said. "I promise."

In fact, Molucco Wrathe was *not* alone in his cabin on board *The Diablo*. Sitting on a pile of silk cushions on the chair opposite the captain was his trusty pet snake and constant companion, Scrimshaw. Together, they were surveying the haul of fine gemstones from that day's raid.

"Feast your eyes, Scrim," said Molucco. "Did you ever see such rare beauties?" In one eye, Molucco wore a jeweller's optic and he lifted a sapphire up in his hand and drew it closer to the lens. Suddenly, he gasped. "After all these years!" he exclaimed. "I've found it. The perfect sapphire!"

Cradling the jewel in his palm, Molucco removed the optic and set it down on the table. Tears of joy streaked his lined face. "Oh Scrimshaw, I'm a happy fellow today. The perfect sapphire. Who ever would have believed it? Why, I'd begun to think there was no such thing." He held out the gem to Scrimshaw to appraise. Scrimshaw slid off his cushion and set off across the table to investigate.

"There's a good boy," Molucco said, gently stroking the snake's skin. "You've been my most faithful companion these past few years," he said. "How old are you now?" He thought back. "Why, it's nigh on twenty years since my brother Barbarro and I found you and your brother Skirmish. Twenty years! That's more than many a pirate's lifespan. We shall have to plan a celebration!" Molucco smiled at the reptile who was twisting and turning amongst the glittering jewels.

"I've had my fill of human company,' Molucco said. "Too many have come and gone, taken advantage or even betrayed me." He took a snifter of rum. "When push comes to shove, my friend, there are just two things I can count on . . . my sapphires and you!" The snake looked up at Molucco and it seemed as if perhaps he understood his master's words. "Here's to you!" said Molucco, raising his glass once more.

"Well now, this *is* a cosy scene, isn't it?"

Molucco gave a start to hear another voice in the room. His eyes roved darkly about the place as he saw three people circle the table – a young man and two attractive young women. The man was dressed, ludicrously, in a cowboy hat. The two women wore cloaks, fastened with glittering brooches. Molucco's eyes were immediately drawn by the gemstones. Glancing up, he saw that both women sported heart-shaped tattoos around their right eyes.

"So you've come to pay me a visit, have you?" Molucco said. "First, you kill my dear brother, Porfirio. Then you make off with my sister-in-law's hand. And now it's my turn to be boarded."

"That's a fair assessment of the situation," answered the man. His companions smiled.

"They told me to expect a visit," Molucco said, perfectly calmly. "Oh yes, they had all kinds of ideas and instructions about how my crew and I should defend ourselves."

The man's smile froze. "You knew we were coming?"

Molucco smiled, addressing Scrimshaw once more. "They weren't expecting that, do you see? They think they have all the answers but they're wrong."

The man removed his hat. "Forgive my incivility. My name is Johnny Desperado and these ladies are Nathalie and Jacqueline. We are, to coin a phrase, Vampirates."

"Yes, yes, I know what you are." Molucco stared at Johnny and chuckled. "Vampirates, eh? You look more like a cowboy to me."

Johnny shrugged. "A man may be many things at once."

246

The two women were looking at Scrimshaw. "He's a beauty," said Jacqueline, reaching out a bare arm from under her cape. "Come and say hello, you handsome fellow." She held her arm steady and Scrimshaw coiled himself about it. Jacqueline laughed softly. "Would you look at that?" she said. "He's like a piece of living jewellery."

"Unhand my snake, madam," said Molucco petulantly.

Jacqueline smiled prettily. "It's he who has *my* hand bound, sir. Not the other way around. He seems to like me."

Molucco frowned. "Well, you've popped by to say hello. Time you were leaving. I'm not in the mood for social niceties."

"That's quite all right," Johnny said. "We won't take up much more of your time, will we, ladies?"

He turned to his companions. They both smiled, their incisors nudging over their open lips.

Molucco turned to Johnny. "What are you doing here? *The Diablo* is a private ship. How did you get past my guards up on deck?"

Johnny shrugged. "We killed them," he said nonchalantly. "Oh, but you might like to know, they put up a pretty good fight."

"Yes." Nathalie licked up a stray glob of blood from beneath her lip.

"You killed them?" Molucco asked, shaking his head. "Why? I don't understand any of this."

"It's really very straightforward," Johnny said. "We've come for this ship."

"Well, you can't have it," Molucco raged. "Go away! It's my ship. Always has been, always will be."

Johnny smiled and shook his head. "Haven't you heard? The times, they are a' changing, grandpa, and we're expanding our fleet." He planted his feet wider apart on the cabin floor. "It's my job to bring this ship under our control tonight."

Molucco thrust back his chair angrily, and stood face to face with Johnny. "If you want this ship, you'll have to kill me first."

The men locked eyes. Molucco's were full of fury but Johnny's were full of fire. Nevertheless, Johnny shook his head. "I would gladly kill you," he said. "But, see, I'm a gentleman and I promised you to these two ladies." With that, he nodded, and Jacqueline and Nathalie closed in on Molucco in a pincer movement.

"Would you like me to take care of the snake?" Johnny asked Jacqueline.

"Oh, yes, good idea." Jacqueline passed Scrimshaw over to Johnny.

"No!" Molucco protested. "Do what you want to me, but don't harm one scale of Scrimshaw's!"

Molucco was in no position to negotiate. He was now completely frozen in the two demons' clutches.

Johnny cradled Scrimshaw in his arms. "You might want to turn away about now, little buddy," he said.

CHAPTER THIRTY-ONE

The Morning After

Ma Kettle opened her eyes and took a moment to adjust to her surroundings. She was lying on her bed, still dressed in her trademark crinolines. Through a tear in her ancient curtains, a sliver of greyish light nudged hesitantly into the room. Ma was disorientated. Could it really be morning already? She reached over to the old whisky barrel she used as a night-stand and fumbled for the glasses which she rarely wore outside this room. The glasses were propped against a cold pot of tea which had sat there, untouched, since it had been brought in. Dimly, Ma remembered Sugar Pie's offer of a soothing brew.

Glasses on, she scrutinised the clock ticking away on the wall, its swaying pendulum shaped like a dropped anchor. A quarter past seven already! No! She had settled down for a nap the evening before and slept right through. She frowned. This was most uncharacteristic. Maybe she was coming down with something. Yes, she thought grimly. *Age*.

It was far from an easy manoeuvre swinging her vast skirts and the legs contained therein off the bed and onto the floorboards below. As she stood up straight, Ma Kettle caught her breath. Memories of the night before were beginning to drift back to her. The busy tavern. Her conversations with Sugar Pie and that young pirate, barely old enough to run a razor over his cheeks. What was his name? Did it even matter? Above all, she remembered waiting for Molucco to arrive. And waiting. And waiting.

He had never come, she thought now, shaking her head. Or maybe he had. Maybe, while she was out for the count in her quarters, he had sauntered into the tavern and helped himself to that bottle of oyster champagne they had put on ice for him. Yes, of course that's what must have happened.

Ma pushed back the curtain. The morning light was weak but still sufficient to make her squint. Outside, a fine rain was falling. She opened her window a touch to let in some air. Something was niggling her. If Lucky *had* come over, then surely he'd have popped by to say hello to her? He was no stranger to her quarters and Sugar Pie would have known to let him through. A cold river of panic flowed through Matilda Kettle's veins.

She cast a cursory glance at her old looking-glass, frowning at her reflection, then exited her bedchamber, without bothering to slip shoes onto her stockinged feet. The tavern was quiet as a graveyard at this time of the morning. It was always the case. Ma's young workers would have flopped down exhausted onto their mattresses not long ago, so by now would be in a deep sleep, grabbing the vital rest needed between one night's mayhem and the next.

Ma liked to walk alone through the tavern most mornings. As she strode between the empty tables and chairs, the place would pulsate with memories of happiness and laughter remembered jokes and incidents from the evening before and the one before that. Her happy thoughts would stretch back night after night after night and through the many years since she had first erected that flashing neon sign on the cliff-top and welcomed pirate crews from far and wide. It seemed only a giddy moment ago but, in truth, it was a long time.

This morning, as she walked through the deserted tavern in her stockinged feet, noticing the empty chairs and half-drunk tankards, Ma wasn't filled with her usual high spirits. This morning, the emptiness got to her old bones. She found herself thinking of all the pirates who had been and gone – who had drunk and danced and laughed here and then gotten themselves killed and dragged down to Davy Jones's locker. "I'm getting maudlin!" she scolded herself. "Better buck up my thoughts before the kids wake up!"

Ma managed to raise the flicker of a smile as she passed beneath the skull-and-bones glitterball which hovered over the dancefloor. She walked on to the door which led out onto the terrace, and pushed it open. The fine rain fell on her painted face and seeped into her stockings but somehow she didn't mind. There was an underlying warmth to the rain. Ma could feel it bringing her gently back to life.

She stepped out onto the wooden boards of the terrace, softly shutting the door behind her. As she did so, she noticed a ship sailing across the horizon; a pirate vessel on its way. It made her smile once more. A new day was beginning. In the end, that was all you could hope for and give thanks for; one more day in this hurly-burly world.

It was then that Ma noticed she was not alone on the terrace. Someone was sitting at the table at the far end, also watching the ocean. She would recognise that silhouette anywhere. Her heart lifted. Molucco Wrathe. She could spot him a mile off, even without her secret pair of glasses; such was the deep connection between the two of them. So, he *had* come to the tavern! But why was he sitting out here in the falling rain? Why hadn't he come to find her? She strode over to his table, determined to get some answers.

She hadn't yet reached the table when she realised that something was wrong. There was no doubt it was Molucco. You couldn't mistake those rainbow-coloured dreadlocks or the blue velvet tricorne hat he wore jauntily over them. But he was perfectly still. Too still even to be sleeping. Besides, no one slept sitting up like that.

Her heart in her mouth, Ma hastened her step. Her stocking snagged on a jagged piece of decking and she felt a splinter pierce her foot. Still, she kept on walking towards Molucco.

She could scarcely bear to look, but she knew she had to. As she stood in front of the table, she beheld the most terrible sight of her life. However long she lived, nothing would ever appal her more. There, facing her, was her own dear Lucky, Captain Molucco Wrathe. He was dressed in his usual finery, but every last drop of blood had been drained from him. His circular blue glasses still rested on his mummified nose.

"Oh, Lucky!" cried Ma, conscious of how inappropriate his nickname seemed now. He was gone – a pirate legend and the love of her life. She had always imagined they would end up growing old together someplace. Now reality slashed through that fantasy. Molucco wouldn't grow any older. It was unbearable. "*My* Lucky!" she wailed. "How *could* you go and leave me?" She had never felt such loneliness.

It was then that she noticed a small movement at Molucco's shoulder. His hair brushed forward, as if blowing in the breeze. But it wasn't the breeze. It was Molucco's pet snake – his dark eyes filled with the same pain and bewilderment as Ma's own.

"Oh, Scrimshaw!" Ma exclaimed, as the snake came fully into view. "Oh, my poor dear Scrimshaw. You were with your beloved master to the end."

The snake stared sadly at Ma, then turned his desolate face

252

and burrowed back into the familiar sanctuary of Molucco's rainbow dreadlocks.

In the captain's cabin on board *The Blood Captain*, the celebrations had gone on — below decks of course — long past daybreak. Sidorio and his two lieutenants lounged around, the many empty bottles in close proximity telling the tale of their revelry.

"And do you know what he says to me then?" Johnny's words were beginning to slur into one another. "I'll tell you what he says . . ."

Stukeley interrupted his friend. "No, *I'll* tell you. He says, 'If you want this ship, you'll have to kill me first.'"

Johnny waved his finger towards Stukeley. "Yesss!" he exclaimed, surprised. "Exactly right! How did you know?"

Stukeley shook his head, grinning. "Because that is the twenty-sixth time you've told us the story."

Johnny shrugged, reached for the open bottle at his side, and took a slug. "It's a story worth telling!"

Sidorio smiled paternally at his lieutenants. "You did good tonight, Stetson," he said, turning his head. "Just as you did when you took *The Albatross*, Stukeley. You've both proved to me that you are ready to become captains."

"I'll drink to that!" Stukeley reached for the bottle nearest to him and held it out to the others. The three bottles chinked. "One for all . . ." Stukeley said, looking hopefully at the others. Sidorio and Johnny gazed back at him, blankly. "And all for one!" Stukeley said. "Just once, you'd think you might remember!"

There was a knock at the door.

Sidiorio glanced up. "Come in!"

The door opened and Obsidian Darke entered the room like a dark cloud. "You asked to see me, Captain," he said, his cold eyes sweeping across the scene and registering his evident distaste.

"That's right, Lieutenant," Sidorio said, reaching into the crate and extending a bottle in Darke's direction.

"No thank you," Darke said. As Sidorio arched an eyebrow in disbelief, he added, "I make it a policy not to drink after sun up."

"Suit yourself." Sidorio unscrewed the cap and helped himself to the liquid inside. "Delicious! You know, Darke, you should loosen up, have a little fun. All work and no play makes Darke a very dull Vampirate."

Johnny laughed and added, "Dull, dull, dull."

Giving their words the barest of acknowledgements, Obsidian Darke carefully moved aside some of the empty bottles and sat down. "When I heard you wanted to see me at this hour, Captain, I thought it must be an urgent matter indeed."

Sidorio grinned. "You mean to rouse you from your beauty sleep?" He nudged Johnny, who cracked up laughing. Stukeley chuckled too, and swigged more blood.

"I did not mean that," Darke said.

Sidorio set his bottle on the floor and wiped the smile from his face. Suddenly he was all business. "I do have something of the utmost importance and urgency to discuss with you. Earlier tonight, Johnny here brought in *The Diablo*. You may have heard of this pirate ship. It's something of a legend. Stukeley was, in former times, one of its crew and I myself sailed on it once, albeit briefly. Now, it's part of our fleet."

"Kudos to you, Lieutenant Desperado." Obsidian Darke turned and nodded formally at Johnny.

"It's *Captain* Desperado, now," Johnny corrected him.

"Indeed?" Obsidian Darke's eyes narrowed. "*The Diablo* was captained by Molucco Wrathe, if I am not mistaken. What of him?"

Johnny giggled. "I let Lola's girls do their work. We left him at his favourite tavern; found him a table with a great view!"

Darke's face was impassive. "A trophy," he said, disparagingly. "And his crew? How many did you convert during this attack?"

Johnny shrugged. "Just a few. Most of them were off getting rat-faced in the tavern."

"I see," Obsidian said, smiling at Johnny. "In other words, you are to be congratulated for invading a deserted ship."

"It wasn't deserted." Stukeley came to his friend's defence.

"There's no need for us to argue over semantics," Darke said, smiling in an utterly humourless fashion.

"No need for us to argue *at all*," Stukeley said. "We were enjoying a very happy celebration before you arrived."

"Nothing," Darke said, "would please me more than for you to recommence your jollity." He turned to Sidorio. "Captain, shall we dispatch our business?"

Sidorio smiled. "It's very simple, Lieutenant. See, as we are expanding our fleet, myself and my co-commander – that's my lovely wife – need to see who has what it takes to step up to the rank of Captain."

Darke nodded. "And?"

"Good news!" Sidorio announced. "You've made it to the final cut. Now I just need to see the fire in your eyes. So I'm giving you a mission. *You* will lead the next attack. I'm looking for great things from you, Darke."

Once more, Obsidian Darke nodded.

Sidorio nudged a well-thumbed sheet of paper in the Vampirate's direction. Darke reached out his long, white fingers and took it.

"It's the list of pirate ships we're taking to build our fleet," Sidorio explained. "I've crossed out the ones already secured by myself, Stukeley and Johnny. You can take your pick of the rest. You have forty-eight hours to prepare for the attack. Choose whichever of the crew you'd like to back you up. Except me. obviously. I never deputise for anyone."

"Indeed," Darke said, passing back the list and rising to his feet. "Will that be all?"

Sidorio nodded. "That's all."

"Which ship have you chosen?" Stukeley asked.

Darke's cold eyes swept across his three comrades. "*The Tiger*," he said.

Johnny laughed.

Stukeley let out a whistle. "You don't mess around, mate, do you?"

"It seems my choice is a source of some amusement to you?"

"No, no," Stukeley said, exchanging a grin with Johnny. "Except you might find *those* pirates just a bit better prepared for the fight."

Darke raised an eyebrow.

"It's the ship of Vampirate assassins," Johnny explained.

Darke did not react. "I will go and begin planning my strategy," he said. Nodding at Sidorio, he turned and made his exit.

As the door closed smartly behind him, Johnny swigged from his bottle again. "I don't like that *hombre*," he said.

"Nobody does," Sidorio replied. "That's what I like about him!" He frowned. "However, he certainly knows how to break the party mood. I'm going to hit the sack."

Stukeley nodded. He pointed at Johnny whose eyes were already closed. "Looks like our little cowboy is ready for the night-train to Slumberville too!"

"Not in my cabin!" Sidorio boomed, giving Johnny a sharp kick with his boot.

"What's that?" Johnny asked, his eyes opening wide in confusion. "Where am I?"

Ignoring Johnny's ramblings, Stukeley addressed Sidorio.

"Captain, there's something I've been meaning to tell you all night but somehow I just never got around to it."

"I'm tired now," Sidorio said. "You've missed your window. Try me again later."

Stukeley persisted. "It's about Connor."

Sidorio's interest was immediately piqued. "What about Connor?"

"It's good news," Stukeley said. "The news you've been waiting for, in fact."

Sidorio drummed his feet on the floor. "Go on."

Stukeley smiled. "His blood hunger has risen," he said.

Sidorio's eyes widened. He grinned, his gold incisors glinting in the lamplight. "Stukeley, my old friend, this news calls for another drink. Wake up Sleeping Beauty over there and crack open another few bottles."

CHAPTER THIRTY-TWO

The Hunt

Darling Grace,
Wakey, wakey! I hope you slept well and had delicious
dreams. The girls and I are heading out from the ship on a
little jaunt this evening and we'd love you to join us. Our
carriages arrive at ten o'clock sharp. Wear something
gorgeous and meet us up on deck.
LLL xxx
P.S. Please bring the attached with you. It may come in
handy later!

Lola's note brought a smile to Grace's face. She had just woken up but it was only eight o'clock so she had plenty of time to get ready. She felt full of energy – in fact rather restless – and a trip away from the ship with Lola, Mimma and the gang sounded just the ticket. Grace wondered if they might bring along some more of those delicious rose-coloured macaroons. She had certainly missed nibbling on them the past couple of nights.

Grace noticed the paper clip peeping over the corner of Lola's note. Turning the paper over, she found a playing card resting under the clip. Intrigued, she slipped it out and held it up to the light. It looked like a regular playing card – the Queen of Hearts – only it was black. Grace smiled, wondering if it was part of a game they were going to play later. Then she set down the card and Lola's note for safe keeping and opened up her closet. She had a very important decision to make: which dress and shoes should she wear for tonight's outing?

Grace was dressed and ready to head out by nine-thirty. She had butterflies in her stomach but she wasn't sure why. How could time be dragging so slowly?

There was a knock on her door and gratefully she ran towards it. Who could it be? Maybe Johnny, she thought with a smile.

Opening the door, she found Mimma standing there, impeccably dressed and groomed as usual.

"I love your outfit," Grace said, as she let Mimma in.

"Yours too!" Mimma said. "I don't think I've seen you in that dress before. The colour really brings out your eyes."

Grace flushed with pride and anticipation of the night ahead. "I'm really looking forward to our outing," she said. "Do tell me where we're going and what Lola has planned!"

Mimma smiled. "All in good time, dear. I guarantee it will be an evening to remember." She snapped open her handbag. "Seeing as you're coming out with us all tonight, I thought you might like me to give you the black heart again." She held up her make-up brushes, ready for action.

"Oh yes!" Grace said. "That's a wonderful idea."

Mimma set to work. As before, she was meticulous. Finally, she set down her brush and led Grace to the mirror to assess her handiwork.

"It looks great!" Grace said. "Oh, but you've done it around my *left* eye. You all wear your hearts around your right eye. Only Lola has hers on the left."

Mimma smiled and put her hand on Grace's bare shoulder. Grace realised she was trembling, for some reason. Mimma's touch helped to steady her.

"You're special," Mimma said. "You're Lola's daughter now."

The others were waiting up on deck as Mimma led Grace out, arm in arm. Lola turned and broke off from the group. She looked stunning in a long coat trimmed with fur and a hunting hat with a spray of exotic feathers tucked in the brim.

"Good evening, Mimma. And who's *this* sophisticated lady?" Lola's head turned slowly from side to side. "Could it be? No, I don't think . . . but it is . . . why, Grace Tempest. Look how you've grown up before our very eyes!"

Grace flushed with pride once more. "Thank you," she said, still a little nervous. "I hope you don't mind my wearing the heart . . . On the left, I mean."

Lola smiled and clasped Grace's hands. "I love it!" she said. Her eyes met Grace's. "My dear, you're shaking. We had better get you into the warm." She turned to address the rest of her crew. "Come on, everyone! Our carriages await!"

The five carriages trundled up the hill road, each pulled by a black horse. Grace thought of Nieve and wondered if Johnny might be out riding her alone tonight. The rider of her carriage didn't look unlike Johnny – though, Grace reflected, not quite so handsome. Each of the young male drivers of the five carriages was dressed formally in a black tail-coat and top hat.

Grace rode in Lola's carriage, along with Mimma and Zofia. They had loaded what looked like three chunky briefcases in with them and these were placed on the floor of the carriage now, wobbling from side to side as the wheels trundled along the uneven track.

"Are those picnic boxes?" Grace asked.

260

The others laughed at that.

"No," said Mimma.

"She's not far off the mark, to be fair," Lola said, turning her face to the carriage window. "We're almost there, now. Look, Grace, isn't that a handsome house? Not unlike the one I myself was raised in."

Lola's gloved hand tapped the window pane. Grace leaned across and glanced out. The track continued up to the very top of the hill. And there, nestling right on top, like a beautiful iced cake, was a white mansion with columns around the entrance.

"It's lovely," Grace said, sitting back against the seat once more. "Does it belong to friends of yours? Are they having a party?"

Lola smiled brightly. "Yes, dear. Something like that."

The five carriages drew up around the ornamental fountain in the centre of the driveway. As Grace stepped down from their carriage, it looked like a fairy-tale setting with the water speckled silver in the moonlight.

Lola strode over to the driver. "Thank you, Rodrigo," she said. "Wait here for us. You know the drill."

"Yes, ma'am," said the driver, doffing his hat at the captain.

Grace looked back, seeing a number of familiar faces stepping out from the other carriages – Jacqueline, Nathalie, Jessamy, Camille, Leonie and Holly. There were sixteen of them in all, each beautifully dressed; each of them carrying a chunky black case.

"What *are* those cases?" Grace asked Lola. "Why don't I have one?"

"Don't fret, dear," Lola said. "You're mainy here in an observational capacity."

"Observing what?" Grace wondered aloud.

Lola didn't answer. She was already at the door, rapping the

261

elaborate brass knocker loudly. There was a brief delay and then the door opened, revealing a brightly-lit hallway inside. A smartly-dressed valet appeared and Lola leaned forward to speak to him. As she did so, the pair disappeared from Grace's view. In any case, she was distracted by Leonie and Holly who had come over to compliment her on her dress and the black heart "tattoo".

"It will be time for you to get a proper one soon," Leonie said.

Lola reappeared on the front steps and clapped her gloved hands briskly. "Come on in, ladies! I'm afraid we'll have to make our own way to the dining room. It seems the valet is indisposed."

Lola stepped inside and the others followed. As Grace entered the hallway, she noticed something lying on the floor. No, not something but *someone*. It was the valet. His face was pale grey and there was a pool of crimson blood flowing from two piercings on his chest.

"On you go, Grace," said Holly, catching her eye. "I'll deal with him." So saying, she crouched down beside the man and snapped open her briefcase. Grace saw her reach inside for some equipment. Was it some kind of medical bag?

"Come on!" Mimma swept Grace off along the corridor.

It was an impressively long hallway but Lola seemed to know exactly where she was headed. Fifteen pairs of heels clicked on the marble floor-tiles. Grace felt butterflies in her stomach once more, as they turned a corner and moved like a Chinese dragon towards a pair of double doors at the end. Lola positioned herself in the centre of the doors and adjusted her hat and coat. Jessamy and Camille took hold of a door each. They exchanged a nod with Lola, they pulled them open. Lola strode into the room.

Jessamy and Camille ushered their crewmates in after the

captain. Mimma took Grace's hand and led her towards the dining table at the centre of the room. An elegantly-dressed group of people appeared to be in the closing stages of a very fine dinner party. Grace counted the heads at the table. Twelve. Then she looked around the table at her crewmates, each standing poised with a black case at their side.

The silver-haired man at the far end of the table rose. "What is the meaning of this intrusion? Who are you?"

Lola unpinned her hat. "Colonel Marchmain," she said. "Surely your memory isn't as poor as all that? I'm Lady Lola Lockwood Sidorio, proprietor of the Black Heart Winery. I made an appointment with you regarding our wares. Surely you haven't forgotten?"

Lola noticed that the elderly but well-groomed woman at the other end of the table was now shooting daggers at the old colonel. He shook his head. "I don't remember any kind of appointment with a winery," he said, shaking his head.

Lola frowned. "Well, this is a little awkward. As you can see, it's not just a matter of inconvenience to myself, I've brought along the whole winery team." Lola gestured around the room at her colleagues. You could have cut the tension in the room with a knife.

"Geoffrey!" exclaimed the woman at the end of the table. "I don't know what's going on here, but please tell this ghastly woman to leave. I will not have my daughter's engagement soirée ruined! Get them out!"

"Leave this to me, Honoria," the Colonel said gruffly. "I have everything under control." He approached Lady Lola, who observed him with cool detachment, hands on hips. "Now look," said the Colonel, "I don't know quite how this confusion has arisen, but I don't recall making an appointment with the Black Heart winery or any other winery. The fact of the matter is I buy all my vino from Clarke's. Always have done." His tone softened. "That said, in light of the fact that you and your colleagues have been inconvenienced, for whatever reason, I would be amenable to setting up a meeting at another juncture to discuss a small order."

As Lola weighed up his words, she slowly peeled off her long gloves. Then she shook her head sharply. "There will be no need for another appointment, Colonel. We're not here to *sell* you wine. This is more of a harvesting mission."

The Colonel stared blankly at her. Grace felt her heart racing. Suddenly, she understood what this was all about. How could she have been so slow?

Lola snapped her fingers. "Ladies, to work!"

Grace stood out in the hallway. She had felt faint in the dining room watching Lola and her crew go about their business. It had been strange. She wasn't sure it was wholly down to repulsion, either. She had felt an element of hunger too – and it was no longer a hunger for patisserie or any such conventional foodstuffs.

Out of the corner of her eye, she saw Holly unplugging her equipment from the corpse of the valet. Holly wiped the nozzle and then zipped it neatly back into the pack she wore around her waist, before turning her attention to the six bottles standing beside her. She screwed a cap onto each bottle in turn and loaded them into her black briefcase. Grace watched in fascinated horror. She remembered her earlier thought that the cases might have contained their picnic – and Lola's words: "*Not far off the mark.*"

A cry and frantic footsteps drew her attention away from the case. She turned and saw a young woman running towards her. She was bleeding from her thorax and, as she ran, blood spattered her pretty tulle dress. "Please!" she cried to Grace. "Help me!"

Grace nodded. "Come on!" she said. "I will . . . I will help you." Holly turned in surprise as Grace took the girl's hand and ran down the steps and through the open doorway out into the night.

At the fountain in the driveway, the girl stopped for a moment, drawing breath with a sob. "They've all been killed. And worse . . ."

"It's all right," Grace said, holding the girl steady in her arms. She found herself face to face with her. The girl was pretty and not much older than herself. Grace remembered the older woman's words before. She looked at the girl. "Tonight was your engagement party, wasn't it?"

The girl nodded, tears trailing down her neck and mingling with her blood. "It's all over now. Everything's over."

"Yes," Grace said. She found herself looking at the warm blood still budding on the girl's décolletage. Suddenly, all she could focus on was the blood. The girl's words, her tears, were lost to her. All Grace could think about was her own hunger, taking over each of her senses, driving her forward.

Before she knew what she was doing, Grace found herself bending forward, licking the blood. She felt the girl recoil but, instinctively, Grace gripped her tighter, pressing her against the edge of the fountain. Suddenly, her butterflies were gone. So too was that strange feeling of hunger. Now Grace knew exactly what she needed . . . She leaned forward once more.

Just then, Grace felt a pair of hands pulling at her waist.

"Grace! Let her go!" It was Lola.

Grace clung tightly on to the girl but Lola's grip won out. As she pulled Grace away, the girl fell, limp, to the gravel below.

Lola looked at Grace and shook her head. "My, my," she said. "You are a little greedy guts, aren't you?" She reached into her pocket and produced a handkerchief, then wiped away the ring of blood from Grace's mouth.

"That's better," Lola said. "Now, you should know that we have a certain way of doing things around here. And that is not it."

Lola's crewmates began exiting the house. They strode over to the waiting carriages, stilettos crunching on the gravel, briefcases in hand.

Lola clicked her fingers. "Camille! Grace has made a start here, could you take over?"

Camille nodded and, snapping open her case, knelt down beside the girl's body.

"Come on, dear," Lola said, leading Grace firmly away. "I think you've had enough excitement for one night, don't you?"

Grace was too dazed to speak. But now Lola smiled. "Don't look embarrassed, my dear. It's wonderful that your hunger has risen. Of course it is! Sid will be just thrilled at the news. But I can't have any member of my crew – and certainly not my own stepdaughter – behaving in such an uncouth fashion. It would destroy my reputation."

Grace hung her head, but Lola reached out her hand and lifted her chin. "Come on," she joked. "Back to our carriage before it turns into a pumpkin!"

As they set off, arm in arm, Lola paused. "Did you bring that playing card with you?" she asked.

Grace nodded, reaching into the pocket of her skirt and removing the black Queen of Hearts card which had been attached to Lola's invitation.

"Perfect!" Lola said, taking the playing card. She turned and threw it towards the dead girl's prone body. The card fluttered like a moth in the night air, before landing on the girl's open mouth. Lola squeezed Grace's arm. "It's my calling card," she explained.

Lola led Grace back to the carriage. Mimma and Zofia were already waiting inside, three cases stowed at their feet. Lola ushered Grace up the steps, then turned to the young driver. "Crack the whip, Rodrigo!" she said. "Our business here is done."

CHAPTER THIRTY-THREE

We Need to Talk about Grace

"They've just started using these new tool-belts and cases," Grace said. "Before, they had to bring people back to *The Vagabond* to drain their blood efficiently but now they have this portable equipment which means they can drain and bottle the blood anywhere."

Darcy shuddered. "Oh, Grace. And you saw this happening? How awful!"

"It's OK, Darcy." Grace shook her head. "I didn't stay in the room for long."

Darcy frowned at her friend. "I didn't mean how awful for *you*." Thinking she might have been a little harsh, she added, "Though, of course, I wouldn't have wanted to see such things. It must have been distressing."

Mosh Zu nodded to himself. "So this is how they organise their so-called blood hunts. An extremely valuable insight." Turning back to Grace, he asked, "And there were twelve victims, you say – trapped and killed by Lola Lockwood's crew?"

Grace nodded. There was a strange look in her eyes which Darcy found impossible to read. There seemed to be a growing gulf between herself and Grace at each of these nightly conferences, and she didn't know what to do about it.

"Is there something else you want to tell us?" Mosh Zu inquired.

Grace looked agitated, then took a deep breath. "One of them escaped," she said. "A young woman. The dinner was to celebrate her engagement . . ."

Darcy gasped, bringing her hand to her lips in horror.

"I was out in the corridor," Grace continued, her eyes wide. "The girl ran towards me. Her dress was torn and her flesh was pierced." She paused, a distant look in her eyes.

Darcy turned to Mosh Zu, hoping to catch his attention, but he was fully focused on Grace, waiting for her to continue.

"The girl asked me to help her. I said that of course I would. We ran out of the house. There was a fountain outside. The most beautiful fountain I've ever seen." Grace's face was beatific.

"And the girl," Mosh Zu asked. "How was she?"

Grace narrowed her eyes, as if refocusing. "The girl was weak – from the bleeding, perhaps . . ."

Or perhaps from seeing all the people she loved massacred on the night of her engagement party, Darcy thought angrily.

"She was weak," Grace continued. "She leaned against the fountain . . . to rest."

Becoming silent, she closed her eyes for a time, as if she was journeying back to that place and moment. When she opened her eyes once more, Darcy froze. Grace's beautiful emerald eyes had disappeared. In their place were deep pools of fire. Darcy was no stranger to such sights – her own eyes went through the same transformation when she was hungry for blood – but she was unprepared for the shock of seeing Grace in this state.

"What happened at the fountain?" Mosh Zu pushed her.

Grace looked pained. "The girl was bleeding. She was weak. I couldn't help . . ." She broke off, then began again. "I couldn't help . . ." She sighed deeply. Her eyes closed once more.

"You couldn't help *what*?" Mosh Zu probed.

Grace opened her eyes. They were back to normal – greener and brighter than ever, like stones washed in a mountain stream. Darcy almost cried with relief.

Grace looked momentarily disorientated, then continued. "I couldn't help her," she said. "There was nothing I could do. Lola and the others came out of the house. They soon got to work on her."

"The poor girl," Darcy said.

Mosh Zu rose from his seat and stepped towards Grace. "How has this difficult experience left you feeling?"

Grace shrugged. "Drained, I guess. And tired."

"You should rest," Mosh Zu said. "The night is almost over."

"Where's Lorcan?" Grace asked. "Why didn't he come to see me tonight?"

"We told you when you first arrived," Darcy said. "Don't you remember?"

Grace shook her head, frowning slightly.

"His combat training is demanding so much of his time and energy," Mosh Zu said. "He wasn't able to join us tonight."

Grace frowned. "I tried to visit him before, but I couldn't get through to him. Is he avoiding me?"

Darcy could not contain her irritation. "Of course he's not avoiding you, Grace! We *all* have difficult and demanding roles to play in this mission. Sometimes it's just not possible for us to be together at the same time."

Grace raised an eyebrow. "All right, Darcy! I was only asking!"

"Quite so," Mosh Zu said, in soothing tones. "As I said before, the hours of darkness will be over soon. I must send Darcy back to her post at the prow of the ship now."

Grace nodded and smiled. "Figurehead by day . . ." she began, but her powers of projection were already fading. Her voice cut out and Darcy watched as, piece by piece, the image of Grace disappeared into the ether. After she had gone, the Captain's cabin seemed to echo with silence and emptiness.

Darcy turned to Mosh Zu. "We need to talk about Grace," she said.

He nodded.

"You saw the look in her eyes," Darcy said. "Didn't you? When she was talking about that girl at the fountain."

Mosh Zu nodded again. "Yes, I saw the hunger."

"We have to get her back," Darcy said, "before she acts upon her hunger."

Mosh Zu did not respond.

"Well?" Darcy said. "What do you think?"

"Oh, Grace has already taken blood," Mosh Zu said, calmly.

"No!" Darcy clenched her hand into a ball. "No!" she repeated, her voice laced with despair.

Mosh Zu nodded. "We, of all people, know that taking blood is not in itself a bad thing. What matters is *how* you take it. Grace took blood from the girl at the fountain, but I strongly suspect that it wasn't her first taste. I believe that someone has been helping to stir up her appetite."

Darcy felt herself reeling from his words. "You really think that Grace fed on that poor girl?"

"Only a little," Mosh Zu said. "Grace's appetite is only just surfacing."

Darcy shook her head. "How can you be so . . . *accepting* of this?"

"Grace is a dhampir," Mosh Zu said. "You didn't know this when you first met her, so you formed your views about Grace and her character based on the notion that she was mortal.

Now, you must adjust your viewpoint. That may take a little work."

Darcy frowned. "I can get past the idea that Grace is a dhampir and that she has an appetite for blood, but there are other changes I'm finding harder to accept. She seems to have become so cold and selfish. She never used to be that way. She's changing, no doubt thanks to the influence of that vicious Lola Lockwood and Sidorio."

Mosh Zu shrugged. "Changing fundamentally *or*, like a chameleon, adapting *temporarily* to the challenging circumstances in which she finds herself?"

"I care very deeply about Grace," Darcy said, firmly. "She's one of my dearest friends. She's done an amazing job on that ship but now it's time to bring her home."

Mosh Zu smiled softly. "Soon," he said. "But not yet."

"Why not?" Darcy asked, unable to keep the irritation out of her voice. She wished Lorcan was here to back her up but, as he wasn't, she'd have to fight this battle solo. "Grace's mission was to go and see how the rebel empire works and to report back to us. Well, she's done that – night after night – in sufficient detail to give us all tortured dreams."

"You're right. The information Grace has relayed to us is exceptional."

"We know enough now," Darcy said. "*More* than enough. Her mission is complete."

Mosh Zu shook his head. "You look only at the effect that others are having on Grace. You should pause to consider the impact *she* is having upon *them*."

Darcy shook her head in disbelief. "You're surely not suggesting that Grace is acting as a civilising force upon the rebels? It certainly doesn't seem that way when they are out every night hunting blood, hijacking pirate ships and wantonly killing anyone who strays into their path!"

"Appearances can be deceptive," Mosh Zu said. "Grace is working her way to the heart of Sidorio's empire, just as the Captain wants."

Darcy froze at the mention of their captain. "Is it *really* what he wants or what *you* want?" she asked. There was steel in her voice as she continued. "I'm sorry, but it's no longer clear to me who's running this ship – him or you."

Mosh Zu's voice remained calm. "Nothing has changed, I assure you. I am merely holding the reins until the Captain's return. Then I will go back to Sanctuary and the Captain will take his rightful place, at the heart of the Nocturnal world."

"Yes," Darcy said. "Yes, that's what you say, night after night. But we only have your word that the Captain *is* going to return. And, with the greatest respect, I'm not sure I believe you any more." She shook her head. "The Captain would never have sent Grace into such a dangerous situation. And, if he had, he'd certainly have rescued her before now. *Before* she took blood."

"No," Mosh Zu said. "You're wrong. The Captain knows exactly where Grace is. He wants and needs her to be there. Darcy, the Captain that you knew – or thought you knew – is gone. When he makes his return, you'll find him a changed man."

"What do you mean by that?"

"Exactly what I say." Mosh Zu's face was serene.

"Stop talking in riddles!" Darcy said. "You always do that and it's infuriating!" She felt more frustrated with him than ever.

Mosh Zu smiled. "Daylight is not far away now," he said. "You must take your position as our figurehead once more."

"In other words," Darcy said huffily, already walking towards the door, "I'm dismissed."

"Something like that," said Mosh Zu.

Johnny was getting ready for bed. It had been another non-stop night and he was more than ready for a good eight hours of shut-eye. He pulled his undershirt over his head and hunted around in his closet for a fresh singlet to change into. As he turned around, he was dumbfounded to find Grace standing right in the middle of his cabin.

"Grace, what are you doing here?!"

"Please, don't be angry!" she said.

He broke into a warm smile. "I'm not angry, *carina*. It's just a surprise. I didn't even hear the door open."

She looked agitated. "I didn't come in through the door." There was a haunted look in her eyes.

"Hey," he said, stepping closer and reaching out his arms. "What's wrong, G?" He drew his arms around her but found that they just moved clean through her and he was left hugging himself. "Hey, where did you go?"

"I'm still right here," Grace said, as he stepped back and gazed at her curiously. "Only I'm not exactly here. This is an astral projection of me. My physical body is still on *The Vagabond*, but I needed to talk to you. This is just a little thing I can do."

"Seems like there's no end to your talents, " Johnny said, with a wink. He slipped the singlet over his head and pulled it down across his tanned chest, then reached out to her again. "Wow! My hand goes right through you. Grace, this is weird . . . but very cool. Can you teach me how to do it?"

"I don't know," Grace said, her eyes pained. "Johnny, I really needed to see you. I need your help."

Johnny's face became serious. "Of course," he said. "Anything for you, Grace. What's up?"

Grace looked imploringly into his eyes. "I need blood," she said. "I'm so hungry for it. I thought maybe you could help me find some."

Johnny nodded. "Wow! Sure! I mean, yes of course."

"Thank you!" She looked deeply relieved.

Johnny folded his arms across his chest. "I'll come over to *The Vagabond* just as soon it gets dark."

Grace looked panic-stricken. "Can't you come right now, Johnny?"

He glanced at the clock at his bedside, then shook his head. "I'm sorry, Grace, but the sun is due to rise in a matter of minutes. Sunlight and Vampirates don't mix . . . as you know only too well." Seeing her obvious nerviness, he racked his brains. "Look, if you need blood you're aready in the perfect place. *The Vagabond* is the main storage depot for all our blood. Just head down to the cellars and crack open a bottle!"

Grace heard his words but looked far from reassured. "I'm scared in case I drink too much or I have a bad reaction to it. I really want you to be there."

"I know," he said, his voice as soft and warm as melting chocolate. "Look, can you wait, what, twelve hours? I'll come right on over as soon as the sun goes down."

"Twelve hours?" Grace said. She bit her lip. "I just don't know if I can wait that long . . ."

"Could you try, *carina*?" Johnny said, smiling encouragingly at her. "For me?"

"All right," she said. "I'll do my best."

CHAPTER THIRTY-FOUR

Connor's Decision

Connor stood on the beach, waiting for Kally and listening to the waves crashing onto the shore. He still felt numb from the news that Molucco was dead. Stukeley had told him that their former leader's blood now filled six bottles kept under lock and key in Lola's "wine cellar". The thing that was most horrifying to Connor was that this kind of information no longer shocked him. He inhabited another world entirely now. There was a time when he had thought of Molucco as a father-figure. How ironic, he reflected, as the spray from a wave hit his face, all that time he'd spent thinking that Molucco might be his new dad, when his true father – Sidorio – was just waiting in the wings.

Connor had had to shed one persona after another in a short space of time – lighthouse keeper's son, orphan, pirate prodigy. Now, he was Connor Quintus Antonius Sidorio – the dhampir. And where did his loyalties lie?

Stukeley had told him about the next attack. By rights, he ought to be guarding the information closely. Yet here he was on this beach once again, waiting to pass on the intelligence to Sidorio's sworn enemy – the Pirate Federation. But this would be the last time he passed on such information. Not because he was switching sides. Nothing as simple as that. This war was raging out of hand and he was no more able to stop it than he was able to prevent the tide from coming in to the shore. He was resigned to that now. He had done his best for Cheng Li and the Federation. He hoped they would use his latest intel to their best advantage. Maybe they would even, by some miracle, repel Obsidian Darke and his crew. But Connor had to be realistic. It was just as likely that Cheng Li would be defeated. That really would close the book on Connor's career as a pirate. For, though Molucco had often claimed the credit, it was Cheng Li who had plucked him out of the ocean and made a pirate of him. But, in spite of his early signs of promise, the dice had been loaded against him from the start.

Seeing Kally's familiar spiky blue hair bobbing into view, Connor dived into the water and began swimming out towards her. As ever, she was pleased to see him, but today he had neither the time nor the inclination for pleasantries. He wanted – he *needed* – to get this over with as soon as possible. "I'm sorry to rush you," he told her, "but we need to get down to business."

She nodded and swam alongside him to the nearby rock. As Connor pulled himself up out of the water, Kally ran a hand through her hair, then rested her arms on the rock and her elfin face on her arms. "OK, dude. Tell me the latest."

Connor experienced a sudden flush of anxiety, feeling the heavy burden of what he had to say. Then an increasingly familiar numbness returned and he became business like once more. "The next attack will be tomorrow night," he said. "And it's the big one. They're going to attack *The Tiger*."

Kally's rainbow-coloured eyes widened.

"Obsidian Darke will lead the attack. I told you about him before, remember?"

"Marble-cold and merciless," Kally said, with a nod.

"That's him," Connor said. "As usual, he'll be able to choose his team from the rest of the crew."

"Wow!" Kally said. "So this is really going to happen. Cheng Li will flip but, from what I hear, she's ready for this. According to Jacoby, she and Cate have some new secret weapon."

Connor's ears pricked up at this. "A new weapon? Do you know what it is? Has she commissioned more swords from Master Yin?"

Kally shook her head. "I'm only told what I need to know. I'm not even sure *Jacoby* knows what it is."

Connor nodded. "Cheng Li likes to keep an ace or two up her sleeve," he said. "Always has. Always will."

"Well, I'd better head off and deliver the bombshell. And tell them your plans, of course. Are you coming with me now or tomorrow?"

Connor heard her words. He'd been expecting them, preparing for them. But, now they had come, he said nothing in response, only gazed deep into Kally's extraordinary eyes.

"Connor?" she asked. "When do you want to make your bid for freedom? The clock's ticking now, isn't it?"

Connor shook his head. "I'm not coming back with you," he said.

"Not today but tomorrow, right?" She gazed at him with concern.

"No, Kal. I'm not coming back. Full stop."

"*What?*"

"Kally, there are things you don't know about me and I plan to keep it that way. The fact is, this is where I belong. In time, I think you'll understand."

She shook her head, fresh tears budding in her eyes. "No. How can you say that you belong here, with these monsters? After what they did to Molucco . . ."

"It's complicated," Connor said. "And we don't have time to get into it now. You need to get my message about the attack back to Jacoby as quickly as possible. Secret weapon or not, Cheng Li and Cate are going to have to pull out all the stops this time."

Kally nodded. "I'll go now," she said. "But I'll meet you back here at the same time tomorrow. You might have more information for me to pass on at that point."

"I've told you everything," he said. "There's nothing more to say. Wish them luck." He paused. "And tell Jasmine that I'm sorry."

"Just meet me," Kally said, biting down her emotions. "As a favour to an old friend."

"I'll think about it," he said.

From high up in the crow's nest, Bart had an exceptional view of the deck of *The Tiger*. He watched as, down below, Cate and Cheng Li put the rest of the crew through their paces during the latest punishing session of combat training. The "gruesome twosome", as he affectionately referred to them, had increased combat training to two ninety-minute sessions each day and, in the past few days, they had thrown some challenging new moves into the mix. Looking down now, he saw that both Jasmine and Bo Yin had got these new moves down pat. No surprise there – sometimes he thought that little Bo Yin had elastic running alongside her muscles. Others of the crew needed more time to master the new attack sequences.

But Cate and Cheng Li had a secret and Bart was in on it. The new moves had been devised thanks to the information Lorcan Furey had provided on his recent visits. Cate had threatened to personally throttle Bart if he revealed to Cheng Li that he knew the score – and he didn't doubt she meant it. He wasn't about to blab. Too much depended on this. Pirate captains were being assassinated right across the oceans: Bojan Petrović, captain of *The Redeemer*; Narcisos Drakoulis, captain of *The Albatross*; and now Molucco Wrathe, captain of *The Diablo*. Bart shook his head at this latest and most shocking murder. Molucco had often talked about the pirate's life being a short but a merry one, but Bart knew that the pirate captain would never have expected to end his days at the hands of a Vampirate.

Looking out across the ocean, Bart found it utterly inconceivable to think that Molucco Wrathe would never set sail again. It seemed as ridiculous as imagining that the sun wouldn't rise. Everyone had had an opinion about Molucco. Bart himself had laid the blame for Jez Stukeley's death at his door, but he was over that now. In truth, he had been for a good while. The crazy old sea dog hadn't deserved to die like that. No one did.

Looking down from this position at the top of the ship, Bart felt a strange sense of peace and calm, despite being in the midst of such troubling times. He wasn't sure where this feeling came from, but suddenly, the movements of the crew below seemed as graceful as a ballet – not that Bart Pearce had ever been to the ballet – and there at the heart of it all was Cate. He'd known her so long, yet he never ceased to be surprised by her talent, commitment and beauty. Not everybody saw it, but to him Cate Morgan was special. Watching her, Bart came to a decision. He checked his watch to record the time – two-forty-nine. He wanted to remember this exact moment. Maybe it took times of crisis to make you realise what was truly important. He realised, with absolutely no sense of embarrassment, that he had the biggest grin known to man plastered across his chops.

Bart watched Jacoby's light-boat skimming across the waves

towards *The Tiger*. Back from his daily report from the fishtail, Kally. According to young Jacoby, Kally had said she'd met Bart in the past and had sent him her best wishes but, for the life of him, he couldn't remember meeting a fishtail and of all the wacko things he'd gotten up to in his three and twenty years he was pretty sure that this was something he would remember.

As Jacoby moored the light-boat and began climbing up the side of *The Tiger*, Bart made his descent back down onto deck. Time for the hourly changeover. The lads arrived on deck at approximately the same moment. Seeing Jacoby, Cheng Li called a time-out. The crew gratefully laid down their weapons and drew breath.

Jacoby strode across the deck towards Cheng Li, who was drinking thirstily from a flask of water. He had a dark expression on his face. Bart saw it and moved towards him. In the crowd, others caught it too. Jasmine. Cate. Bo Yin. Every face looked at him expectantly.

Cheng Li threw down the flask. "So, what news, Jacoby?" she inquired.

For once, the deputy captain didn't dress up the information he had to convey. "We're the next target," he said.

There was utter silence on deck. Every member of the crew froze at Jacoby's words.

Cheng Li did not miss a beat. "You all heard that? Good!" She reached for her sword and lifted it so that it glinted in the afternoon sunlight. "We knew this moment was coming. And we're ready. The Vampirates have made their first mistake. This is the point where everything changes. You are all poised to write your names in pirate history!"

Bart turned at the knock on his cabin door.

"Come in!" he called, swiftly covering the old sea-chest he'd been rummaging through with a shirt. "It's open."

Jacoby appeared in the door-frame, looking agitated. A door-to-door visit from the deputy captain was a first.

"What's up, buddy?" Bart asked. "You look like a man on the edge."

"Actually, that's not far from the truth," Jacoby said. "I'm really sorry to disturb you, Bart, but I didn't know who else to talk to. It's about Connor."

Cate shook her head. "Connor's not coming back?"

Bart nodded. "That's what he told Kally."

"But why?" Cate asked.

"I don't know." Bart shook his head. "Catie, none of us know. But it must be pretty serious for Connor to make such a decision."

Cate frowned, turning her eyes away and watching the dying light across the ocean. The nightly drama of light and shadow, sky and water, never grew dull for her.

"I made two big decisions today," Bart said.

They were close together at the deck-rail now. Cate turned away from the sunset and looked curiously at her long-time comrade, now her boyfriend. The word still felt strange to her – it gave her the same sense of awkwardness as the few times she'd worn a dress – but she was in absolutely no doubt about the depth of her feelings for Bart Pearce. He had become her fixed point in an increasingly turbulent world. As steady as the mast, as strong as the sail. That was how she thought of him.

"Tell me about these decisions," she said.

"I'm going after Connor," Bart said. "And please don't try to talk me out of it, Catie. I've arranged it with Jacoby. I'm going along with him to his morning rendezvous with Kally. I'm going to get her to take me to Connor so I can talk some sense into him." He stopped speaking. Cate said nothing.

Bart looked deep into her eyes. "I thought for sure you'd tell me this was madness, that Connor can take care of himself, that there are bigger issues at stake here . . ."

Cate smiled. "Exactly what issues are bigger than the safety and happiness of a dear friend?" she asked. Then she smiled. "Besides, when it comes to the battle, my prize fighters are Jasmine and Bo Yin. If *they* told me they were bunking off, I'd give them a serious talking-to. But you – you're another matter entirely, you old lummox."

Bart stroked Cate's cheek tenderly. "And there I was suffering from the delusion I was becoming indispensable to you," he said. "Now look, seriously, Catie, I'm not deserting you in your hour of need. I fully intend to be back by nightfall, with Connor at my side. We'll give it to the Vampirates right beside you."

"That sounds good," Cate said. "But things may be more complicated with Connor than you anticipate. If he needs time, give it to him. Just bring him home safe – and yourself while you're about it. And that's an order from your superior officer!"

Bart smiled and saluted her.

Cate flushed with embarrassment, though she figured she ought to be used to Bart's ways by now. But that perhaps was what made the two of them work. He was so loud and gregarious, so given to bold gestures. She was much quieter, more self-contained. He brought her out of her shell and she calmed him down. She smiled, wrapping her arms around his waist. "You said you'd made *two* big decisions today. The first was about Connor. What was the second?"

"Tell you what," Bart said, speaking softly and looking deep into her eyes. "The other piece of news can wait until I get back and all this craziness is over."

He smiled at her once more and, as she looked into his eyes, she had a fleeting glimpse of eternity. *As steady as the mast, as strong as the sail.*

CHAPTER THIRTY-FIVE

Forbidden Fruit

"I came as soon as I could," Johnny said, slipping into Grace's cabin.

"It's really good to see you," she said, closing the door tightly behind him.

It felt strange having Johnny right here in her cabin. Strange, but exciting – as if he was somehow forbidden fruit. She could tell he had made an effort for her, as if they were going on a date. He was dressed in a fitted black shirt, jeans and his riding boots. As she stepped closer, she could smell his delicious woody cologne, familiar to her now from the nights pressed up close against him on horseback.

Grace realised that Johnny was looking at her just as intently as she was at him. His handsome face cracked a smile, revealing his extremely white teeth. Amongst them were his two pronounced incisors. Now they didn't bother her one bit or make him seem any less handsome. If anything, the reverse.

"Did you manage to hold out until I got here?" he asked her.

She nodded, smiling.

"Good girl!"

She shrugged. "Well, I kind of made you a promise."

He nodded, smiling once more. "OK, so what's the plan? How do we slip into the cellars without anyone noticing?"

"Lola and the key members of her winery team are out harvesting again tonight," Grace explained. "They've gone further inland this time so we should have a clear run for the next couple of hours."

Johnny nodded. "I saw their carriages hurtling off along the coast road as I was making my way over. That's cool that they're out of the picture. What about the cellars themselves, though? I imagine they're locked, aren't they?"

"I don't foresee any problems with us getting inside," Grace said, reaching into the pocket of her skirt and producing a ring of keys. "I appropriated these from my stepmother's cabin earlier."

Johnny nodded, impressed. "Did you astral project yourself in there or do you have yet more magic tricks in your repertoire?"

Grace shook her head. "Actually, this was just a case of good old-fashioned theft." She smiled. "Sometimes, I like to stick to the classics."

Johnny whistled lightly. "You know, Grace Tempest, when I first met you, I had no idea what a bundle of fun you would turn out to be. Seems you're quite the rebel, eh?"

Grace flushed at his compliment. "Come on," she said, handing him a lantern and lifting a second for herself. "We have a cellar to break into."

The Vagabond was quiet as the grave below decks. As Grace and Johnny made their way down to the lowest level of the ship, they didn't pass a single soul.

"We made it!" Grace said, passing her lantern to Johnny and trying the first of the keys on Lola's chain in the cellar door. It was too much to hope that she'd pick the right key first time but it only took her a handful of tries before the lock clicked open.

"We're in," she whispered to Johnny, feeling a thrill of excitement and reaching out for his hand. As he took hers, he gave it a squeeze. Together they stepped through the door into the dank cellar.

They found themselves in a vast cabin. It seemed to Grace to be as big as the one at the base of *The Nocturne*, the one they used for Feast Night. But instead of a dining table and chairs, this room, true to expectations, was given over to row upon row of bottles.

Johnny let out a whistle as they walked hand in hand down an avenue of bottles. "I never knew Lola had so much stock. I mean, I knew she was stepping up production but we have enough to keep us going for years here!"

Grace stopped and, withdrawing her hand from Johnny's, pulled out a bottle. It was labelled with the Black Heart winery crest and on the reverse were some tasting notes. "Young, fruity, with a hint of spice . . ." She turned to Johnny. "What do you think?"

"Let's give it a try," he said, taking the bottle from her hands.

"What do we do?" Grace asked, feeling a strange electricity running up and down her spine. "It's a screwtop, so do we just open it here and drink it down? Or shall we take it back to my cabin?"

Johnny giggled. "I like it down here," he said. "It feels kind of naughty, doesn't it?"

Grace nodded, finding that she was smiling too.

"You said yourself that Lola and her posse are out for at least a couple more hours. I reckon we can take our time." He held out his lantern. "There are some glasses over there and, look, we can use that old blanket as a picnic rug. Make ourselves all nice and cosy. Come on, partner!"

He ambled along the avenue again, bottle of wine in one

hand, lantern in the other. Grace followed after him, feeling a heady sense of excitement.

"I've got to do this," Darcy told Lorcan. "You do understand, don't you?"

Lorcan's eyes registered concern but he nodded. "I'm not sure it's the wisest move," he said. "But yes, of course, I understand. I'd come with you but look at the state of me! I wouldn't want Grace to see me like this. Besides, I never really mastered the art of astral travel."

"It's OK," Darcy said. "You stay here and get cleaned up or take a well-earned rest. I've never seen anyone work so hard. No wonder you're growing fresh muscles nightly!" She brushed his arm lightly with her fingers. "I'll go and talk to Grace. I'm sure it will set all our minds at rest."

Lorcan nodded. "I hope so," he said, opening his arms and drawing Darcy into them. "Be careful, though, you hear me? And be sure to tell Grace how much I miss her and want her back here . . ."

Darcy looked up into Lorcan's eyes. "In your arms?"

"Well, yes," he said, a little awkwardly.

"Don't worry," Darcy said, smiling. "I know it's Grace you want."

"You're very important to me, Darcy," Lorcan said. "You know that, don't you?"

She nodded. "We're like brother and sister, you and I. Why I'll be speaking with a Connemara brogue before you know it!" She hugged Lorcan tenderly, then slipped out of his embrace. "I'm going to go back to my own cabin and project from there, if you don't mind."

Lorcan nodded. "Come and find me as soon as you get back, you hear?"

*

287

Darcy Flotsam prided herself on being one of the most accomplished practitioners of astral travel aboard *The Nocturne*. Whilst many of the Vampirates – she corrected herself, whilst many of the *Nocturnals* – Lorcan included, struggled with the basics of projection, she was sufficiently skilled that she could select from two different modes of travel. The first would take her directly to a place that she knew – this was the way Grace made her nightly rendezvous in the Captain's cabin. The second, more subtle, method enabled Darcy to travel to a person, rather than a place. This was how she had once travelled to Grace aboard *The Diablo* and this, she decided, was how she would now travel to her aboard *The Vagabond*.

But even when you were skilled at the psychic arts, you had to allow a certain margin for error. As Darcy wrinkled her nose at the musty odour which suddenly enveloped her and glanced about at her now decidedly gloomy surroundings, she thought she must have travelled to the wrong location. It took her a moment to detect the floorboards beneath her feet but, following them, she skimmed along to the end of the dark corridor. As she did so, she heard soft voices and laughter ahead.

Darcy felt her heart lift. One of the voices belonged to Grace. Whatever strange place this was, her abilities had not failed her. She gave herself a mental pat on the back and proceeded in the direction of the voices. She was aware that Grace wasn't alone but that was OK. If she was careful, she could quietly observe her friend and, when the coast was clear, perhaps give her a little sign of her presence.

As her vision grew more acute, Darcy wondered what all these shelves on either side of her might contain. Then, she discerned the unmistakeable shapes of bottles; row upon row of them. It took her a moment to make the connection and then she felt sick to her core. She remembered Grace's grim tales of Lola Lockwood's night harvests. So, she thought, these are the cellars. It made sense – there was a darkness and gloom to this location which was not about the lack of lighting or the dank environment, but surely emanated from all the lives cut short and drained into the bottles surrounding her. Darcy shuddered, but refused to be deterred. This was never going to be a walk in the park and she badly needed to talk to Grace. Providing she accomplished that mission, she could endure this veritable chamber of horrors.

Seeing a pool of light fanning out around the corner, Darcy hung back a moment. She must be close. And yet the voices and laughter had receded. Confused, she floated to the very end of the corridor and, steeling herself, glanced in the direction of the light. As soon as she did so, she regretted it.

There was Grace, sure enough. She was stretched out on some kind of blanket, an open bottle and two half-empty glasses at her side. But Grace wasn't alone, she was with a young man. Darcy couldn't get a good look at him as his back was turned towards her, but he was lying alongside Grace. Then he moved and Darcy saw the one thing she hadn't prepared herself for. The young man and Grace were kissing.

Darcy frowned, thinking instantly of Lorcan. She brought her hand across her lips. As she did so, the couple broke their kiss. Darcy knew that she should retreat but somehow she couldn't. She watched as the man turned and reached for the bottle.

"Ready for a top-up?" she heard him say.

Grace nodded. "Yes please!" Then, she drew herself up into a sitting position. As she did so, she caught sight of Darcy and gasped. Darcy shot back around the corner.

"What's up?" Johnny said, turning to Grace.

"You have to go," she said to him.

"Why?"

Grace's mind was racing. "It's one of Lola's crew," she said. "She must have come back early for some reason."

Johnny looked around, confused. "I don't see anyone," he said. "Are you sure it wasn't a trick of the light?"

"Trust me," Grace said. "You have to get out of here." She began pulling him up from the blanket.

"What about you?" he asked, stumbling onto his feet and reaching for his boots, which he'd shrugged off to get more comfortable.

"I'll talk my way out of this," Grace said. "But you have to go. Now!"

"All right!" he said. "But come and find me later. Astral project or whatever you need to do to tell me you're OK."

She nodded. "Of course."

As Johnny disappeared into the shadows, Grace stood up and began walking in the other direction. "Darcy," she said. "I know you're there. Come out so I can see you."

"All right." Darcy said soberly, stepping out in front of her.

Grace reached out her hand and tested it by passing it through her friend's neck. "Good. This is just an astral visit, then."

"Yes," Darcy said. "But I still saw what I saw." Her voice was low and raw.

Grace frowned. "You look even more disappointed in me than usual," she said. "I know you've been dying to say stuff to me these past few nights. Well, now there's no Lorcan or Mosh Zu around, you can feel free to say exactly what you want."

"I came to see you because I was worried about you!" Darcy said, distressed at her friend's tone. "And, after what I've just seen, clearly I was right to be concerned."

"On the contrary," Grace said. "I'd have thought that it's more than evident that I can take care of myself." She smiled. "And that I'm making new friends."

"Grace!" Darcy's eyes went wide. "How do you think Lorcan would feel if he heard you say that? If he knew about you and that boy on the blanket?"

"Well," Grace said. "We won't have to wait long to find out, will we? No doubt you're just itching to hover back to *The Nocturne* and spill the beans."

Darcy was speechless for a moment. She shook her head. "Lorcan has real feelings for you, Grace. He's opened himself up to you in a way I've never seen him do in all the years I've known him. Can you really brush him aside so casually?"

"I'm not brushing anyone aside," Grace said, dismissively. "I was just having a little drink."

"I saw you," Darcy said. "And, from where I was standing, it wasn't a glass you had pressed to your lips."

Enraged, Grace reached out to slap her friend's face but, of course, her hand simply flew through the air. It caught her own cheek and stung like mad.

"Serves you right," Darcy said. "If I could have slapped you back, I would have."

"Because I'm having a little fun with Johnny?" Grace said.

"Oh," Darcy nodded. "So *that's* Johnny, is it? I might have guessed."

Grace shook her head. "How dare you judge me!" she said. "Do you have any idea what I've been through these past few months, these past few weeks in particular? *Do you?* I don't think you do. Not you or Mosh Zu or Lorcan. You're all so busy with your 'important missions' that I never see you except at our night-time conferences. Lorcan's even stopped coming to them. If anyone's brushed anyone aside, it's him."

Darcy sighed. "That just isn't true, Grace, and you know it."

Grace shook her head once more. "Let's face facts, Darcy. It *is* true and it's probably rather pleasing to you. I mean, you've always carried a torch for Lorcan, haven't you? Don't bother denying it. It must have churned you up when he chose me instead of you, even when he thought I was mortal. Well, the coast is clear for you. I'm with Johnny now and, if you want to

291

know the truth, he's a thousand times more fun to hang out with than Lorcan Furey. So hurry back to *The Nocturne* and help yourself." She folded her arms. "I just hope it ends better for you than your disastrous spin with Jez Stukeley."

Darcy's eyes stung with hot tears. "What have they done to you?" she asked. "You were so sweet, so kind, before Sidorio and Lola Lockwood got to you."

"Oh, dry your eyes," Grace said callously, "before you get wood-rot! I was never as sweet or as kind as you make out. I'm Sidorio's daughter. You know what they say: the fruit doesn't fall far from the tree."

Darcy struggled to string words together. "This isn't you talking, Grace. It can't be."

Suddenly, she noticed the dry, red stain around Grace's lips. Of course! Darcy had been so taken aback by witnessing the kiss that she'd forgotten what Grace had been drinking. Now, it all made sense. She smiled with relief.

"What are you grinning at like some carnival Aunt Sally?" Grace asked.

"It isn't you talking. All this horrible stuff. It's the blood."

Grace rolled her eyes. "Believe what you want to, Darcy, but please leave me alone. Surely you're almost out of power by now."

"Oh, I'm going," Darcy said. "But I'll be back. You can bet on it." So saying, her image faded from view.

Grace found herself alone in the cellar. Her cheek still stung from her own slap. She lifted her hand towards it. *Stupid!* She wandered over to the blanket and sat back down, reaching out once more for her glass. As she lifted it to her lips and felt the silky liquid glide down her throat, she felt instantly calmer.

"Do you think perhaps you've had enough for one night?"

She glanced up and missed a breath, finding Johnny standing

there in front of her. He looked more handsome than ever. Forbidden fruit.

"I told you to go," she said, smiling nevertheless.

He smiled back at her. "See, I don't always do what I'm told."

"Me neither," she said, stretching out her legs and passing him his glass as he sat back down beside her. He took a sip.

"So I couldn't help but overhear some of that heated exchange," Johnny said.

Grace flushed, then rubbed her cheek. "Did you see me slap myself? That must have been highly amusing!"

"Actually," Johnny said, his eyes bright, "it really was."

Grace frowned. "It really hurts!"

"I like a woman who can throw a punch – even if it is at herself." Johnny lowered his glass, then leaned closer and kissed Grace softly on her cheek. "Do you think that might just take the pain away?"

"I'm not sure," she said. "You may have to do it a second time, or even a third . . ."

He shrugged. "Not a problem." But he hung back for a moment, looking suddenly nervous. "Grace, you don't have to answer this but I'm going to ask you anyway. When you said I was a thousand times more fun than Lorcan, did you mean it?"

Grace looked up into his chocolate-brown eyes. She shook her head very slowly, registering his disappointment even as she did it, though he did his best to hide it.

"No, Johnny," she said. "Not a thousand times more fun. A *million* times."

CHAPTER THIRTY-SIX

Sidorio's Son

Connor sat on the rock on the beach where he had his daily meetings with Kally. This, he had no doubt, would be the very last of their rendezvous. But where was she? Her timekeeping was usually impeccable. Today, she was already half an hour late. Should he be worried for her safety? He frowned. If Kally was in danger, what could he do to save her? There was a whole lot of ocean out there to comb for one diminutive fishtail.

An hour later, Kally still hadn't arrived. Connor had grown hot sitting in the sun. He decided to take a dip. He peeled off his shirt and dived into the cool water. He lingered underwater for a time, enjoying the silence beneath the surface. He felt a little envious of Kally. This was her world and she could stay down here for as long as she chose to, not having to rely on the limited amount of air in a pair of human lungs. As he framed the thought, Connor smiled to himself. In the past few weeks, his body had gone through several profound changes. He was no longer vulnerable to vertigo. His strength was growing on a daily basis. And when he was wounded, as in his bout with Sidorio, his flesh was far quicker to heal. Wasn't it possible therefore that he would now be able to stay underwater for longer? He decided to try the experiment. He checked his watch and began swimming away from the shore.

Ten minutes later, Connor's head bobbed up through the water's surface. Even then it wasn't because he'd run out of oxygen – his lungs felt perfectly comfortable – but because he was feeling cold and wanted to get back into the sun. Elated by this fresh demonstration of his new physical powers, he lay in a star shape on the surface letting the midday sun bathe him with its warm rays.

After a time, he grew bored of floating and swam back across to the rock to dry off. Lying in the heat, his body grateful for the rest, he drifted off easily to sleep.

"Connor!" He woke to find a familiar pair of rainbow-coloured eyes staring at him from beneath a spiky blue fringe.

"Kally!" He was relieved. "You're so late. I was worried about you."

"Were you?" She seemed pleased. "Well, I'm glad you came and double-glad you waited, dude. I have a nice surprise for you."

"A surprise?" Connor felt his sense of calm instantly vanish. Surprises were no longer welcome, as far as he was concerned.

Kally turned, brought her fingers to her lips and sounded a whistle. Connor watched her curiously, then stood up on the rock, turning his gaze in the direction she had whistled. He saw a familiar light-boat skimming across the waters towards them.

Connor frowned. "Kally," he said, "what have you done?"

Shrugging, Kally slipped backwards and dipped underwater. Connor was left to watch and wait as the small boat made its way over to the beach. Now, it was close enough for him to see who was on board. He saw Bart wave at him. There had been many times when Connor had been thrilled to see his old friend. This wasn't one of them. Nevertheless, he lifted his own hand. Then he dived back into the water and swam over to the beach.

Connor was waiting on the sand as Bart anchored the small vessel and waded through the shallows. Bart smiled as he crossed the sand towards him. "It's so good to see you," he said, opening his arms and drawing Connor into a hug.

Connor nodded but stepped backwards. "It's always good to see you, Bart. But I wish you hadn't come."

Bart frowned. "What did you expect? That you'd send back the message that you were staying here and we'd all just accept it?"

Connor squinted into the sun. He didn't know what to say. There was the truth, of course, but that wasn't an easy conversation to jump into.

"You mean too much to us, Connor," Bart said. "And I'd hope that, after everything we've been through together, you'd feel the same way."

"The sun's really bright here," Connor said. "Why don't we take a walk?"

Bart nodded and they set off, side by side, along the beach.

"So, are you going to tell me what's going on with you?" Bart asked.

"It's complicated," Connor said. "I don't really know where to begin."

Bart smiled. "Just talk to me, buddy. Like you always have."

Connor took a deep breath. "The first thing to say is that my decision to stay here isn't a rejection of you guys. Nothing could be further from the truth. This is all about me, what I'm going through."

Bart frowned. "I was worried from the start of this mission, bud. I thought it was madness for Cheng Li to send you out here solo."

Connor shook his head. "It's not the mission," he said.

Bart stopped in his tracks and turned. "I don't understand."

Connor paused too. "I've been going through a lot of changes," he said.

Bart reached out a hand and placed it on his shoulder. "I know, buddy. I've watched you grow up before my very eyes. From that first night when you came on board *The Diablo*. Remember that?"

Connor nodded.

Bart put his arm around Connor's shoulder as they continued along the beach. "We were at each other's side when Jez was killed and we helped each other through that. And when you killed for the first time, you know how worried I was about you."

Connor nodded. "I know."

"You're like a brother to me, Connor Tempest," Bart said. "I'm here to help you through whatever curve-ball life throws at you. Cate feels the same way. And Jacoby and Cheng Li and Bo Yin. Connor, everyone misses you. Everyone wants you to come home."

Connor took a deep breath. "What about Jasmine?" he asked. "Has she said anything to you about me coming back?"

Bart shook his head. "Not in so many words but I know she's fond of you too. Why do you ask?"

Connor threw caution to the wind. "Something happened between me and Jasmine when we went to Lantao."

"I see." Bart's eyes narrowed. "Well, she's kept that to herself and, as far as I know, she and Jacoby are still a couple." Seeing Connor wince, he added, "Connor, I can understand you being torn up about this. You're a decent guy and Jacoby's a mate of yours. If you and Jasmine have fallen for each other, that's OK. Come back and sort it out. In my experience, these situations are rarely as bad as they seem."

Connor smiled. "Thanks for the advice," he said. "But it's a lot more complicated than that."

Bart shrugged. "It's a long beach and I'm in no hurry."

Connor suddenly stopped in his tracks, scanning the water. "Where's Kally?" he asked.

"She's fine," Bart said. "Splashing around somewhere. I told her I wanted some alone time with you."

"We should turn around," Connor said. "I need to head back to *The Blood Captain*. And you must get back in your boat and return to *The Tiger*."

Bart shook his head. "We've barely started talking, buddy," he said. "I came all this way for you. Give me some more time."

"The clock is ticking," Connor said. "You know about the attack tomorrow night on *The Tiger*. You should be there to fight."

"I'll be back in good time for that," Bart said. "With you at my side."

"I'm not coming back, Bart," Connor said. "I know it's hard for you to understand but there are things you don't know about me."

"Then tell me," Bart said, frustration evident in his voice. "Because all you've given me so far is some cock-and-bull story about you and Jasmine Peacock. I'm not getting back into that boat until you give me a much better reason than that." His eyes bored deep into Connor's and Connor knew his friend would stand by his words.

"All right," Connor said. "I'm going to tell you everything. But then you have to go back, without me."

"Start talking," Bart said.

"You know Cheng Li's story that she persuaded Sidorio I'm his son, right?"

Bart chuckled. "Sure, I know it. They say there's no fool like an old fool. I guess that holds true for immortals too."

Connor felt his heart hammering as he opened his mouth once more. "He believed it because it's the truth. I *am* Sidorio's son."

Bart was speechless for a moment. "This is a joke, right? You're about to deliver a killer punchline?"

Connor shook his head. "It's no joke. Our mother had a relationship with Sidorio and she bore him two children. Grace and I are both dhampirs – half-mortal, half-vampire. There's a lot more to the story but those are the key facts you need to know."

Bart was, unsurprisingly, taken aback. "How long have you known this?" he asked.

"Not long," Connor said. "Cheng Li found out before I did. She told me, and Sidorio, as we were making our retreat after the attack on his wedding."

"You've known *all* that time but you didn't tell me?" Bart said.

Now it was Connor who was lost for words. "What was I supposed to say? How could you possibly understand?"

"I'm your friend, Connor," Bart said now. "Whatever happens to you, I want to be there for you. All right, this is fairly extreme. So, you're half-human and half-vampire. Well, that's got to be better than one hundred per cent vampire, right?"

Connor shrugged. "Maybe. I don't know. Like I said, I've been going through a lot of changes," he said. "You remember my vertigo?"

Bart nodded. "Of course."

"Gone," Connor said. "And if you thought I was strong before, you should see me now. Plus my body has this new ability to heal."

Bart shook his head in amazement. "You're sounding like some kind of superhero," he said. "This is great, Connor! When you come back to *The Tiger*, you're going to be an unstoppable force."

"I keep telling you," Connor said. "I'm not coming back."

Bart's face was pained. "But I still don't see why. I mean, I completely get how all this crazy stuff would shift your world-view, throw you off centre. Of course it would. And here you are dealing with it all on your own . . ."

"I haven't exactly been on my own," Connor said. "Grace is here too. And Stukeley."

"Jez?" Bart said. "Of course."

"He's been showing me the way," Connor said. "After all, he's been on a similar journey."

"But he's a regular vampire, right?" Bart said. "Not a dhampir, like you?"

Connor nodded. "That's right, but he and I do have one thing in common."

"You have lots of things in common with me and all your other pirate mates too," Bart said, forcefully.

Connor couldn't hold back any more. "Yes," he said. "But there's one big thing that separates us now and joins me to Stukeley and Sidorio and the rest of the Vampirate crew."

"You don't need to say it." Bart closed his eyes.

"I do," Connor said. "Because if I say it, you might just understand that nothing can ever be the same. If I say it, you might just jump back in that light-boat, sail away and forget you ever knew anybody by the name of Connor Tempest."

"No," Bart said, raising his hands to his ears. "I don't want to hear it."

"I'm hungry for blood!" Connor cried. He reached out and tried to displace Bart's hands. "I, Connor Tempest, need and want blood."

Bart dropped his hands and shook his head. There were tears in his eyes. "Not you," he said. "Not you." Then almost a whisper: "Not you."

Connor frowned. "I didn't want to put you through this. I don't want to put any of the others through it. That's why it's better if I stay here. Now, perhaps, you'll understand."

Bart nodded, his face crestfallen.

"I'm going back to the ship now," Connor said. "It'll be dark soon and they'll wonder where I am." He looked up at Bart. "I'm hopeless at goodbyes," he said. "So I'm just going to turn and keep walking along this beach and you're going to get into your boat and go. OK?"

Bart nodded. "OK," he said, the small word heavy with all the sadness of the world. He stood on the sand, watching impotently as Connor set off on his lonely journey.

CHAPTER THIRTY-SEVEN

The Uninvited Guest

After his painful encounter with Bart, Connor stepped out onto the deck of *The Blood Captain* with a heavy heart. It hadn't been easy telling his long-time friend to go away and forget about him. In truth, Connor had never felt lonelier. Just when he needed friends like Bart the most, something inside him was telling him that – for their protection more than his own – he must push them all away.

The deck was deserted and Connor was grateful to be the first of the group to arrive. A cool night breeze was blowing and Connor inhaled it, hoping the deep breaths would help calm his tormented mind. He walked over to the deck-rail and gazed out at the ocean. The sky was already velvet-black and the sea took on the same dark tones. It was like looking out into an infinite void. Connor was unsure if it was the thought or the breeze which made him shiver.

Suddenly he felt a hand on his shoulder. Instinctively, his shoulders arched as he turned to see who it was.

"Good evening, Connor."

Connor found himself staring into the cold appraising eyes of Obsidian Darke.

"Lieutenant Darke, good evening."

"You seem somewhat agitated," Darke said. "Something on your mind?"

"No." Connor shook his head. "I'm just hanging out, waiting for the others to go over to *The Vagabond* for Tiffin."

"Tiffin," Darke said. "A nonsense, if you ask me. A hive of vampires buzzing around as if they're at a cocktail party. A complete and utter waste of time – even for those of us with unlimited rations of time at our disposal."

"If you think that," Connor said, "why bother going?"

Darke considered his words, then shrugged. "Your father wants me there and we must all march to the beat of your father's drum. Isn't that so? He is, after all, King of the Vampirates. For now, at least."

Connor frowned. "We all have to make our own choices," he said. "Be our own men."

Darke smiled, though the corners of his mouth barely curved upwards. "How young you are, Connor Tempest. How very young." He stepped back. "Well, I shan't wait with you for the rest of the pack. The sooner I get there, the sooner I can make my excuses." He turned and made his way across to the other side of the ship where a gangplank extended out to *The Vagabond.*

Connor turned back to the deck-rail, grateful to be free from Darke's cloying company. He wasn't, however, alone for long. Hearing footsteps, he turned to see which of the others had made it out first. As he looked up, his heart plummeted.

"What are you *doing*? I told you to go!"

"I know," Bart said. "But I couldn't leave like that. You mean too much to me – to all of us. I had to come and talk to you just one more time."

Connor shook his head. "Talking won't solve this," he said. "We could talk for days and we wouldn't find a resolution."

"I'm not ready to give up on you, buddy," Bart said, wrapping his muscle-bound arm around Connor's shoulder.

Connor shrugged off Bart's hug and turned to face him. "You have to get off this ship right now," he said. "Every second you stay here places us both in severe danger."

Shrugging, Bart turned and leaned against the deck-rail. The message was clear — he wasn't going anywhere. Connor frowned. What could he do? He knew that Bart was acting out of the goodness of his heart, but this was madness and highly dangerous.

Behind them, the deck door creaked open. Connor glanced across as two figures stepped out onto deck. Stukeley and Johnny saw Connor and raised their hands in greeting. They strode over to join him. Connor's blood ran cold.

"Who's your friend?" Stukeley asked, as he and Johnny arrived at Connor's side.

Bart turned and presented his face to them. Johnny was nonplussed but Stukeley's face turned a whiter shade of pale. "What are you doing here?" he asked coldly.

Bart grinned. "Is that any kind of greeting for your old mucker? Seems to me I gave you a friendlier welcome when you returned to *The Diablo* not so long ago."

Stukeley was unmoved. "We've all traversed a lot of water since then," he said. "You're on our ship now and you're not welcome. Especially now that you're part of the Vampirate assassination squad on board *The Tiger*." Stukeley glared at Bart.

Connor's eyes darted between his two old friends. He watched as Bart shrugged nonchalantly and extended his hand to rest on Stukeley's shoulders. "Seems like your memory is getting highly selective, old pal," he said. "Didn't you and your cowboy companion here do a deal with my captain, Cheng Li — head of the assassination squad? Didn't you in fact join forces with her in an attempt to assassinate Lady Lola Lockwood, wife of your commander-in-chief?"

Stukeley exchanged a dark look with Johnny, then looked back at Bart. No further words were spoken but it was apparent that some form of stand-off had been reached.

"Is your *amigo* joining us at Tiffin?" Johnny asked Connor, brightly.

"No," Connor said.

"Yes," Bart answered simultaneously.

"No," Connor said again, louder.

Stukeley smiled. "Actually," he said, "I think Bart *should* come along. It could be fun."

Johnny grinned. "Well, he can't come in those clothes. They don't even pass for smart casual. You know Lola's a stickler for such things."

"Can one of you lend me something to wear?" Bart asked.

Johnny grinned again. "As you can see, *hombre*, you're a little bigger than us three. I'd be happy to lend you some clothes but I don't think you'd be able to fasten them."

Stukeley nodded. "He's right on the money, as per. There's only one person on this ship with the same collar size as you."

As if on cue, the deck door was thrust open again and Sidorio swaggered out onto the deck. As usual, he was dressed elaborately in a custom-made outfit by Lola's favourite tailor. The captain pounded over to the others in a cloud of pungent aftershave. "Evening, all." Noticing Bart, he raised an eyebrow. "Who are you?"

Connor stepped into the fray before any of the others could. "This is my friend Bart," he said. "He's come to visit me. Just overnight. Assuming that's OK with you."

Sidorio looked Bart up and down, then turned to Connor with a smile. "Whatever you wish," he said. He extended his hand to Bart. "Any friend of my son's is a welcome guest on my ship."

Connor watched as Bart and Sidorio shook hands. This whole meeting was surreal. He wondered if Stukeley would say anything about where Bart had come from, but he held his tongue – for now. It was Johnny who broke the silence.

"Captain, we were just saying that Bart needs something more formal to wear for Tiffin. We wouldn't want to offend Lady Lola. He's only packed a capsule wardrobe and he could really do with borrowing a shirt and some pants from you."

"Pants?" Sidorio boomed, eyes raised.

"He means trousers," Stukeley said. "Pants is the American for trousers."

"Oh!" Sidorio looked mightily relieved. "Connor, you know where my cabin is. Take your friend over and find something for him to wear. Us three will head over to *The Vagabond* as an advance party. Lola, as you know, hates to be kept waiting."

"Yes, Father," Connor found himself saying. Anything to keep the peace. He was aware of Bart flinching as he said it.

Firmly he led Bart across the deck and through the door leading into the ship's interior.

When they were safely inside, Connor turned to Bart once more. "This is madness!" he said. "Stukeley and Johnny will be telling Sidorio all about you right now."

Bart shrugged. "Perhaps," he said. "But I'm assuming their captain doesn't know about their secret pact with Cheng Li. I think that stick of dynamite should buy me a few hours of protection, don't you?" He smiled.

Connor shook his head. "You're not dealing with mortal minds any more," he said. "You need to understand that things play very differently around here."

"Don't worry about me," Bart said. "I can take care of myself. Let's small-chunk this – one step at a time. Our next challenge is to find me something that fits but which isn't made of either leather or chainmail. And absolutely no feathers!"

Lola peeled herself away from Sidorio's side as Grace entered the room, flanked by Mimma and Nathalie. Lola smiled to herself, noticing how like three gothic peas in a pod they looked. The girls had done exceptional work on her stepdaughter.

"Grace, darling, how charming you look tonight. Sid will be so touched you're wearing his mother's brooch *again*. And I see Mimma's done you another heart tattoo."

"Yes," Grace nodded, her eyes bright. "I was thinking I should get it tattooed on properly."

"I suppose so," Lola said, drawing her away from the others and leading her into an unclaimed corner of the room. "We need to have a little chat, dear."

Grace rolled her eyes. "What have I done now?" she asked.

"Hmm," Lola said. "I wonder." She folded her arms. "Let me give you a clue. It involves a key, my cellar and a certain swarthy *vacquero*."

Grace realised there was no getting out of this. "I'm sorry," she said.

Lola frowned. "I've told you before, Grace. I have high standards for my crew – and even higher ones for members of my family." Her expression softened and she extended a silk-gloved hand to Grace's shoulder. "If you wanted blood, you need only have asked. After all, I am the world's leading connoisseur of the stuff. Skulking around in the cellars with Johnny, well it's just not how *people like us* behave!"

Grace's eyes were wide and hungry. "You'd really give me blood?" she said.

"Of course." Lola's eyes sparkled and she beckoned over Jacqueline who was carrying a silver salver bearing a bottle and two glasses. Lola lifted the bottle and poured a modest amount

307

of the ruby liquid into each glass. Then she extended one to Grace. "Wait!" she commanded, imperiously. "First we tilt, then we swirl. Then we luxuriate in the aroma. And then – *and only then* – do we drink it."

Lola lifted the glass to her lips and took a sip. Grace upended the glass and drained it thirstily in one. Lola exchanged an exasperated look with Jacqueline. "Like father, like daughter," she said. "Just what I need – another project."

Mimma appeared at their side, smiling excitedly. "Excuse me, Captain, but your husband is asking for you. It seems that Connor has arrived with a friend."

"Really?" Lola's interest was piqued. She turned to Grace. "Jacqueline will keep you topped up during Tiffin," she said. "But you must learn to sip *not* glug. I will not have a binge drinker in the Lockwood Sidorio clan." So saying, she turned and walked away to join her husband once more.

"Darling," Sidorio said, his hand reaching across to stroke the small of her back, "I'd like you to meet a good friend of Connor's, Bart Pearce. He's visiting for the night."

Lola extended her gloved hand to Bart and smiled. "Welcome to *The Vagabond*, Bart." She laughed coquettishly. "I heard Chef Escoffier was serving rare beef tonight, but I had no idea this was what he meant."

Bart bowed his head to Lady Lola and kissed her gloved hand. "It's a pleasure to meet you, Lady Lockwood. I mean Lady Sidorio! Connor has told me so many nice things about you."

"Really?" Lola arched an eyebrow, then smiled at Bart. "Please, call me Lola." She looped her arm through his. "Now, let's get you a drink," she said, leading him off with Connor and Sidorio following close behind.

Bart looked apologetically at his host. "I don't mean to be rude, but I'm afraid I don't really drink what you're serving."

Lola waved his hand. "I know that, silly, but I do have a few

308

more conventional vintages in my cellars, you know. When my husband tipped me off you were coming, I had the girls go down to find a bottle of the 2505 Shiraz. I take it that might be to your taste?"

"Well, yes!" Bart said, as surprised as he was relieved.

Smiling, Lola clicked her fingers and Zofia appeared at her side with a bottle and a glass. "Bart, Zofia. Zofia, Bart. Zofia will take care of your particular drinking needs tonight, won't you, dear?"

Zofia nodded and smiled prettily. Lola spun Bart around towards the table. "If only I'd had more notice of your visit I'd have asked Chef to prepare more food."

Their eyes swept across the table which was, as usual, groaning under the weight of Chef Escoffier's creations.

"It looks like there's plenty to me," Bart said.

Lola placed her glove on Bart's forearm and gave it a squeeze. "A man of your dimensions needs a good feed," she said. "But don't worry, Grace seems to be off her food at the moment, so you can have her share! Look, there she is, Connor's twin sister – not that you'd know it to look at them."

Bart nodded. "We know each other," he said.

"You do? Oh, isn't life amusing? Six degrees of separation? Pah! More like two, I say. Grace! I say, Grace! Come on over and say hello to an old friend."

Grace reached for Johnny's hand and together they approached Bart and Lola.

"Hello, Grace," Bart said, opening his arms to hug her hello.

She looked at him strangely and did not embrace him, one hand squeezing Johnny's tightly, the other locked around her glass. "Bart, how surprising to see you here. Have you met my very good friend, Johnny Desperado?"

Bart nodded. "Yes, we met before," he said, turning jovially to Johnny. "How's your night going?"

"Swimmingly, thank you," Johnny said, tipping his Stetson towards Bart. "And yours?"

"Very enlightening," Bart said.

Lola reached forward and swiped the Stetson from Johnny's head. She sent it flying into the corner of the room, where it landed on a hat-rack. "Johnny dear, you know the rule. No hats indoors. And frankly why you'd want to cover up that lovely head of hair is a mystery to me." She ran a gloved hand through his thick, dark locks.

Grace frowned and tugged at Johnny's hand. "Weren't you about to tell me something in private?" she said.

Johnny glanced at her. "Was I? Oh, er, yes, of course I was." He followed as she led him off towards a private corner.

Lola grinned at Bart. "Don't they make a lovely couple?" she said. "Well, Bart, do sit down." She glanced over her shoulder. "You too, Connor. You know how delicious Chef's food is."

"Yes," Connor said, sitting down and pulling out the seat next to him for Bart.

"We'll catch up later," Lola said, her gloved hand massaging Bart's shoulder. Then, she looped her other arm through her husband's and propelled him away.

Bart nudged Connor. "This isn't going bad at all, buddy," he said. "Great food. Good Shiraz. Beautiful ladies. And your stepmum, Lady Lola – she's a hoot. I'm so glad our assassination attempt failed and I got the chance to meet her properly."

Connor frowned. "Don't be deceived by appearances," he said. "And don't let your guard down for a moment. You might just die laughing."

But Bart grinned, irrepressible as ever. "Buddy, I told ya before. I can take care of myself. Now pass me the jumbo shrimp and try to *relaxez-vous!*"

CHAPTER THIRTY-EIGHT

The Fourth Buccaneer

Bart nudged Connor. "Grace has changed quite a bit, hasn't she?"

Connor shrugged. "Has she?"

"Clothes, hair, black heart tattoo, Vampirate boyfriend . . . yup, I'd say she's certainly changed some since last I clapped eyes on her."

Connor glanced up at his sister. She was standing hand in hand with Johnny, regaling her girlfriends about something or other. They seemed to be hanging on her every word. Evidently, she was Ms Popularity within the Vampirate ranks. She appeared to be having a good time – maybe it was even for real. If so, good on her! Doubtless, she was finding the whole transition to being a dhampir a whole lot easier than he was.

"Buddy, do you reckon that's *blood* in Grace's glass?" Bart asked him.

"I don't know," Connor said, somewhat bored. "What's this new obsession of yours with Grace?" Nevertheless, he found himself looking over once more, just in time to witness her take a long sip from her glass. As she did so, the hunger was evident in her eyes. Could she *actually* be knocking back blood like it was grape juice? It was possible. He couldn't condemn her. As

311

his eyes circled the room, he was suddenly aware of all the blood in close proximity. In glasses. In bottles. He could smell it. Taste it. He wanted it. Now.

"Connor?" He felt Bart grip his arm. "Buddy, did you hear what I said?"

Connor was torn from his reverie. He turned to Bart and noticed his friend's expression. "What's wrong?" Connor asked. "You look like you've seen a ghost."

"Not a ghost!" Bart rasped. "For a moment there, you had actual fire in your eyes."

Connor shrugged. "It happens when I get the hunger. It happens to us all."

There was a haunted look on Bart's face. "I remember when I first saw Jez – I mean Stukeley – look that way. And now you share the same look."

"Don't worry," Connor said. "I'm not about to lean over and puncture your neck, if that's what you're concerned about. I have it under control."

Bart frowned. "How can you be so sure?"

"Can we *please* talk about something besides blood?" Connor asked impatiently.

Bart nodded, heartened to see that his friend's eyes were now back to normal once more.

"Tell me about my old friends." Connor found the words exiting his mouth before he had time to censor them. "Tell me about Cate."

"Of course!" Bart exclaimed, smiling. "In fact, there's something I've been meaning to tell you all day. You know how close Catie and I've gotten of late?"

Connor nodded.

"Well, I've made a decision. When I get back to *The Tig*—" He swallowed his words, aware of his audience, then lowered his voice. "When I get back, I'm going to ask her to marry me."

"You are?" Connor's face broke into a huge grin. "That's awesome news."

Bart nodded and patted his pocket. "I found my gran's wedding ring. It was in that old sea-chest I've been lugging around with me all this time. I'm going to give that ring to Catie."

"I'm really happy for you," Connor said, reaching out to hug his friend.

"I hope you'll think about coming back for our wedding."

"Sure," Connor said, for want of anything better to say. "I'll think about it."

Watching from a distance, Lola prodded Sidorio. "The hunky Australian certainly seems to have cheered up Connor. That's the first time I've seen him smile properly in nights."

Sidorio nodded, but frowned. "You do know which ship Bart's from, don't you?"

"*The Diablo*, right?" Lola said. "Presumably he was one of the lucky pirates out on the lash when Johnny and the girls took over the ship."

Sidorio shook his head. "He *was* on *The Diablo* originally, with Connor and Stukeley – when Stuke was on the other side. But now, he's been seconded to *The Tiger*."

"*The Tiger*?" Lola's eyes widened. "The ship of would-be assassins? The ones who tried to off me at our wedding breakfast? The next ship on our list?"

Sidorio nodded. "Yes, my dear, the very same." He turned to her. "Don't you find it quite some coincidence that he should turn up out of the blue tonight – the very night before we mount our attack?"

"You think the little pirates know something?"

Sidorio shrugged. "We can't rule it out," he said. "Though I don't see how they could. Do you?"

"No." Lola shook her head. "Maybe he *is* just here to see his old friend. It's clear they have a genuine bond." Her eyes were glued to Bart now. "I wonder, though . . . do you think he's here to tell Connor something? No, not to tell him but to *ask* him something. About us? About our ambitions, perhaps?"

Sidorio shrugged. "Who knows? But I don't want him going back to *The Tiger* before Obsidian Darke and his team head out there tomorrow night. It's in our interest to keep that pirate here, under our radar, for the next twenty-four hours."

Lola nodded. Then her eyes grew diamond bright. "Darling, I have an even better idea. Seeing as he makes Connor so very happy, why don't we keep Bart here indefinitely?"

"What are you suggesting?" Sidorio asked.

Lola leaned closer and whispered in her husband's ear.

"A-hem, a-hem!" Stukeley interrupted. He had climbed onto a chair and was signalling to the rest of the room. "Ladies and gentleman, if I could have your attention for one moment."

"If you break that Chippendale, you'll have far more than my attention to deal with!" Lola cried. There was a ripple of laughter.

"I promise I'll be careful," Stukeley said to Lola, then turned back to address the group. "We have a very special guest in our midst tonight and I'd like you all to charge your glasses in readiness to raise a toast to him."

Connor and Bart looked towards Stukeley with alarm. He had captured everyone else's attention too. Zofia stepped forward to top up Bart's glass. She offered Connor a glass of wine too, which he reluctantly accepted. It was, all things considered, better than the alternative.

Around the room, the rest of Lola's team busily refilled every glass, until each Vampirate was poised. Stukeley continued his toast. "As many of you know, back in the bad old days, I was a pirate."

There were hisses and boos around the room. Once more Connor and Bart frowned. Where was Stukeley going with this?

314

Stukeley tutted. "Oh, you are a miserable lot," he said, working the room. "Yes, I was a pirate, working alongside young Connor here and this strapping lad, Bartholomew Pearce. Indeed, the three of us were such a tight-knit unit, that we were given our very own nickname . . . the Three Buccaneers. And we had this saying, didn't we, lads?" He glanced at Connor and Bart, his eyes bright. "*Didn't we, lads?*"

They nodded mutely.

"Yes," Stukeley continued, more loudly. "And this is how it went." He raised his glass aloft. "One for all!" He turned expectantly to the others. "Come on, boys! One for all . . ."

Connor and Bart rose to their feet, glasses in hand, but as they opened their mouths to speak, another voice was heard.

"And all for one!" Johnny cried, standing and raising his own glass.

Sidorio's distinctive laugh boomed around the room. "It seems that where once there were three buccaneers, now there are four!" he said.

"Very good, darling!" Lola laughed throatily and raised her glass aloft. "Friends, family, crew-members!" Her eyes swept the room and settled on Bart. "Honoured guests! A toast to the *Four* Buccaneers."

"The Four Buccaneers!" chorused the rest of the gathering. Glasses were raised and Bart watched as, all around him, blood was drunk in his honour. His eyes moved from Lola to Sidorio to Stukeley – who jumped down from the antique chair to join him. Bart's eyes travelled along the row of Lola's attractive crew – was it his imagination or were they all staring at him? – and onto Grace, with her strange new tattoo and her cowboy boyfriend. At last, his eyes settled on Connor. Bart saw Connor raise his glass to his lips and the blood-hunger flicker in his old friend's eyes. Was Connor now drinking blood too? He could no longer tell the difference.

Bart set his own glass down on the table but his hand was shaking and his glass tumbled over, spilling a fan of red across the stark white damask tablecloth. "I'm sorry," he said, turning to Connor. "I'm sorry, I can't do this. I need air . . ." He pushed back his chair and weaved through the crowd, desperate to find the door.

Connor abruptly set down his own glass and headed for the exit.

Lola stepped forward to survey the wine-spill but her efficient crew were already cleaning up the table.

As Lola left her husband's side, Obsidian Darke seized the opportunity to approach Sidorio.

"Captain," Darke said, reaching into his jacket. "I have made my list for the attack tomorrow night." He removed a square of paper from his inside pocket and opened it out before passing it to Sidorio. "This is the crew I would like to support me."

Sidorio glanced down at Darke's predictably precise handwriting and smiled. "You've chosen well," he said. "What you lack in quantity, you have more than compensated for in quality. These are all of my best fighters, present company excluded, of course."

Darke nodded. "Do I take it that I have your permission to enlist these men and women, Captain?"

Sidorio nodded, folding the list and passing it back to Obsidian Darke.

"Excellent," Darke said, putting the square of paper away again. "There are two more names I wanted to add to the list but I was unsure of the protocol."

Sidorio arched an eyebrow. "Which other names?"

Darke cleared his throat before continuing. "Connor and Grace."

Sidorio's interest was piqued. "You'd like my son and daughter to participate in this attack?"

Darke nodded. "Of course, I have heard of your son's fighting

316

ability. And I saw it with my own eyes when he got the better of you a few nights back. If what I hear on the grapevine is true, your daughter is equally talented."

"They have good genes," Sidorio said, with some pride. "Darke, you may take Grace into the attack with you but Connor is unavailable." Sidorio smiled broadly. "Tomorrow night will be my son's initiation into blood-taking."

"I see," said Darke. "Well, of course, that's a momentous . . . moment in any young vampire's life . . ."

Sidorio waggled his finger. "Connor's not merely a vampire," he said. "He's a dhampir."

"Quite so," Darke said. "Well, it appears that I shall have to make do with one twin only." He nodded at Sidorio. "Captain, I thank you for the loan of your daughter."

"Make sure no harm comes to her," Sidorio said. "Or there will be consequences."

Darke nodded. "Understood, Captain." Seeing Lola making her way back towards them, Obsidian Darke hastened his speech. "And now I shall return to *The Blood Captain* and map out the attack in more detail."

"I hope you're not leaving on my account," Lola said, as she returned to her husband's side.

Darke shook his head. "As ever, it is business that calls me away. Thank you for a most entertaining Tiffin." He turned and made a hasty path to the door.

"That man gets more odious every night," Lola said.

"Yes," Sidorio agreed. "I'm beginning to hope that one of the Vampirate assassins gets the better of him."

Lola laughed and chinked her glass against his. "I'll drink to that," she said.

Darke lost no time in striding across the deck towards the gangplank leading back to *The Blood Captain*. It was windy out on deck and he had raised his hood. As it flapped in the breeze, he glimpsed Connor on the other side of the deck, talking to his pirate friend. For a moment, he considered turning back and speaking with them. But the night air was brisk and time, as ever, was short. As was his habit, Obsidian Darke kept his head down and proceeded briskly about his business.

Connor and Bart stood together at the guard-rail of *The Vagabond*. "I've got to go," Bart said.

"Yes." Connor nodded.

Bart looked down at his light-boat, idling in the water below. "I'd tell you to jump in, buddy, but I see now that it could never work."

Connor sighed. "If only it were that simple. I'd love to come back to you and Cate and Jasmine and the others. You guys gave me a home when I had none and I'll always be grateful for that."

"Everything's different now," Bart said. "You're right. You belong here, with Stukeley and the others. I know what a great friend he can be – and I hope he will be a good one to you now, because, buddy, you badly need someone in your corner."

"Let's not draw this out," Connor said, doing his best to rein in his emotions. "I told you before I'm rubbish at goodbyes."

Bart nodded, his eyes empty and broken.

"Will you tell the others the truth about me?" Connor asked him.

Bart hesitated for a moment, then shook his head. "No," he said. "They don't need to know."

Connor smiled gratefully. "Would you tell Jasmine that I wish things could have been different?" Then he shook his head. "Actually, better you don't say anything to her. Hopefully she'll find happiness again with Jacoby." Tears pricked at Connor's eyes. "I'm *so* pleased about you and Cate," he said. "You two belong together. You're everything that's good and true . . ." His voice faltered and he was unable to finish.

Bart stepped forward and hugged his friend. "You don't need to say anything more, buddy. And neither do I. We both know what we mean to each other."

Connor nodded, hugging Bart and trying to shut out the thought that it would be the last time he did so. As Bart finally released him, Connor spoke softly. "I'm going back to my cabin on *The Blood Captain*. I need to be alone for a while."

Bart nodded and, as Connor walked away across the deck, he climbed over the guard-rail and made his descent to the light-boat waiting below.

Bart wasted no time. He had to get away from this place and back to normality as swiftly as possible. He couldn't afford to think about Connor or Jez. It was too painful, too paralysing.

He lit his hurricane-lamp and strung it to the mast of the boat, then pulled up the anchor. As it landed with a thud in the centre of the small craft, Bart realised how heavy his heart felt. Ignoring this, he scanned his charts. He had no fishtail to guide him on this return journey but he would do just fine, navigating home by the stars. It would keep his mind occupied.

Once he'd gained a little distance, he permitted himself to turn back and take one last look at the two Vampirate ships, moored side by side in the water. Then, to his horror, he spotted three more ships moored alongside. At the end of the line was *The Diablo*, the latest addition to the Vampirates' ever expanding fleet. There was no mistaking the galleon's distinctive lines. He knew they'd taken it but somehow he hadn't quite believed it. Now he saw it was true. He shook his head. No more, he thought. They wouldn't succeed in taking *The Tiger*. He turned away, vowing not to take another backward glance.

As he did so, he noticed a pair of hands on the starboard side of the boat. "Kally?" he said, surprised. She had said that she was heading back to *The Tiger* before night fell.

"Who's Kally?" asked a familiar voice as a svelte figure, clad in a scarlet scuba suit covering all but her face, hands and feet, climbed deftly into the light-boat.

Bart watched dumbfounded as the head of the scuba suit was peeled back. Lola Lockwood shook out her raven locks. "That's better," she said, smiling at him.

"What are you doing here?" he asked. "I'm heading home now."

Lola looked a little offended. "After the welcome I gave you, Bart, I'm a little offended you didn't say goodbye to me in person. And have your forgotten that you are still wearing my husband's clothes?"

Bart was trying to get the measure of the situation but he was tired and hadn't reckoned on this strange turn of events. He realised that, whatever else, he had to keep Lola talking.

"Is that what this is about?" he asked, essaying a smile. "You're coming to claim your proper goodbye? To get your husband's clothes back?" He began unbuttoning the shirt, but Lola shook her head.

"Goodbye is such a final word," she said. "This is only *au revoir*."

As he continued unbuttoning Sidorio's shirt, Bart's fingers suddenly froze. He noticed the pearl-handled dagger in Lola's hand. Where had that come from? His own sword was beyond his reach. *No worries*, he calmed himself. He was a heck of a lot bigger than her. He could easily overpower her and throw her over the side. He remembered the last bout of combat training Cate had given him and prepared to defend himself.

But before he knew it, Lola had Bart in a stranglehold. He felt utterly paralysed by her grasp. They were locked together in

320

a horrible parody of an embrace. Lola's mouth was close to his ear and she spoke to him softly now. "I thought a dashing young pirate like you would wish to die by the dagger. Yes, darling, that's right. I'm going to kill you now. But there's no need to be frightened." Her eyes gazed upon him with a strange tenderness. "I'm going to stab you very cleanly through the heart. It will be sudden and largely painless."

She was mad, utterly mad, but Bart was powerless to do anything but listen to her ravings. "You'll fall into something akin to a deep sleep," she said. "We call this state the anteroom, because it's a holding point for the next stage of your journey." Her voice was as gentle and reassuring as a mother singing a lullaby to her baby. "You'll sleep and, during that time, we'll take you back to the ships. There, my husband will complete the process. He will sire you, Bart. And you will be one of us. Connor will be so happy, don't you think? I could tell he didn't want you to leave and now you never will. So you see, my sweet little pirate, it truly *isn't* goodbye but only *au revoir.*"

As she spoke these last soft words, Lola took the pearl-handled dagger and, true to her promise, stabbed it clean through Bart's chest. But before the point even pierced his flesh, Bart Pearce knew that his big old heart was irreparably broken. He thought of Connor. He thought of Jez and Molucco. He thought of Cate. And then, nothing.

CHAPTER THIRTY-NINE

Family Portrait

Connor pushed open the door to Lola's cabin and was surprised to find it quiet and empty. No, not empty . . . as he closed the door behind him, he realised there was one other person in the room: Grace. She was standing beyond the table, in front of an easel which had been draped in red velvet. Now, as she became aware of Connor's presence, she turned to face him. At first, it was a shock to see her sporting the black heart tattoo around her left eye, but then he realised that she had in fact been wearing it the past few nights – though it was only now that he seemed to be seeing her properly for the first time.

"Where is everyone?" Connor asked, approaching the table. A spread of food had been laid out for them, although by usual standards, the quantity was modest – more like a picnic supper than a feast.

"They're all getting ready for the attack," Grace said. "There's a note here from Lola." She pointed to the table but Connor didn't bother picking it up. "She says that she and Sidorio will be along later and we should go ahead and help ourselves."

Connor hesitated, somehow reluctant to sit down at the table.

322

"The attack tonight," Grace said. "It's against your ship, isn't it? *The Tiger*."

Connor nodded. "Yes – though strictly speaking, *The Tiger* is Cheng Li's ship."

Grace's eyes met his. "Aren't you worried for her and your other comrades?"

"Sure, I'm concerned," he said, "but if anyone can defend themselves against Vampirates, it's the crew of *The Tiger*. In fact, if anyone needs to worry, it's Obsidian Darke. He's the one leading the rebel attack."

Grace shivered at the mere mention of Darke. There was something disquieting about him. She stepped towards the table and surveyed the spread. As usual it looked delicious but, since she had started drinking blood, her hunger for Chef Escoffier's treats had dwindled. Grace suddenly turned back to Connor, her eyes bright. "You've warned Cheng Li about the attack, haven't you?"

Connor smiled, but said nothing.

Grace nodded, piecing together the jigsaw in her head. "*That's* what Bart was doing here. You've sent a message back with him."

Connor shook his head. "You're close but actually Bart's appearance took me by surprise. The message went back ahead of his visit."

Grace pulled out a chair and sat down. "I envy you, Connor. Throughout all of this, you've always known what side you're on. Your life has so much clarity – you're a pirate on an undercover mission. Whatever's happened here, however much Sidorio and Stukeley ingratiate themselves with you, you've never lost sight of your mission. You were simply here to spy on the rebels and send back intelligence, and that's what you've done. And now, I suppose your mission is successfully concluded and you'll be returning to *The Tiger* – assuming it survives tonight's attack."

Connor pulled out the chair beside her. "It *will* survive the attack," he said, sitting down. "Cheng Li and Cate have been preparing for this scenario for months." He paused, his voice softer now. "But I'm not going back."

Grace's eyes registered surprise. "What do you mean?"

Connor held her gaze. "Exactly what I say. I'm a dhampir now. Of course, I always was – I just didn't know it. So now I have this constant hunger for blood. How can I possibly go back and live amongst normal people?"

"Mortals," Grace corrected him.

"Like I say, normal people. I'm no longer mortal. I'm a dhampir, Sidorio's son. I hate it, of course. I hate the hunger and the violence. Frankly, I hate just about everything about my life aboard *The Blood Captain*. But, most of all, I hate this thing I've become. I'd give anything to go back to my old life, but that isn't an option. I can't fight my true being but I *can* protect the people I really care about – and that means staying as far away from them as possible."

"Oh Connor," Grace said, reaching out her hand to him. "I'm so sorry you feel this way. I wish we'd talked sooner."

He shrugged, squeezing her hand but letting it go. "What's the point in talking? We'll probably get through this. We usually do."

Grace frowned. "Connor, I hate to see you like this. You're immortal now. We've both been blessed with this amazing gift. You can't just plan on 'getting through' eternity – there has to be more to it than that. We have to make our lives meaningful!"

Connor smiled bitterly. "Bart and Molucco both have this motto: a pirate's life should be 'short but merry'. I never really saw the point of it before, but when I think of the alternative – *this* alternative – I completely get it."

Grace shuddered. "Are you really saying that you'd swap places with Molucco? He's dead now, isn't he?"

Connor nodded. "Yes, and yes."

"Oh, Connor," Grace said again, shaking her head.

"Let's talk about you," he said. "Seems like you've adapted to life here pretty easily, unlike me."

"Too easily," Grace said. "Don't forget, I came here on a mission too. Well, two missions, in fact. My official mission was similar to yours – to spy on the rebels and report back to the Nocturnals." Seeing her brother's blank face, she reminded him, "That's what Mosh Zu and Lorcan have renamed their crew."

"Yes, I remember," he nodded. "And how has your mission gone?"

Grace nodded. "I've done my bit, reporting back to them each night via astral travel." Suddenly she paused, glancing at him. "Hey, how about you? How did you send your messages back to Cheng Li?"

Connor smiled. "I sent them via a fishtail – a kind of mermaid. How else?"

Grace nodded, impressed. "Well, like I say I've done my bit. I've told them how things work around here – Lola's blood harvests, that kind of thing. I think they feel it's been useful."

"You don't sound so sure," Connor said.

Grace shrugged. "I'm sure about their feelings; it's mine I'm less certain about. Although I came here on an official mission, I had my own private mission as well. I wanted to change the way things worked here. I thought I could use my influence, this new position as Sidorio's daughter, to change the way they did things. Naively, I actually thought I might be some kind of civilising force."

"What happened to change your mind?" Connor asked.

"This," Grace said, sweeping her hand across the table. She picked up a tiny rose-coloured macaroon and placed it on her palm. "These pretty little cakes – and everything else they've been feeding us from our very first night here – are laced with blood. They've been using them to stoke my hunger. Yours, too, of course."

Connor nodded. It all made sense.

"You seem to have managed to control your hunger much better than me," Grace said. "I'm out of control, Connor. I'm so ashamed to admit this but a few nights back, on one of Lola's blood hunts, I almost killed a girl. Isn't that terrible?"

Connor shrugged, his expression dark. "There's already one killer sitting at this table," he said. "Why not two?"

Grace frowned, hating hearing him so down on himself. "You had good reasons for killing that guard. You acted to save your comrade's life. But Lola's sprees are just sport. All that blood, bottled up in her cellars, is totally unnecessary."

Connor shook his head. "Surely it's completely necessary. Everyone on these two – or rather, *five* – ships needs blood to survive, Grace. Us included."

"Yes," Grace conceded. "But there *is* another way – the way of the Nocturnals. I lost sight of that in this fog of hunger but now I'm beginning to see clearly again." She faced Connor square on. "The thought of someone taking blood was never so terrible to me because I've seen how it can be done in a disciplined, responsible way – through the donor system." She crushed the blood macaroon in her fist and brushed the crumbs onto the floor. "People don't need to die for us to thrive."

Connor was impressed by his sister's sudden show of strength. "You said you envied my clarity of purpose but it seems like you're the clear-sighted one, Grace. If you're able to accept your hunger for blood, then you know the ship you *should* be sailing on; the people you need to be surrounded with. From where I'm sitting, it looks like you have it all worked out, sis."

Grace shook her head. "It's nowhere near that cut and dried, Connor, you know that. I like it here. I've always found the

326

Vampirates fascinating. I love their culture and I love hearing their personal histories. It wasn't the worst thing to discover that I truly belonged in this world. I thought it was going to be horrible coming on board *The Vagabond*, but in many ways it's more fun than *The Nocturne*. I've made great new friends here – Mimma, Jacqui and Nat . . ."

"And Johnny?" Connor added.

Grace blushed. "Yes, and Johnny. He's very cool. I met him before, you know – at Sanctuary. He thinks he's such a bad boy but deep down he's just a pussycat."

Connor raised his eyebrows. "From what I hear, he led the attack on Molucco. Your pussycat may be another man's killer tiger."

Grace's face was guarded. "Johnny's very susceptible to other people's influence," she said. "He was in his mortal life and he has been ever since he crossed over. He's been moulded by Sidorio and Stukeley, but he's just as open to good influences . . ."

"Like you," Connor suggested.

"Well, yes," Grace said.

"I thought that you already had a boyfriend," Connor said.

Grace frowned. "I do," she said. "And I care deeply for Lorcan. He's been so brilliant, right from the start. The last thing I want to do is hurt him, but I think I may already have done that."

Connor squeezed her hand. "You're young," he said. "We both are. We always knew we had our whole lives ahead of us; we just didn't realise we'd been granted the bonus eternity package. Grace, after everything we've been through, I think we're allowed some time to make mistakes, to find out what we believe and who we are."

Grace smiled. "Yes," she said. "You're right."

"It was nice having this chance to talk, just the two of us," Connor said. "It's crazy really – we've been on each other's doorsteps for the first time in ages and yet we've barely spoken two words to each other each night."

"Yes," Grace said. "But we both had a lot going on. It was good just to know you were close."

Connor smiled at her. "Thanks, Grace. That means a lot."

She squeezed his hand once more. "I'm always here for you," she said. "You may be shutting other people out from your life but, please, don't shut me out." She smiled. "I think what I'm starting to realise is that we're far more in control of our own destiny than we've given ourselves credit for."

Just then, the door opened, and Lola swept inside, Sidorio close upon her heels.

"Hello, darlings," Lola said, striding towards the table. She frowned. "What's up with you two? You've barely touched a thing."

"I'm not hungry," Connor said, unapologetically.

"We were too busy talking," Grace added. "It was nice to have some family time."

"Talking of family," Lola said, turning to Sidorio, "I have a surprise for you, my love."

Three pairs of eyes turned expectantly to Lola. Smiling, she strode past the twins to the end of the table, approaching the easel draped in red velvet. "Signor Caravaggio delivered our family portrait earlier this evening. I forced myself not to peek until we were all together. Come closer, everyone, and I'll unveil it!"

The twins stood up from the table and walked over to join Lola. Sidorio followed.

Lola gripped the velvet cover by the corner and pulled. "One . . . two . . . three!"

Grace gasped.

Connor frowned.

Sidorio smiled.

Lola jettisoned the cloth and clapped her hands. "Oh, isn't it marvellous? Hasn't he done a wonderful job?"

"Yes," Sidorio said, drawing Lola to his side. "My family."

"*Our* family," she corrected him, beckoning the twins to come and join them.

Connor lingered at the portrait, reluctant to join in any group hug. The picture was absolutely grotesque. They had all been painted with the fire of hunger in their eyes and both he and Sidorio had blood dripping from the sides of their mouths. Although the painter had achieved a good likeness of each of them, he had also employed a hefty dollop of artistic licence. They certainly hadn't needed to sit for so many hours for *this*.

"It's very good," Grace said, punchily. "Where are you going to hang it?"

Sidorio shrugged but, as ever, Lola was ahead of her husband. "Darling, I thought you should have it on *The Blood Captain*. After all, that's the lead ship in our fleet. And that way, even when Grace and I aren't physically on board, you'll have a lovely reminder of the two most important women in your life."

Sidorio nodded and leaned across to kiss his wife. "Perfect," he said.

Lola lifted the picture and presented it to her husband. "Why don't you take it with you now?" she suggested. She turned to the twins. "Well, seeing as neither of you has touched your food, I declare Tiffin to be over. Besides, the night holds much excitement for you both." She smiled enigmatically.

"What kind of excitement?" Grace asked.

Lola turned towards Sidorio. "I'll let your father explain," she said.

Sidorio smiled, his gold teeth glinting. "Lola's right. Tonight *is* a very special night for you both," he said. "Grace, you are to report to the deck of *The Diablo*. Obsidian Darke has requested that you join his attack force."

Grace's face went white. "He wants *me* to join the attack on *The Tiger*?"

"Isn't it exciting?" Lola said. "Run along, dear, it's not long till they sail. Oh, and you might want to rethink those shoes."

Before Grace could protest, Sidorio approached Connor. "My son, this will be the night of your initiation. Tonight, you will become a fully-fledged dhampir as you and I take blood together." Sidorio smiled proudly at his son. "Go now to your cabin on board *The Blood Captain*. You'll find a note from me there, and the first of three gifts to mark this momentous night."

CHAPTER FORTY

The Quick and the Undead

Grace felt adrenaline course through her as *The Diablo* sped across the ocean in pursuit of *The Tiger*. She had never been involved in a battle before and had absolutely no idea what to expect. Nor did she have any clue as to why Obsidian Darke should have claimed her for his team – or why Sidorio and Lola had agreed to his request. Was she being sent into the battle arena to prove herself or merely to die? Less than an hour ago, she'd been talking calmly to Connor about their immortality but she hadn't reckoned on being dispatched to war that very night! True, there had been no Vampirate fatalities in the previous three attacks – at least none that had been reported back – but tonight was fundamentally different. They were attacking a ship of dedicated Vampirate assassins. A cold dread took hold of Grace. She'd had no combat training – save a few lessons during her brief sojourn on this very ship – and, if things proceeded as expected, this was going to be a very violent confrontation indeed.

After parting from Connor and the others, Grace had gone back to her cabin. She had found a new pair of boots and an antique sword lying on her bed, along with another of Lola's handwritten notes:

*I think both of these may prove useful to you. The sword
once belonged to another Grace – an Irish pirate by the
name of O'Malley. I "borrowed" it from the Pirate
Academy. Mum's the word!*
LLL xxx

Now Grace gripped the hilt of the ancient sword in her right
hand. Her other hand clasped Johnny's tightly. He'd been
shocked to see her arrive on deck and quickly reassured her that
he'd watch out for her in the fight. She was grateful to hear it.
It was all very well Lola giving her a legendary pirate's sword but
she hadn't the first idea how to use it. It really ought to be
Connor standing here in her place – he'd know exactly what to
do – but it seemed that Sidorio had other plans for her brother
tonight.

Grace glanced towards the prow of the ship, where Obsidian
Darke stood alone, his back turned to the rest of the crew. He
was barely lit by the moonlight. *The Diablo* was sailing with no
lights so as to arrive at *The Tiger*'s side without warning.
Although, Grace reminded herself, Connor had already sent
them a warning, so even if the actual moment of attack was a
surprise, the fact of it should not be. It was eerie sailing on a
ship in utter darkness, making your way through the night.
Around her, the ocean had become a void. With her vision
limited, Grace's other senses intensified. She could hear the
heavy rigging creaking overhead but, as she glanced upwards,
her eyes couldn't even pinpoint the top of the mast.

Darke, whom her eyes returned to now, was a similar
enigma. In many ways, Grace found him a more chilling
presence than Sidorio – who had lately revealed a more human
side. In contrast, she had been unable to break through Darke's
defences. Perhaps it was a good thing. Grace could only guess

at the layers of dark sediment which had accreted over so many years to form Darke's character.

As the galleon rolled from port to starboard and back again, Darke's footing seemed preternaturally solid. Silhouetted by moonlight — arms folded, head fixed on the horizon — he resembled a statue. Not the graceful statues you found in museums but the more brutal kind, raised by dictators — of themselves — in parks and squares, to remind a subjugated people of their lot in life.

Johnny nudged Grace and pointed ahead. There in the middle of the dark ocean was a brightly-lit ship: *The Tiger*. Its mainsail was down and its deck lights on. Grace felt a wave of nausea. The ship looked so vulnerable. Could it be that Connor's message hadn't reached Cheng Li?

Now Obsidian turned to address the rebel troops. "We're nearly there," he cried, his thunderous voice carrying not only across the deck but further, out across the ocean. "You've already had your instructions. I have only one thing to add." At that point, a shaft of moonlight illuminated Darke's hard face and cold eyes. "Kill or maim any pirate who crosses your path. But leave the captain to me."

As *The Diablo* slammed into the side of *The Tiger*, the two wooden hulls cracked and splintered on impact. Vampirates began leaping the gap between the two ships even before the three wishes slammed down into position.

"Stay close!" Johnny cried, gripping Grace's hand and leading her to the middle wish. "Watch your step," Johnny told her now. "The wishes get slippery and you need to watch out for sudden movement too. It's best to move fast."

Grace followed in Johnny's wake, doing just as he instructed. As she jumped down onto the deck of *The Tiger*, Grace felt a fresh wave of adrenaline pumping into her veins. No wonder

Connor had grown addicted to such moments. She was filled with fear and yet, in a way, she had never felt so alive.

Although the pirate ship had seemed unprepared for attack, this was clearly a ruse, for now the members of its crew came streaming out from every corner, waving swords and roaring battle cries. The fight had begun.

Grace stuck close to Johnny. She had already made a decision. She would be merciful and only use her sword to defend herself. She just hoped she was capable of that. As she witnessed the speed and force of the fighting around her, she backed away to the very edge of the deck.

Her overriding impression was of speed and confusion – and blood, so much blood. She had imagined these battles as like one of Connor's soccer games, but the reality wasn't anything like that. There was no order here. It was hard even to tell who was on each side. By and large, the Vampirates and the pirates were dressed in similar battle attire and both sides wielded similar-looking swords. Already, several bodies had fallen onto the deck, creating obstacles for those left standing.

Suddenly, Grace saw a familiar face charging past her.

"Cate!" she called out, immediately recognising Connor's mentor and her own former comrade. Cate either didn't see her or chose to ignore her, as the weapons supremo headed into the centre of the deck and – seconds later – speared a Vampirate right in front of Grace's eyes.

"Get in!" Cate congratulated herself as she raced on towards the heart of the deck.

Grace had never seen her this way before. Cate might be a pirate rather than a Vampirate but, right now, she too had fire in her eyes.

Obsidian Darke moved single-mindedly through the battle zone, watching grim-faced as members of his team were struck down. It was too early to call which side had the upper hand. His dark eyes watched Stukeley cutting a swathe through the pirate ranks. He realised he had underestimated Sidorio's lieutenant. Having seen him so often playing the clown at Tiffin, it was an adjustment to watch him now as a powerful warrior. Darke's eyes sought out Johnny and Grace, but he was unable to locate them amongst the melee.

As two pirates simultaneously charged him, Obsidian Darke expertly dispatched them both. He didn't even see them as genuine adversaries – merely irritants to swat away. He had only one target and nothing was going to prevent him from getting to her. At last, he saw her up ahead at the prow of the ship. Cheng Li – captain of *The Tiger*. Leader of the self-styled Vampirate assassins. At last, she was in his sights. Darke dipped his head and charged.

Cheng Li was monitoring the progress of the battle and the number of dead and wounded falling on her pristine deckboards. In the opening stages, it had seemed to her that Cate's strategy, and especially the insights she had gained from her sessions with the delectable Lorcan Furey, were reaping dividends. Watching her young crew dispatch the cocksure demons had filled Cheng Li with a warm and fuzzy feeling inside. But then, several of the "dead" had risen from the deck, in spite of their livid wounds, and returned to the fray – worse, it seemed as if they were now possessed of a new energy and determination.

"Cate!" Cheng Li cried. "Spread the word. We need more instant kills!"

Without missing a beat, Cate ran down the centre of the deck, carrying the message. "Make sure you finish them off, people!"

Jacoby heard the cry and picked up the theme. "If in doubt, decapitate!"

Cheng Li nodded. This fight was far from over but she had no doubt that she would emerge the victor. It could be no other way. All her life had been building towards this mission and this moment. It was the single most important battle in the history of the Pirate Federation. After tonight, when pirates spoke in hushed tones of reverence about a Li, it would be about her and not her father.

Up ahead, the Vampirates had gained some headway and Cheng Li noted with displeasure that two of her best young fighters had fallen. Their killers moved on remorselessly, in a pincer movement, both heading for Cheng Li. She lost no time propelling herself into the air in another move devised by Cate and Lorcan. Before she even landed, she had kicked one of her opponents across the deck and into the guard-rail. He smashed onto the floor, stunned, leaving Cheng Li time and space to deal with the other aggressor.

The Vampirate had evidently taken time out to feast on one of his previous victims. Blood was running down his mouth to his chin. Cheng Li gritted her teeth. Even such a repulsive sight as this was not going to put her off her game. She executed another of Cate and Lorcan's special manoeuvres, jumping clean over the vampirate, then twisting in mid-air and striking out with her silver sword from the other direction.

Annoyingly, her blow – just fractionally – lacked the requisite force and, though the blade speared the Vampirate's belly, it was not deep enough to remove him from the fight for long. Cheng Li reached out to reclaim her sword and have another go but the Vampirate was ahead of her. Suddenly her sword was in *his* hands and *he* was bearing down on *her*. She was more indignant than fearful. How on oceans could the duel have turned so quickly in the wrong direction?

The Vampirate lifted the silver sword to strike. Unfazed, Cheng Li coolly reached behind her back to draw her twin *katanas*. But as her hands made contact with her back, she realised that something was wrong.

"Looking for something?" the demon asked her, obviously amused. Cheng Li followed his gaze to the edge of the deck, where her *katanas* now lay, impotent and useless. He must have cut the straps when she jumped over him. Furious with herself for not realising, she now faced up to the prospect of imminent attack by this Vampirate, while – no! – a second moved into position behind her.

Cheng Li cursed the Vampirate. She cursed herself. Tonight was the night she was due to write her place into the history books. Now she'd be lucky to merit a footnote in Molucco Wrathe's chapter. It couldn't end here. It just couldn't. But, as the grinning vampirate – blood spilling from his chin onto her beautiful deck – brought down his sword, Cheng Li prepared for an uncomfortable reunion with her father in the afterlife. She could just imagine the disapproving look on Chang Ko Li's face.

Now the second Vampirate – the one looming behind her attacker – raised his own sword. Cheng Li froze. Was she destined to be killed by not one but two demons?

Having notched up another outright kill, Jacoby took a breath and scanned the deck. He was filled with exhilaration and pride as he saw his crewmates performing at their dazzling best. He watched Cate fight two Vampirates simultaneously. Her face might be red but she had yet to break sweat. Just past her, Jasmine was gaining the upper hand also. She had mastered Cate's new moves as expertly and effortlessly as he'd have expected. Watching her skewer her vampire opponent like a demon kebab, Jacoby felt a new wave of respect and affection for his girlfriend. And there, just to her side, was that indefatigable fighting machine, Bo Yin. There was no one more athletic on their crew. Bo was running rings around her attackers.

Jacoby turned, ready to run back into the fray. As he did so, he caught sight of Cheng Li at the prow. She was trapped – with two Vampirates bearing down on her. Jacoby's blood ran cold. He didn't have time to reach her. The captain was on her own and it looked like Jacoby was about to receive an unwanted promotion . . .

Cheng Li's eyes moved from her first attacker to the second Vampirate, hovering behind him. Whichever way this played out, it wasn't looking promising for her.

The second Vampirate roared in the ear of the first, "Let her go!"

"Beat it!" cried the first Vampirate, angrily. "I was here first!" He raised his sword and Cheng Li prepared for the end. But, to her amazement and confusion, the second Vampirate now raised his own sword and calmly and cleanly decapitated his comrade. The first demon's vile face registered considerable surprise as his head flew past her en route to the ocean.

Meanwhile, his abandoned body turned confused circles, until a strong hand pushed it to one side and sent it spinning across the deck.

"I told you before," boomed the imperious voice of Obsidian Darke. "The captain is mine."

CHAPTER FORTY-ONE

The Allies

Cheng Li stared into the face of her killer. It was just the two of them now, cut off from the rest of the battle, standing at the prow of the ship. The Vampirate's grey-black eyes bored into hers. He turned and retrieved Cheng Li's sword, which the first would-be assassin had been carrying, prior to his decapitation. Curiously, the Vampirate handed Cheng Li's sword back to her.

"You're going to need this," he said. "And those *katanas* too, I think."

Cheng Li raised an eyebrow as the Vampirate stretched out his arms and the *katanas* flew into his hands, as if drawn by a magnetic impulse. Now, he passed these weapons back to her too.

"Is it a duel you want?" Cheng Li inquired of her adversary.

He contemplated her words, then shook his head. "Not with you, Captain Li. There is much work to be done. We shouldn't waste time sparring with one another."

Cheng Li frowned. "I don't understand," she said. "You mean you're *not* going to kill me?"

"Correct," he said, his voice sounding suddenly more

human. "Turn around and I'll repair your holsters so you can carry those *katanas* once more."

Her first thought was that it was a trick but, nevertheless, she turned, figuring that he would have killed her by now if that was his intention. She felt the Vampirate tighten the straps on her back and slot the two blades back into their sheaths. Then, to her further surprise, he placed his hands on her shoulders and turned her around to face him.

"I'm confused," she said. "What's going on here? Who *are* you?"

The corners of the Vampirate's mouth now lifted in a smile. "My name is Obsidian Darke and I am a Vampirate captain."

"Exactly," Cheng Li said. "You led this attack. Presumably you intend to kill me?"

He shook his head. "I'm not your murderer, Captain Li. I am your ally. My name perhaps is meaningless to you, so let me explain further. I am the captain of *The Nocturne* and its crew – the Nocturnals. I went into hiding for a time and left instructions for my comrades to prepare for the coming war. During this time, I was embedded within the rebel empire of Sidorio, watching his every move. While I was there, you made an alliance with Lorcan Furey, my lieutenant. He was acting on my behalf."

Cheng Li shook her head in disbelief. "So you're not just *a* vampirate captain," she said. "You're *the* Captain."

"Yes, Captain Li." He nodded and smiled. "It's good to be back."

Cheng Li was elated not only by her eleventh-hour reprieve but also by this unforeseen turn of events. Now she knew she was not about to die, she wanted to know how things were going. She looked beyond her ally to survey the scene on deck. "The battle awaits," she said.

Obsidian Darke nodded, then raised his hands in the air

once more. This time, his hands summoned a mist. It came on so suddenly and so completely that instantly the battle came to a standstill. The stunned combatants, on both sides, froze as they waited for the mist to clear. No one could see an inch beyond their face. The deck grew eerily silent. Then there was a bump, and a crack on the starboard side, and *The Tiger* lurched. It felt as if another ship had pulled up alongside them.

The mist lifted as quickly as it had arrived. Cheng Li's heart was racing. A third ship *had* arrived at their side – *The Nocturne* – and now the rest of the Nocturnal army, led by Lorcan Furey, entered the fray.

Obsidian Darke turned to Cheng Li. "I believe the tide has just turned," he said.

Cheng Li's eyes were bright. "Let's finish this," she said. "Together."

Seeing Lorcan and their allied forces streaming into position filled Cate with a fresh burst of energy. She surveyed the deck and saw yet another female Vampirate sporting the black heart tattoo. Maybe this was another of the evil crew who had murdered Molucco Wrathe. Cate had already dealt with two of the others personally – why not make it a hat-trick? This one was, strangely, lingering at the edge of the deck. It would be an easy victory. Cate let out a battle cry and ran at her, silver sword aloft.

Grace had been stunned both by the descent of the mist and then by the sight of Lorcan arriving on deck. But it wasn't just Lorcan's arrival that had taken her by surprise, it was also his appearance: he looked completely different to how she remembered him. She had noticed, during her last few astral visits, that he was putting on muscle due to his nightly training bouts, but it was only now that she realised that his evolution into an imposing young warrior was complete. She waved at him and began assessing how easy it might be to negotiate her way across to him through the fray.

But before she could work this out, Grace was faced with a far more urgent problem. Cate was running straight at her, fury in her eyes and sword spinning in her hand. Grace wanted to cry out to her to stop but, by the time she'd introduced herself, she'd be dead. Actions were going to have to speak louder than words. Nerves pulsing through her body, she drew her own sword. Seconds later, silver clashed against steel.

To her amazement, Grace managed to successfully defend herself against Cate's first blow, but there was no time to congratulate herself. The weapons supremo was already lining up her next attack. Grace ought to have been terrified but, curiously, her fear had drained away. In its place, she felt a calm and focused energy.

As Cate swung her blade a second time, Grace found that her own sword was already in the perfect position to repel it. Unrelenting, Cate lined up the next attack. Once again, without forethought, Grace moved her sword into position ahead of Cate's blade. Cate lined up another strike. Quicker than ever, Grace's sword shot through the air. This time, she sent Cate's sword back with some force. Grace buzzed with adrenaline. It was as if she could read Cate's every move before it happened! It was exhilarating.

Cate was surprised at how well the Vampirate girl was fighting. She was a natural swordswoman. It was a pleasure to fight somebody so competent with the sword – most of her previous combatants had shown little flair in that department and relied instead on raw aggression, which they had in spades.

As she looked deep into her opponent's eyes, she couldn't believe what she saw.

"Grace!" she exclaimed. "Grace Tempest!"

"Yes," Grace cried. "I wanted to tell you before, but you'd have sliced me in two before I got my name out."

"What are you *doing* here?" Cate asked, incredulous.

"It's complicated," Grace replied. "And there's no time for lengthy explanations. But, Cate, I'm not here to fight you or any of the other pirates. I was sent on this attack against my will."

Cate frowned, remembering Molucco and weighing up the odds. "Grace, you're not on my crew. And if you're not on my crew, you're the enemy."

Grace shrugged, her eyes aflame. "If that's how you feel," she said. "Let's fight!" Her sword was already pulsing with energy. She was ready.

Jasmine was starting to feel a little fatigued after her many bouts. She had a wound to her left shoulder blade but it didn't seem to be major. The pain was bearable and the blood-flow seemed to be staunched for now. In spite of this setback, she was pleased with her success and that of her comrades. Now the allies had arrived, the Vampirates were falling thick and fast.

But the problem of finishing off the Vampirates was still ongoing and Jasmine soon found herself under attack from a familiar face.

"I killed you five minutes ago," she cried, indignantly.

"Guess again!" said the Vampirate with a grin.

As the Vampirate charged, Jasmine instinctively jumped backwards to open up more space for the fight. As she landed, instead of meeting solid deckboards, her feet met flesh. Jasmine lost her balance and fell down on top of a slain Vampirate. Her own attacker lost no time. He leaned over her with a twisted grin and reached out his sword. With a dead Vampirate underneath her and a decidedly "undead" one on top, there was nothing Jasmine could do but pray.

Her attacker's grin suddenly froze and Jasmine saw a spike run through his chest.

"Roll, Jasmine!" a familiar voice cried. Obediently, Jasmine rolled to her side as the speared Vampirate crashed down to join his inert crewmate. Looking up, she saw Bo Yin withdraw her sword from the Vampirate's back.

Bo Yin grinned as she reached out a hand to help up her comrade. "You owe me one, Jasmine Peacock!"

Jacoby smiled in delight as he watched Lorcan and his team getting stuck into the fight. The tide had definitely turned in their favour. It was time to shift this battle up a gear. The deck of *The Tiger* was littered with the fallen of both sides. The stench was grim, the deck slick with blood as well as seawater, and it was getting harder and harder to move around. Jacoby looked across to the empty deck of *The Diablo* and assessed the distance. Then, raising his sword aloft, he pushed through the crowd and propelled himself over the side of *The Tiger*, onto *The Diablo*. Once more, the ancient galleon was under pirate control.

Jacoby stood on the deck, hands on hips, coolly staring back at the Vampirates over on *The Tiger*. One of them returned his gaze directly, his eyes dark and brooding. Jacoby knew this man. As Jez Stukeley, he'd been a legendary pirate fighter. From what Jacoby had observed tonight, Stukeley was still at the top of his game. He would be a worthy adversary.

Grinning, Jacoby beckoned him across. "Come on, then." He drew his sword. "Come on over if you think you're hard enough!"

Eyes aflame, the Vampirate began to run towards him.

Grace's sword clashed against Cate's once more. Although she had vowed to use Grace O'Malley's sword only to defend herself, as the fight progressed, Grace was finding that she was equally adept at initiating her own attacks. She wondered at this new ability. Was it derived from this sword in particular – with the spirit of Grace O'Malley somehow guiding her hand – or was it in fact another manifestation of her dhampir powers? Whichever, Grace was filled with satisfaction as she struck Cate's sword with such power that it fell from the pirate's grasp. Instinctively, Grace edged further forward to prevent Cate from retrieving her weapon.

"Wait!" Cate raised her hand. "I surrender!" Her face was pale. "Before you kill me, tell me one thing." She paused for breath. "What have you done with Bart?"

Grace frowned, aghast. "I'm *not* going to kill you," she said. "I was *never* going to kill you."

"Tell me where Bart is," Cate said. "He went to visit Connor two days ago and we haven't seen him since."

Grace nodded. "He did come to visit Connor. He was on the ship last night, but he got upset and left to come back here."

"Look around you, Grace. Do you see him?" Cate's face was ashen now. "He never came back."

Now, Grace drew down her sword. "I don't understand. Where is he?"

CHAPTER FORTY-TWO

The Third Gift

"There," Sidorio said. "My final gift. Like I say, not *quite* ready for you."

Connor couldn't speak. Looking into the heart of the cabin, every fibre of his being froze. There, laid out on a low bed, was Bart. Or rather, Bart's body. Was this some trick, some hallucination brought on by his first proper taste of blood? No. It was what it was. He could see it and sense it. Sidorio's third gift. This, this *horror* was truly Sidorio's idea of the best gift of all.

"What have you done?" Connor rasped. "*Why* have you done this?" He shook his head, then opened his mouth and let out a deep, keening wail.

Sidorio placed his arm around Connor's shoulder. "Hush," he said. "Calm yourself and let me explain."

"How can you possibly explain this?" Connor was incredulous, hot tears streaming down his face. "You've killed my best friend. And now you present his body to me and expect me to *thank* you?"

Sidorio frowned at Connor's anguish. "Actually, Lola killed him. This was something we both wanted to do for you – together. You're missing the point, son. His *body* isn't the gift.

I told you before – he's not yet ready for you. I'm going to sire him. I'm going to breathe eternal life into Bart. *That* is my gift to you."

Connor shook his head. "You're mad!" he said. "You and Lola both. You're stark, staring mad."

As Stukeley traded blows with Jacoby on the deck of *The Diablo*, he couldn't help but be impressed by the young pirate's flair.

"You're good at this," Stukeley observed, as their swords clashed.

"I know!" Jacoby threw his strength into forcing Stukeley backwards.

Stukeley laughed, dusting himself down and preparing for the next bout. "Arrogant, too. I used to be just like you, you know."

"Alive, you mean?"

Stukeley laughed, raising his sword to repel Jacoby's attack once more. "Alive or undead, it makes no difference," he said, as they parried along the deserted deck. "What matters is the skill with which you wield your weapon." Their swords clanged together once more. "And you," Stukeley said, catching his breath, "you wield the steel well, my friend."

Jacoby grinned. "My sword is made of silver. All the better to destroy you with, Vampirate!" His eyes met Stukeley's. "What's with all the compliments? Next thing you know, you'll be trying to recruit me to the dark side."

"That's not such a bad idea," Stukeley said. "We can always use skills like yours on the team. You should think about it, pirate."

"Over my dead body!" Jacoby cried, lifting his sword aloft once more.

Stukeley laughed. This time, he had gained the upper hand

in the skirmish. After a volley of sword strokes, his rapier made contact with the flesh of Jacoby's forearm. As he drew blood, he laughed. "Death *is* usually part of our recruitment process," he said.

In contrast to the empty *Diablo*, the deck of *The Tiger* was still crowded with combatants. Johnny didn't have much room to manoeuvre, but it hadn't stopped him notching up a good few victories. He was having fun – so much so that he had temporarily lost track of Grace. He had promised to look out for her in the fight and, to the best of his ability, he had. But this last bout had left him closed in at the centre of the deck, not far from the mast. Now he tried to break through the crowd to go and find her. As he did so, he felt a hand grab him by the back of his collar and jerk him backwards.

Johnny spun around to face his adversary and found himself looking into a familiar pair of sky-blue eyes. "Well, well," he said. "Lorcan Furey. How are you, old pal? It's been a while."

"I'm not your pal," Lorcan said, his gaze severe. "The last time I saw you was at Sanctuary, where you behaved like a demented rodeo rider. I had to step in to rescue Grace from you."

"Well yes," Johnny said. "I'm sure that's how *you* saw it. I'm sure you go to bed each day and dream about rescuing damsels in distress. Happy to have been of service." The movements of the fighters on either side of them pushed Johnny and Lorcan closer towards each other. Lorcan stretched out his arms to shove Johnny away again. Johnny grinned. "Looks like someone's been working out."

"Do you ever shut that hyperactive mouth of yours?" Lorcan snarled.

"Sometimes," Johnny said, smiling. "Like, maybe when I'm kissing a beautiful dhampir."

Lorcan's eyes blazed fire at Johnny. "If you've laid one finger on Grace," he said fiercely, "you'll have me to answer to." He shoved Johnny roughly, but nothing could wipe the grin from the cowboy's face.

"Seems to me Grace has grown up some since you last saw her," Johnny said. "She can make her own decisions now and I didn't hear her complaining any when we were out riding all those nights, snuggled up nice and close."

"Stay away from her, you hear?" Lorcan said. "You're no good for her."

Now Johnny frowned. "You're not interested in what's good for Grace. You just want her for yourself. You may have been the first Vampirate she happened upon, but now she has someone to compare you to. Now she can make a more . . . *informed* choice."

Lorcan shook his head. "You may have worked some superficial charm on Grace," he said. "But there's nothing you could do to rival the deep bond she and I share."

"I know, I know," Johnny said. "It was you that plucked her from the oceans. It's a tired story, *amigo*."

Lorcan's eyes were bright. "We go back much further than that. I held her in my arms when she was only a baby."

Johnny rolled his eyes. "And you don't think there's anything freaky about wanting to be her boyfriend?!"

"I don't *want* to be her boyfriend," Lorcan said, darkly. "I *am* her boyfriend."

Johnny shook his head. "Don't be so sure, *amigo*. The way Grace has been acting lately, it's by no means certain that you're still in the picture. No, I'd say the jury is very much still out on that. But, hey, we don't need to argue this out between ourselves. Grace is up on this very deck. Let's go find her and have her explain the state of play."

Lorcan was visibly alarmed to hear that Grace was on the

ship, in the midst of this fierce battle. It was the very last place he believed she should be. But he reined in his fear and kept his eyes trained on Johnny. "We can talk to Grace in a moment," he said. "But first, I'm going to rough you up a little."

"Really?" Johnny said, clearly amused.

Lorcan nodded, at last finding the space to draw his sword. "I don't usually enjoy inflicting pain, but in your case, Desperado, it's going to be a pleasure."

Sidorio frowned. "Connor, I just don't understand you. I'm racking my brains, doing everything I can to try to make you happy but you don't seem at all grateful."

"*Happy?*" Connor was virtually speechless. "*Grateful?*"

Sidorio nodded. "I know how close a friendship you had with Bart. I could see how happy his visit made you. But it could never work – him being a mortal and you a dhampir." He smiled and stretched out his hands. "This was the obvious solution. Once I breathe life back into Bart – once I sire him, as I did Stukeley – the three buccaneers will be properly reunited for all eternity! No father could offer his son a greater gift than that."

Connor looked from Bart's lifeless corpse to Sidorio's smiling face. He shook his head. "I didn't ask for any of this. Being your son. Being a blood-hungry freak. You say you want to make me happy. Don't you see? I *was* happy before – when I had a career as a pirate and good friends in my life." His eyes flashed fire at Sidorio. "Now I'll never be happy again – thanks to you and your insane wife. I only have one regret – that I failed to kill Lola when I had the chance. If I'd been successful, Bart would still be alive tonight."

"Connor, I can see you're hurt but please, don't say such things. Your stepmother only wants the best for you. As do I. And Bart *will* live again." He stepped towards Bart's body.

"No!" Connor shouted. "Stay away from him!"

Sidorio turned, evidently perplexed. He opened his arms in a paternal gesture but Connor retreated from him. When he reached the wall, he slumped against it and dropped down, curling into a ball and sobbing uncontrollably.

Sidorio walked over and leaned against the wall beside his son. "I know what it is to be lonely, Connor. Perhaps you're forgetting that I too have been on this journey, so I know exactly what you are going through. I was killed – by Caesar, of course – and then granted the gift of immortality. And, be in no doubt, this *is* the greatest gift a mortal can receive." His tone grew softer. "Nonetheless, it *is* lonely to begin with. We all know that. You are immediately cut off from your friends and family. You know that you will remain ageless as they grow old and diseased and die. You have a choice: do you stay and endure that constant torture or do you take yourself away? I made my choice. I turned my back on my old life and went out into the world. I had some amazing adventures but, I will confess, I often felt lonely. For the longest time, I kept myself to myself, refusing to let anyone get close."

Connor felt the tears drying on his skin. He listened, intrigued in spite of himself to hear Sidorio talk this way. "The first hundred years are the worst. I don't want that for you. Things are better for you, in any case. You will never be alone. You have your sister. You have me and Lola and Stukeley. You are surrounded by people who love and truly understand you, Connor. Don't you realise how fortunate you are?"

Connor emitted a hollow laugh. "You really think you understand me?" he said, shaking his head. "You understand *nothing*."

Sidorio looked bereft. Connor turned his face away and drew himself to his feet. He walked over to Bart's prone body and reached out to take his friend's hand. It was cold and limp, utterly drained of life. Fresh tears flowed down his face. "I'm so sorry, Bart," he said. "You only ever showed kindness and generosity towards me. You didn't deserve this. It's all my fault and I'm so sorry."

"Connor." Sidorio had risen to his feet and was, once more, at his son's side. "You have nothing to apologise for." His gold fangs were prominent now. "Would you like to stay and watch me perform the siring?"

Connor looked incredulously at Sidorio. Hadn't the madman – the monster – understood one word that he'd said to him? Was he that stupid; that deranged? Clearly, the answer – on both counts – was yes. The only thing that spoke to Sidorio was action and, specifically, violent action.

Connor did the only thing left in his power. He drew his sword and aimed it squarely at Sidorio's chest. The tip of the blade cut through Sidorio's designer shirt and pressed against his flesh.

"Listen carefully," Connor said. "If you so much as touch my friend, I will run you through with my blade. Again and again and again. You may be immortal but I'll find a way to destroy you. I promise you, I'll find a way."

CHAPTER FORTY-THREE

Truth and Consequences

Connor's sword pressed into Sidorio's flesh. Father and son locked eyes – Connor's blazing with anger; Sidorio's filled with dismay. Sidorio was carrying a sword himself, in a holster attached to his belt, but he didn't even reach for it.

Footsteps drummed along the corridor, growing louder as they came close. The door to the cabin was slightly ajar and now it was pushed open.

Lola stepped inside and swiftly closed the door behind her. "What's going on here?" she demanded.

Sidorio's head swivelled towards her. "Connor's third gift wasn't to his taste," he said.

Lola addressed Connor directly. "Put down your sword." Her tone was civil but firm.

Connor's eyes lingered on Sidorio but, slowly, he drew down his sword.

"That's better," Lola said. "Now, let's talk about this. Like civilised people."

Connor let out a hollow laugh, but allowed her to continue.

"What exactly is the problem, Connor?"

He turned and looked at her in repelled wonder. "What do

you *think* is the problem, stepmother dearest? You killed my best friend."

"Well, yes," Lola said, confused and a little impatient. "And now your father is going to sire him for you so he'll have eternal life."

Connor's voice was firm. "No one's going to be siring Bart. Not tonight. Not ever."

Lola arched an eyebrow and glanced over at Sidorio. She could see the concern etched across his face. Her eyes turned back to meet Connor's.

"No doubt this was your idea," he said. "An act of revenge because I tried to kill you."

Lola shook her head, smiling indulgently. "Revenge? No, Connor. Don't you remember what I told you when I first welcomed you on board *The Vagabond*? That all past transgressions were forgotten and that our relationship would begin anew from that moment. I meant every word. Since I discovered you were my husband's son, I have welcomed you onto my ship, into our home, with open arms. I have acted only out of kindness and generosity to you. I take my stepparenting responsibilities very seriously. And this is how you repay me — by raising your sword to your own father? Connor, I'm disappointed in you."

Connor shook his head. "You still don't get it, do you? Neither of you do. You fiends killed Bart. I'll never forgive you for that as long as we all live."

"You seem to forget that we're all immortals here," Lola said. "That's a long time to bear a grudge, dear. Besides, you shouldn't be forgiving us — you should be *thanking* us. Few parents could bestow such gifts on a child."

"I'm not interested in your gifts," Connor said.

"Don't be so dismissive," Lola said. "Your father and I are constructing an empire, the likes of which the world hasn't seen

354

in a very long time. Naturally, we want you and Grace at our side." Lola sighed. "Connor, if you could just jettison this unappealing adolescent angst and open your eyes to the very real opportunities here, I think you'd see that we are offering you the most dazzling of futures."

Lola exchanged a glance with Sidorio. He nodded, buoyed up by her stirring words.

Connor remained unmoved. "I don't want anything from either of you."

Lola frowned. "This is getting a little trying," she said. "I'm sorry if there have been crossed wires here, but we truly thought that by breathing immortality into Bart's impressive but nonetheless mortal body, we would make you a happy young dhampir." Her dark eyes bore into Connor's.

Connor held her gaze. "You thought wrong," he said.

"Here's what I suggest," Lola said, refusing to accept defeat. "Take some time to rest and cool down – I'm afraid the Sidorio clan do have a tendency to burn quick to anger. You can't fight your gene-pool! If you go and think about this quietly, I'm confident you'll see that you've got the wrong end of the stick. Then Sidorio can proceed with siring Bart and we can all move on. As a united family."

Connor was silent for a moment. Lola smiled reassuringly at Sidorio, content that she had regained control.

Then Connor opened his lungs and let out a fearsome cry of anger. "No!" he shouted. "I'm not going to cool down or think this over. And, once and for all, no one is going to sire Bart. As for being part of a family with you . . . forget it! I'm leaving the ship tonight and I'm taking Bart with me. The least I can do is give him a proper burial."

Shaking, Connor pushed past Sidorio and lifted Bart from the bunk. His friend's body was heavy but, even without his new-found strength, Connor would have broken his own bones if necessary to remove Bart from that cabin. Hoisting Bart's body over his shoulder, he turned to leave the room. His sword was poised in case either Sidorio or Lola tried anything.

Sidorio followed him out into the corridor. "Connor," he said. "Please, don't run out on us like this. Don't let it end this way."

Connor turned to him, his eyes raging with fire. "*I* didn't end this. *You* did. You and that she-devil wife of yours."

Connor turned purposefully and walked off down the corridor. At the end of the passage, he turned into the main stairwell of the ship – and found to his horror that he was walking towards the family portrait. Sidorio must have hung it up there earlier.

Connor could hear Lola's and Sidorio's footsteps close behind him. Making sure that Bart was secure on his shoulder, he stepped up close to the portrait. Then he lifted his sword and slashed a diagonal through the canvas. It was especially gratifying slicing Lola's face in two. He lifted his sword and cut the remains of the picture into ribbons. His heart hammering, he drew down his sword and set off up the stairs.

Lola grabbed Sidorio's arm as they took in the vandalised portrait.

"Oh no," she cried, aghast. "After all Signor Caravaggio's fine work!"

"Do you think he could paint another?" Sidorio said.

Lola shook her head. "It would be too embarrassing to even ask." She shuddered. "How much sharper than a serpent's tooth it is to have a thankless child!"

Sidorio looked blankly at her.

"I was quoting Shakespeare," Lola said, impatiently. Seeing the hurt in her husband's eyes, her tone grew softer. "Mr William Shakespeare wrote plays, darling. In fact, there's one I think you'd rather like. I have it in my library. I'll read some of it to you later, Sid. Perhaps that will soothe your frazzled nerves."

Back on the deck of *The Diablo*, Johnny's and Lorcan's swords met once more.

"Of course," Johnny said nonchalantly, as he swiped at Lorcan, "the really *big* scoop on Grace is that she's developed a great liking for blood since you last saw her."

Lorcan swung his sword against Johnny's. "Don't waste your breath on cheap lies," he said. "You're going to need every bit of energy you can muster."

Johnny's eyes were bright. "It's no lie, *amigo*. Grace loves the ruby-red stuff." He spun his sword through the air, defending Lorcan's attack. "And why shouldn't she? She *is* a dhampir."

"A dhampir doesn't need blood to survive," Lorcan said.

"True," Johnny agreed amiably, between parries. "They have a choice, unlike you or me. But Grace has definitely given blood the thumbs up. Good for her, I say. It's one of the reasons why she fits in so well on our ships. See, we don't beat ourselves up about our appetite. Not like your lot – the ship of self-hating vampires."

Their swords clashed once more and locked together. Now Lorcan threw all his weight at Johnny, pushing him back along the deck. "The Nocturnals are not *self*-hating," he said. "We just hate Vampirates like you. You give us all a bad name."

Johnny shrugged. "I think you just proved my point. No wonder Grace got bored of you lot and decided to defect to the fun side." He dug in his heels so that he was bringing his own strength to bear against Lorcan. It was, for the time being, a deadlock.

Lorcan smiled grimly at Johnny. "The only reason Grace came over to your ship was to spy for us," he said. "Whatever she's done – whether it's going riding with you or pretending that she's into blood – it's only been part of her mission. We've been playing you, cowboy and you're just too dumb to realise it."

Johnny's expression changed. His cockiness drained away in an instant. "I don't believe you," he said. "I know what went down between Grace and me."

Lorcan was merciless. "Sure you believe me. I can see it in your eyes. You've fallen for Grace. You've wanted her from the very first time you saw her at Sanctuary. You tried to steal her from me then – when I was blind and sick. That's the kind of lowlife you are, Desperado. But you couldn't have her then and you can't have her now. Face it, you were just part of her game plan."

Lorcan shoved Johnny backwards. Their swords separated at last.

Johnny's face was dark. "I'm going to kill you, Furey," he spat. He charged at Lorcan, and this time, Lorcan was wrong-footed. A space opened up in his defences and Johnny's sword found its way through. His blade sliced through Lorcan's hair. As a clump of dark locks fell to the deck, Johnny's sword continued towards Lorcan's neck, pressing in just below his right ear lobe. Johnny stared at his rival, his eyes full of fire. "Maybe I can't have Grace. But now, *amigo*, neither can you."

Cheng Li and Obsidian Darke were fighting side by side and proving an unstoppable force. As they each dispatched their latest victims, Cheng Li turned to the Vampirate captain.

"I always had you figured for a pacifist," she said. "Not a man of action."

"I used to be a pacifist." His voice was low. "But times have changed and I needed to change with them. It wasn't an easy transformation, but it was a necessary one."

Cheng Li's eyes swept across the deck. "I think we're winning this," she said.

"We have to," Obsidian said, his eyes as dark as his name. He raised his sword and ran back into the fight.

Lorcan felt the cold steel of Johnny's blade against his neck and glanced up at his dark, mocking eyes. He could tell the cowboy Vampirate was relishing this. He wondered how long he would draw out the moment of victory.

"Stop!"

Johnny and Lorcan froze to hear the familiar voice – the voice which had such power over them both.

Now Grace was at their side, her own sword in her hand. Her emerald eyes looked from Johnny to Lorcan and back again.

"Put down your sword, Johnny," she said.

Johnny exhaled slowly. "I can't do that, Grace. I'm sorry." He pressed the edge of his blade harder against Lorcan's flesh. Another millimetre and he'd draw blood.

"Wait!" Grace said. "I heard what Lorcan told you. I can understand why you're angry."

"Is it true?" Johnny asked, his eyes avoiding them both and fixed only on the tip of his sword.

Grace hesitated.

"*Is it true?*" Johnny repeated. "Grace, if you don't want me to do something bad, you need to start talking fast."

"Some of it is true," Grace said.

"Which part?"

"Stop hounding her," Lorcan rasped. "Just do what you have to do. Isn't that the cowboy code?"

"Shut up!" Johnny fumed. "Grace, I asked you which part was true."

"I did come to you, at first, on a spying mission. And I didn't trust you in the beginning. I've always liked you, Johnny. I know Lorcan won't thank me for saying that but we all know it's true. I'm allowed to like both of you. After what happened at Sanctuary, it was hard to trust you again, but you showed me a whole new side on those midnight rides. I enjoyed getting to know you – the real you." She paused. "And Johnny, the real you would know that if you want any kind of future with me, harming Lorcan would be the very worst thing you could do." As she spoke the words, she stepped closer.

Johnny's eyes darted from Grace to Lorcan and back again.

"I don't know what to believe," he said.

"Believe *me*," said Grace.

"She's only saying this to save my skin," said Lorcan.

"Wow," said Johnny. "You really do have a death wish, don't you? Well, the time for talk is over. I'm gonna make your wish come true." He drew back his sword and readied himself for the killer blow.

As his sword swung forward, it was met by another blade. But this time it wasn't Lorcan who faced Johnny along the length of their swords. It was Grace.

CHAPTER FORTY-FOUR

Choices

Grace looked at Johnny down the blade of her sword. "I'm not scared of using this if I have to," she said. Her confidence was buoyed up by the knowledge that, if necessary, she could wield Grace O'Malley's sword with consummate skill.

Johnny gazed in wonder at Grace. "I really don't want to fight you," he said.

Grace looked into his eyes. She found herself thinking of the twists and turns in their relationship. Joker Johnny who had kept her spirits up during those difficult nights at Sanctuary. The loner who'd confided in her about the bad choices he'd made in his life and after crossing. The Johnny who'd attacked her and told her, as he'd left to join Sidorio's team, "It ain't that I *can't* be good. It's just that I'm so much better at being bad." She had lost faith in Johnny then, but since arriving on *The Vagabond*, she'd got to know a different man. She thought of their midnight rides and their crazy adventure down in Lola's cellars. Remembered his frantic expression earlier that night when he'd seen her on the deck of *The Diablo*. She suspected that he'd been sent on some kind of charm offensive by Lola but, even if this was true, she didn't doubt that his feelings for her were genuine. One exchange above all others was etched in her mind.

"When you said I was a thousand times more fun than Lorcan, did you mean it?"

"No, Johnny. Not a thousand times more fun. A million times."

She remembered the vulnerability in his eyes then. He bore the same expression now. Seeing Lorcan and Johnny together made her feel guilty. She had feelings for them both – not quite the same feelings but strong feelings, nonetheless. It had been an exaggeration, brought on by the adrenaline of the night and the taste of blood, to say that he was a million times more fun than Lorcan. Her relationship with Johnny was easier in many ways but there were shades and complexities to her relationship with Lorcan that gave it deeper roots.

"I know you don't want to fight me," she said. "And now you need to let Lorcan go." She glanced over her shoulder. "You're losing the battle. Your team needs you."

Johnny looked past Grace, his eyes sweeping across the deck. She was right. His team was being decimated. There was no sign of Stukeley and there, in the heart of the battle zone was Obsidian Darke, fighting one of his own Vampirates. What was going on?

Johnny turned back to Grace. "You're right. I have to go. Wait for me, OK? Stay out of the fighting and wait until we go back over to *The Diablo*."

Grace shook her head. "I'm not coming with you," she said, with a certain sadness.

She expected him to go, then – he needed to rejoin the fight – but he seemed rooted to the spot, his eyes flickering with pain. "So I really was just part of your mission."

"No, Johnny," Grace said. "I told you before that I like you. I wasn't lying. I can't go back with you to *The Vagabond* and *The Blood Captain*. You were right – I *do* have the hunger for blood

362

but I can't bear the thought of someone dying in order for me to have it. The way that Sidorio and Lola run their ships repels me. It almost drove me to killing someone for blood myself. That's why I have to go back to *The Nocturne*. You say it's a ship of self-hating vampires but you're wrong. It's a ship of vampires who acknowledge their need for blood and have found a responsible way to fulfil it."

Johnny nodded. His eyes looked a little brighter. "I hear what you're saying. I wish it could be different but I understand that, for now, it can't." He held out his arm to her and tapped the words tattooed there. "Like it says right here, Grace – the ride is far from over. For all of us."

He winked at her, then gave her a salute as he ran off across the deck. Grace watched him enter the fray. She fervently hoped he would emerge unscathed.

There was still a lot of swordfighting going on but many of the rebel Vampirates had already been forced back onto the three wishes and were retreating onto *The Diablo*. Grace glimpsed one fight continuing on the deck of the other ship. Stukeley and Jacoby Blunt. Intrigued, Grace watched the well-matched duel for a moment. As yet more of the rebels ran for cover, her view of the fight was blocked. Turning her eyes back to *The Tiger*, she saw Jasmine Peacock tending to a wounded comrade – a girl not unlike a younger version of Jasmine herself. Grace searched for Johnny in the melee. Her eyes located him. He had jumped onto the ship's railing and was signalling the official retreat. Grace let out a deep exhalation of relief. It was over.

She felt a hand on her shoulder. Turning, she found Lorcan. He opened his arms and drew her into a tight hug. After all this time apart, being in his arms again felt like coming home.

"Thank you for saving my life," he said.

"Any time," she replied, her voice raw with emotion.

*

363

As the last of the surrendering rebels leaped back across from *The Tiger* to *The Diablo*, Johnny approached Obsidian Darke and Cheng Li. He was now the lone rebel left on the deck. The gap between the two vessels was widening, minute by minute, and he didn't have much time. But now that Obsidian had switched sides – and with Stukeley already somewhere on *The Diablo* – Johnny had assumed command of the rebel forces and he had no intention of racing away, tail between his legs.

He planted his feet squarely in front of his opponents. "So, Lieutenant Darke, you were playing us all along?"

Obsidian's shadowy eyes connected with Johnny's. "This was never a game," he said. "Lives have been lost here tonight – on both sides. These are matters to take very seriously."

Johnny nodded towards the bloodstained slash across the front of Darke's shirt. "It's a shame your opponent didn't aim a little higher. It might have been your side sounding the retreat."

Cheng Li addressed Johnny now. "Tonight marked the beginning of a new alliance between the Pirate Federation and the Nocturnals," she said. "We have a message for your captains." She exchanged a glance with Obsidian, then proceeded. "Tell Sidorio and Lola Lockwood that the war they so badly wanted has now begun."

Obsidian nodded. "My only regret is that Sidorio and Lola weren't here tonight. Then this might have been the end rather than the beginning." His eyes swept across the deck. "You've seen how roundly we defeated the rebel forces tonight," he said. "Report that back to them. Tell them that with our unbreakable alliance, the rebel Vampirates will never win."

Nodding grimly, Johnny turned and began his own journey back across the wishes. He wasn't looking forward to reporting this – any of this – to the captains. Well, at least, he wouldn't be alone. As usual, Stukeley would be right there at his side.

"Let me look at you, again," Lorcan said, his hands resting on Grace's shoulders. He smiled and shook his head. "You're more beautiful than when I last saw you. And you'll be even more so when you wipe that horrid heart off your face."

Grace frowned, but he didn't seem to notice. "You were so strong against Johnny," he said. "You sounded so convincing. Why, I almost believed you myself."

Grace bit her lip as she looked into his blue eyes. "Lorcan, I wasn't lying to Johnny. Everything I told him was the truth." She felt his body grow tense, but she had to be honest with him. "I do like Johnny," she said. "And I do like blood. I know you'd prefer that neither of those things were true but I can't lie to you just to spare your feelings." He was frowning as she continued. "So much has happened to me recently. I've gone through so many changes. If we're going to make things work, you and I, we have to be completely honest with each other."

Lorcan's frown began to dissolve. "It's a relief to hear you talking about making things work. For a moment there, I thought – I feared – we were over."

Grace shook her head. "Lorcan, I said that I liked Johnny. I didn't say I was in love with him."

His eyes grew bright again. "So, are you saying you're in love with me?"

Grace was distracted by movement in the centre of the deck. The victors were starting to line up along the edge of *The Tiger*, watching *The Diablo* as it began to make its retreat.

"This isn't the time or the place to discuss our feelings," Grace said. "Come on, we should join the others."

She turned and strode across the deck, full of energy and

purpose. Lorcan watched her go, feeling as if he'd been pushed away. She had said there was no time to talk but all he'd needed to hear was one word – yes.

At last, the allies could rest. Pirates and Nocturnals came from all corners of the deck to stand together as *The Diablo* pulled away into the night. Its lights had been switched on now and, seeing the line of victors, the rebel forces began to form their own equivalent line along the edge of the deck.

The allies were solemn as they observed their defeated foes. They knew that in the coming war not every battle would be theirs. Already, tonight, many of their own had paid the ultimate price for this victory. Many, on both sides, had sustained wounds.

Obsidian Darke stood side by side with Cheng Li. Captain Li looked out towards *The Diablo*, feeling justified pride at the story of this night. She would be the toast of the Federation after this but, actually, that mattered far less than the thought that she and her team, working alongside the Nocturnals, had together achieved something important as well as historic. This victory wasn't about writing her name in the history books – though that wouldn't be the worst thing that could happen – but about beginning to achieve a lasting peace on the oceans; ensuring that the pirates of the future might sail on far less troubled waters.

At Cheng Li's right hand was Cate Morgan, pre-eminent weapons supremo and attack specialist. Tonight's battle had been her proudest hour in military terms and would consolidate her outstanding reputation in the pirate world. She had raised her game – her art – to a whole new level working with Lorcan Furey and devising combat techniques to repel the superhuman enemy. In spite of this, Cate couldn't help but feel a sense of emptiness. As she too looked out across the ocean, she could think only of Bart. He ought to be standing alongside her right now. She tried to kindle the hope that he was on his way home but, in her heart, she knew that he was never coming back.

Next to Cate stood Jasmine Peacock, and then Bo Yin. Both young women had sustained wounds in the battle. Each bore her scars proudly, knowing that she had distinguished herself as a talented and mature fighter. Jasmine and Bo were only at the beginning of their pirate careers. Who knew what glorious things they could achieve in the battles to come?

The rest of the pirate crew lined up next to Bo Yin while on the other side of Obsidian stretched out the line of Nocturnals. Next to Obsidian stood his lieutenant, Lorcan Furey. Lorcan's eyes were turned to the other ship and to Johnny in particular. The rebel Vampirate was a threat in more ways than one, and he wasn't going to let him get away with it.

Lorcan's thoughts turned to Mosh Zu. The Vampirate guru hadn't participated in the battle but he had played a vital role in preparing the Nocturnals. Lorcan had grown frustrated with him at times, to the point of doubting his reassurances that the Captain would return. Now, he bowed his head and acknowledged that he hadn't been able to see the full picture. He thought of another important comrade who was also missing. Darcy Flotsam. She had played her own key part against the rebels. She may not have wielded a sword but her contribution was none the less valid.

Grace Tempest walked behind the line of allies and stepped into the place which Lorcan and Obsidian had kept for her. As she stood there at the edge of the deck, the ocean breeze blowing in her hair, she felt a sense of connection – of power and solidarity – with the others in the line. They had each in their own way played their part in a seemingly impossible mission. She glanced back along at the others, marvelling at this strange but powerful new alliance between the pirate and

Vampirate world. United, there was no threat they couldn't address.

Looking across at the departing ship, she thought how deceptive appearances could be. In truth, she might easily have been standing on *The Diablo* now. There were strong ties to bind her to Johnny and the others. Sidorio was still her father. Even more importantly, Connor was still on *The Blood Captain*. Grace wondered how his initiation into blood had gone. She thought of their conversation earlier that night. It had been painful to hear his disgust at becoming a dhampir. Whatever happened in the future, she had to work to help him adjust and become comfortable in his own skin.

But Connor could take care of himself and, for now, her place was here with the Nocturnals. She could see that Johnny was still watching her, as his ship receded into the night. With some difficulty, she pulled away and turned her face towards Obsidian Darke.

Was he *really* the Vampirate Captain? It was such a big adjustment to make. When he had been disguised beneath a mask and cloak, he had instilled deep fear in others but never in her. Now that he bore a human face, she found him far more disconcerting.

Hearing footsteps behind her, Grace turned and glanced over her shoulder. She saw Mosh Zu and Darcy walking together across the deck. They must have crossed over from *The Nocturne*. Grace was pleased to see them again, but nervous. She and Darcy had last parted company in an angry fashion and it had all been Grace's fault. Would Darcy forgive her? As the two comrades reached the line, Mosh Zu set off to take his place at the end. Before Darcy could follow him, Grace reached out a hand and grabbed her, pulling Darcy into the space beside her. Darcy looked surprised but pleased. She smiled sweetly at Grace and it seemed clear that she too was anxious to put any unpleasantness behind them. They stood side by side. The line-up was complete.

Suddenly the silence was broken. "Jacoby!" Jasmine cried. "Jacoby!"

All eyes turned to Jasmine and then followed the direction of her pointing finger. She was gesturing at *The Diablo*. The ship was almost completely shrouded in darkness now but two new figures had stepped forward to enter the line-up. Johnny was no longer alone at the centre of the ship. He had been joined by his fellow deputy, Stukeley. And there, at Stukeley's side, was Jacoby Blunt.

"Jacoby!" Jasmine cried again.

Jacoby stared out across the widening gulf, but he didn't seem to see her. He didn't seem to see any of them. There was a strange, disconnected look in his eyes. Was he the Vampirates' prisoner? No one seemed to be holding him and his shirt was soaked with blood. A cold current of fear pulsed through Jasmine's heart. Had the unthinkable already happened?

Her question remained unanswered as the gap between *The Tiger* and *The Diablo* widened and the Vampirate vessel was, at last, swallowed up by the night.

Chapter Forty-Five

Heartbeats

"Connor," Kally said. "Are you sure you want to do this? It's not too late for Sidorio to sire him. You could still bring Bart back."

Connor remember the night six weeks earlier when he, Bart and the rest of Cheng Li's crew had gathered at the Full Moon Saloon. Connor saw, as clear as day, Bart smashing his fist against the palm of his other hand. "A short life but a merry one. That's what I signed up to. When I die, bury me deep as hell where no vampire can dig me up and have me join his crew."

The fire in Bart's eyes as he had said those words was still vivid in Connor's head as he turned back to Kally. "No," he said, shaking his head. "As tempting as it is, for my sake, I just couldn't do that to him." He had made a promise to his friend and he would honour it. He looked back across the water to Bart's corpse, laid out on the sand. "He deserves a proper death and the peace that follows. That's the one thing left I can do for him."

"You're sure?" Kally asked once more.

Connor nodded. He was about to swim back for Bart but hesitated, turning to Kally. "Before we set out," he said. "There's something I wanted to tell you."

She looked up at him, her rainbow-coloured eyes full of curiosity.

"Yesterday, I had a dream about you," Connor said. "It was about meeting you in *Calle del Marinero* and sailing with you guys on *The Lorelei*."

Kally's eyes brightened. "Connor, you remembered! At last!"

Connor nodded. "I dreamed we went swimming from the boat. It was night-time. You and the other fishtails were already under the water. Bart, Jez and I followed after you. The water was dark at first, but then it was filled with coloured lights, like lasers." Connor smiled at the memory. "The lights were coming from you and the other fishtails. You were *so* beautiful, Kal – like an underwater angel."

As Connor stopped speaking, he saw that there were fresh tears in her eyes. "You really did remember," she said at last.

"Yes," he said, swimming closer to her. "And I remembered one more thing." He paused. "You were falling in love with Bart."

Kally said nothing. She closed her eyes, but this didn't stop her tears. Connor leaned forward and drew the fishtail into his arms. He held her there as she released the sobs that had been building inside her. As he comforted her, Connor couldn't help but think of Cate. She had loved Bart too – for such a long time. She was going to be devastated when she learned of his death – perhaps all the more so, if she knew that he had been planning to propose to her on his return. The ring had been in Bart's pocket and now Connor had it. His first thought had been to deliver it to Cate but he was no longer sure whether that was the right thing to do. Maybe it would just cause Cate too much pain.

At last, Kally grew peaceful again and opened her eyes. "What's next for you, Connor?" she asked. "Will you go back to Sidorio? Or to Cheng Li? Or will you embark on some new journey altogether?"

Connor had no answers. "I don't know what I'm going to do," he said. "All I do know is nothing will ever be the same again. I can't even begin to think about my future until I've said goodbye to Bart."

Kally nodded. "Come on, then," she said, gently. "Let's take him out for a swim."

Connor took one of Bart's arms and Kally the other. Together, the three friends began their journey out to the deep ocean.

"There's this prayer," Connor told Kally, as they swam away from the beach. "Bart spoke it at Jez's funeral. I think I'd like to say it for him."

"Great idea," Kally said.

"I know how it begins," Connor said, "but I'm not sure I can remember the whole thing."

Kally smiled up at him. "Whatever you can manage will be fine," she said.

Connor began speaking the words as he swam.

"Mother Ocean, Father Sky,
Send this pirate to his rest.
He was one amongst the best —
Set his spirit free to fly.
Brother Sun and Sister Moon,
Bathe him in your balmy light.
Now no longer need he fight —
The one you called back far too soon.
Lightning, thunder, wind and rain,
Let his cutlass blunt and rust—"

Connor broke off. Tears were streaming down his face.

"It's OK," Kally said. "It doesn't matter if you can't remember any more. Bart will understand."

Connor shook his head. "I do remember it. I don't know how but I do. The worst part is, in my head, I can hear Bart speaking it at Jez's funeral. And now—" He broke off. "And now . . ."

Kally nodded and smiled reassuringly at him. They swam on for a time in silence. They were a good distance away from the shore now. Both the air and the water were cooler here. Connor was aware of Kally watching him, though his head was turned away from her. He didn't want to catch her eye. He was sure he knew what she was going to say.

At last, Kally spoke. "Connor, I think we're far enough out now."

He sighed, and stopped swimming.

"Are you ready?" she asked.

Treading water, he shook his head, sadly. "I could never be ready for this moment." He looked once more at Bart's face, fresh tears coursing down his own cheeks. "All right," he told Kally. "We'll do this. Just let me say goodbye to him."

She nodded. Connor gripped Bart's hand and tried to stem the flow of his tears. "Bart, all I really want to say is that you've been the best friend I've ever known. From the very first night we met – you let me take your bunk, remember? – to the last." He took a breath. "I'm going to miss you so much, buddy." He shook his head. There was so much more he wanted to say but he was too upset to give voice to the words.

"That was perfect," Kally told him. "Do you think it would be all right if I kissed him goodbye?"

Connor nodded. He watched as Kally stroked the hair back from Bart's forehead, then traced her fingers along his cheek. At last, she kissed him lightly on his lips. "Sleep tight, beautiful Bart," she said.

Kally released her hand from Bart's and waited for Connor to do the same. Connor could feel the weight of Bart's body sinking beneath the surface. His heart lurched. He wasn't ready. This was so final. His hand kept hold of Bart's and now he felt himself being pulled under the water, following his dear friend.

Connor kept hold of Bart's hand as they sank slowly down from the bright, clear waters to the dark waters below. Kally followed close beside. As the waters grew too dark to see ahead, her tail became illuminated and suddenly the ocean was filled, as Connor had remembered in his dream, with a rainbow of lights.

And so the three of them continued their journey right down to the ocean bed. In spite of everything he hated about being a dhampir, Connor was grateful that he could now breathe underwater and so accompany Bart on his final journey.

One thing which he still couldn't do, but which Kally could, was to speak underwater. "This is a beautiful spot, don't you think?" she said now.

Connor glanced around at the coral and other vegetation on the ocean floor. It was like a garden in a way, full of colour and life. As they laid Bart down and made him comfortable, a brilliantly-coloured shoal of fish swam by, lingering for a moment, as if greeting the new arrival.

Kally touched Connor's arm. "He'll never be lonely here," she said. "I promise you, Connor."

Connor nodded. Bart looked peaceful now. He knew it was time to say goodbye.

Connor took one last look at that friendliest of faces, then felt Kally tug at his own hand.

"Ready to swim back up?" she asked.

He nodded. At last, he was.

On *The Vagabond*, Lola opened her cabin door to find Sidorio sitting, waiting for her. It was evident that he was in a pensive mood.

"I gather we've sustained our first defeat," Lola said. "But it's only a temporary setback, my darling. When the dust settles, we'll reconfigure our crews and come back stronger and harder than ever, I promise." She strode over to the freshly-filled decanter and poured vintage blood into two glasses. She offered one to Sidorio. He accepted it but, unusually for him, did not immediately drink.

Frowning, Lola took a much-needed sip from her own glass. Sidorio bore a haunted expression. "What's the point of this?" he asked.

"The point of what?" Lola asked, disturbed but disguising her feelings with a casual, upbeat tone.

"All this fighting," Sidorio said. "The expansion of our empire. Remind me, Lola. What are we doing it *for*?"

Lola could no longer control her feelings. "I can't believe you're asking me this!" she said. "It scares me to hear you talk this way."

Sidorio's sorrowful eyes met his wife's. "Connor has gone and it's clear he won't be coming back. He doesn't want any part of our world. And now it transpires that Obsidian Darke was a fraud – the captain of *The Nocturne* in disguise. He led my crew into battle and half of them to their destruction. He played us for fools."

Lola frowned at this confirmation of earlier rumours. "What about Grace?" she asked. "I always thought she had more potential than her brother."

"Gone," Sidorio said, shaking his head slowly. "Grace chose to side with her former allies. She went back to *The Nocturne* with Darke and his crew." He turned to Lola, his eyes empty and desolate. "Both my children have gone and they're not coming back. Don't you see why that makes all of this feel utterly meaningless?"

Lola took another steadying sip of her drink and stepped

closer to Sidorio, running her fingers across his smooth head. "Sid, I can see you're feeling low but I promise you'll feel differently again soon." Her voice grew steelier as she proceeded. "We began building this empire before we even discovered that Connor and Grace were your blood kin and, now they are gone, we must continue our work."

He gazed up at her. "I'm sorry, I just don't know if I have the fight in me any more."

"You must find it again," she said, fire brimming in her dark eyes. "Connor and Grace were always going to prove problematic heirs. The human side of their nature would always have held them back – and us too." She drank another draught. It was fine blood – liquid velvet on the tongue. "I know this is difficult but you have to let them go."

"I can't just . . . let them go," he said. "Whether they are pure-bloods or half and half, Connor and Grace are mine. They're the only children I'll ever have."

Lola smiled and set down her glass. "That's where you're wrong," she said. Now she reached for Sidorio's free hand and lifted it until his thick palm rested on her belly. As she did so, he watched her, his eyes wide with wonder. He glanced down at his hand, noticing that Lola's stomach was rather more curved than he remembered it. How had this escaped his notice? His eyes travelled back to meet hers. They seemed to dance with light.

"Do you feel the heartbeats?" she asked him.

"Heart*beats*?" He directed all of his focus to his hand and Lola's belly, utterly still and silent. At first, nothing. Then, to his amazement, he did feel them. Two beating hearts. He shook his head and smiled up at his beautiful, extraordinary wife.

TO BE CONTINUED . . .

Author Note

WARNING: PLOT SPOILERS!

I had to bring Lola Lockwood back to life! Or, rather, I had to bring Lola Lockwood Sidorio back to the undead. She is such a fun character to write and has such an enjoyably unsettling effect on all the characters around her. When I introduced her in BLACK HEART, I was never in any doubt that she would be destroyed in the book's closing pages. But, almost as soon as I did it, I realised that I was no more willing than Sidorio to let her go. When the book was published, her legion of fans convinced me she had to return. I tried to keep the twist a secret but if you attended my Edinburgh International Book Festival event in August 2009 you'll know that I let the cat out of the bag there. Thanks for keeping Lola's secret for a few months!

EMPIRE OF NIGHT also sees the return of Kally – the fishtail who we last glimpsed in my World Book Day 2007 story, DEAD DEEP. Kally is such a feisty character that I thought it would be fun to bring her into one of the main novels at some point but it was a fluke that she swam her way into EMPIRE OF NIGHT. It didn't happen until quite late in the plotting process. I had decided that Connor needed a discreet but convincing way to communicate with Cheng Li from *The*

Blood Captain. After much wracking of my brain, I realised that the answer was obvious. I mean – what better way to send secret messages across the ocean at warp speed than via a fishtail?

There are, as you'll have seen, a few new characters in this book. Firstly, there's the trio of Mimma, Nathalie and Jacqueline who Lola assigns to keep tabs on Grace. These three made their debut in a short story I wrote for PUFFIN POST magazine last year called NIGHT HARVEST (you can now read this at vampirates.co.uk). The names of these dangerous ladies are borrowed from good friends in Australia. Hello Mim, Jacqui and Nat! Thank you, guys, for letting me depict you as ruthless vixens!

The other major "new" character is Obsidian Darke. It was really important to me that when the Vampirate Captain came back into the story, he should do so in a very strong way and I was excited when I came up with the idea of disguising him and planting him at the heart of the story. I like how frustrated Lorcan and Darcy get about his failure to return when in fact he's already there in the thick of the action! Of course, Grace only discovers Obsidian's true identity at the very end of the book. One of the things I'm looking forward to exploring further in the next VAMPIRATES adventure is how she gets on with her old mentor in his new and decidedly different incarnation. He's still an enigma but a rather different one now that, at last, his mask has been removed.

This book also features two celebrated characters I have shamelessly plundered from history – the Italian artist Caravaggio (1571-1610) and the renowned French chef Auguste Escoffier (1846 – 1935). It may interest you to know that Escoffier did indeed once famously create a "white and pink feast" and I have replicated this pretty faithfully in Chapter 17, including Escoffier's famous dessert – the Peach Melba!

Whilst this book sees the arrival of some new characters, it

378

also sees the sad departure of a couple of key cast-members who've been with us since the very beginning. I'm not going to mention their names here – just in case you have raced ahead to read this before finishing the story. What I will say is that I didn't let go of either character lightly. It's unusual – indeed unprecedented – for me to cry whilst writing, but tears were streaming down my own face as I wrote Chapter 45!

That moment of weepiness aside, in the main EMPIRE OF NIGHT was a really fun book for me to write, probably the most enjoyable in the VAMPIRATES sequence to date. As usual, I'm indebted to all the people who supported me along the way. Don't panic – I'm not about to launch into an Oscars-style speech. I think most of the key players know how grateful I am. Being a writer can be a lonely business, which is one of the reasons that I so much enjoy getting out and about and talking to my readers around the UK and indeed around the world. I was "on the road" at various points during the writing of EMPIRE OF NIGHT. In April 2009, I did my first US author tour and my day at the wonderful Housman Elementary School in Houston made me think afresh about the character of Johnny who also hails from Texas.

Sometimes, chapters or scenes loom ominously ahead of me and it helps to talk them through before I get into the writing. I had just such a "block" about Connor and Sidorio's duel in Chapter 20. After a spirited session with a group of inspiring students at South Molton Community College in Devon, I came away bursting with ideas and, more importantly, enthusiasm to resume writing. I am also indebted to Hedd ap Emlyn from Wrexham Libraries who explained to me the finer points of horse-riding while driving me to my homeward-bound train after three days of events in North Wales. Grace's midnight ride with Johnny would be infinitely poorer were it not for Hedd's insights.

Finally, a huge thank you to all the Nocturnals out there, who – week in, week out – send messages to my blog at vampirates.co.uk. An author couldn't wish for a more dedicated readership. If you haven't visited the site yet, do come and join in the chat.

Trust the tide!

Justin Somper
March 2010

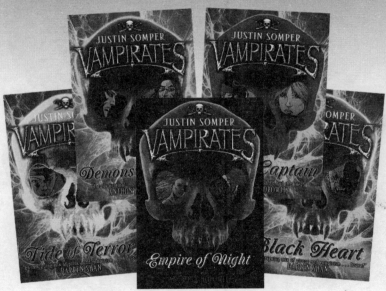

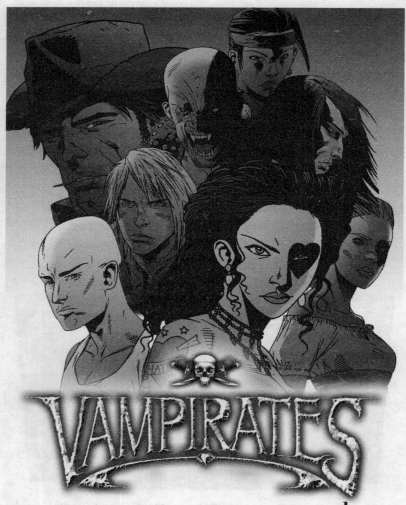